ALSO BY KATE O'REILLEY

IN GOOD HANDS
COMING SUMMER 2013

IT'S NOTHING PERSONAL

Quandary Publishing
PO Box 631129
Littleton, CO 80163-1129

First Quandary Publishing paperback edition January 2013

QUANDARY PUBLISHING and colophon are registered trademarks of Quandary Publishing, LLC.

For more information about special discounts and bulk purchases, please contact Quandary Publishing, Special Sales at 720-989-4478 or quandarypublishing@gmail.com

Manufactured in the United States of America

ISBN: 978-0-9886633-1-2

For my husband and daughter,
with never-ending love

ACKNOWLEDGMENTS

First and foremost, I want to express my love and gratitude to my husband and daughter who have always been, and will always be, my biggest fans. They stood by me through the worst of times. Hopefully, I will be able to repay them someday with the best of times.

Thank you to the countless people who were willing to sacrifice their time to offer me feedback. To my amazing editor, Liz Parker, who was never was afraid to tell me the truth, and was never wrong about it, either. Your edits and impressions were priceless. May there be many more meetings at coffee houses in our future. On more occasions than I would like to admit, you saved me from myself. I also thank my stepdaughter, Kim, who gave me not only invaluable editorial advice, but, most importantly, her friendship. To Don and Robin, no amount of gratitude can express my debt to you – your feedback transformed my manuscript.

And to my Monday crew: Sharon, Robin, Val, Sandy, Brittany, and Jay (our 'honorary' gal pal) – an unlikely group of people that learned to love and cherish one another. We all faced our challenges, but the reward – our collective friendship – was worth the pain. To all of you, thank you for holding me up when I felt like crumbling, and for encouraging me every step along the way. To Sharon, in particular, we came together at the worst points in either of our lives. Over that time, you have supported me, inspired me, made me laugh, and watched me cry. I wish you and your family nothing but happiness.

IT'S NOTHING PERSONAL

A NOVEL

KATE O'REILLEY

Quandary Publishing, LLC

ONE

January 20, 2010

Dr. Jenna Reiner's Land Rover fishtailed as she turned into the parking lot of St. Augustine Hospital, nearly striking a cement post. Inside the relative safety of the parking garage, she felt relieved to have finally escaped the icy roads. Little did Jenna know, things would have been much simpler if she would have had the good fortune to slide off the road and into a ditch on her drive to the city. Unfortunately, life dealt her a different fate. She arrived safely at work and began the day that would change her life forever.

The clock on the dashboard read 7:12. Time was against Jenna. She had only eighteen minutes before her first case was scheduled to start. "Dammit," she muttered, as she rushed to gather her things from the back seat. Lassoing her stethoscope around her neck with one hand, she unloaded her briefcase and extended its handle with the other. Trudging across the parking lot, wheeling her bag behind her, she had to dodge a minefield of chunks of dirty, sloppy snow.

Entering the main lobby of the hospital, Jenna felt a rush of heated air. In order to make up for lost time, she nearly sprinted down the narrow, dimly lit hospital corridor toward the elevators. The rubber soles of her operating room clogs were wet from the grime of the parking lot. With each step against the worn, discolored tile of the hospital hallway, Jenna's shoes let out a series of high-pitched, relentless squeaks that echoed behind her.

Jenna approached the elevator and the doors opened spontaneously. She breathed a sigh of relief, jumped in, and punched the button for the third floor. Only a few feet away, Jenna spotted a couple of patients and hospital workers advancing toward her. She knew she did not have the luxury of wasting time waiting for the stragglers, nor did she have any particular desire to be overly polite. Pretending not to see them, Jenna repeatedly pressed the close button, and the doors shut before the others could enter. The elevator reached the third floor, and she anxiously glanced down at her phone. It was now 7:18, which allowed her barely enough time to meet her patient, prepare the operating room for anesthesia and, God willing, get one last chance to use the restroom.

She strode toward the main doors of the operating rooms and frantically swiped her identification badge in front of the sensor pad. The sensor's light switched from red to green, and the double doors swung open. Jenna bolted inside with her bag trailing in a wild track behind her. Passing the assignment board, she located her designated operating room, OR 2.

Jenna grabbed a blue surgeon's cap, tied it snugly in place at the back of her head, and carefully tucked her ponytail of brown hair inside. Glancing in the mirror, she nonchalantly pulled out a few wisps of hair from in front of each ear – just enough to look more feminine, but not enough to get her in trouble for having exposed locks. Grabbing a mask, Jenna secured it over her face. Her deep, blue eyes were her only visible facial feature, and they stood out well against the cap and mask. Satisfied with her appearance, Jenna headed off to her operating room.

Upon opening the door to OR 2, Jenna was chilled by the familiar, yet always unpleasant, draft of frigid air that emanated from the operating rooms. The Talking Heads' song, "Once in a Lifetime," blared from the operating room speakers. The lyrics somehow seemed appropriately matched to her mood.

Inside the operating room, Hillary, the scrub tech, and Rebecca, the circulating nurse, were busy counting surgical equipment. Hillary, dressed in a sterile surgical gown and gloves, fingered each item as Rebecca stood by and checked them off from her count sheet. Jenna walked in to hear Hillary identifying each item on her table, "Ten ray techs, five laps, two blades, one hypo . . ."

The women paused when they saw the doctor enter the room.

Rebecca spoke over the music. "Dr. Reiner, I just wanted to let you know that Dr. Hoover's caught in traffic, and she's going to be at least thirty minutes late."

One of Jenna's biggest pet peeves was to be running behind schedule, but now that it was the surgeon's fault and not hers, she was grateful for the delay.

"Rebecca, you're a life saver," Jenna said as she smiled underneath her mask and slowed down her hectic pace. She made her way past the tray of surgical devices and toward the head of the operating room bed, where her equipment and medications were located. Clumsily, she wedged her briefcase into the only crevice not taken up by anesthesia gear. Jenna then devoted her attention to performing her routine check of the ventilator, monitors, and equipment. Like a prima ballerina performing on stage, she floated through her routine.

During Jenna's preparations, she discreetly reached into her bag and pulled out a Diet Pepsi. Rebecca caught sight of Jenna's indiscretion and glared at her, but the doctor knew better than to take Rebecca's feigned scorn seriously. Looking Rebecca directly in the eye, mocking innocence, Jenna asked, "What?" Then, defiantly, she opened her forbidden soda. The cracking of the metal tab and the small explosive release of carbonation resonated throughout the room. Rebecca shook a disapproving finger at Jenna, but the twinkle in her eyes indicated otherwise.

Hillary winked at Jenna and said, "Hey, Doc, we've all got our vices. Your secret's safe with us."

Thrown off guard by Hillary's gesture, Jenna blushed and quickly turned her back on the scrub tech.

Rebecca and Hillary resumed their count, and Jenna was ready to check out narcotics for her first patient. She stepped in front of the Accudose machine, entered her personal identification code on the keyboard, and pressed her index finger over the red, illuminated biometric sensor. After confirming a fingerprint match, the automated machine came to life.

Grabbing the surgical schedule taped to her anesthesia machine, Jenna scanned it for her patient's name. Her first patient was Michelle Hollings, a twenty-two-year-old female scheduled for breast augmentation. Just another routine case, Jenna surmised, as she proceeded to enter the patient's name into the machine. Under Michelle Hollings' account, Jenna typed "Fentanyl" and touched the screen to select the 5 cc ampule from the menu. One of the small drawers sprang open, revealing a bin containing six glass vials filled with the drug. Jenna took one, verified the initial count, and closed the drawer.

She was about to retrieve Versed when Rebecca asked, "Hey Dr. Reiner, I'm guessing you haven't seen the patient yet?"

"No, Rebecca. I'm hoping she's young and healthy, so it shouldn't take me more than a couple of minutes."

"Well, since Hillary and I are done with our count, I'm gonna go see the patient and then hopefully score some coffee before Dr. Hoover shows up."

"Go for it. I'll be right behind you," Jenna replied, without looking up.

Rebecca scurried off to meet the patient, leaving Jenna and Hillary alone in the operating room.

Jenna finished checking out a 2 cc vial of Versed. With her narcotics in hand, she exited the Accudose machine. The machine clattered as its drawers automatically locked.

For several minutes, both Hillary and Jenna quietly went about their respective tasks. The silence made Jenna uneasy. She barely knew Hillary, who was relatively new to St. Augustine. They had worked together only a few times. While Jenna had to concede the newcomer always conducted herself professionally in front of the surgeons, she also saw an element of "white trash" in the scrub tech. Hillary had bleach-blonde hair with black roots, brown eyes encircled with heavy eyeliner and mascara, and an excess of tattoos and facial piercings. However, her impression was based upon more than Hillary's physical appearance. Hillary's manners were unrefined. She pictured Hillary more as a bartender in a seedy watering hole than as a healthcare professional. If Jenna had to choose two words to describe the scrub tech, they would be "dark" and "scrappy." Hillary had the air of someone who had lived a hard life.

There was something else about Hillary that put Jenna on edge. She had not noticed it until the two of them were alone. Jenna had a disconcerting feeling that

Hillary was watching her. Yet, every time Jenna glanced at Hillary, the scrub tech was looking in another direction. The sense of paranoia made Jenna feel foolish. She tried to put it out of her mind as she engaged Hillary in small talk.

"So," Jenna asked, "how do you like St. Augustine so far?"

"You know, it's been fine. Everyone's been pretty cool. I'm not used to your winters, though. What's up with all the snow and ice? I was sliding all over the place on my way in. It scared the crap out of me."

"Well, you get used to it, I guess. Where'd you come from?"

"I just moved here from California. I've been going through some pretty rough shit lately. I have a little girl who lives with her dad in San Francisco. I'm just trying to get my life back on the right track so I can regain custody. I haven't seen my daughter in over a year."

The fact that this person Jenna hardly knew would divulge such intimate, sordid details about herself left her feeling anxious to leave. She glanced up at the clock, which read 7:45.

Jenna moved over to her anesthesia cart. The cart was nothing more than a glorified, multi-drawer tool chest containing non-narcotic drugs and anesthesia supplies. She drew up the remaining intravenous medications needed for the case. Per her routine, Jenna took all of her syringes, opened the bottom drawer of her anesthesia cart, and concealed them in a bin beneath bags of intravenous fluid. After stashing her medications, Jenna took one last glance around to make sure everything was in order for the start of her first case. Satisfied, she grabbed her stethoscope and headed out of OR 2.

On her way out, Jenna told Hillary, "Well, I hate to cut things short, but I need to go see the patient. Good luck with everything, and I really hope things work out for you."

"Thanks, Doc. Think I have enough time to break scrub and go get some coffee?"

"I can't imagine why not. My guess is we won't be bringing the patient back to the room any sooner than fifteen minutes from now."

By the time Jenna walked out of the operating room, Hillary had already ripped off her sterile surgical gown and threw it into the waste bin.

Jenna could not shake the eerie feeling she got from being alone with Hillary. The woman conveyed a sense of danger.

Hillary was finally alone in the operating room. Unfortunately, Jenna's suspicions were correct. The scrub tech had been secretly watching Jenna as she hid her drugs and knew exactly where to look. Hillary opened the bottom drawer and lifted the bags of IV fluid. Immediately, she found what she craved. She plucked the 5 cc syringe filled with clear fluid and labeled with a blue "Fentanyl" sticker from the pile of other medications. Slipping two fingers into her breast pocket, Hillary pulled out an identically labeled syringe filled with saline. Swapping one syringe for the other, she covered the drugs, and closed the drawer of the anesthesia cart. Everything was exactly as Jenna had left it. Hillary smiled as she headed to the locker room.

TWO

Jenna reached the preoperative patient area, which was bustling with surgeons, anesthesiologists, residents, nurses, and lab technicians, all in constant motion. Ignoring the chaos, Jenna maneuvered her way toward the dry-erase board that served as the OR schedule. She searched the board for her patient and darted off to room four. Jenna delivered three rapid knocks on the door and entered.

She grabbed Michelle Hollings' chart from the table at the foot of the bed. After confirming she had the right patient, Jenna introduced herself.

"Hi, Michelle. I'm Dr. Reiner. I'm going to be your anesthesiologist for your breast augmentation with Dr. Hoover today. It's nice to meet you."

Jenna shook Michelle's petite hand. Moving in closer, Jenna noticed that Michelle's fingernails were decorated with hot pink polish and little, sparkly flower decals. Jenna also caught a glimpse of Michelle's diamond nose ring.

"Nice to meet you, too," replied Michelle. "This is my boyfriend, Bradley. He's the one footing the bill."

Jenna turned her attention to an attractive man in his forties seated at Michelle's bedside. Dressed in a black suit and sporting a Rolex watch, Bradley seemed like an unlikely match for Michelle Hollings. He looked up from his Blackberry and grinned.

Jenna smiled politely at the boyfriend. "So is this a present for you or her?"

As Jenna asked the question she noticed the gold band on Bradley's left ring finger. There was no corresponding ring on Michelle Hollings' hand.

In response to Jenna's question, Bradley's expression transformed into a guilty sneer.

At the same instant, the patient and her boyfriend blurted out, "Both," and started laughing. Jenna chuckled as well, trying to hide her distaste for Michelle's choice in men.

On the other hand, Jenna could appreciate Bradley's interest in Michelle. The young woman was extremely attractive. She had long blonde hair, beautiful green eyes, and a perfect body. Jenna glanced at Michelle's vital signs, mostly because she was dying to know Michelle's height and weight. Exactly as Jenna suspected, Michelle had ideal dimensions, standing at 5 feet, 10 inches tall and weighing 115 pounds. Jenna, who stood 6 inches shorter and weighed 15 pounds more than her patient, was inwardly envious.

"All right then," said Jenna, as she reviewed Dr. Hoover's history and physical from the chart. "From what Dr. Hoover has to say about you, you have no health problems, you don't take any medications except birth control pills, and you have no allergies. Is all that correct?"

"Yep, pretty much."

"And no smoking, drugs, or excessive drinking?"

"Nope." Michelle shot Bradley a conspiratorial grin.

"I see they did a pregnancy test on you this morning, which was negative.   Have you had any problems with anesthesia in the past?"

"Nope. Usually, I do pretty good."

"I assume you've had nothing to eat or drink since midnight, right?   You didn't stop at Starbucks for a latte on the way in?"

Michelle giggled nervously.   "Unfortunately, no. No latte, or anything else for that matter.   But it does sound damn good right about now."

"Well, I thank you for being a compliant patient. I have only one last question.   Do you have any loose, missing, or chipped teeth?   Anything in your mouth that's not permanent?"

"Just my tongue ring," said Michelle, opening her mouth and proudly displaying a silver stud.

"That will have to come out before we take you back," Jenna said firmly.   "Any other piercings will also need to be removed."

"I was afraid you'd say that," pouted Michelle. "Does that also include my piercings . . . down there?" Michelle dipped her head in the direction of her crotch.

Jenna tried to sound unbiased.   "Yeah, even the ones down there."

Over the course of the next few minutes, Jenna performed a quick physical exam.   She peered into Michelle's mouth and assessed her airway.   Next, Jenna listened to Michelle's heart and lungs, which sounded completely normal.

After Jenna finished examining Michelle, she said, "Now's the time where we have to go through the risks associated with anesthesia, and then I need to get you to sign the anesthesia consent. Even though I have to tell you all the things that could go wrong, I want to start by reassuring you that I do not anticipate any problems."

Michelle sat up straight, signaling Jenna to continue.

"The most common complaints after surgery are nausea, vomiting, pain, and a sore throat. I will give you anti-nausea medication to help prevent you from feeling sick and narcotics that will hopefully allow you to wake up pain free. However, the nurses in the recovery room have more medicine, if you need it. If you get a sore throat, lozenges help, and it should resolve in a few days."

Jenna paused for a moment. She could see the glazed-over look in Michelle's eyes. After giving Michelle a moment to process the information, Jenna continued.

"It's rare, but sometimes we can have serious complications from anesthesia. For this procedure, I have to intubate you, which means that I put a breathing tube down your throat and into your windpipe while you're unconscious. Then I use a ventilator to help you breathe during the surgery. That was why I looked in your mouth and asked about your teeth. Those things help tell me if it should be easy or hard to get the tube in place. Based on my assessment, your airway looks very easy. However, there is a small chance that I could chip a tooth, cut your lip, or damage a vocal cord while trying to place the tube.

"There is also a possibility that you could have an allergic reaction to any of the medicines that I give you. If I see any indication that something like that is happening, I have other medications in the room to treat you.

"The most serious complication, and this is true for any patient, any surgery, and any type of anesthesia, is a serious and potentially life-threatening heart or lung complication."

With the mention of the possibility of death, Michelle Hollings clutched tightly to Bradley's hand, but otherwise maintained her composure. From what Jenna could tell, Bradley did his best to look interested and concerned, but she also caught him checking his Blackberry several times.

"Michelle," Jenna asked, "do you have any questions about the anesthesia or the risks?"

"No. I'm just ready to get on with it. I'm looking forward to my new rack," Michelle grinned.

"Me too," said Bradley, a bit overly enthusiastic.

With that, both Dr. Jenna Reiner and Michelle Hollings signed the appropriate lines on the anesthesia consent form. Jenna left the room and ran into Rebecca in the hallway.

"Dr. Reiner," said Rebecca, "Dr. Hoover just got here. She said she already got surgical consent from the patient in her office yesterday, so she just needs to pop in and say a quick hello. Is there anything you need, or are you okay if we head back to the operating room in about five minutes?"

Jenna was already halfway down the hallway. She called back over her shoulder, "Just make sure the patient takes out all her piercings and gets some Versed before you come back. Otherwise, I'm good, and I'll see you back there. Thanks!"

THREE

Jenna returned to her operating room to find it unoccupied. She found it odd that Hillary was not scrubbed back in and standing watch over the surgical equipment before the patient arrived. A critical part of Hillary's job was to ensure the integrity of the sterile surgical instruments – something that required her physical presence.

Approaching her area at the head of the operating room bed, Jenna opened the bottom drawer of the anesthesia cart and retrieved her stockpile of drugs. Each syringe, with the exception of Propofol, contained a clear liquid. If it weren't for the preprinted labels Jenna had affixed to each syringe, it would be virtually impossible to distinguish one medication from the other. Ritualistically, Jenna arranged the syringes on the silver tray of the anesthesia machine in the exact order that she intended to administer them to her patient – Versed, Lidocaine, Fentanyl, Propofol, and Rocuronium.

At 8:15, Jenna was still the only one present. It had been well over ten minutes since she left Rebecca in the hallway. With all of her drugs laid out in the open, she was forced to remain in the room until the patient appeared. Pulling out her phone, she engaged in a quick round of Solitaire. After several more minutes, she finally heard the sound of voices approaching the operating room doors.   Jenna   waited   as   Rebecca   maneuvered   the cumbersome   hospital   gurney,   with   Michelle   Hollings onboard, into the room and lined it up next to the operating room table.

Overly bright and cheery, Rebecca quipped, "Hey, Dr. Reiner. Here's our friend, Michelle. Michelle, this is the operating room. I'd introduce you to the rest of the gang, but they don't seem to be back yet."

Rebecca's last sentence was said with reproach, as she cocked her head in the direction of the surgical equipment and glanced inquisitively over at Jenna. Jenna correctly interpreted Rebecca's expression and tone, as both women questioned Hillary's whereabouts. Outside the view of her patient, Jenna shrugged her shoulders and shook her head disapprovingly.

"So, Michelle," asked Jenna, "how's that cocktail treating you?"

Completely   lucid,   Michelle   responded,   "What cocktail?"

Michelle's anxiety was evident as her eyes darted from one daunting piece of surgical equipment to the next. Jenna said compassionately, "Don't worry. I've got more."

Jenna grasped the syringe of Versed and injected its contents into Michelle's intravenous line. Not only would the Versed make Michelle feel as though she had a few drinks, it would also cloud her memory from that point forward.

The second dose of Versed seemed to have an impact on Michelle. Wearing a silly smirk, she slurred, "Oh yeah, I'm feeling it now."

Jenna guided Michelle from the hospital gurney over to the operating room table. Once the patient was positioned correctly, Jenna started her pre-induction routine. First, Jenna secured a mask over Michelle's face that delivered one hundred percent oxygen. She then applied the standard monitors to Michelle – a blood pressure cuff, EKG leads, and an oxygen saturation monitor. While Jenna went about her business, she overheard Rebecca on the phone with the charge nurse.

With unconcealed annoyance, Rebecca asked, "Can you find out where Hillary is, and tell her we have the patient in the room? We are about to start the case, and there's no scrub tech!"

Jenna stopped eavesdropping and returned her focus to her patient.

"Okay, Michelle, we're ready to go off to sleep. I'm giving you the good stuff. You're going to get really sleepy, really fast."

In rapid succession, Jenna injected Lidocaine, Fentanyl, and Propofol. Jenna pushed the Propofol into Michelle's intravenous line. The milky white fluid travelled down the IV tubing from the injection port and disappeared into Michelle's bloodstream. At that point, Jenna warned Michelle, "This last medicine that you are getting might burn a little bit at your IV site, but it makes you fall asleep quickly. I'm rubbing your arm as you drift off, which helps some with the discomfort. I promise, we are all going to take very good care of you, and we'll see you in a few hours."

Thirty seconds later, Michelle's eyes flickered and then drifted shut as the rest of her body went limp under the effect of the drugs. Jenna then held a mask securely over Michelle's mouth and nose, squeezing oxygen into her lungs from a bag on the anesthesia machine. After Jenna witnessed Michelle's chest rise and fall from the artificial breaths, she injected the Rocuronium. Within thirty seconds, the paralytic took effect and each hand-delivered breath entered Michelle's lungs with increasing ease.   Once   Michelle   Hollings   was   completely unconscious and paralyzed, Jenna tilted her patient's head back and placed the metal blade of the laryngoscope into her mouth.   The light at the tip of the instrument lit up Michelle's   throat.   Jenna   peered   in   and   slid   an endotracheal tube past Michelle's vocal cords, into her windpipe.

Jenna was taping the breathing tube in place when she glanced up and noticed Dr. Lisa Hoover standing by the doors.   Reaching over to the anesthesia ventilator, Jenna attached the breathing circuit to the endotracheal tube, and turned on the machine.   The bellows on the ventilator rhythmically squished down like an accordion and then stretched out again.   With each descent, Michelle Hollings' chest rose as her lungs were inflated with a mixture of oxygen and anesthesia gases.

Jenna smiled at her colleague and announced, "She's all yours."

"Thanks, Jenna."   The surgeon then turned her attention toward Rebecca and asked curtly, "Do we have a scrub tech for this case, or am I flying solo?"

As if on cue, Hillary appeared.   Her arms were wet up to the elbows from scrubbing them at the surgical sink in the hallway.   In order to avoid contaminating herself, Hillary held her arms up in the air and away from her body as she backed into the doorway, careful to avoid touching anything.   Hillary walked over to the surgical table and dressed herself in a sterile surgical gown and a pair of gloves.

"Sorry I'm late.   No one told me you guys were in the room."

Rebecca shot Hillary a cold, critical stare and shook her head in disgust. No one else in the room acknowledged Hillary's apology and, for several minutes, it was painfully silent.

The hush was soon broken by the sound of Dr. Hoover's iPod playing her collection of modern rock over the operating room speakers. Dr. Hoover left the room to scrub, returning with the same ceremonial entrance that Hillary had performed a few minutes prior. Hillary helped the surgeon gown and glove.

Rebecca was ready to prep Michelle Hollings' chest for surgery, but before she did, one unpleasant task remained.

The nurse asked, somewhat embarrassed, "Dr. Hoover, the patient has a piercing in her pubic region. She said she could not get it out on her own. Do you want me to remove it?"

Rebecca had already parted Michelle's legs. Dr. Hoover came over and took a look. "Yeah, that needs to come out."

"I was afraid you'd say that," Rebecca responded, sounding defeated.

Jenna walked down to the foot of the bed and peeked at Michelle's piercing. A silver stud with little bulbs on each end was embedded in her clitoris. Jenna laughed and left Rebecca to her 'duty.'

Hillary unexpectedly piped in to the conversation. "I've got one, too."

Jenna replied, "I don't mean any offense, but why would you do that to yourself? Doesn't it hurt?"

Hillary shrugged and answered matter-of-factly, "It's just another way to express yourself. I just know thatsome people think they're cool. Once they heal, they don't hurt at all. I guess it's all about individual choice."

"I guess," was all that Jenna could articulate for a reply.

With the piercing removed and the chest prepped and draped, Dr. Hoover prepared to start the procedure. Before the surgeon made her first incision, Rebecca grabbed the patient's chart and turned off the music.

"Time out," said Rebecca. Everyone paused and gave the nurse their full attention. "This is Michelle Hollings, twenty-two-year-old female, no major medical problems, no drug allergies. She is in the supine position and is here today for a bilateral breast augmentation. Implants are in the room. Preop antibiotics are running. No beta-blockers were ordered or administered. Compression stockings are on and functional. Warming blanket is in place. All in agreement?"

Following a series of mumbled "yeses" and "yeps," Rebecca turned the music back on. Dr. Hoover and Hillary moved to the right side of the patient's chest, and the surgeon ran the blade of her scalpel over the lower part of Michelle Hollings' breast.

In response to the incision, Michelle Hollings' blood pressure and heart rate increased. Quickly, Jenna increased the concentration of anesthetic gas being delivered. She then logged back into the Accudose machine and checked out 10 milligrams of Morphine. Like Fentanyl, Morphine is a powerful narcotic, but lasts much longer. Based on Michelle's lack of response to the first dose of Versed she received in preop, Jenna assumed that the girl was probably not naïve when it came to drugs. Consequently, Jenna did not hesitate to inject the entire dose of the narcotic. After several minutes, Michelle's heart rate and blood pressure remained elevated, so Jenna administered another 5 milligram dose of Morphine. Finally, the drugs took effect.

"Looks like we have a party girl on our hands," Jenna declared.

"Oh yeah?" asked the surgeon. "Is she sucking up the goods?"

Jenna replied, "4 milligrams of Versed, 250 micrograms of Fentanyl, and 15 milligrams of Morphine. Yeah, I'd say she's a fun date."

The remaining two hours of the case passed uneventfully. At the conclusion of the surgery, Jenna turned off the anesthesia gases, gave Michelle medicine to reverse the effects of the muscle relaxant, got her breathing on her own, and removed the endotracheal tube. Jenna then transported Michelle and her new, very large breasts, to the recovery room. Once there, Jenna gave report to the recovery room nurse. When she informed the nurse of the amount of narcotic and Versed she had given to Michelle, the nurse whistled softly and whispered, "For a breast augmentation, on such a tiny, little thing? Wow!"

"Amazing what partying can do for your metabolism," Jenna remarked and then walked away.

Jenna was headed to the preop holding area when she felt the vibration of her pager on her hip. Unclipping it from her waistband, she squinted to read the tiny print.

"To all Doctors: Blizzard Warning in Effect. All remaining elective surgeries at all facilities cancelled for today. Only call doctors need to remain in-house."

Having been confined in the windowless operating room all morning, Jenna had no idea the weather had gotten so bad. She strolled into the hallway and glimpsed out the window. The snow was falling at a relentless pace – big, wet flakes coming down in droves. On the streets below, people were battling the wind and drifts just to cross the street. Cars were already becoming nearly entombed.

Immediately, Jenna worried about her daughter. Mia was in fifth grade. If the hospital deemed things bad enough to cancel cases and forfeit revenue, then certainly the schools would be closing soon, too.

Reaching into her breast pocket, Jenna pulled out her phone and quickly texted her husband.

"Hey, Tom. Can you get Mia from school? I'm leaving now, but you're closer. See you guys soon. Love, Jenna. P.S. A nice bottle of red and a warm fire sounds great, if you're 'up' for it."

Not thirty seconds later, Tom texted back.

"Definitely UP for that. Already picked Mia up. School closed an hour ago. Drive safe – roads are awful. Love you!!"

Jenna smiled as she headed toward the elevator, thinking to herself the day was not turning out too badly after all.

FOUR

June 5, 2010

Hillary and her parents had been sitting at the kitchen table for hours, discussing the mess she had created. Harold Martin struggled to comprehend the amount of devastation that his daughter had caused. His stomach balled up when he thought about the degree of trouble Hillary faced. Infuriated and exhausted, Harold clutched Hillary's arm and began to yell at her. The ringing of the phone, however, immediately silenced him. Hillary shook her arm free from her father's grasp and stomped over to the telephone. Her mother and father watched her trembling hands pick up the receiver.

There was no reason for Hillary to check caller ID. She had been dodging phone calls and meetings with Detective Morris for over a week. Her moment of truth had come.

"Hello," Hillary answered, barely more than a whisper, as she turned away from her parents.

"Is this Hillary Martin?" asked the deep, authoritative and, by now, recognizable voice on the other end.

Her parents sat motionless as they strained to catch every word of Hillary's end of the conversation.

Hillary could barely force the words from her mouth.

"Yeah, this is Hillary."

"Hillary, this is Detective Morris. I need to set up a time to meet with you down at the station. We need to question you regarding allegations of drug tampering and diversion that occurred while you were employed at St. Augustine Hospital. It seems like we've had our fair share of difficulty connecting. If you are available today, I'd like to meet with you at three o'clock. Would that work for you?"

Tears of self-pity and fear slowly slid down Hillary's cheeks. "Yes sir, I will see you there."

Detective Morris had played nice cop with Hillary Martin for over a week now. During that time, she had repeatedly lied to him, eluded his phone calls, and failed to show up for scheduled meetings. Today he was not taking any chances.

Pointedly, Detective Morris asked, "Do you have a ride down to the station? If not, we will send a car to pick you up."

Hillary understood this was his way of telling her that this was her last chance to come in voluntarily. Not appreciating being backed into a corner, Hillary made no attempt to disguise her irritation. "My parents will give me a ride. We'll be there at three."

"Do you have an attorney, or do we need to arrange to have someone represent you?"

"You already know everything. What's some dumb-ass lawyer going to do for me now?" Hillary hissed.

Before Detective Morris had the chance to say anything else, she hung up.

Hillary's parents remained seated at their modest, maple kitchen table. The cups of coffee in front of them had long since grown cold. Harold grabbed his wife's hand and held it tightly. Janice sullenly looked around at her cheerful kitchen. Filled with memories, the room had always been her favorite place in their home. Janice loved the chipper, yellow wallpaper speckled with pretty, white daisies. The pine floors were marked up by years of love, laughter, and horseplay. Hillary's mother glanced over to the stove, where she had dotingly cooked her family's favorite meals. To Janice, her kitchen symbolized her family's lives. *At least their former lives,* she thought sorrowfully.

The morning sun filtered through the windows of the breakfast nook. Instead of radiating warmth and comfort into the cozy space, the sunlight cast a condemning spotlight on Hillary, as she took her seat at the table.

Hillary's mother stared at her daughter as if she were looking at a stranger. Janice strived to remind herself that Hillary was once an innocent child. However, each memory was promptly overshadowed by the chilly presence of the woman sitting across from her.

Glancing at one of her most cherished photographs hanging on the wall, Janice sighed. Hillary was about three years old with ivory skin, long black hair, and big brown eyes full of mischief and joy. Janice smiled to herself as she reflected on what a truly beautiful and amazing little girl Hillary had been. The picture had been taken on a beach vacation in Key West as Hillary played in the sand, lost in her own imaginary world. Her parents snapped the photograph without Hillary's knowledge. No posing, no cheesy smiles, no looking awkwardly into the camera. It captured the natural sparkle, tenderness, and grace of their only child.

Hillary squeezed her mother's hand and said softly, "I remember that beach."

"You do?" Janice's voice cracked. "You were so little. Those were good times."

Janice looked back at Hillary. Hillary's formerly flawless skin was now marred by piercings and tattoos. Her once twinkling eyes now bore the dark patches and sunken look of many years of hard living and drug use. Hillary's previously black hair was bleached out, uncombed, and greasy. Janice studied her daughter, dressed in a tattered, black T-shirt and overly tight jeans. To her, it was obvious that somewhere along the way, the delightful little girl filled with promise and hope had transformed into a monster. Although this acknowledgement broke Janice Martin's heart, she knew it was true. The little girl she loved so dearly would never have committed the acts carried out by this woman sitting at her table.

Hillary stroked the back of her mother's hand with her thumb. "Mom, you did a good job. Don't ever forget that. All this had nothing to do with you, or Dad. You both did everything right. I'm just a fuckup."

It broke her parent's hearts to admit it, but Hillary was right.

Instead of responding, Harold and Janice each put their feelings of shame and anger aside and grasped Hillary's hands. They sat there at the table, forming a triangle filled with love and despair. No one spoke a word. Over the past week, Hillary had confessed everything to her parents. There was no sense in rehashing the shock and disgrace that her actions brought upon her family.

Eventually, the cuckoo clock interrupted the Martins' time together. The little bird only cried out one

"Cuckoo" and then retreated into his wooden box. Janice Martin, shaken from her trance, looked at Hillary and said, "Well, I guess we better all get ready. We'll need to leave here in an hour."

The Martins' unlocked hands and stood from the table. Hillary rushed over to her parents and buried herself in their embrace. While her mother and father held her, Hillary sobbed uncontrollably. Finally, she pulled away and stared at them with eyes that were wet, red, and puffy. A clear stream ran from Hillary's nose toward her lips, but she made no attempt to wipe it away.

Through her sniffles, Hillary pleaded, "Mom, Dad, I'm so sorry. Please, no matter what I've done, please never abandon me."

Harold's words were unsteady. His characteristic strength and confidence had long since dissolved.

"Hillary, your mother and I will always be there for you. We promise you that."

Both of her parents nodded, with tears in their eyes.

Hillary smiled gratefully and then walked away to get ready for the meeting she dreaded.

An hour later, Hillary and her parents left for the police station downtown. During the drive, the Martins were silent. Hillary watched the familiar images of the city pass by from her window in the backseat. When they passed the football stadium, she remembered the fall games she went to with her dad. Driving by the McDonald's reminded her of Happy Meals on the run, while her mother chauffeured her from one activity to the next. Hillary had the window open and embraced the warm June air. She had an overpowering urge to cherish every moment of the car ride.

Hillary and her parents arrived at the police station, and her mother started to steer their car into the parking lot.

"No, Mom," said Hillary firmly. "I'm going in alone. Just drop me off in front."

At first, Janice was hurt that Hillary did not want them to come with her, but she also had to respect her daughter's wishes. She reluctantly pulled in front of the police station and glanced back at her daughter. Hillary's hair was still dirty and stringy, she had not bothered changing clothes, but she had put on some makeup. Unfortunately, the dark eyeliner only accentuated the bags under Hillary's eyes.

Hillary sprang up between the front seats and gave each of her parents a kiss on the cheek. Without saying another word, she opened the car door and walked up the cement steps to the entrance of the police station. Reaching the glass doors, Hillary contemplated looking back toward her parents. Instead, she chose to focus straight ahead and entered the station.

Janice watched her daughter disappear into the gloomy building. Once Hillary was out of sight, Janice's body went limp, and a torrential flood poured from her eyes. Harold reached over from the passenger seat and turned off the car's ignition. He held his wife tightly as they both wept. Neither of them said the words, but at that moment, they both knew their daughter was gone forever.

FIVE

Hillary shuddered as the glass door of the police station slammed behind her.   She could not escape thoughts of iron bars clanking shut and locking her in, which was how she feared her day would end. The warm, summer air instantly vanished, replaced by a cold blast from the building's air conditioner. Hillary forced herself to move forward, each step requiring a quantum amount of strength.

Inside the lobby, Hillary spotted an information desk staffed by a middle-aged, overweight female cop, busy on a phone call. The officer caught sight of Hillary approaching and defensively held her finger up in Hillary's face in a shushing gesture. Hillary closed her mouth and waited. While the policewoman continued her conversation, Hillary turned around and studied her surroundings.

This was not Hillary's first time inside a police station.   She had been arrested several times for petty crimes – shoplifting, underage drinking, and possession of marijuana.   This station resembled all the others.   The cracked tile floor was permanently stained by years of dirt and grime.   Fluorescent lights provided a depressing, artificial glow.   Uniformed officers meandered this way and that. Some carried cups of coffee, while others guided handcuffed men and women to their destinations. Random, undecipherable squawks from police radios provided a unique form of white noise. People from every sector of society, ranging from drug dealers to middle-aged soccer moms, filled the station.

Five minutes later, the phone call ended. With blatant irritation, the officer asked Hillary, "Can I help you?"

Unappreciative of the officer's attitude, Hillary smacked her gum a couple of times and then answered, "Yeah, I'm here to meet Detective Morris."

"Your name?"

"Hillary Martin."

Hillary impatiently tapped her fingers on the officer's desktop. The woman scowled at Hillary's hand, refusing to do anything until the drumming ceased. Thirty seconds later, Hillary stopped.

The policewoman pointed to a row of chairs across the lobby. "Go take a seat."

Hillary wanted nothing more than to give the officer a piece of her mind, but she held her tongue and walked away. It turned out that Hillary did not have time to sit in one of the filthy chairs before she noticed two large men in dress shirts with identification badges around their necks headed straight for her. Once the officers were within feet of her, Hillary read their names. The taller, older man with graying hair, a small gut, and a prominent bald spot on top of his head was Detective Bob Morris. His cohort, Detective Joe Pacheco, was younger, leaner, and much more attractive.

Never having met either of these detectives face-to-face, Hillary was taken aback by the fact that they certainly seemed to recognize her.

Detective Morris introduced himself and his partner. Hillary stood in front of the men with her thumbs tucked in her back pockets and simply nodded. She was much too nervous to speak or shake hands.

Not wasting any time, Detective Morris pointed toward the back of the lobby and said, "Follow me."

Hillary felt her mouth go dry as she trailed behind Detective Morris, while Detective Pacheco took up the rear. She could not shake the impression that this line up was strategic, in case she tried to bolt. The threesome maneuvered through a maze of tight hallways and corridors until they came to a room at the end of a hall. A sign on the door read, "Interview Room 4." Detective Morris opened the door and gestured for Hillary to enter.

The room itself was intimidating by its mere simplicity. The space was small, no more than 10 feet by 12 feet. In the center sat a standard foldout table with two plastic chairs on one side and a single chair on the other. A video camera was mounted in a corner of the room near the ceiling. Hillary followed the trajectory of the lens and realized it was pointed directly at the chair she assumed she would occupy. A red light below the lens flashed on and off. She was already being videotaped.

Detective Morris followed Hillary inside the room. Pointing to the solitary chair, he said, "Please, take a seat."

Hillary sat down and noticed there was a one-way glass on the wall behind where the detectives took their chairs. Staring at her own reflection, knowing that strangers were likely behind the glass watching her, made Hillary feel self-conscious and vulnerable. There were three bottles of water on the table. Detective Morris offered one to Hillary, took one himself, and gave the last one to Detective Pacheco. With shaking hands, she accepted the bottle and twisted off the cap. Noisily, she swallowed one large gulp, wiping her mouth with the back of her hand.

"Ms. Martin," said Detective Morris, "just to lay the framework for our interview, I need to make sure you understand that your statements today are completely voluntary. You can end this interview any time you want. You also need to understand that anything you say can and will be held against you in a court of law. Is this all clear?"

Hillary slouched in her chair and tucked her unwashed hair behind her ears. Without looking up, she answered, "Yes."

Detective Morris continued, "Do you also understand that you have the right to have an attorney present during questioning? If you can't afford one, the court can appoint one for you."

"Yes." Hillary continued to speak in the direction of the floor.

Detective Morris handed a document and a pen to Hillary. "If you still wish to proceed with this interview without an attorney, I need to have you sign at the bottom of this form."

The gravity of the situation smothered Hillary as she held the pen. Glancing at Detective Morris, much like a daughter asking her father for advice, she questioned, "Do *you* think I should have an attorney?"

Detective Morris responded with cool professionalism, "I can't advise you one way or the other. It's up to you. But if you want one, now is the time to make that request."

Hillary placed the paper on the table, signed her name, and snickered, "I guess you guys pretty much know what's been going on already"

With the formalities completed, Detective Morris said, "Probably a good place to start is for you to tell us why *you* think you're here."

Hillary's response was flat and detached, "I'm here because, you know, I need to turn myself in. There are charges against me from St. Augustine Hospital involving drugs."

Detective Morris kept his focus on Hillary as he shifted topics. "Can you tell me how long you've been a scrub tech and where you've worked?"

Hillary lifted her head slightly, but still avoided any eye contact. "I got my first job in 2007, in Nevada. A year later, I moved with my boyfriend to Los Angeles. I was pregnant, and he had gotten a really good job there. We were trying to make the best life we could for the baby. Before my daughter was born, I worked in L.A. as a scrub tech for a while. And, of course, I worked at St. Augustine."

Detective Morris asked, "Were you fired or disciplined at either of the first two facilities where you worked? In Nevada or California?"

Hillary's voice was raspy. "I left the job in Nevada on good terms. I only quit because we were moving. In L.A., I was fired because of attendance issues. I had a lot of problems with the pregnancy and missed a lot of work. I always had doctors' notes to excuse my sick days, but they didn't care. It was just as well anyway, because the baby was about to come."

"So after you lost your job in L.A., and before you moved out here to work at St. Augustine Hospital, what did you do for money? You did have a baby to support, right?"

Hillary answered sadly, "Well, yes and no on the baby part. I did have a baby, a little girl named Amber.

Me and her dad split up pretty much right after she was born. I couldn't work *and* take care of Amber, so her dad took her up near San Francisco, and they lived with his mom. She helped take care of the baby while my ex worked. I moved in with some friends in L.A., but I didn't have a car, and I couldn't find any hospital jobs nearby. I did some waitressing for a while. Then, last fall, I called my folks. I think they could tell I needed help – I guess they could hear it in my voice. Anyway, they invited me to come back home. Once I moved out here, I got hired at St. Augustine almost immediately. I guess it was a lucky break."

Detective Morris tapped his pen on the wooden table. He leaned closer to Hillary and asked, "Since I'm not in the world of medicine, and I'd like to understand things as best I can, can you explain what a scrub tech does and the qualifications for the job?"

Hillary's eyes brightened. For the first time since the interview began, she sat up straight and turned to face the detective directly. With her head held high, Hillary confidently explained her job.

"Well, in order to become a scrub tech, you have to go to a certified program for about eighteen months. The scrub tech's job is to assist the surgeon on cases. Before the surgery started, I would go into the OR and open the instruments onto the surgical table. Then I would have to scrub in."

Sensing Hillary enjoyed playing the role of the expert, Detective Morris strived to maintain the momentum. He interjected, "What does that mean . . . 'scrub in?'"

Hillary became more animated and comfortable with every word. "Oh, that means I scrub my hands and arms with a special soap and sponge. Then I put on a sterile gown and gloves. The point is that no surface of my skin or clothing is exposed, or else I would contaminate the sterile surgical equipment. Sorry, I forget that not everyone knows what goes on in the OR."

"No need to be sorry. I find this fascinating. Please continue."

In response to Detective Morris's compliment, Hillary smiled. Speaking with authority, she continued, "Once I was sterile, I would set the instruments up for the case. Then, me and the circulating nurse would count everything on the table. When the surgeon came in, I would help him or her get into a sterile gown and gloves. Then I'd help place sterile drapes over the patient. During the case, I would pass instruments to the surgeon and assist them on whatever they needed help with. When the case was done, me and the circulating nurse would recount all the instruments, you know, to make sure nothing got left inside the patient. Once the case was done, I would gather up all the instruments and send them down to be sterilized."

"As a scrub tech, did you ever have to access medications for the surgical procedure?"

"The only meds that I had anything to do with were the ones used by the surgeon. Stuff like local anesthetics or steroids. The circulating nurse would open those meds and dump them into bowls on my surgical table. Then I would draw up the medication into a syringe and hand it to the surgeon."

"Are any of those medications that the circulating nurse would put on your table narcotics?"

"No," replied Hillary. "Only the anesthesiologist has the narcotics."

Detective Morris saw Hillary had already consumed her entire bottle of water and was starting to fidget with the bottle.

He asked her kindly, "Would you like more water?"

"Yeah, that would be great."

With that, Detective Pacheco took his cue as the junior detective and left the room to fetch more water. Detective Morris took advantage of the break in the conversation and asked, "Hillary, I need to make sure, before we go any further, that you still wish to voluntarily continue with this conversation and that you do not want an attorney."

Hillary defiantly interlaced her fingers and straightened her arms in front of her. The sound of knuckles cracking permeated the air. Hillary forcefully rolled her neck in alternating circles, as if preparing for a street fight. Once she was done, she said, "I'm fine. Let's keep going."

SIX

Detective Pacheco strolled back into the interview room with a cold bottle of water, which he politely handed to Hillary.

Detective Morris resumed his questioning. "So, Hillary, when did you get hired at St. Augustine?"

"Back in November of last year. I can't remember the exact date."

"And before you worked at St. Augustine, did you have any problems with drugs or substance abuse?"

"Yeah," Hillary replied. Images of high school occupied Hillary's consciousness – snorting coke in her friends' basements, skipping school to get high, stealing alcohol and money from her parents. These memories gave way to more recent events. She thought back to her time in L.A. and the filthy apartment she shared with four other people. Flies swarmed around dirty dishes piled in the sink. Garbage littered the floor. Hillary could almost feel the scratchy fibers of the stained carpet against her bare legs as she sat on the floor, shooting up in the sweltering heat of summer. Subconsciously, she grabbed her left arm as she recalled holding a hypodermic needle to her skin and pushing the sharp metal tip into her flesh. She longed for the rush she derived from injecting heroine into her vein.

Detective Morris watched Hillary intently. Her head was down and her hair fell forward, covering her face.

"When did your problems start?"

Hillary picked at a string hanging off the left thigh of her jeans, bracing herself for the horrible reality she was about to disclose.

"Well, it probably started when I was a kid. When I was about twelve, I broke my arm and had to have surgery to fix it. I was in a *lot* of pain, and I was taking pain pills for it. Even as a kid, I liked the way the pills made me feel. They just took everything and made it go away. I would sneak extra pills when my mom wasn't looking. I think that's what got the ball rolling. From that point forward, I'd pretty much take whatever I could get my hands on. Alcohol, weed, pills, whatever."

Detective Morris switched topics. "According to St. Augustine, the Department of Health, and the CDC, their investigation has revealed that you tested positive for hepatitis C during your pre-employment physical at St. Augustine. According to officials from the hospital, a nurse informed you of the test results when you were hired. She encouraged you to follow up with a specialist. Do you remember that?"

"I don't remember the exact details. I didn't feel sick, so I pretty much blew it off."

Hillary's lower lip trembled. She struggled in vain to hold back the tears before they slid from her eyes. Instinctively, she wiped her nose with the back of her arm. Detective Morris slid a box of tissues toward her.

Leaning forward, Detective Morris rested his arms on the table and remained silent. He stared at Hillary until she could feel his piercing gaze. She was compelled to look up at him.

With their eyes locked, Detective Morris asked, "Hillary, a big part of this case rests on whether or not you knew you had this infection while you worked at St. Augustine. Did you or did you not know you had the virus before you started working there?"

Hillary squirmed in her chair. All eyes were on her, pinning her down. "Yeah, I knew."

Emotionless, Detective Morris continued, "Do you admit to taking Fentanyl intended for patients and using it to inject yourself?"

Hillary rubbed her sweaty palms on her thighs. Her right foot tapped uncontrollably under the table. She bit down hard on her lower lip, leaving an impression of her teeth embedded in her skin.

"Yes." Hillary choked on her words.

"Was it only Fentanyl? Did you ever divert any other drugs?"

"No. I never took anything else."

Detective Morris scooted his chair in so that he was even closer to Hillary. The screech of the metal legs grinding against the floor caught Hillary off guard, and she impulsively raised her head. For several moments, the only sound in the interview room was the humming of the air conditioner. Finally, t and asked, "Can you tell me exactly how you stole the Fentanyl and what you'd do with the syringes?"

"Getting needles and syringes was easy. I would just grab some saline from wherever, draw up 5 cc into a syringe, and put a Fentanyl sticker on it. The Fentanyl labels were on top of all the anesthesia carts. They were real easy to get, too. Then I would keep the syringe in my pocket and wait for a chance to switch it out for the real deal. If the anesthesiologist walked out of the room and left their drugs, I'd sneak over and make the switch."

"So you would switch a syringe of Fentanyl that was drawn up by the anesthesiologist, intended for the patient, and then replace it with a syringe of saline?"

"Yep," Hillary answered bluntly. Although her tone indicated indifference, Detective Morris noticed Hillary swallow nervously.

He continued, "And once you had a syringe of Fentanyl in your pocket, when and where would you use it?"

"It all depended. Sometimes I'd save it and use it at home. Other times, I'd use it at work."

"I'm curious, with all the people around in the OR, how exactly would you administer the drug while you were at work?"

"I'd go into a stall in the women's restroom."

"And then you'd tie up your arm with a tourniquet?"

"Yes."

"And inject?"

"Mm-hm."

"And no one, not one of your colleagues or supervisors or any of the doctors, no one ever noticed that you were . . . ?"

"High? Nope. I guess I knew my limit. I was smart enough not to overdo it."

"Okay," Detective Morris continued, "I'd like to get back to the syringes. From what you've told me so far, it sounds like you would steal a syringe that was clean and contained Fentanyl and replace it with a syringe that was also clean, but contained saline. However, we now have at least six patients who have hepatitis C with your exact genotype, and four more that will likely be confirmed to have your genotype within the next several weeks. Can you help me understand how these patients contracted your strain of the virus?"

Hillary glanced up at the flashing red light on the camera and then at her reflection in the one-way mirror behind the detectives. Staring blindly at her image, she said, "There were times when I would keep the used syringes. I guess I got lazy. As time went on, I wouldn't always get a new syringe every time I made the swap. Sometimes I'd just fill the used syringe with saline and put it back in the cart."

Detective Morris masked his outrage and calmly asked, "Okay. So you said earlier you were aware that you had hepatitis C. When you were swapping syringes, trading out Fentanyl for saline, and doing that with a contaminated syringe, did the thought ever cross your mind that you could be infecting other people?"

"No," she responded flatly as her eyes shifted to her lap.

"Why not?"

Hillary clenched her fists under the table, digging her fingernails into her palms. "It just didn't."

"Do you now understand that you were responsible for infecting patients?"

Hillary focused on the scratched surface of the table and nodded.

"We need you to answer out loud."

Hillary inhaled deeply and replied, "Yes."

"How many times would you estimate that you stole Fentanyl from the anesthesia carts and replaced it with another syringe?"

Hillary shrugged, "I really couldn't say. I don't know an exact number."

"Well, we just want to try to get some kind of handle on the magnitude of this situation. Do you think it was closer to ten or a hundred? Did you do it every day?"

Hillary's head whipped up as she spat out, "Oh no, not every day! It mostly depended on whether it was available or not. I'd estimate maybe fifteen to twenty times total."

"Do you remember any particular anesthesiologists whom you may have habitually targeted?"

Hillary's eyes and mouth opened wide, and she raised her eyebrows. "It wasn't like that. It was based completely on opportunity. If I saw the drugs lying out on the anesthesia cart and no one was in the room, I'd make the swap. Some days, I had the chance and took it. Other days, not so much."

Detective Morris persisted, "Which kind of leads us to how you were ultimately caught. You were in a room that you weren't assigned to. Isn't that part of how you also found the opportunity to divert? By going into other rooms and looking for narcotics?"

"On that day, the day I think you're talking about, I finished setting up my room early and had time to kill before my case started. I was friends with a nurse who was working in one of the other rooms, and I wanted to tell her about this new guy I was seeing. I hadn't gone in there looking for Fentanyl, but when I walked past the anesthesia cart, I noticed there was a syringe of it sitting out, and I made the switch.

"The scrub tech in the room noticed that I was lurking around the anesthesia cart, and she asked me what I was doing. I told her I was looking for a Band-Aid. She didn't buy it. I'm pretty sure she was the one who reported me to the charge nurse. Anyway, I just left the room.

"Later that morning, I was scrubbed in on my case, and another tech came in to relieve me. I thought I was just getting a break. When I walked out of the OR, the charge nurse and the nursing supervisor were waiting for me in the hallway. They immediately escorted me down to the ER, where I was given a drug screen."

"And the drug screen came up positive for Fentanyl?"

"Obviously that's true, or I wouldn't be here today," said Hillary, agitated.

Detective Morris ignored her sarcasm. "What did St. Augustine do from there?"

"They immediately suspended me. They told me they would arrange for a meeting to discuss things. I knew my job was over, so I pretty much blew off all their phone calls and letters from that point forward. I never bothered to show up for any of their meetings."

Changing subjects, Detective Morris asked, "Do you know how you were initially exposed to hepatitis C?"

Hillary mumbled, "Um, probably in L.A., before I moved out here. I was shooting up heroin. I did it for about three months. I was sharing needles with some people up there."

The detective rubbed the stubble on his chin and furrowed his brow.

"Hillary," he said with reproach, "you just told me that you got hepatitis from sharing dirty needles. Yet, you want me to believe you didn't think that your dirty needles would infect patients?"

Hillary remained quiet.

Detective Morris leaned back and stretched his legs. He inhaled deeply, filling up his chest.

After holding his breath for several seconds, he released, and the hard rush of his breath travelled across the table.

Hillary could feel the warm air and smell the stale scent of coffee as the blast hit her face. She shifted back in her chair to escape it.

Detective Pacheco recognized his cue and spoke into the microphone. "This concludes our interview. Still present in the room are Hillary Martin, Detective Morris, and Detective Pacheco. Time is 17:05, and the date is June 5, 2010. Ms. Martin will now be read her rights and taken into custody."

The red light on the camera continued to blink. Hillary sat motionless with her arms crossed against her chest.

Detective Pacheco instructed her, "Please stand and place your arms behind your back. You are under arrest for diversion of and tampering with narcotics."

Stiffly, Hillary obeyed his orders. Staring at the one-way mirror, she felt the heavy metal handcuffs being tightened around her wrists. Her mind drifted as Detective Pacheco read her Miranda rights and led her out of the room. Before following them, Detective Morris looked into the one-way mirror and nodded.

Keith Jones, the CEO of St. Augustine Hospital, frowned back at the detective, knowing his expression was invisible to the officer. Mr. Jones dialed his attorney.

"We need to meet. Now. But before then, make sure this story stays out of the press for at least a few days. I don't care what it costs, just make it happen."

Not waiting for an answer, Keith Jones hung up and marched out of the police station.

SEVEN

June 14, 2010

Jenna woke at 5 a.m. to the incessant beeping of her alarm clock. Her fingers expertly located the snooze button as she dove under the silky sheets and lazily lingered in bed. Her back was to Tom, but she could feel the mattress shift as her husband began to stir. Tom rolled toward Jenna and pressed his warm body against hers. She wiggled herself closer to her husband, moaning as their skin touched. Tom gently kissed the back of her neck, working his way to her ears. His hot, moist breath sent shivers through Jenna. He slid his fingers underneath her silk panties. Jenna was wet with anticipation. Tom plunged his fingers inside her, slowly dancing in and out, tantalizing her with his touch.

"Good morning, Mr. Reiner," Jenna purred. She peeled off her panties and guided Tom inside her.

"Good morning, sexy," Tom whispered into her ear.

Jenna's breathing became erratic as Tom's thrusts grew more forceful and aggressive. Within minutes, they cried out into the silent house as they both climaxed.

She giggled as she pulled away from her husband. "We better learn to keep it down. One of these days, we're going to wake Mia."

The morning sun was beginning to rise, filling their bedroom with a soft glow. Jenna could just make out the contour of Tom's muscles. Looking at him, with his blonde hair and light blue eyes, she started to get aroused again.

Jenna forced herself to check the time and groaned. Ginger, their Golden Retriever, interpreted Jenna's sound as an invitation. Without hesitation, the dog jumped on the bed and snuggled up to Jenna.

Tom laughed. "Looks like, at the very least, we piqued our dog's interest."

Unenthusiastically, Jenna climbed out of bed. The sweet scent of sex lingered on her body. She pulled on her fluffy, pink robe and sauntered barefoot down the cool, travertine tile hallway into the kitchen. Jenna let Ginger outside to do her business and made coffee. With two warm mugs in her hands, she returned to their bedroom and handed a cup to Tom.

"Thanks, babe," Tom replied, propping himself up in bed.

Jenna grinned as she leaned over her husband and kissed him hungrily. He attempted to pull her back into bed, but Jenna shook her head seductively and walked into the bathroom. She turned on the shower, waited for steam to rise from the glass walls, and stepped inside. Closing her eyes, Jenna relaxed under the stream of hot water. From the bedroom, she heard Tom turn the television on.

Jenna was scrubbing her hair when Tom began shouting. She could not understand what her husband was saying, but he kept calling her name. With her head still covered with shampoo, Jenna threw a towel around her body and ran into the bedroom, dripping a trail of water and suds along the way.

Tom was sitting upright in bed, pointing at the television. He turned up the volume. The tail end of a commercial blared from the TV.

Jenna was perplexed and mildly annoyed. "Tom, what the hell is going on?"

Tom hushed his wife and stared at the TV. The broadcast returned to the morning newscast. A petite, blonde reporter from Channel 8 was standing outside of St. Augustine Hospital with a microphone in her hand.

Jenna fell silent as she watched the report.

"Channel 8 News has just learned that a surgical scrub technician who, up until recently, worked at St. Augustine Hospital, may have put thousands of patients at risk for acquiring hepatitis C. The scrub tech's name is Hillary Martin, and she is infected with the hepatitis C virus. In a videotaped police interview, Martin admitted to stealing syringes filled with Fentanyl, an extremely powerful and addictive narcotic. Martin also confessed to injecting herself with the drug. She would swap the stolen syringes with used ones filled with saline and remnants of her own virus-laden blood. Anesthesiologists, unaware of the theft, may have used the contaminated syringes on surgical patients during their procedures.

"Representatives from St. Augustine hospital have yet to confirm Martin's alleged actions, stating that the investigation is ongoing. Standing here, we have Keith Jones, the CEO of St. Augustine Hospital. Mr. Jones, what can you tell us?"

The cameraman zoomed in on Mr. Jones, an attractive, middle-aged man, with short, gray hair and an athletic build. Jenna was immediately drawn to his eyes.

They were small, dark, beady, and ominous. Something about Keith Jones intimidated her.

A man of power and control, Mr. Jones demonstrated nothing less as he spoke to the camera in a commanding voice. "St. Augustine strives to provide the very best in patient care. Our patients' health and safety have always been, and continue to be, our highest priority. We urge all patients who had surgery at St. Augustine between November 2009 and April 2010 to come to our hospital for free, confidential hepatitis testing. We are shocked at the allegations that have come to surface and are diligently trying to work out the best plan of action to make sure our patients receive the care they deserve. Thank you."

Mr. Jones turned and walked away before the reporter could attempt another question.

Tom turned down the volume and looked directly at Jenna.

"Do you know the tech?" he asked nervously.

Jenna thought for a minute and then shook her head. "I don't think so. I mean, I suppose I may have worked with her."

Jenna nibbled at her thumbnail. Tom reached up and pulled her hand away from her mouth. He knew his wife was deeply troubled.

"Jenna, what are you thinking?"

"Things are only going to get worse," she said glumly. Jenna left her husband alone on the bed and returned to the shower.

Between her interlude with Tom and the news story, Jenna was running late. She rushed to get dressed.

Mia came down from her room to kiss her mother goodbye for the day. Jenna buried her head in Mia's long blonde curls and hugged her tightly. Before letting go of her daughter, Jenna sneaked a glance at the television.

It was a few minutes after 7 a.m., and the local news had switched over to the national affiliate.   To Jenna's horror, the lead story was St. Augustine Hospital and the hepatitis C outbreak. The event was officially *big* news.

Jenna smiled when she kissed Mia, careful to protect her daughter from her own mounting anxiety. Glancing at Tom, Jenna sensed his apprehension.

Tom moved closer to Jenna and whispered in her ear, "Call me if you hear anything new."

Jenna nodded solemnly.

"Have a good day at work and school," Jenna said to Tom and Mia as she left the house. "I love you both."

On the drive in, Jenna listened to the story being recapped on the radio. After the third iteration, she had enough. She turned the radio off and drove the rest of the way in silence.

Approaching the street in front of St. Augustine Hospital, Jenna was astonished by the amount of chaos. Every major local news affiliate had a van stationed directly in front of the hospital, and a sea of satellite dishes extended into the air. A number of police cars were present with officers standing outside the entrance.

Jenna pulled into the parking lot. Before getting out of her car, she sighed heavily, hoping the release would prepare her for things to come. Hastily, she made her way through a side door into the lobby of the hospital.

Inside, there was complete pandemonium. Tables, staffed by nurses and hospital administrators, had been set up across the entire length of the lobby. Hand-printed posters were taped to the walls that read "Hepatitis

Testing/Information." Hundreds of horrified people, presumably patients, descended upon the tables, searching for answers.

Suddenly, Jenna felt conspicuous in her surgical scrubs. Afraid of being accosted by an angry or frightened patient, she quickened her pace and disappeared into the safety of a back stairwell that led up to the operating rooms.

Jenna walked directly to the doctors' lounge. The room was crowded with other anesthesiologists, all of whom were speaking at once. She moved toward the back of the room, catching portions of conversations along her way.

"Do you leave your drugs sitting out?"

"How could this have happened, right here, in our ORs?"

"I wonder who she stole from."

Dr. Rob Wilson strode into the lounge looking deeply troubled. His already ruddy complexion took on a deeper hue of red, and his wrinkles were accentuated by his frown. Rob Wilson, standing at 6 feet, 4 inches and weighing over 250 pounds, was a man who, on physical stature alone, was difficult to ignore. His professional accomplishments also demanded respect. Dr. Wilson was both Chief of the Anesthesia Department at St. Augustine and President of Jenna's group. Her colleagues took note of his presence, and their conversations began to die down. Eventually, the sound of multiple doctors shushing one another overpowered the last conversations, and the room became silent.

"All right," Rob said, "I know you all have a lot of questions. Let me just start by telling you what I know. There has been a cluster of patients testing positive for hepatitis C who lack the traditional risk factors. The common thread among these patients is that they all had surgery at our hospital between November of last year and April of this year.

"Coincidentally, at the same time that these cases were being investigated by the State Health Department, one of the surgical scrub techs from the main OR was caught using Fentanyl. Her name, as many of you now probably know, is Hillary Martin, and she worked here during the time period in question. She was known to be positive for hepatitis C at the time she was hired.

"About ten days ago, Ms. Martin turned herself in to authorities. Martin has admitted to stealing syringes of Fentanyl from our anesthesia carts. She would inject herself with the drug and replace the dirty syringe, refilled with saline, back on our carts before any of us noticed the theft. Unfortunately, if what she says is true, then at least some of us unknowingly injected hepatitis C virus directly into our patients' bloodstream while they were under our care."

The doctors were speechless, and the collective body heat was causing the room to become stuffy.

Rob caught his breath and continued, "At this point, ten patients have tested positive for hepatitis C. We have no idea how many more will turn up as we proceed with mass testing.

"We will try to get more news to you as it becomes available. At this point, I must discourage all of you from discussing this matter with other members of the OR staff or other anesthesiologists who are not part of our group. The potential legal implications of this debacle are nothing short of epic. As such, I must also ask that all of you refrain from engaging in any discussions with the media. For now, that's all I know. I suggest that the best thing we can do is get back to work and continue to take excellent care of our patients."

Once Dr. Wilson had concluded his speech, the noise in the room quickly escalated as Jenna's colleagues pelted him with questions. Jenna, unable to tolerate the frenzy, quietly slipped away.

Despite having been warned about discussing the scandal, it was the main topic of conversation throughout the operating rooms. By the end of the day, the speculations and rumors only made Jenna more upset and uncertain.

Shortly after 3:30 p.m., Jenna's cases were over, and she was mentally exhausted. Slipping out one of the back doors of the hospital, she made it to her car undetected, and drove home in silence.

Pulling into her driveway, Jenna whispered to herself, "Please, God, don't let this involve me."

EIGHT

June 15, 2010

At 3 a.m. Jenna lay in bed, wide-awake with a pounding headache and a profound sense of dread. The racket from the chirping of crickets outside her open window sliced through her. Jenna had hoped that the Ambien she consumed the night before would have allowed her to sleep. Unfortunately, the sedative was unable to conquer her racing mind. Giving up on any hope of rest, Jenna grabbed her glasses, quietly rolled out of bed, and tiptoed down the hallway. Ginger's paws clicked against the tile as the dog trailed behind her. When Jenna reached the kitchen, she could hear Tom snoring. In the early morning stillness, she swallowed four tablets of Advil and made a cup of tea.

Jenna headed to her home office. Not wanting to wake the rest of her family, she left the lights off. Carefully, she felt her way behind her antique, cherry desk and sat in the leather chair. Alone in the darkness, Jenna wiggled the computer's mouse. The light from the monitor was barely enough to illuminate the keyboard, but it was sufficient for Jenna's purposes. She opened her email. Midway down the screen, her attention was drawn to an email from Dr. Rob Wilson.

With a trembling finger, Jenna clicked on the mouse and opened the document. She was completely engrossed when Tom's voice startled her.

"Hey there! Can't sleep?" he asked.

Jenna nearly toppled over her tea. She could barely make out Tom's frame. "Geez! You scared me to death! What are you doing up?"

"I should ask you the same thing," Tom muttered as he switched on the lights. "Everything okay?"

Jenna squinted as the brightness hit her eyes. Tom walked behind her and massaged her neck. For a moment, Jenna closed her eyes, enjoying the warmth of Tom's powerful hands against her bare skin.

"Actually," she groaned, "I didn't sleep a wink last night. My world is upside down. Everything I've ever been taught to trust – the hospital, the staff – are all suspect. I just opened an email written by Keith Jones, Mr. Big Shot CEO himself. It's addressed to all St. Augustine physicians. Rob Wilson forwarded it off late last night."

Tom peered over Jenna's shoulders. "This ought to be interesting."

Jenna leaned closer to the screen and pushed her glasses up, "Yeah . . . interesting alright. It says the hospital is extremely remorseful regarding the unconscionable acts of their former employee. They intend to remain open and honest in their communications, and they want the physicians to know that most patients are not at risk."

Tom listened intently. "So far, it sounds like either they are the most honest, compassionate, for-profit corporation known to man, or the cover up has begun."

"I'd vote for the latter," Jenna replied grimly.

Jenna's back stiffened as she continued reading the email.

"Oh my God! You're not going to believe this!" Jenna cupped her hand over her mouth. "Any patients who acquire hepatitis C as a result of Hillary Martin's actions will be provided free medical care for life, including liver transplantation, if necessary."

Tom stood in silence for a few minutes while he digested what Jenna had said.

"What's your take on this memo?" he asked.

Jenna swiveled the office chair around to face her husband and slowly shook her head.

"I really don't know. It feels . . . big . . . huge. It looks like the hospital has already lawyered up. I get the sense that they are trying to walk that fine line between appearing like they care yet, at the same time, aggressively covering their ass."

Tom nodded. "Yeah, I agree. This is something that could ultimately take St. Augustine down for good. It remains to be seen how many patients are infected, but it's pretty much guaranteed that each and every one of them is going to sue, and probably for big bucks. The testing of thousands of patients alone is going to cost them a fortune, not to mention providing a lifetime of medical care for every infected patient."

Jenna was gripped by an alarming revelation. "I hope St. Augustine doesn't throw anesthesia under the bus as a scapegoat."

Tom looked pale. Stroking Jenna's cheek, he said, "You and me both."

Retreating into the kitchen to make some coffee, Tom left Jenna alone with her growing apprehension.

Jenna turned back around to face the computer and called up the website for the local news affiliate. Not surprisingly, the lead story was the hepatitis scare at St. Augustine Hospital, but there was little more information than the day before.

Thirsty for more details, Jenna typed Hillary Martin's name into a Google search. The first hit was a Facebook page. Unsure if it was *the* Hillary Martin, Jenna rapidly clicked to the link.

The photographs on the screen reignited memories of the scrub tech with whom Jenna had worked, but barely knew. With Hillary Martin's crimes now revealed, the images on the screen were deeply disturbing.

Jenna sat motionless, mesmerized by the photos. Her concentration was broken by the scent of fresh coffee, as Tom entered the office holding two steaming cups.

"Thanks," Jenna said, gratefully accepting the additional caffeine. She blew over the surface of the mug and cautiously took a sip.

"Don't mention it." Tom walked around to Jenna's side of the desk and pulled a chair up next to her. Right away, Tom took in the images on the computer screen and asked, "Who the hell is that? Please don't tell me that's our next nanny."

Jenna was too mortified to appreciate Tom's humor. Instead, she responded with a barely audible whisper, "No Tom, it's not our next nanny. Say hello to Hillary Martin."

Tom took a closer look at the pictures. He had not yet noticed the tears spilling down Jenna's cheeks. When Tom finally glanced at his wife, Jenna was nearly catatonic. Her mouth was agape, her eyes wide, and her pupils dilated.

"Jenna," Tom said as he pulled his wife into his arms. "What's wrong, baby?"

Whispering shallowly, Jenna confessed, "I remember working with her! There was this patient I took care of a while back that had a clit ring. During the surgery, we were all commenting on it. Hillary Martin was the scrub tech for that case. She told us she had one, too. It stands out in my mind because who would admit to such a thing? Especially to people you don't know very well."

Tom looked at his wife and asked, "Do you remember anything else?"

Jenna tried to think back, but it had been many months ago. Like a bolt of electricity, a memory struck her. Jenna stood and started pacing, shaking her head as she muttered repeatedly, "Oh no! No, no, no."

The world crashed in upon Jenna. The lights in the room swirled around her. A tingly, buzzing sensation enveloped her body. Her heart raced, her mouth went dry, and she gasped for air. An immovable lump in her throat made it impossible to speak. She could hear Tom's voice, but it sounded distant and distorted. Everything she had worked for seemed to be in jeopardy. Worse, what if her patient was infected? Jenna was drowning in guilt, grief, and fear.

Tom shook Jenna by the shoulders and forced her to focus on him. "What? Jenna, what's wrong?"

Jenna's heart sank. "I remember she disappeared before the start of the case. I went to see the patient, and when I came back, she was gone. They had to track her down. Tom, what if she stole my drugs?"

Tom did not answer. He did not have the heart to tell Jenna what he was thinking.

NINE

Later that morning, Jenna fought to clear her head as she prepared for her first case. However, as she drew up drugs for her patient, she was reminded of the devastation that Hillary Martin had left in her wake. For the past week, Jenna had been struggling to adapt to new hospital rules. Anesthesiologists were no longer allowed to draw up controlled substances until the patient physically entered the operating room. Serving as a constant reminder, a copy of the policy was taped prominently to the front of every Accudose machine. At first, before the story broke, Jenna thought the new policy was the result of some government regulation. Only now did she understand its significance.

Jenna glanced at the memo, and it struck her that it was dated June 7, 2010. This was a week before she, or any of her colleagues, had any knowledge of Hillary Martin's crimes. Coincidentally, it was also two days after Hillary Martin turned herself in to the authorities.

The timing of the policy left Jenna feeling deceived. Her new reality consisted of a world where the operating room was no longer considered safe, and the staff could not be trusted. More troubling, it was not only the staff that Jenna could no longer count on. She strongly suspected that the hospital administration, including Rob

Wilson, was controlling, withholding, and possibly covering up information.

The nurse wheeled in Jenna's first patient. Immediately, Jenna turned her back and logged into the Accudose machine. She resented being forced to neglect her patient while she drew up drugs. It placed her in the uncomfortable position of having to rely too heavily on the nurses. Too many things could go wrong, and Jenna was powerless to defend against it.

With her drugs ready, Jenna was now able to focus. Everything the nurses did needed to be rechecked. EKG leads were in the wrong location, the oxygen saturation probe was on the wrong hand, and not one of the nurses had bothered to provide supplemental oxygen to the patient. Jenna silently went about the business of correcting their mistakes, trying to mask her frustration.

Dr. Jon Miner, the surgeon, entered the room as Jenna was in the process of intubating.

"Hey, Jenna," Jon said as he watched her carefully tape the endotracheal tube in place.

Jon and Jenna had a friendly relationship, but as Jenna glanced up, she noticed that the usual warmth in Jon's brown eyes was missing.

Jenna forced herself to paste on a convincing smile. "Hey, Jon. I see you must have survived the madness of the lobby. Congratulations."

The two doctors waited for the nurse to prep the patient for surgery. With the nurse preoccupied with her task, Jon moved in close to Jenna and said discreetly, "It's crazy around here."

Jenna crinkled her forehead and frowned as she replied softly, "Yeah. It's getting scarier by the minute. Personally, I worry about how we anesthesia doctors will be impacted."

Not one to mince words, Jon told Jenna, "Honestly, I think you guys could be in a lot of trouble. Aren't you supposed to be responsible for your drugs? If that scrub tech was able to somehow steal narcotics because anesthesiologists weren't securing them, I think that opens you guys up to lawsuits."

Jon's words intensified Jenna's premonition that she might end up with an infected patient.

Jenna was defensive. "I guess it might all depend on how you did or didn't secure your drugs. I mean, if you left them sitting on the top of your cart in plain view, in an unoccupied room where anyone walking in could easily see them and take them, that would be one thing. But if you hid them somewhere, or took other measures to keep them out of sight, that seems to me to be a different story."

"Well, I'm not trying to scare you, but I had an interesting conversation with one of my neighbors last night, who just happens to be the father of Lyle Silverstein." Jon's words sounded foreboding, but the name meant nothing to Jenna.

"Who is Lyle Silverstein?"

"I can't believe you don't know," Jon said, somewhat condescendingly. "Obviously, you haven't faced a lawsuit yet in this town. Lyle Silverstein is one of the most aggressive, nasty, ruthless, and vindictive malpractice attorneys in the state. He also happens to be one of the most successful. So anyway, I ran into his father while grabbing my mail last night, and, naturally, this topic came up. His dad actually said with pride that Lyle is already representing several infected patients, and he expects to get more. According to Silverstein senior, Lyle is calling this his 'retirement package,' and he is gearing up for huge settlements. What probably matters most to you is that Lyle plans to go after both the hospital and the anesthesiologists. Like I said, if you end up with an infected patient, you could be in some serious trouble."

Jon sensed the nurse was eavesdropping. He shifted closer to Jenna and lowered his voice. "Jenna, do you think you could be at risk?"

Jenna's fear escalated. A headache started to sweep over her, along with a wave of nausea. She answered Jon in a secretive whisper, "I don't know. I mean, I *never* left my drugs just sitting out. Anyway, I just don't see how they could pin this on the anesthesiologist. The operating room is supposed to be a secure environment. It's not our fault the hospital hired a criminal."

"Well Jenna, the anesthesia doctors may not have been the ones that pulled the trigger on the proverbial gun, but at least some of you left the gun loaded, cocked, and sitting out. Without the gun sitting there, none of this would be happening."

Jon's harsh words left Jenna feeling wounded.

She asked shrilly, "You think we are at least partially responsible for all this? How can you think something like that?" Heat rose up Jenna's neck.

Unable to face Jenna's shocked expression, Jon left the room to scrub for the case. He never answered her question.

The next four hours of the case passed uneventfully. Jon chatted mainly with the nurses, while his selection of jazz blared from the operating room speakers. Normally, Jenna would have been annoyed by the loud music – today was different. At least it relieved her from feeling obligated to engage in any further conversation with Jon. For the duration of the case, Jenna stayed hidden behind the surgical drapes, silently lost in thought.

The case finished up around noon. In the recovery room, Jenna was in the middle of giving report to the nurse when she felt a hand grip her shoulder. She glanced back to see Jon, standing behind her. He whispered in her ear, "Jenna, I can't change the way I feel, but, for what it's worth, I really hope that none of your patients were infected."

Jenna smiled nervously and whispered, "Me too."

TEN

Jenna's stomach growled as she left the recovery room and headed toward the cafeteria in search of food. Passing the nurses' lounge, she noticed it was unusually crowded. Spotting Rebecca, Jenna sprinted to catch up with her in the hallway.

"Hey, Rebecca. What's going on in there?"

Rebecca spoke softly, as if she were divulging a secret. "Keith Jones is going to update the staff on the hep C stuff."

"Is this meeting just for nurses, or can I go too?"

Rebecca responded kindly, "I don't see why you can't attend. Go on in. There's some pizza in there, so feel free to help yourself."

"Thanks," Jenna said. She headed into the crammed nurses' lounge and stood inconspicuously near the doorway. Even though the pizza smelled delicious, her appetite had disappeared.

Most of the rectangular lounge was occupied by a large dining table. The relatively small amount of remaining space was inadequately suited to accommodate what appeared to be at least fifty staff members who had gathered for the impromptu meeting. Every chair at the long dining table was taken, some being shared by two nurses. Other staff members stood against the walls. Even though most of the staff took advantage of the free lunch, they chewed their food in silence, not wanting to miss a single detail of what Keith Jones was about to say.

Jenna surveyed the room. Finally, at one end of the table, she spotted the CEO. They had never been introduced. In fact, the first time Jenna ever had a face to put with his name was the day she saw him on the news. However menacing Keith Jones appeared to be on TV, in person he was more formidable. The CEO was undeniably handsome, but in a hard, chiseled sort of way.

With practiced style, Keith Jones held up his hands, signaling everyone to quiet down. The gesture was unnecessary. Every person in the room had already fallen completely quiet. Keith Jones confidently addressed the crowd, "Thank you all for coming. I know it's your lunch period, but with so many staff members, this seemed like the best way to gather the most of you in one place. Hopefully, you all got something to eat. Just so I have a sense of who is in attendance, are most of you operating room nurses and scrub techs?"

Many of the staff simply nodded. One of the operating room nurses noticed Jenna standing by the door and said, "We also have an anesthesiologist here. Dr. Reiner." At the mention of her name, the crowd collectively turned their heads toward Jenna, who blushed at being singled out. She looked directly at Keith Jones. His relentless stare perturbed Jenna, but she forced herself to return his gaze. Instantly, she got the impression that he was familiar with her. It was a fleeting awareness, yet undeniably present.

Suddenly, Jenna felt like a trespasser and regretted having come into the lounge. She addressed Keith Jones, while the entire room remained focused on her. "I thought this meeting was open to everyone. I don't want to intrude, so I can leave if the meeting was not meant for physicians."

Keith Jones continued to concentrate on Jenna. His haunting scrutiny made her feel like he knew her deepest, darkest secrets. In a tone that revealed nothing, Mr. Jones said, "No, Dr. Reiner, it's fine that you're here. Please feel free to stay." Following his approval, the eyes and ears of the staff shifted their attention back to the CEO.

He resumed his address, "As you are all probably aware, we have had some very unfortunate events occur recently at St. Augustine. I'm going to assume that, by now, you all know the basic details of Hillary Martin and her crimes. If not, I encourage you to visit the employee website.

"At this point, you all are strongly discouraged from talking about this issue in any area where patients may be present, as well as speaking to members of the press.

"From a preventive standpoint, all staff anesthesiologists have been advised as to changes in policy regarding the handling and securing of controlled substances. Under no circumstances are any drugs, but most importantly controlled substances, to be left out on anesthesia carts without an anesthesiologist present in the room. Any violation of this policy should be reported immediately to the charge nurse or the chairman of the anesthesia department, Dr. Rob Wilson. Now, if there are any questions, I can attempt to answer them."

Impulsively, Jenna raised her hand before she had the good sense to stop herself. Keith Jones had already been gazing in her direction and did not hesitate to call on her, "Yes, Dr. Reiner?"

Jenna strained to keep her voice even in order to conceal her fear of Keith Jones as she asked, "I just want to clarify exactly what you mean by how our drugs should be stored. I understand that our drugs cannot be sitting out in plain sight. My question, however, is whether it is acceptable to store our drugs within the drawers of our anesthesia machine? Is that considered secure?"

Keith Jones glared at Jenna as if she were the criminal. "At this point, unless drugs are locked within your anesthesia cart or are being carried on your person, they are no longer considered secure. Just so you all know, locks will be installed on all carts by the end of this week."

Several nurses raised their hands, and Keith Jones shifted his attention elsewhere. Jenna slipped out of the nurses' lounge undetected. The interaction left Jenna deeply disturbed. She tried to dismiss it, but Jenna could not shake the feeling that he was somehow sizing her up for a particular reason.

Jenna arrived home early in the afternoon. The house was quiet and empty, but Jenna could hear Mia and her babysitter, Kim, in the backyard engaged in a water-balloon war. The two girls were so wrapped up in their game that neither of them noticed Jenna's arrival. Jenna watched in delight as Mia giggled and squealed.

Hiding behind a lawn chair, Mia taunted Kim, "You can't get me!"

Kim shouted back, "Just did!" The splash of water exploding from the impact of a balloon hitting the chair threw both girls into a laughing fit.

From the deck, Jenna could see Mia's golden hair was soaked and matted to her head. Her daughter's eyes twinkled with joy and innocence.   For a moment, the luxury of seeing her only child so happy allowed Jenna to overlook the strangeness of the day. A genuine smile crept over Jenna's face as she tried to put things in perspective.

ELEVEN

June 16, 2010

Jenna woke early and left the house by 6:00 a.m. She had been notified the night before that Rob Wilson would be holding a meeting at her group's office building at 6:30. Attendance was mandatory, and anyone who missed the meeting would be fined. All OR start times had been postponed. Jenna had never seen anything like this in her entire career.

At 6:20, Jenna arrived at the offices of Mountain Anesthesia Services. In the conference room, foldout chairs had been set up to accommodate the sixty or so members of her group. Jenna took a seat in the back. Five minutes later, every chair was occupied.

Rob Wilson, dressed in black slacks and a pressed white shirt, walked in at exactly 6:30. He strode to the front of the room. His voice was powerful and loud. There was a microphone present, but Rob Wilson had no reason to use it.

"Good morning, and thank you all for arriving promptly. This meeting is intended to make sure we are all on the same page with respect to the hepatitis issue. Mountain Anesthesia Services has been working diligently in cooperation with attorneys from our malpractice carrier and representatives from St. Augustine Hospital. Our attorneys have produced a list of guidelines intended to help all M.A.S. doctors in dealing with this issue."

Jenna nervously glanced around the room as she tried to read the faces and thoughts of her colleagues. Everyone appeared unusually serious and subdued. Other than that, nobody was giving anything away.

Rob Wilson continued, "To begin with, you all must refrain from contacting any patients you may know personally, or any potentially infected patients. If an M.A.S. physician becomes aware that one of his or her patients was infected with hepatitis C during the critical time period, we advise that under no circumstances should you contact those patients. If a patient that you treated contacts you directly, do not discuss this matter or any other aspect of their care. Instead, refer them directly to St. Augustine Hospital. Counsel has further advised us to refrain from offering any apologies to patients, as such statements could later be interpreted as admissions of guilt if litigation occurs."

It was the first time Jenna had ever heard the term "counsel has advised." To her, it sounded particularly formal and daunting.

"I know this next point is going to bother most of you. St. Augustine has a list of the infected patients to date and therefore also knows which of us are involved. At this time, our malpractice carrier has advised us *not* to request a copy of this list. We have been advised to wait until St. Augustine completes its investigation and then voluntarily provides us the list."

His statement caused an uprising amongst the doctors in the room. Many of Jenna's colleagues stood up, gesturing wildly and shouting in outrage. Rob's thunderous voice was drowned out.

"We have a right to know!"

"These are our patients!"

"How can they keep that information from us?"

The noise level increased, but Jenna tuned them all out. She thought about Keith Jones and whether this explained the ominous look he had given her the day before.

Rob Wilson did his best to remain calm, but his face flushed. His fellow physicians continued to bombard him with anger. In an effort to regain control, he pounded his fist on the table and bellowed at the group.

"Alright, everyone, we all need to calm down. This is the advice from our attorneys. As unsavory as it is, it would be foolish and ill-advised to ignore their recommendations.

"Also, if any of you are contacted by the media, counsel has strongly advised that all M.A.S. physicians refrain from offering any commentary or speculation."

In his concluding remarks, Rob Wilson dropped an unexpected axe. "You must all understand that failure to abide by these guidelines could be grounds for suspension or termination. It is imperative that we all act cohesively."

Jenna could not believe what she had just heard. She felt agitated, nervous, betrayed, belittled, and angry. Jenna knew Hillary Martin would pay dearly for her crimes. For everyone else pulled into this nightmare, the fate of the scrub tech did not matter. Patients would sue and since Hillary Martin had nothing, the lawsuits would be aimed elsewhere. Jenna was certain that meant both the hospital *and* the doctors.

She thought about Keith Jones. He struck her as a self-centered, underhanded son-of-a-bitch. As the head of St. Augustine Hospital, Jenna was certain Mr. Jones would eventually place public blame on the anesthesia doctors.

How far Keith Jones was prepared to go in order to save his hospital remained to be seen.

The meeting officially adjourned, and Jenna was eager to escape. She had no desire to dissect Rob Wilson's words with any of the other doctors. Jenna was walking to her car when she had a thought that literally stopped her dead in her tracks.

What would I do if Mia had gone in for a simple surgery and had come out infected with hepatitis C?

Jenna felt fury and rage swell up inside her at the thought of her daughter having been harmed. Her answer came to her without hesitation.

I would sue everyone involved and take him or her for all that they had. I wouldn't stop until everyone who bore any responsibility suffered miserably. I would seek revenge.

At that exact moment, Jenna fully comprehended the degree of trouble she faced if she indeed had an infected patient.

TWELVE

August 2010

The Reiner family returned from a well-deserved, two-week vacation in Hawaii.   In Jenna's absence, life slowly returned to near normal for the medical community at St. Augustine Hospital.   Media coverage dwindled. Patients continued to be tested for hepatitis C, but the majority had already been through the process. The lobby of St. Augustine had been restored to its pre-hepatitis, non-chaotic state.   Conversation amongst members of the hospital staff reverted to more mundane topics. Patients stopped asking about the outbreak.

Jenna's first day back to work unfolded uneventfully, with easy cases and uncomplicated patients. After her last case, Jenna stopped by the OR control desk to pick up her mail. Absent-mindedly, she sorted through the stack of envelopes and magazines that had accumulated during her absence, while her mind drifted back to her family's vacation. Visions of Mia frolicking in the ocean played in Jenna's mind. Mia had looked radiant with her wet hair tangled from the seawater, her light tan shining in the sun, and her blue-green eyes sparkling with unabated happiness. Jenna joy relished the memory.

Her thoughts of Mia were instantly overshadowed by a sense of impending trouble when she came across the last envelope in the pile. In her hand, she held a letter from St. Augustine Hospital, addressed to her, and marked with a big red stamp, "CONFIDENTIAL." Jenna ripped open the envelope and yanked out the letter.

At that moment, Jenna's entire life was dissolving. Everything she had strived to achieve was blowing away, like a pile of dust. Standing in the small room, Jenna felt the air grow thick and heavy. It hurt to breathe. Scorching bile rose up from her stomach, coating the back of her throat. She stared at the letter, but the words bled into one another – a sheet of blurry black waves upon a white background. Jenna needed to flee before anyone could see her. Attempting to escape, her legs buckled beneath her. Unsteady and weak, she pushed herself into motion.

Jenna hastily shoved the letter in her bag and bolted for the back staircase. Clumsily, she lifted her briefcase and charged down three flights of stairs, skipping one and sometimes two steps as she made her descent. Sprinting across the parking garage, Jenna reached her car. Breathless and sweaty, she unlocked the driver's door and jumped in. Her tires squealed against the pavement as she exited the garage and pulled out on to the main street.

Immediately, Jenna dialed Tom. He answered on the second ring.

"Hey, Jenna. Think you'll make it home in time to meet Mia at the bus stop?" he asked casually.

On the other end, Jenna tried to talk, but she was wracked by sobs. Tom was instantly concerned.

He shouted into the phone, "Jenna? Jenna! Are you okay? What's going on? Jenna, talk to me!"

Jenna's entire body shook. She knew she had to get off the road. Spotting a grocery store, Jenna abruptly changed lanes and nearly sideswiped a woman driving an expensive convertible.   Ignoring the angry honks and hostile gestures from the enraged woman, Jenna pulled into the parking lot and stopped her car. Meanwhile, Tom continued shouting frantically at her through the phone.

"Jenna! You have to talk. Come on, you're really scaring me."

Jenna was now gulping for air, barely able to get out the words, "I'm . . . getting . . . sued."

Tom was panic-stricken.   "Jenna, I can't understand you. You need to calm down. Take some deep breaths, and then tell me what's wrong."

He heard his wife suck in air and blow it out several times. Finally, her wailing seemed to subside.

Tom gently asked, "Are you okay?"

All Jenna could do was eek out the word "no" before she started crying again. Several minutes passed before she regained a very modest level of composure. Whimpering softly, Jenna told her husband, "Tom, I'm getting sued. I got a letter from St. Augustine. What am I going to do?"

"Where are you right now?"

"I pulled off into a parking lot of some grocery store. I nearly took out some socialite in a convertible as I pulled in."

"Can you read me the letter?"

Tom could hear the rustling of paper in the background. Jenna choked on the words as she spoke.

"This letter is to notify you that your patient, Michelle Hollings, has retained Allison Anders of Silverstein, Howell, and Anders P.C."

"Oh, baby. I'm so sorry. Are you okay to drive? Do you want me to come get you?" Tom had never seen Jenna lose control like this before.

Jenna leaned her face against the glass of the car door, smearing makeup across the window. The coolness soothed her flushed skin. Closing her eyes, she said, "I'll be alright. I just need to calm down for a few more minutes before I get back on the road. Can you take care of Mia?"

Tom reassured his wife, "Don't worry about Mia, I'll be there for her at the bus stop. Take all the time you need, but don't drive until you're calm. It's not fair to the innocent debutantes on the road."

Jenna forced herself to chuckle at his attempt at humor. "Thanks. I'll call you when I'm on my way home."

THIRTEEN

For several minutes, Jenna sat in her SUV, gazing out the window, but seeing nothing. She rolled down the windows and opened the sunroof, allowing a warm, late summer breeze to sweep through the car.

Leaning her head back and staring up at the puffy clouds, Jenna tried to figure out what to do next. The hum of traffic as people drove home from work permeated the air. In the rearview mirror, Jenna noticed two men walking in the direction of her car. They were probably harmless, but Jenna was already rattled. Slightly panicked, she locked the doors, rolled up the windows, and pulled out of the parking lot.

Jenna got back on the road and was surprised when her phone rang. The number on the screen displayed an unfamiliar area code.

Cautiously, Jenna answered. "Hello?"

The unfamiliar man on the other end had a gentle, southern drawl.

"Hello. May I please speak with Dr. Jenna Reiner?"

Jenna remembered Rob Wilson's warning about the press and became instantly paranoid.

"May I ask who's calling?" Jenna's guard was up.

"Yes ma'am. This is Randy Stevens. I'm one of the senior malpractice attorneys with The Doctor's Mutual Group."

Jenna felt slightly embarrassed. "Oh, I'm sorry. This is Jenna Reiner. I didn't recognize the number on caller ID. I hope I didn't come off as rude."

"Not at all, Dr. Reiner. I hope you don't mind me calling you, but Rob Wilson just called and informed me of the letter you received today."

Jenna's wariness escalated. The only person that Jenna had told about the letter was her husband, and that was only minutes ago.

Confused, she asked, "Rob Wilson? How would he know?"

"Rob Wilson was privy to that information based upon his position of Anesthesia Department Chair. St. Augustine provided him with a list of names this morning."

"What do you mean? I'm not the only one who got a letter? How many letters were sent out?"

Jenna's mind was spinning, one worry melding into the next.

Randy answered without hesitation, "At this point, we know of twenty-eight doctors that received letters today. That's more than the number of cases formally linked to Hillary Martin. Obviously, some of these letters will turn out to be nothing. Hopefully, yours will be among them.

"It's important for you to understand that, at this point, you are not being sued. Hopefully that relieves some of your anxiety. The letter could mean anything. This patient may not even have hepatitis, or she may have hepatitis that is unrelated to Hillary Martin. This incident has received a lot of press coverage and, unfortunately, there are always people out there looking for an easy payoff."

The number of letters Randy Stevens quoted terrified Jenna. Once again, she started to weep. Although Jenna tried to keep it from coming through in her voice, her attempts were futile.

Jenna asked, "How will I know? I mean, how will I know if I'm one of the lucky ones where it turns out to be nothing?"

"Unfortunately," said Randy, "we just have to sit back and wait. If this patient is going to file a formal lawsuit, her lawyers will let us know soon enough. For now, just keep going about your business as best you can."

"Easy for you to say," said Jenna, more bitterly than she intended.

Randy did not take offense. He said kindly, "I know. I'm not the one who has to go through this. If you ever need to talk or have any questions, please call me – anytime. I have your email address, and I will send my office and cell phone numbers to you. We've hired local attorneys to represent the members of your group. I will also send their contact information. I expect they will be in touch with you very soon.

"I know that Dr. Wilson has already advised you not to discuss this matter with anyone, but I need to make sure you understand that. Even conversations you have with trusted friends and colleagues can be used against you, if this ever goes to court. You can talk to me, the local attorneys who represent you, your spouse, your psychiatrist, and your priest. That's it. Everyone else is off limits, okay?"

"Okay," responded Jenna. Randy Steven's instructions made her feel isolated.

"From this point forward, Dr. Reiner, I want you to send any documents you receive directly to me and the local attorneys."

Randy truly felt sorry for Jenna. From their short conversation, Randy surmised Jenna Reiner did not have the arrogance or inflated self-confidence that he witnessed in most physicians. He correctly sensed that Jenna Reiner was a humble and honest person who was in over her head and scared out of her mind.

"Dr. Reiner," Randy asked, "do you have kids?"

The mere thought of Mia brought a sense of calm to Jenna. "Yeah, I have little girl. Mia just turned eleven."

"My best advice for you right now is to spend time with her and your husband. Remember, they are what really matter in life. Don't neglect the basics – exercise, sleep. It's easier said than done, but don't let this consume you. If not for your sake, then for your husband's and your daughter's. Because, believe me, the stress quickly filters down onto those you love the most."

"Thank you. You're right. And, please call me Jenna."

"Only if you agree to call me Randy. Is there anything else I can do for you tonight, Jenna?"

"Pour me a stiff cocktail," Jenna joked. She was immediately self-conscious about her comment. The last thing she needed was her attorney suspecting she had a substance abuse problem. Every move she made from this point forward would be subject to scrutiny. Attempting to recover, Jenna said, "Just kidding. No, I think we've discussed everything we needed to. Like you said, there's nothing to do but wait and see."

"Unfortunately," said Randy empathetically, "that's all we can do."

FOURTEEN

September 2010

A week had passed since Jenna received the letter from St. Augustine. Following Randy's advice, she did her best to go about life as usual, but found it impossible. Jenna felt as though she were stranded in the ocean, treading water, waiting to see if eventually the sharks would get her.

On Thursday, Jenna finished her cases by early afternoon. Feeling restless and hoping to clear her head, she decided to hurry home and take Ginger for a jog before Mia got out of school. Jenna marched through the hospital lobby, completely preoccupied. Before exiting the building, she stopped by the doors and fished through her bag for her car keys. Bent over, rifling through hospital badges, gas receipts, and handfuls of pens, Jenna did not notice the attractive young man wearing jeans and a polo shirt headed directly for her.

"Jenna Reiner?" asked the man in a friendly, familiar tone.

Instinctively, Jenna stood and acknowledged the stranger. He had light brown hair, green eyes, and impeccably white teeth.

"Hi," Jenna smiled. "Do I know you?"

In an instant, the interloper thrust an envelope at Jenna's chest. She grasped it before it fell to the ground.

The man hissed at Jenna, "No, but I know you. Dr. Jenna Reiner, you've just been served."

Before Jenna could articulate a response, the man turned his back and stormed out of the lobby. Jenna was left standing alone while strangers milled around her. She compelled herself to look at the envelope. It was from Silverstein, Howell, and Anders, P.C. The guillotine had dropped.

Jenna bolted to her car and hopped in. Petrified, she ripped open yet another unwelcome letter. Jenna held it in her trembling hands, but she could not force herself to remove its toxic contents. Instead, she dialed Randy Stevens. His secretary put Jenna through without delay.

"Hello, this is Randy Stevens," he said with the same kindheartedness that he had extended to her one week earlier.

"Randy, it's Jenna Reiner. I just got served a letter today from that attorney's office."

"Oh," said Randy, with a new tone of seriousness. "Can you read it to me?"

"I haven't even read it myself."

Jenna pulled the letter from the envelope, unfolded it, and read the words that she had been dreading for months.

"Dr. Reiner: This letter is to inform you that your patient, Michelle Hollings, has retained our services and seeks damages against you. While under your care on January 20, 2010, Ms. Hollings contracted hepatitis C. Her blood has undergone genetic typing to determine the DNA sequence of her hepatitis C virus. It demonstrates 99.98% relatedness to that of Hillary Martin's viral genotype.

"Had you not demonstrated recklessness and carelessness in securing your narcotics, Hillary Martin would certainly never have had the opportunity to contaminate a syringe intended for Ms. Hollings. Also, you failed to detect that the syringe had been tampered with and, instead, heedlessly injected the virus into Ms. Hollings' bloodstream during her anesthetic. You have direct culpability in her unfortunate contraction of this devastating disease."

Jenna was left breathless. "It's signed by Allison Anders."

Unimaginable pain welled up inside Jenna. The horrendous allegations became her reality, and her grace period had come to an end. For several minutes, Jenna was speechless. She sat in the driver's seat, clutching the wrinkled letter. Randy could hear Jenna's irregular breathing over the phone. He did not interrupt the silence. Instead, he patiently gave Jenna time to pull herself together.

Finally, Jenna cried out with guilt and shame that she had never felt before. "The letter says *I* gave her the virus. *I* pushed the virus into her bloodstream, and it's *my* fault. If it hadn't been for *my* recklessness and *my* actions, the patient wouldn't be infected."

For the past week, Jenna had secretly worried that she was the one who ultimately injected the virus into Michelle Hollings' bloodstream. Jenna's anguish that she may have hurt one of her patients, even unintentionally, weighed heavily upon her conscience. To see her inner fears printed and articulated by a stranger cut her to the core.

Jenna whispered, as much to Randy as to herself, "It's my fault."

"No, Jenna," said Randy sternly. "It is most definitely *not* your fault. You weren't the drug abuser. You weren't the thief. You are just as much a victim as the patient. You were preyed upon and taken advantage of by a criminal. This event is unprecedented. There was absolutely no way you could have seen it coming."

All Randy could hear on the other end were muffled sobs.

"Jenna, are you listening to what I'm saying?"

"Sort of."

Randy sounded distant, jumbled, and foreign. Overcome with humiliation, remorse, and profound sadness, Jenna also felt tainted. She had been branded a villain, and there was no going back. Jenna figured it was only a matter of time before the whole world knew the extent of her incompetence and the ugliness of her actions.

Relentless in his approach, Randy continued to pummel her with logic.

"You have to understand that their claim of a ninety-nine percent DNA match to Hillary Martin's virus is just that – it's a claim. It may or may not be true, but at this point in the game they haven't provided any evidence to back it up. Their words are designed to intimidate and scare you. I will have to admit that this letter is particularly nasty, but remember they are only words. It's no more than kids on a playground taunting each other. Do you understand?"

Jenna did not answer his question. Instead, she asked sorrowfully, "What do doctors do if they aren't doctors anymore?"

"What do you mean?" asked Randy, deeply troubled by Jenna's tone.

"I mean, what if this destroys my career and my reputation? What if this destroys *me*?"

Jenna was suffocating in misery. Her darkest fears poured from her mouth.

"What if no one wants to work with me anymore? Once these lawyers are through with me, what am I going to be left with? My colleagues will shun me. They will condemn my actions. Patients may recognize my name and refuse to allow me to be their doctor. Things will never be the same. All the years, all the pain, all the hard work . . . it will be meaningless.

"Other doctors that have been through lawsuits – have any of them just decided it's not worth it anymore and dropped out of medicine? There must be some that have thrown in the towel. What do those doctors do?"

Randy thought carefully about how to respond. It was unusual for a physician to come to terms with what a malpractice suit could do to their career so early in the litigation process. Jenna Reiner was either very prophetic or extremely pessimistic. Either way, her insights had Randy deeply concerned.

He finally said, "Most physicians don't leave medicine. Honestly, I hate to say it, but there really aren't many good options. If you didn't stay in medicine, you would have to completely start over doing something else."

"That's what I was afraid you'd say," said Jenna hopelessly. "So, what's next?"

"I will contact Jim Taylor, who will be your local attorney. I'm sure he will call you tonight and will probably want to meet with you tomorrow. Give the letter to Jim when you meet. He will forward a copy to me. I'll be in touch."

"Okay," Jenna said flatly. Hanging up the phone, she felt numb and empty.

Jenna started her car and sobbed all the way to Mia's school. She did not call Tom to tell him she was on her way. Jenna was incapable of speaking, so there did not seem to be any point.

When Mia saw Jenna's SUV waiting for her outside the schoolhouse, her face lit up. Mia bolted to the car, flung open the passenger door, and immediately asked Jenna, "Hi, Mom. Can we go get ice cream?" It was their ritual whenever Jenna got off early enough to get Mia from school.

Mia's grin disappeared when Jenna turned her head to face her daughter. Jenna's eyes were swollen, and her face looked tired and sad. As Jenna sat in the driver's seat, strapped down by her seat belt, Mia saw in her mother's face the same look the tigers had in the zoo exhibit – broken and trapped.

Mia had never seen her mother in such a state. The little girl sprang over the console and hugged Jenna tightly.

"Mommy, what's wrong?'

The simple question was more than Jenna could bear. She broke down.

Jenna had to tell her daughter the truth. She clutched Mia's little body and whispered into her hair, "Everything."

FIFTEEN

The next day, Jenna found herself downtown amongst the skyscrapers, traffic, and business people. Jostling through the crowds, she made her way to the corner of Broadway and Market. Walking into the immense lobby, Jenna felt irrelevant and small. The two-story high ceilings, glass exterior walls, and the black, polished marble floors all gave the impression of opulence and intimidation. She glanced at the time on her phone – 3:50 p.m. Jenna was scheduled to meet her attorneys for the first time at 4:00. She entered the elevator, pressed the button for the twelfth floor, and watched the doors close. On the twelfth floor, Jenna stepped out into the expansive lobby of Moore and Everett, LLC.

Behind the reception desk, an older woman with a round frame, gray hair, wire-rimmed glasses, and soft, kind eyes greeted Jenna.

"Hi there. Can I help you?"

The woman's easy-going nature helped put Jenna at ease.

"Yes. I'm Jenna Reiner. . . Dr. Jenna Reiner. I have a four o'clock appointment with Jim Taylor."

"Please sign in on the registry and have a seat. I'll let him know you're here."

Jenna scribbled her name and walked over to a group of leather chairs positioned in front of a wall of windows. Once seated, Jenna took in her surroundings. The people walking through the lobby moved with a sense of purpose and urgency.

Restless, Jenna stood and gazed out the large window down on the little people and cars below her. She wondered if any of their lives were falling apart, or was she the only one?

Ten minutes later, a clean-cut man who appeared to be in his late fifties approached her. He wore perfectly pressed slacks, a collared shirt with no tie, and expensive, Italian loafers with tassels on top. The man had an honest face, brown hair with a hint of gray at the temples, was of medium height, and an average build. He was the kind of person that Jenna would have never given a second glance if she met him on the street. However, as he came up to her, she quickly appreciated his decency.

"Are you Dr. Reiner?" asked the man.

"Yes." Jenna held out her hand to shake his. "Are you Jim Taylor?"

"I am." His handshake felt gentle and comforting. Not the firm, bone-crushing grasp that she expected from a lawyer.

Jim gestured toward a long hallway. "We have a conference room set up back here. After you . . ."

With the manners of a gentleman, Jim let Jenna lead the way. He directed her through a maze of offices and cubicles, until they finally reached a large conference room. In the center, ten black leather chairs surrounded an oversized oak table.

Jim told her, "Please, have a seat wherever you'd like. Can I get you some coffee or anything else to drink?

My partner, Nancy Guilding, will be working these cases with me. She should be here in just a second."

Jenna sat down in one of the center chairs and said, "I'd love some tea, thank you."

Jim buzzed a secretary, who quickly appeared with a carafe of coffee and another filled with hot water. The woman set an assortment of tea bags and sugar cubes on a silver tray in front of Jenna. Another assistant filed in behind the first, carrying a tray of coffee mugs. Jenna was taken aback by the luxury and formality of her surroundings. Part of her found it comforting to know she had prestigious lawyers defending her. Another part of her shuddered as she grasped the seriousness of her situation.

The assistants filed out of the room, and a woman in her late forties entered. The woman dressed conservatively, wearing a plain, gray skirt and jacket, with a white blouse underneath. Her shoes were simple leather flats. The woman's black hair was cut in a short, conservative bob, and she wore brightly rimmed glasses. Her smiled was warm and nurturing. She advanced toward where Jenna was seated and introduced herself, "You must be Dr. Reiner. I'm Nancy Guilding, but please, call me Nancy."

Inexplicably, Jenna felt safe in the presence of these strangers.

Jenna stood and shook Nancy's hand. "It's nice to meet you. And please, both of you call me Jenna."

Jim and Nancy each took a seat across from Jenna. Jim asked for copies of both of the letters Jenna had received regarding Michelle Hollings, which she quickly handed over. Picking up the telephone, Jim buzzed for one of his legal assistants. Within minutes, a tall, blonde woman entered the conference room.

"Jenna, this is Melanie Johansen, one of our paralegals. She'll be assisting us on your case."

Jenna smiled politely at the woman. "Nice to meet you."

Handing over the letters to Melanie, Jim asked, "Can you make copies for the three of us and start Dr. Reiner's case file?"

The notion of having her own case file sent a chill through Jenna. She could already envision the spines on three-ring binders dedicated to her, "Michelle Hollings v. Dr. Jenna Reiner." Anyone who saw one sitting around would know that Jenna was the accused.

Minutes later, Melanie returned with the requested copies. She handed them to Jim and left. "Just let me know if you need anything else," Melanie said, softly closing the door behind her.

Jim distributed the copies. The three of them sat for several minutes in silence, as Jim and Nancy read the letters. Jenna felt uneasy with nothing to occupy her time. Nervously, she took a gulp of tea, burning the roof of her mouth on the piping hot drink. Feeling foolish, she tried to ignore the pain.

Finally, Jim looked up at Jenna and asked, "The first thing I want to know is, how are you holding up through all this?"

Jenna plastered on a tight smile. However, her bravado soon vanished. Stunned by Jim's compassion, she felt her defenses dissolve. Gazing down at the table, tracing a grain of the wood with her finger, Jenna said quietly, "Not so good."

Jim continued gently, "Can you tell me what 'not so good' means?"

"Well," Jenna sighed, "to begin with, never having been sued before, I have absolutely no idea what to expect.

Beyond that, I feel like a failure. I'm scared to death. I can't sleep. I can't concentrate. I'm falling apart."

A tear traced a line down Jenna's cheek. She was too embarrassed to meet her lawyers' gaze. They could hear the disgrace in her voice, but they did not need to see it in her face. "I'm filled with such incredible guilt. The thought that I may have filled my patient's blood with a deadly disease, even if I didn't know it – it's killing me. It's like waking up in the hospital and finding out the red light you ran resulted in killing the other driver."

Jenna's voice became shaky, and mascara collected in dark pools below her eyes. Nancy passed her a tissue box. Jenna accepted it gratefully and wiped away the black smudges.

Jim paused for a moment, making sure Jenna was finished before he spoke. "Jenna, all these things that you're feeling are completely normal. Being sued is one of the most traumatic things that can happen to a physician. Our job is to get you through it and to help you make the best decisions along the way.

"As of right now, for the record, you are not formally being sued. However, we expect those papers to be filed by the patient's attorneys with the court any time now. This is not going to go away. I think our job today should be to get to know each other. Does that sound okay?"

Something about the calm manner in which Jim conducted himself helped Jenna regain her composure. She raised her head and nodded.

Nancy spoke for the first time since her introduction to Jenna. "I know our world is completely foreign to you, so I want to make sure that you understand some important fundamentals. First of all, anything you say to either of us is confidential. Secondly, even if we ask you a question where you think we may not like the answer, please be honest with us. When defendants lie, they get in trouble. They tell so many lies, they can't keep them straight, and then they get caught. The truth is easy to remember, so don't forget that.

"Another really important thing for you to understand is that this is all about money. It's not about justice or the truth. The law firm that the patient has retained is notoriously merciless. They don't play nice, and they don't play fair. You need to mentally and emotionally prepare yourself for that right now. If you don't, I guarantee it will destroy you. They are going to say terrible things about you. Just remember, it's nothing personal."

Nancy's warning startled Jenna, sending a jolt through her. She had not known what to expect, but she certainly did not expect this.

Although Jenna feared the answer, she asked, "So, what should I anticipate from here on out?"

Jim spoke, "I wish I could give you a detailed schedule or timeline, but it usually doesn't work like that. I can tell you that lawsuits are best characterized by peaks and valleys. There will be months where very little seems to happen. Then, out of the blue, we'll inundate you with requests for documents, affidavits, and meetings. I would expect things to be pretty low-key for a while. If you ever have any questions or just need to talk, call us. We will email you all of our contact information, including our cell phone numbers. Never be afraid to use them. Deal?"

"Deal." Although Jenna appreciated her attorneys' offer, their twenty-four-hour availability brought her little comfort.

The meeting ended, and Jenna somberly exited the mammoth building. Instead of returning to her car, she tried to clear her head by walking around the busy downtown streets. Jenna's mind was a million miles away as she blended with the crowds of workers, shoppers, and city-dwellers. Aimlessly stepping off the curb to cross the street, Jenna walked directly into the path of an oncoming taxi. The driver slammed on his brakes to avoid hitting her. Tires screeched, and the rusted bumper of the yellow cab stopped only inches short of striking Jenna. The angry cabby honked and raised his arms. Jenna looked right through him. She was not sure whether she should be grateful that he avoided killing her or angry that she was spared.

SIXTEEN

After Jim and Nancy escorted Jenna to the elevator, they returned to their conference room. Once inside, Jim refilled each of their mugs with hot coffee. Nancy dropped a cube of sugar into hers, while Jim flopped into one of the leather chairs.

"So, what do you think?" he asked, leaning back with his hands clasped behind his head.

Nancy dissolved the sugar with a stirring straw, watching the rich black fluid swirl in her cup like a miniature tornado.

Carefully slurping her hot coffee, she replied, "My first impression is that I like her."

"Me too," Jim said. He and Nancy had been friends for years, but it never ceased to amaze him how similarly their minds worked. It was part of what made them such a good team.

Nancy kicked her shoes off underneath the table. It had been an exhausting day. She enjoyed this small reprieve. Taking a moment to collect her thoughts, Nancy pictured Jenna sitting at the conference table. She had the appearance of a little girl in a fancy restaurant who was trying valiantly to mind her manners.

Completely at ease, Nancy spoke candidly. "Jenna is not your typical doctor, not by any stretch of the imagination. For the past twenty years, how many doctors have we seen who have been thrust into the role of defendant? Hundreds? Of those, I can't remember one that hasn't arrived dressed professionally, like they would for their clinic days. Most of them exude confidence – usually too much so. They try to take control of the meeting, dictate its course. When asked direct questions, they give away very little information and certainly nothing more than is absolutely necessary. Honesty doesn't always come easily to a doctor whose medical license is on the line."

Jim reflected on some of the more pompous physicians he and Nancy had defended over the years. She was right. Many of them were distasteful.

Nancy continued, "Jenna, on the other hand, is completely unassuming. She shows up wearing khaki capris, a modest T-shirt, and strappy sandals. If I met her in public, the last thing I'd guess about her is that she's a physician. I like her humility and her honesty. You asked her how she's doing, and she let you know."

"I agree," responded Jim. "She didn't seem to hold anything back. It was refreshing."

Nancy rubbed her temples, straining not to forget a single impression. "Right now, I think she's scared out of her mind. I get the feeling that she is barely holding it together. The way her voice quivered when she spoke and her unsteady hands tells me she's close to the edge. At times, she almost seemed like an abused dog, you know? Like when you reach out to show her kindness, her instinct is to pull back before she gets smacked."

"I picked up on that, too," Jim said. "I don't think she ever imagined finding herself facing this type of situation, and I think she's overwhelmed. On the other hand, I do believe she is one of the more virtuous physicians we've met in a while. Of course, her instinct is self-preservation, but she doesn't forget the others involved. I think in spite of what she fears for herself, a big part of her grieves for the patient."

Nancy nodded as she leaned back in her chair, nibbling on the tip of her pen. "I see things the same way. It's obvious Jenna feels genuinely awful about her patient becoming infected."

"It sure is," Jim said, taking off his reading glasses and placing them on the table. Unbuttoning the cuffs on his shirt, he rolled up his sleeves while he reflected on the doctor. After a few moments, he put his spectacles back on and said thoughtfully, "Jenna's an interesting contradiction of vulnerability and feistiness. I think we are going to have to be very careful how we deal with her throughout this lawsuit. I wouldn't go so far as to call her fragile. She never would have survived the rigors of medical school and residency if she had paper-thin skin. I only hope we can exploit her inner strength."

"Me too." Nancy stretched her arms above her head and yawned.

Jim smiled warmly at his colleague and trusted friend. "Why don't we call it a night? Tell your husband I'm sorry for keeping you late. I owe him a beer."

Nancy laughed as she stood to leave. "He's keeping track, Jim. At this point, you owe him a brewery."

SEVENTEEN

Over the course of several weeks, Jenna became increasingly glum. One night, after Mia had gone to sleep, Tom found Jenna huddled up on the couch, her head resting on Ginger's soft fur. The only light in the room came from the muted television. Tom sat next to Jenna, but she did not notice his presence. He reached over and took her hand. Only then did she lift her head.

"Jenna, are you going to be okay?"

"I don't know."

Tom's patience was fading. He had tired of Jenna's sulking. In his mind, her period of mourning needed to come to a conclusion.

Exasperated, Tom said, "I don't understand why you are internalizing this so much. You should be *pissed*. I mean, *REALLY PISSED*! Some sick, drug-addicted skank decides that not only is she going to steal your drugs to get high, but she's also going to leave her dirty virus in a syringe to be used on patients. I bet Hillary Martin probably sat there and watched you and the other doctors push the plunger. Maybe that gave her a rise, too."

"Tom," Jenna shouted, losing control, "I'm not you! Just because you would get pissed off, doesn't mean I'd do the same! I'm too sad to be angry right now."

He barked back, "Jenna, I'm sick of it. You're like a ghost. You barely talk to me. We hardly even touch. You go through the motions of being a mother, and that's it. Mia misses you. She's been crying herself to sleep lately, wanting to know when you'll be happy again. Honestly, I don't have an answer for her. I can't stand watching you mope around all the time. You need to realize that you did not commit this crime! If you keep it up and continue to carry on this way, people are going to start to think that maybe you *are* guilty. You better snap out of it. If you don't, you are going to screw yourself and, very possibly, our family!"

The thought of her daughter sobbing every night upset Jenna more than anything else Tom had said. His selfish inference to their waning sex life infuriated her. Feeling anger build up inside her, Jenna was grateful that Mia was a sound sleeper, and her bedroom door was shut.

Jenna's upper lip curled, and she snarled, "Tom, how could you possibly understand anything about this? You have never had someone else's life in your hands! You didn't invest over twelve years trudging through college, medical school, and residency, just to end up here! I've been accused of doing something that could end up killing an innocent person. Tell me, how could you possibly relate to that? So am I angry about it? Absolutely! But mostly I'm hurt, devastated, ashamed, humiliated, sorry, and petrified. Every bad thing you could imagine – that's what I feel. Don't you dare tell me how to act! What I need, more than anything, is for you to listen, let me cry, and let me vent. Most of all, I need you to make me feel protected."

Without saying another word, Jenna stood, stormed into their bedroom, and slammed the door shut. It was the first time she had ever walked out on Tom. Her heart pounded in her chest. Jenna went into their bathroom and examined her reflection in the mirror. She was a shadow of her former self. Her eyes were perpetually bloodshot, and her face was tarnished by a seemingly permanent frown. Jenna reached into the top drawer and pulled out her bottle of Ambien. She twisted off the top and flung it carelessly onto the floor. Turning the bottle to the side, Jenna tapped out three of the tablets – triple her usual dose – and downed them with a gulp of water. She stood gazing into the mirror, sobbing, as the pills eventually took effect. The room began to spin, and objects became fuzzy. Like a drunken sailor, she staggered to her bed, fell on top of it, and passed out. Jenna slept in her clothes. Tom never joined her that night.

The next morning, she woke up feeling hazy and confused. With the residual Ambien still coursing through her bloodstream, Jenna forced herself to get ready for work. She showered, dressed, softly kissed Mia goodbye as she slept, and then left the house without speaking to Tom.

Jenna stopped at Starbucks, bought two cups of coffee, and drove to work in silence. When she pulled into the parking lot of the hospital, she had absolutely no recollection of the drive.

EIGHTEEN

In spite of two more cups of coffee between cases, at lunchtime Jenna remained lethargic. There was a short gap before her next case, and she seized the opportunity to grab some food. While waiting for an elevator, she heard a woman calling her name.

"Hey, Jenna, wait up."

Jenna instantly recognized the cheerful voice. It was Katharine Harper. Katharine and Jenna had been friends since medical school. Although Katharine chose to specialize in critical care medicine and Jenna in anesthesiology, the women had remained chummy throughout their careers. Katharine Harper was driven to succeed. Although she was an African American woman in a field dominated by Caucasian males, from the beginning of her career Katharine had set out to prove herself. However, years spent within the confines of the hospital had added gray hair to her head and extra weight to her mid-section. Even so, she had an easy-going nature and a twinkle in her wide, brown eyes that drew people in. To Jenna, Katharine's appeal was her bright personality and her unshakable integrity.

After years of hard work, Katharine had achieved the position of Medical Staff President of St. Augustine.

Jenna was certain that Katharine knew about Michelle Hollings. After all, Katharine had been intimately involved with the Hillary Martin scandal from its onset. Jenna's shame brought on a burning sensation in the pit of her stomach.

In an instant, Katharine was behind Jenna with her warm, soft hand on Jenna's shoulder. Jenna inhaled, attempted a smile, and turned to face her colleague. At that moment, the elevator doors opened, and both doctors stepped inside. The doors shut, and it was only the two of them. Katharine looked at Jenna with compassion and asked softly, "Is something wrong?"

The walls were closing in on Jenna. "Of course not. I just didn't sleep very well last night. Tom and I got into a fight."

"Did you kick his butt?" Katharine teased, jabbing Jenna lightly in the ribs.

The elevator doors opened, and Jenna's eyes filled with tears. Before she could get away, Katharine grabbed her hand and said, "Walk with me."

Jenna, stunned by Katharine's brash gesture, did as she was told. Katharine escorted Jenna outside. It was late summer, and the air was still warm and enticing. Katharine pulled her over to a wrought iron bench situated below a maple tree, full of green leaves that rustled in the breeze.

Glancing around nervously, Jenna was relieved to see they were alone. Katharine was staring at her. Jenna wanted to look away but, out of respect, she could not. Then Katharine said the words that Jenna feared, "Jenna, I know."

"You know what?" Jenna asked innocently.

"Jenna, I know every doctor out there who has an infected patient. I've seen the list, I know that you're on it, and I'm so sorry. I meant to call, but I'd much rather talk to you in person. You don't look so good, my friend."

In response to Katharine's observation, Jenna turned her head. She could not allow Katharine to see her tears. However, the sound of her whimpers gave her away. Katharine spun Jenna around. Jenna raised her hands to her face, attempting to hide her shame.

She quivered, "I'm not supposed to talk to you or anyone else about this. Only my attorneys and Tom."

"Well," said Katharine authoritatively, "I'm here to tell you – screw that. You're a mess. You look like crap. This is obviously weighing on you. *Heavily*. From what I see, it doesn't look like your lawyers or your husband are all that you need. Right now, you also need a good friend, someone who truly gets it.

"Let me tell you something. I've been sued before, too. I know what it can do to you. I know what it did to me. I also happen to have the inside scoop. There are certain things I can't talk about, but there's one thing I can tell you. You may feel like you're the only one standing out there in front of the firing squad. Let me reassure you, you have plenty of company, and it runs the gamut. There are excellent and not-so-excellent doctors who are on the list. Hillary Martin did not discriminate."

"Really?" *Safety in numbers*, Jenna thought to herself.

"Really," Katharine answered. "Furthermore, I don't think you did anything wrong. I don't think any of your colleagues did anything wrong, either. We had a criminal in our operating rooms. How do you protect yourself against something like that? The answer is, you can't. You are an excellent anesthesiologist. You need to convince yourself of your innocence and then fight for it."

Cautiously, Jenna asked Katharine, "Do you think the hospital is going to lay all the blame on the anesthesiologists? They have a lot to lose."

Katharine was quick to answer, "Well, look at it from this standpoint. Right now, there are over twenty confirmed cases. That means twenty anesthesiologists, give or take, all had similar practices regarding how they secured their narcotics. In my opinion, that alone defines the standard of care. If the hospital tries to say that many anesthesiologists were practicing below the standard of care, then they would have to explain why they failed to detect your ineptness or to enforce stricter rules."

"Yeah," said Jenna, "that does make sense. I hadn't thought of it in those terms."

Katharine reached out and hugged her friend. They embraced for several moments. Finally, Katharine pulled back and told Jenna sternly, "For now, you have got to get your act together. Take a couple of days off, if you think it will help. You may want to consider seeing a psychiatrist. This is a huge stress. You have to remain strong to get through it.

"With respect to this conversation, as far as I'm concerned, it never happened. Okay? You are always safe to talk with me, anytime."

Jenna had never felt so close to another woman. She kissed Katharine lightly on the cheek and whispered, "Thank you . . . for everything."

Their moment ended when Katharine's pager alarmed. She pulled it from her pocket and read the display.

"Dammit," Katharine said. "I've got a patient trying to die in the ICU. I'm going to have to run."

The women went their separate ways, and Jenna grabbed her phone and dialed Tom. He answered on the first ring.

"Baby, I'm sorry. You're right. I've been trying to tell you how to handle this based on how I would handle it. I don't want to add stress to your situation. From now on, I'm going to make it a point to simply listen. If you want my opinion, ask me, and I'll give it to you. Otherwise, I just want to be there for you in whatever way helps you the most."

Jenna spoke softly into the phone, smiling for the first time in weeks, "Thanks. I love you."

For the second time that day, Jenna found herself overcome with gratitude for the simplest of gifts. She watched a majestic Monarch butterfly flutter in front of her. Jenna stared at the colorful creature until it finally flew away. She never noticed Keith Jones, peering down on her from his office window.

NINETEEN

October 18, 2010

Hillary Martin had been incarcerated for more than four months. Her prominent, dark black roots served as visible markers of time. She had also lost considerable weight and the blaze orange jumpsuit that had fit snugly back in June was now baggy. Jail-issued flip-flops revealed tiny specks of old black polish on Hillary's toenails. Her fingernails had been chewed down to the quick, leaving ragged edges. Without makeup, her skin was pasty white and dotted with pimples.

A female guard appeared outside her cell and said brusquely, "Martin, you've got company. Let's go."

Accustomed to the drill, Hillary held out her arms, and the guard snapped the chilly, metal handcuffs around her wrists. Escorted by the burly woman, Hillary Martin marched slowly past the other inmates' cells. She could feel the harsh stares from the other prisoners as she made her way, but she kept her head down.

In a small meeting room inside the county jail, Hillary's attorney, Jack Lewis, waited patiently. In spite of their daughter's protests, Harold and Janice Martin had liquidated every asset they possessed to hire Jack to represent their daughter. Hillary's parents may have been modest people, but they were savvy enough to know that a court-appointed lawyer would be inadequate for a case of this magnitude. Jack Lewis may not have been the best attorney that money could buy, but he was the best attorney *their* money could buy.

Ignoring Jack, Hillary entered the room and focused on the single window, which overlooked the parking lot. It was an overcast fall morning. Soggy, dead leaves littered the ground. A brisk wind rattled the glass panes. It was the kind of weather she hated.

The guard removed the handcuffs and left the room, locking Jack and Hillary inside.

"Why don't we sit down and talk?" Jack motioned for Hillary to take a seat. She finally shifted her attention from the world outside to her attorney. Hillary stood for several moments, staring defiantly at Jack Lewis. With his balding head, paunch belly, and unruly eyebrows, Hillary found Jack revolting. In fact, she openly loathed him.

Jack sat down and waited. Eventually, she took a seat. He rested his hands on the table, quietly grinding his teeth in agitation.

Anxious to end their interaction, Jack did not waste time. "Hillary, we are at a crossroads here. You are set for trial exactly a week from today. It's do or die time." He tossed a stack of documents on the table in front of her, and the pages scattered.

Hillary flinched. For the first time since they met, Jack finally had her attention.

"There are forty-two counts against you from the federal government. If you are found guilty, you could be looking at life in prison. Do you understand?" He spat the words at her.

Hillary watched her counselor, expressionless. Her eyes were dead and empty, as Jack imagined her soul might be, too. He reminded himself that he was not hired to like her, but rather to defend her.

Gruffly, she asked, "So, what are my options?"

Jack tapped his pen against the table and said, "Option number one – we proceed with the trial next week. I'll be honest. The evidence against you is overwhelming. We are nearly guaranteed to lose."

"What's option number two?"

Jack's expression became grim. "Option number two – we attempt a plea bargain."

"What kind of plea bargain?" Hillary asked suspiciously.

"You would agree to plead guilty in exchange for a reduced sentence. The problem is we don't have much bargaining power."

Jack eyed Hillary until he was certain she was listening. "The decision is yours."

Standing abruptly, Hillary shoved her chair back and began pacing the room. The chair tipped over and created a loud thud as it hit the floor. The guard outside heard the ruckus and peered through the door. Jack waved the guard away, reassuring her, "Everything's okay."

Picking up the plastic chair, Hillary swung it back toward the table. She positioned it backward and took a seat. Watching her straddle the chair caused Jack's stomach to turn.

"So, what are your thoughts?" he pried.

She buried her head in her hands. When Hillary lowered her hands to the table, Jack noticed her pupils were dilated, and her cheeks were red and blotchy.

"You said that we don't have much bargaining power for a plea deal, but that's not completely true."

Jack leaned closer to Hillary and whispered, "What do you mean?"

"I'm the only one who knows the whole truth about what I did." There was a diabolical glimmer in Hillary's eyes.

Jack glanced out the door. Satisfied the guard was honoring their attorney-client privilege, he moved closer to his client and asked very quietly, "What is the truth?"

With a precarious smirk, Hillary revealed her secret. "I wasn't the only one contaminating those needles, and hepatitis C isn't all they need to worry about."

TWENTY

October 19, 2010

At five o'clock on Tuesday morning, Jenna crept in to her house and flopped on the couch, exhausted. She was dressed in dirty, bloodstained scrubs and had just arrived home from a brutal, twenty-four-hour call shift. Kicking off her shoes, the offensive odor from her swollen feet assaulted her. Jenna's back ached, and her eyes burned. In an hour, Mia would need to be awakened for school. Until then, she could rest.

Jenna had just drifted off to sleep when Tom's high-pitched alarm clock sounded at 6 a.m., shattering the silence of the house. Jenna trudged up the stairs to her daughter's room. Mia was cuddled up in her in bed with the covers pulled over her head. Jenna lifted the blankets and kissed her daughter's soft cheeks. Mia's skin felt hot, and her hair was damp from sweat. Slowly, Mia opened her eyes.

"Mommy, I don't feel good," Mia croaked. Then, without warning, she vomited. Warm, yellowish-green fluid coated her bed, her pajamas, and her mother.

Jenna pulled her wet shirt off, dragging Mia's stomach contents into her hair along the way. Then she helped Mia disrobe and ran to turn on the shower. Gently,

Jenna helped Mia get under the spray. Standing in her bra and scrub pants, Jenna scrubbed her daughter's hair as the shower stall filled with the opposing scents of shampoo and bile.

From downstairs, Jenna heard the phone ring. A few minutes later, Tom called her name. Whoever it was would have to wait. Mia needed her full attention. Jenna was rinsing Mia's hair when Tom peeked into the bathroom. His hand covered the receiver. "It's Rob Wilson," Tom murmured. "He says it's urgent."

Jenna grabbed a towel, drying the suds off her arms and wiping vomit from her hair. She stepped out of the bathroom and whispered back to Tom, "Mia's sick. Can you get her into our bed?"

Tom handed the phone to Jenna. Knowing that nothing good could ever come from such an early morning phone call, she struggled to take in air.

With great trepidation, she answered, "Hello."

"I'm sorry to bother you post call." Rob sounded sincere.

"That's okay. What can I do for you?" Jenna attempted to keep her voice from cracking.

"Jenna, you were served a subpoena from the Federal District Court yesterday. They delivered it to the office late in the afternoon. I knew you were on call and didn't want you to worry about it while you were at work."

How considerate, Jenna thought. Rob saved her from having an emotional meltdown while there were still cases to do and money to be made.

Jenna was standing in the kitchen as Tom led Mia past her, on their way to the bedroom. Mia walked by and Jenna reached out and rubbed her arm.

Turning her attention back to Rob, Jenna said, "I don't understand. What do you mean, a subpoena?"

"That's all I know. I already forwarded it to Jim Taylor and Nancy Guilding. You need to call them as soon as possible."

Jenna broke into a cold sweat. *Was she on trial already? What was going on?* She ended the phone call with Rob and immediately dialed Jim Taylor's direct number. With her adrenaline surging, it was a challenge to press the right numbers on the receiver. From down the hall, Jenna heard vomit splash into the toilet as Mia retched again.

It was not yet 6:30. Jenna fully expected to get voicemail, but Jim answered on the third ring. "Hi Jenna. Nancy's here with me. We have you on speaker phone."

"Rob Wilson told me I got served a subpoena. Am I in trouble?"

As far as Jenna knew, only criminals got served with subpoenas. She felt weak and leaned against the granite countertop for support.

Nancy spoke in a motherly tone. "No, you are not in trouble. A handful of summons were served to doctors yesterday. Hillary Martin is scheduled to go on trial next Monday. You are ordered to testify."

Jenna's heart was beating so rapidly, she felt certain it might burst. Her next question slipped out of her mouth, "Why me?"

Jim piped in, "We're not entirely sure. What we do know is that the federal prosecutor has served twelve doctors, ten of whom are anesthesiologists from your group, and the other two are surgeons. We are placing calls to the prosecutor right now to try to gain more information. Hopefully we'll know more by the end of the day."

Jenna's mind was in overdrive. "What are they going to ask me? What if I say something wrong? Can they use that against me in my malpractice case?"

Nancy tried to reassure her, "We assume they are going to ask you what you remember about Hillary Martin. We will be there in court, but since you aren't the one on trial, we won't be able to object to any of the questions they ask you."

"In other words, I'm on my own to hang myself."

"Not entirely," said Nancy. "Once we get more information, we'll meet with you and help you prepare."

"Who else got a subpoena?" Jenna demanded.

Jim read off a list of her colleagues.

"Do all of us have hepatitis-positive patients? Is that the common denominator?"

Jim said gravely, "At this point, it would be pure speculation, but I think that's probably the case. We're at a disadvantage. We don't yet know the identity of every anesthesia doctor who has an infected patient. We won't know, in fact, until the very last lawsuit rolls in. However, the State Health Department and the administrators at St. Augustine do possess that information. It's highly likely they shared those names with the federal prosecutor."

Nancy chimed in, "Jenna, you're going to be fine. Try not to worry. You're stronger than you think."

Jenna did not respond.

She hung up and walked into her bedroom. Mia was curled up in a ball on the bed with her eyes closed. Jenna lay down, facing her. The stench of vomit lingered on Mia's breath, and the sheets were damp from her wet body. Jenna carefully pulled the blankets over herself and her daughter and fell into a fitful nap.

TWENTY-ONE

October 22, 2010

On an overcast Friday morning, Jack Lewis drummed his fingers on the table as he waited for Hillary to be ushered into the dank, depressing meeting room at the jail. Jack was functioning on a week's worth of very little sleep, no exercise, vending-machine meals, and a heavy conscience. He was sure that the revelations of the past week would disturb him for many years to come. At long last, Hillary had divulged the true details of her crimes.

Hillary silently entered the chamber. Impatient for her handcuffs to be removed, she thrust her arms forward toward the guard. Once the guard shut the door and locked them in, Hillary rubbed her wrists, attempting to erase the sensation of the frigid steel pinching her skin. Jack found it hard to believe, but Hillary actually looked worse than she had on Monday. She was jittery, agitated, and unfocused. Hillary did not seem to realize he was in the room. Bewildered, Jack watched her, feeling like a voyeur. She squeezed a pimple on her chin until it burst and started to bleed. After wiping away the blood with the palm of her hand, she remained mesmerized by the red streak left behind.

Jack was becoming uncomfortable. He grunted in an attempt to gain Hillary's attention. The gesture worked. Hillary was startled back into her bleak reality and took a seat. Her right leg jerked restlessly under the table. Jack tried to overlook it, but the shuffling grated on his nerves.

Tersely, Jack said, "We only have three hours before we are scheduled to be in court. I need to present the details of the plea agreement to you, and you need to stay focused."

Hillary stopped twitching her leg. The blood on her face had coagulated into a dark, red ball.

"Okay, shoot."

Retrieving two stacks of legal documents from his worn, leather briefcase, Jack handed one copy to Hillary and kept the other for himself.

He told her, "I've fought hard for you all week. However, the federal prosecuting attorney is unwilling to make any major concessions in the plea agreement. Do you understand what I am telling you so far?"

"Yep."   Hillary slumped in her chair.   Her callousness tested Jack's patience.

"Okay, so you plead guilty to five counts of tampering with a consumer product and five counts of obtaining a controlled substance by deceit. If you do that, the remaining thirty-two charges will be dismissed, and no further charges will be filed."

Hillary turned her head toward the window. Iron bars partially obscured her view of the gray sky. The distant thunder of a plane roared overhead. Hillary was about to look away when she caught sight of a pretty, little sparrow on the window's ledge. She briefly glanced down at the smeared blood on her hand. By the time Hillary looked back at the window, the bird had flown away.

She turned her attention back toward Jack. "How long?"

Jack found it excruciatingly painful to play the role of the messenger. He resisted the urge to look away from Hillary as he gave her the news.

"Twenty years, without the possibility of parole."

The room fell nearly silent. The only sounds were the "clunk, clunk, clunk" of an officer's footsteps outside the door.

Hillary was hoarse, her throat dry. "What should I do?"

Jack found Hillary offensive. He fought to remind himself that she was a young woman in her mid-twenties, with many years ahead of her. She was a mother who loved her child, and she had parents who loved her. A collection of contradictions, Hillary caused Jack to vacillate between repulsion and pity.

"I can't tell you what to do," Jack said coolly. "This is a decision you have to make for yourself. You will live with the consequences for the rest of your life. All I can do is make sure you understand the implications of your choices. In my legal opinion, it would be highly unlikely that you would receive a lighter sentence from a jury."

"How long until I have to decide?"

"I will meet you at the courthouse in two hours, and I will need your decision then. That gives us just under one hour to prepare."

Hillary stood and walked to the door. She rudely whistled at the guard outside, like an owner summoning her dog.

The guard approached the door and Hillary ordered, "Take me back to my cell."

Jack watched the back of Hillary's head of tangled, unruly hair as she shuffled away from him, returning to her cell. Once she disappeared behind the clank of a solid metal door, Jack gathered up his documents and strode out of the jailhouse into the frosty fall air. Walking to his car, Jack felt certain about only one thing – he had no idea which direction Hillary would choose. Knowing that she would leave him hanging until the last minute, Jack was fully prepared to defend her, regardless of her choice.

Two hours later, Jack Lewis sat at the courthouse in a windowless meeting room. He sipped bitter, lukewarm coffee while he waited for Hillary to arrive. Within minutes, he heard the rattling of chains and footsteps approaching the door. Hillary arrived with her wrists handcuffed and bound to a belt around her waist. Her feet were shackled together. Each step was an awkward shuffle forward. For her part, Hillary seemed unfazed at the indignity of being tied up like an animal. The officer unlocked the restraints and left the room.

Jack knew they had very little time to finalize things before facing Judge Redmond. "Have you made a decision?"

"I have," she said stoically. "I want to take the plea."

Jack did not show any emotion. He pulled out the plea agreement from his briefcase and handed it to Hillary. She thumbed through the document page-by-page, tormenting Jack by wasting precious moments.

He had fill of Hillary's antics. Whether he had her attention or not, he started at the beginning and explained the terms. "The agreement states that in exchange for a sentence of twenty years in federal prison, you agree to provide certain things."

"Like what?" asked Hillary, irritated. She slid down in her chair, her legs extended and crossed at the ankles, impinging into Jack's space.

"First, you need to release any and all medical and employment records to the federal government."

"No biggie."

"Secondly, you need to supply blood and any other tissue samples, as reasonably required by the federal government to aid in their investigation."

"Fine, so I piss in a cup. Is that it?"

"Not entirely. You will be required to give a deposition to the federal prosecutor that honestly and accurately details your diversion activities. They expect you to submit to a polygraph test following the deposition. You will have to tell them everything you have told me over this past week. No bullshit. If there is even the slightest hint that you are being deceitful, the plea deal will be revoked, and no further plea deals will be considered."

Jack asked firmly, "I need to know, is this still what you want?"

"It's pretty much all I've got at this point."

Jack handed her his pen. Hillary twirled it around in her hand, like a tiny baton. Before signing, she placed the tip in her mouth and rolled her tongue over the silver button. Finally, she flipped to the flagged pages, signed the agreement, and passed the document to Jack with his pen on top of the stack.

Their time was over. The guard came to the door and replaced Hillary's wrist and ankle restraints. The three of them walked out of the meeting room. Jack purposefully left his defiled pen behind.

TWENTY-TWO

The guard led Jack and Hillary into the courtroom through a side door. Every seat in the gallery was occupied. Hillary followed Jack to the defendant's table. She could feel hundreds of eyes upon her. The air was heavy as Hillary surveyed the crowd. Most of the faces were unfamiliar, but they all wore the unmistakable look of shock, revulsion, and sadness. Unable to face their scowls, Hillary focused on the wooden floor ahead of her.

Jack pulled a chair out for Hillary. The scrape of the wooden legs across the floor resonated throughout the courtroom. Hillary took her seat and spotted her parents in the row directly behind her. Hillary's mother wore a heavy wool dress that made her look plain and frail. Her father sat with his shoulders hunched over as if he were trying to dissolve into the wooden pew. The three made eye contact, and Hillary smiled, ever so slightly.

Hillary was about to turn back around when she noticed Dr. Jenna Reiner seated in the same row as her parents. Jenna's eyes bore into Hillary's, holding her captive. Silently, Jenna mouthed the words she had come to say. Her lips moved with such precision, the words would not have been any clearer had she shouted them. "Fuck you!" The expression of immense grief on Jenna's face was in stark contrast to her expletive. For a brief moment, Hillary started to fully comprehend the enormity of the damage she had caused.

The court bailiff entered. "All rise. The Honorable Judge Richard Redmond has entered the courtroom."

A tall, bald man with a wiry frame and piercing eyes strode into the courtroom. Judge Redmond nodded curtly at the bailiff and took his seat at the bench. From his perch, the judge scanned the courtroom. For a fraction of a second, every spectator experienced the scrutiny of the judge. Finally, Judge Redmond turned his attention on Hillary, much like an eagle would do before seizing its prey. Hillary tried to look at him, but could not. She was weak and defenseless under his relentless gaze.

Judge Redmond pounded his gavel and spoke with authority. "I understand that we are here today to discuss a plea agreement. Is that correct?"

Jack and the federal prosecutor stood to address the judge. Nearly in unison, they replied, "Yes, Your Honor."

The judge again focused on Hillary. Instinctively, she stood, grasping the table for support.

"Ms. Martin," said the judge, "before you enter into this plea agreement, I need to be certain that your attorney has fully explained the agreement to you, including its repercussions and requirements, in a language that you understand. Is this correct?"

The world crashed down upon Hillary. No longer was she in control, manipulating the situation, and calling the shots. Unfamiliar with vulnerability, Hillary's legs quivered. She tried to speak, but there was no air in her lungs. In barely more than a whisper, Hillary said, "Yes, Your Honor. I understand it completely."

The judge cleared his throat, never for a second taking his eyes off of Hillary Martin. "Ms. Martin, how do you wish to plea?"

"Guilty, Your Honor," she replied, this time slightly louder.

"Do you enter this plea on your own free will and not under any coercion or external influence?"

"Yes, sir."

The judge smacked his gavel once. The thud echoed throughout the crowded courtroom, like a gun being fired.

"The court rejects your guilty plea."

Hillary and Jack involuntarily gasped. She looked at Jack with fear and desperation. The courtroom was silent for a moment and then erupted into a stream of whispers and bodies shuffling.

Frowning at the crowd, Judge Redmond struck the gavel more forcefully. Silence immediately ensued.

Judge Redmond's words to Hillary were harsh. "The heinous nature of your crimes and your complete disregard for the consequences of your actions is unprecedented and appalling. The victims of your crime put their trust and their lives in the hands of the hospital staff, yourself included. You violated that sacred trust. These patients were helpless to defend themselves. While they were most susceptible, your ruthless actions inflicted a lifelong and possibly lethal disease on these helpless people.

"The terms of the length of sentence, according to the plea agreement, do not adequately take into account the views of the victims. Accepting this plea agreement would inordinately restrain my discretion in sentencing.

"You may still continue with a guilty plea, but I will determine the length of your sentence. You would still be required to abide by the terms of the original plea agreement. I must warn you, if you choose to proceed with a guilty plea, the sentence I impose upon you will be much stiffer than the twenty years originally dictated by this agreement. Or, you may choose to revoke your guilty plea and proceed to trial next week, as scheduled."

Jack respectfully asked, "Your Honor, may I request a recess to consult with my client?"

"Court will take a fifteen minute recess." Judge Redmond crushed his gavel onto the sound block. The deafening crack shot through the courtroom. Every spectator sat motionless as the judge rose and returned to his chambers.

Once the judge retreated, the courtroom was on fire with conversation.

Jack and Hillary huddled at the defense table, attempting to block out the sound behind them. Hillary whispered menacingly, "What the fuck is this? You never warned me that anything like this would happen." Her face was bright red, her fists clenched.

Jack responded calmly, "I never expected anything like this. This judge is tough. The problem is, if we proceed to trial, Judge Redmond will preside. I've never seen a plea deal rejected before, but Judge Redmond is well within his rights to do so."

Hillary glanced over her left shoulder at her parents. Janice Martin was crying softly. Her head was buried into Harold Martin's shoulder.

Then, Hillary peeked in the direction of Jenna Reiner. Jenna glowered at Hillary, shaking her head in unabated disgust.

For one of the few instances in her life, Hillary thought of the people she loved, instead of herself. A trial would cost her parents greatly. Not only in attorney's fees, but in their standing within the community and their ability to carry on normal lives. Trial or not, she would never see her daughter again, of that she was sure. Her life was essentially over. The only thing a trial would accomplish would be to cause further grief, embarrassment, and destruction to the few people in this world that still cared about her. Her only chance to minimize their pain would be to end this, now. That was all Hillary had to give them.

Hillary turned back around and said to Jack, "I'm pretty much fucked either way. Or am I missing something?"

Jack was as serious as Hillary had ever seen him. "No, Hillary, you're not missing anything."

Her words were as cold as ice. "Keep the plea."

The fifteen-minute recess was over, and Judge Redmond re-entered the courtroom.

With cold, critical words, the judge addressed Hillary, "Ms. Martin, you've had the opportunity to discuss matters with your counsel. Have you reached a decision on how you would like to proceed?"

Hillary rose to her feet. "Yes, Your Honor."

"Very well. Do you wish to revoke your plea of guilty and proceed to trial, or do you want to persist with your plea, knowing that the terms of sentencing will be left to my discretion?"

Hillary stood tall. "I would like to continue with my guilty plea. I do not wish to proceed to trial."

Unsympathetically, Judge Redmond said, "The court accepts your guilty plea. You are hereby sentenced to fifty years in a federal penitentiary, without the possibility for parole. Court is hereby adjourned."

The judge delivered a final blow of the gavel. Without another word, he stood and left the courtroom.

Attempting to ease the blinding pain in her heart, Hillary rubbed her chest. She gulped for air. Janice Martin instinctively lunged forward over the wooden railing and held her daughter. Neither mother nor daughter had time to say anything before an officer of the court moved in and separated them. Harold Martin pulled his wife down to the bench where they had been seated during the proceedings. He wrapped his arms around her and used all his weight as an anchor to separate Janice from her daughter.

Behind Hillary, the victims and their families held each other and cried.

Hillary was quickly handcuffed and led out of a back door of the courtroom. Jack stood motionless, alone at the defense table.

TWENTY-THREE

Jenna knew attending the court proceedings was a risky endeavor, but she could not resist the opportunity to express her hatred toward Hillary Martin. Certain that Tom and her attorneys would have forbidden her to come, Jenna chose not to tell any of them of her intentions.

As soon as Judge Redmond concluded the proceedings, Jenna bolted from the courtroom. With her goal accomplished, she was anxious to leave before anyone recognized her.

Discreetly, Jenna crossed the lobby of the courthouse. At the main door, she heard the click of stiletto heels striking the marble floor. A tall, slender, blonde woman in a tailored business suit shoved her way in front of Jenna and blasted through the door, leaving it to slam shut in Jenna's path.

"Nice," Jenna uttered sarcastically, flinging the door back open. The obnoxious woman never looked back.

Jenna was about to walk away when she heard someone shout, "Ms. Anders! Allison Anders! Can we get your comment on Hillary Martin's sentence?"

On the top steps of the courthouse, Jenna froze, her eyes and mouth open wide in disbelief. A dozen steps below her, Jenna watched a petite, brunette reporter chase after the blonde stranger. She recognized the newscaster immediately. It was Tamara Knight, the lead anchor for Channel 8 News. A brawny cameraman struggled to keep pace with her.

At the mention of her name, the attorney stopped and turned in the direction of the news crew. Curling her lips into a smile, she purred, "Of course." The cameraman shined the spotlight on Allison, and she quickly smoothed her hair. Under the glow, Allison's green eyes were captivating, and her perfectly coiffed bob glistened. She was strikingly beautiful. Standing at the edge of a small crowd of onlookers, Jenna noticed that Allison Anders' makeup was even more perfect than that of the pretty journalist.

The cameraman counted down with his fingers. "We're live in three, two, one."

Gazing into the lens of the camera, the newsperson spoke into her microphone. "This is Tamara Knight from Channel 8 News. I'm on the steps of the Federal District Courthouse, speaking with attorney Allison Anders. Ms. Anders represents many of the patients whose lives have been tragically devastated by the actions of former St. Augustine Hospital scrub technician, Hillary Martin. Ms. Anders, what do you think of the verdict that was handed down today?"

Allison's eyes narrowed and her smile receded. In a thick, New York accent, she replied, "My clients are not satisfied at all by today's ruling. The fact that Hillary Martin was sentenced to fifty years in prison won't keep this same sort of thing from happening again. The hospital needs to own up to its part. St. Augustine needs to assume responsibility for both creating and allowing an environment to exist where this tragedy could have occurred in the first place. Furthermore, the anesthesiologists who took care of these patients also need to share in the blame. If it hadn't been for their careless handling of narcotics, Hillary Martin would have never had the opportunity to commit her crimes. My clients demand that justice be served."

It was a flawless performance. Every word, every gesture, every facial expression had been rehearsed and finessed for maximum impact.

The interview concluded, and the cameraman shut off the spotlight. Allison politely shook hands with Tamara Knight and walked away.

Jenna darted around the corner of the courthouse. Her palms were clammy, and she was sweating profusely. She had come face-to-face with the woman who would set out to destroy her.

As Jenna stood panting on the sidewalk, her phone vibrated in her purse. A text message from Jim Taylor read, "Plea deal struck with Martin. No trial next week. You're off the hook. Call with any questions."

Jenna whispered to herself, "Tell me something I don't know."

TWENTY-FOUR

October 25, 2010

At exactly eight o'clock in the morning, an unmarked van pulled up to the rear entrance of the Federal District Courthouse. Hillary Martin emerged from the back, with armed guards surrounding her. She looked every bit the criminal. As she lumbered along, shackled by chains, a small crowd of enraged bystanders yelled obscenities at her. Some held signs branding her a "Murderer" and a "Drug-Addicted Whore." Throngs of television cameras captured the scene for the evening news. Reporters shouted Hillary's name, hoping to get a statement or coax her into turning their direction. She refused to acknowledge them. Once inside, Hillary was led to the U.S. Attorney's offices on the third floor of the building.

Two male officers steered Hillary into an interview room and ordered her to sit at the far end of the table. With each step, metal dug into the bare skin of her ankles. Hillary shuffled to the chair and clumsily plopped down. One officer removed her handcuffs and bulletproof vest, but left the ankle restraints in place. The officer stood behind Hillary while his cohort guarded the door.

Within minutes, a middle-aged man with short black hair and a goatee marched in, carrying a Styrofoam cup of coffee. Hillary recognized him from the court proceedings the week before.

The man addressed her from across the room. "Hillary Martin?"

"Yes." Hillary remained seated, refusing to show respect.

"I'm Federal Prosecutor Frank Montano." Montano made no attempt to shake Hillary's hand or otherwise come close to her. He took his seat at the opposite end of the table.

"I will remind you, Ms. Martin, that you are under oath," Montano said with reproach. "There are certain things we need to ascertain from you today, and I expect nothing less than the truth. Do I make myself clear?"

Hillary's jaw clenched. Indignantly, she answered, "Yes."

"Ms. Martin, during your acts of diversion of Fentanyl at St. Augustine Hospital, did you fully understand that certain diseases, like HIV and hepatitis, could be transmitted through bodily fluids? Particularly through blood?"

Desperately wanting to hide from the truth, Hillary paused before she answered. Reluctantly, she mumbled, "Yes."

"During that period of time, did you fully understand that those diseases could be spread via a contaminated syringe or needle?"

Montano's condescending tone incited Hillary. She glowered at the prosecutor and said bitterly, "Yes."

The federal prosecutor persisted, unfazed by Hillary's defiance.

"Is it true that before you started working at St. Augustine, you were explicitly told by a nurse at the employee health clinic that you had hepatitis C? Furthermore, did the nurse not provide you with a hard copy of those lab results? In case you don't remember, I have a copy of those results with your signature of acknowledgement at the bottom."

Hillary started to fidget. Her nostrils flared as she responded, "Yes."

Montano could see the perspiration collecting on Hillary's brow. Sensing her growing discomfort, he continued his assault.

"Regarding your diversion of Fentanyl at St. Augustine Hospital, you indicated to the police that you would sometimes take the drug home and shoot up there. Is that correct?"

"Yes." Hillary knew exactly where Montano was headed. She tried to slow her breathing, in hopes that her heart rate would follow suit.

"Did you ever share the needles and the stolen Fentanyl with other people?"

Montano held his breath as he waited for her response. This was the most critical question he would ask. Up until this point, investigators were only attempting to identify patients who were positive for hepatitis C with a viral DNA sequence that matched that of Hillary Martin's. If there were other individuals involved in contaminating the needles and syringes, the genotype match would become a meaningless tool for identifying victims. Worse, there could be other diseases involved. The magnitude of the crisis was about to escalate.

Hillary gazed at her reflection in the one-way mirror behind Montano. Her chest felt constricted. "Yes,"

Hillary whispered. She took a big breath and forced out the truth in a guttural cry, "*Yes!*"

TWENTY-FIVE

December 15, 2010

Jenna woke early, put on several layers of clothing, and took her dog for a run. Although the temperature was near freezing, the solitude of her neighborhood at five o'clock in the morning helped calm her nerves. By six o'clock, she returned home, breathless and invigorated. Walking through the front door, she found herself greeted by Mia, who was sauntering down the stairs, rubbing the sleep out of her eyes.

"Hi, Mommy," Mia said groggily.

"Hi, Princess." Jenna walked over and hugged her daughter.

Mia giggled, "Gross, Mom! You're all sweaty."

Jenna laughed as she grabbed Mia tight, trapping her. Mia struggled to break free, but to no avail. Jenna kissed the ticklish crook of Mia's neck one last time and then hurried off to take a shower.

At eight o'clock, Jenna arrived at the hospital. She only had three short cases, and then she was free. By mid-morning, the day was going along smoothly. The operating room staff was joking around, and everyone was in good spirits. Jenna allowed herself to forget about the impending lawsuit and enjoy the banter.

With only one case to go, Jenna walked into the congested preoperative area. Anxious to get the case finished, she hoped to finish some Christmas shopping before she had to pick Mia up from school. Jenna was introducing herself to her last patient when her cell phone rang. She snuck a peek at the display. It was Jim Taylor. Jenna excused herself and stepped into the hallway to take the call.

Jim said with remorse, "Jenna, we just got served by Allison Anders. Unfortunately, you are formally being sued."

Jenna felt the room spin. For the first time in her life, she felt faint. Her muscles went limp, and the images around her blurred. Instinctively, she dropped to the ground. The floor swayed to and fro beneath her.

Two of the preop nurses rushed over. The color had vanished from Jenna's skin, turning her a worrisome shade of gray.

"Dr. Reiner! Are you okay?" Susana, the charge nurse, shook Jenna by the shoulders as she shouted the words.

The only thing Jenna heard was a high-pitched ringing, and her vision slowly turned to black. Someone placed a chilly, wet towel on the back of Jenna's neck. Another person ordered Jenna to take a sip of juice. Slowly, things came back into focus. Jenna's phone lay on the ground, beside her. A concerned crowd of nurses and physicians encircled her.

The usual frenzied pace of the preop area had come to a halt. Jenna had become quite a spectacle. She looked up at the nurses and her fellow physicians – everyone was staring. A flood of heat spread over her face and neck. Once onlookers saw that Jenna was okay, most went back to their own affairs. Susana remained and helped Jenna to her feet.

It took Jenna a few more seconds to realize that the whole event had taken place directly in front of her patient's bay.

"Are you alright?" Susana asked.

Jenna could only shake her head as tears pooled in her eyes, threatening to spill over. Not wanting to create any more public drama, she ran to the locker room and locked herself in one of the bathroom stalls. Jenna buried her head in a mound of toilet paper, hoping to muffle the sounds of her sobs.

When she came out, Susana was waiting for her.

Jenna covered her face with her hands. "I'm so sorry. I can't do the next case. That patient saw and heard everything. I need to get out of here."

Susana put her arms around Jenna. "Take the staircase. I grabbed your stuff from the OR, so you don't have to go back. Don't worry about the next case. I'll call your office and tell them you're sick. Now go."

"Thank you," Jenna mouthed.

Grabbing her bag, Jenna bolted out of the hospital and drove directly to the offices of Moore and Everett.

On the drive, she called Tom. They both knew this was coming, but the reality sucked the air from Jenna's lungs. Tom could hardly understand what his wife was saying through her sobs and erratic breathing. Ultimately, Tom got the gist of what had transpired, and he instantly felt his wife's pain.

"Just call me when you're done. Drive carefully, and don't worry about Mia. I'll make sure she's taken care of."

"Thanks," she whispered. Jenna then hung up and parked. She marched into her lawyers' building and rode the elevator up to their offices. This would be the first meeting with her attorneys that really mattered.

TWENTY-SIX

Jenna was directed to take a seat in the waiting area next to the floor-to-ceiling windows. She walked over and reflected on the city below. The scene was so pretty. The city was dusted in snow and decked out in holiday lights and decorations. It dawned on her that she had planned to spend the afternoon shopping for gifts for Mia, not here discussing how her life was falling apart. It made her feel violated and resentful.

A single, involuntary tear slid down Jenna's cheek. Inconspicuously, she wiped it away. She could cry all the way home and all night long if she needed, but not here.

Soon, Jim and Nancy arrived in the lobby. They spotted their client motionless, with her body pressed against the window.

Not wanting to startle her, Jim spoke softly, "Jenna?"

She drew in a large breath and turned around to face her attorneys. It was evident to both of them that she was terrified. They approached and shook Jenna's hand. Nancy caught Jenna off guard as she moved in close and gave her a quick, reassuring hug.

The threesome went back into the conference room and sat down. Jim handed Nancy and Jenna a stack of documents and kept an identical set for himself.

Reading the top page, Jenna felt like she had been punched in the midsection. She fought for oxygen as her heart fluttered. The words felt like knives, piercing through her soul. On the top of the first page, in black and white, there were allegations she could never erase, never make go away. "Plaintiff: Michelle Hollings v. Defendants: St. Augustine Hospital and Jenna Reiner, M.D." She was officially a "Defendant."

Calmly, Jim said, "Let's go through the complaint and make sure you understand it in its entirety. We reviewed it before you got here. The first few pages are mundane formalities, so we can skip past them."

Jenna could see Jim's mouth moving and hear his voice, but she was not processing anything he said. Scrambled thoughts plagued her mind. Jenna strained to focus on words she could not bear to hear. Slowly, Jim's voice registered and began to make sense.

"Next, we come to the 'General Allegations' section. This is where they lay down their case."

For the next two hours, Jim reviewed the seventy-five points it took for Allison Anders to painstakingly detail how Jenna and St. Augustine had messed up at every turn. According to the allegations, the hospital failed to detect Hillary Martin's diversion activities and drug addiction. Jenna failed to secure her narcotics, leaving them vulnerable to Hillary Martin's diversion practices. Michelle Hollings contracted hepatitis C because of their collective mistakes. Both the hospital and Jenna were to blame, and Michelle Hollings deserved to be compensated for her pain and suffering.

Seemingly, there was no shortage of pain and suffering for Ms. Hollings. According to the complaint, her life had been utterly destroyed by her infection. Required to take dozens of oral and injectable medications each week, Ms. Hollings was traumatized by having to inject herself with needles. Side effects of the therapy caused Ms. Hollings to suffer from constant joint pain, drug-induced weight loss, flu-like symptoms, depression, and emotional and physical exhaustion. She was left unable to function in either a professional or social capacity. Obtaining affordable or effective health insurance coverage would be an unattainable goal.

Jenna thought it could not get any worse. It did not seem like there was anything left to ruin in Ms. Hollings' life. Jenna was sure that Jim had to be at the end of the complaint, but the insults continued.

"Michelle Hollings lives in a state of constant apprehension as to whether her contraction of hepatitis C will result in cirrhosis, end-stage liver disease, the need for liver transplantation, or even premature death. She may never be able to have children."

Jenna stared at the malicious words in disbelief. She balled her fists. On the verge of tears, she fought to hold back.

"Is that all?" she cried.

Jim promptly responded, "Jenna, I know it's hard to hear these allegations. You need to distance yourself. Just because they say these things, doesn't make them true. That's why you have us. One by one, we will expose their claims for the nonsense that they are."

Jim gave Jenna a minute to absorb all that she had heard. Knowing the next part would likely be the most hurtful, he dreaded what he had to tell her next. Whatever trauma Michelle Hollings had endured was mirrored in the devastated expression on Jenna's face.

Forcing himself to forge ahead, Jim continued, "The last part of the complaint lists the individual claims. In total, St. Augustine is being sued for eight different claims that range from negligent hiring practices to reckless and intentional infliction of emotional distress."

Jim proceeded to Jenna's involvement, "You are being sued for two claims."

"Well, I guess that's better than eight," Jenna said, helplessly. "What are they?"

"The first claim is for medical negligence. The claim states that you had acquired Ms. Hollings' trust and confidence, and you violated that trust when you failed to ensure that your narcotics were adequately secured and monitored. It also asserts that you failed to properly monitor Ms. Hollings' level of pain and the effectiveness of the Fentanyl prior to and during her operation. They allege that as a direct and proximate result of your negligence, Michelle Hollings has suffered injuries, losses, and damages."

Losses and damages. The words resonated in Jenna's head.

Jim continued, "The second claim against you is negligence per se."

Jenna immediately asked, "What's that?"

"Negligence per se means that you violated a law or a rule. It's different than medical negligence in that with medical negligence, the claim is that your actions were below the standard of care. That is, your actions deviated from what your peers would do under similar circumstances.

"With negligence per se, the claim isn't that your actions failed to meet the standard of care, but that they violated a law. In this instance, it doesn't matter what your peers would do.

"What this claim states is that you violated rules under the Controlled Substances Act. The Act makes it unlawful for Schedule II controlled substances, such as

Fentanyl, to be stored in an unlocked, unmonitored, or otherwise unsecured manner."

Jenna flipped to the last page of the twenty-six-page document. Interrupting Jim, Jenna read aloud, her voice rising with disgust and indignation with each passing word.

"Wherefore Michelle Hollings *prays* for judgment against Defendant St. Augustine Hospital and Defendant Dr. Jenna Reiner, in an amount to be determined by the trier of the fact, for compensatory damages in an amount sufficient to compensate her for her losses as set forth above, special damages, and for costs, expert witness' fees, attorneys' fees, filing fees, pre-judgment interest, post-judgment interest, and such other further relief as the Court may deem appropriate, just, and proper."

Jenna threw the document on the table. Her face was flaming red with disdain.

"Do we have to pay for her clothing and meals, too? Maybe she needs a manicure before the trial! We better factor that in, as well. Maybe we should put her up in a five-star hotel while we're at it." Jenna was yelling, not at her lawyers, but at the document and the people behind it.

The degree of theatrics and lies astounded Jenna. Her initial feelings of shame and guilt lifted and were replaced by anger, disbelief, and revulsion.

Jenna could imagine Allison Anders in some ridiculous lawyer commercial.

"Have you or someone you love been hurt by your physician? Is your life forever ruined because your doctor messed up? Do you need a huge amount of cash to ease your pain and suffering? Well, call the attorneys at AAA Money Sharks, and we will get justice and money for you!"

Several hours had passed, but to Jenna, time seemed to stand still.

Sadly, she confessed, "One thing they said was absolutely true. I did leave my drugs unattended. How can I possibly defend that?"

Jim's eyes brightened. "That's why you have us."

TWENTY-SEVEN

During the meeting, Jim had watched Jenna closely. He was having a hard time reading her. When Jim had first seen her looking out the window of the lobby, she had looked so vulnerable, so shocked, so devastated. Jenna still looked that way, but there had been a very subtle, yet noticeable, shift. Jim thought he saw a flicker of feistiness in her eyes and an inner resolve that was starting to come to life.

Nancy sensed it, too. She had been observing Jenna's expressions as Jim meticulously reviewed the complaint. Nancy saw the pain and humiliation in Jenna's face when she initially saw her name listed as "Defendant." There were moments when she was certain Jenna was going to break down in tears, but she never did. Nancy also noticed Jenna had moments where she looked truly appalled and offended. These were the emotions they needed to foster in their client.

Jenna started to speak, but was embarrassed by the smack of sticky, dried saliva as she opened and closed her mouth. With tremulous hands, she reached for a bottle of water from the center of the table and gulped its contents.

With her mouth no longer dry, she asked, "Where do we go from here? I need to know what to expect."

Jenna's eyes narrowed, and her lips pursed. She was regaining control.

"In the big picture," Jim explained, "where we go from here is a long, arduous process. The next step is called discovery. Formally, it's where both sides request information from a variety of sources, and we start to build the foundation for our defense. In actuality, mostly it's a period of bickering and jostling between opposing counsel. Once we get toward the end of the discovery period, depositions are taken. Have you ever given a deposition?"

"No," replied Jenna, with the innocence of a child. "Honestly, I'm not even sure what a deposition is."

Jim smiled kindly, "That's okay. No one expects you to know what any of this stuff means. A deposition is a formal interview where the person being deposed is under oath. We will take depositions of all the expert witnesses who are called to testify, both for our side and theirs. You will also be deposed."

Jenna raised her eyebrows. "Me?"

Nancy watched Jenna's mounting anxiety. It was astonishing to witness Jenna's resolve shift – brave Jenna one minute, vulnerable Jenna the next. Regardless, Nancy knew she could not afford to mince words. Jenna needed to start preparing for a vicious battle.

"Besides your performance in court, your deposition will probably be the most important thing you contribute to your case. To be brutally honest, the purpose of your deposition is singular. It's Anders' chance to get you to hang yourself with your own words. She will try to get you to admit that what you did was wrong. She will attempt to twist your words, trip you up, and make you appear dishonest. She will hammer you with the same questions over and over again for hours in hopes that you will eventually contradict yourself. All while you are being videotaped, audiotaped, and every word you say is transcribed by a court reporter."

"Sounds wonderful," replied Jenna bleakly.

Nancy reached out and patted Jenna's hand. "I know it sounds horrible, and it is. But I'd rather have you mentally geared up for a grueling experience. When we get close to the time of the deposition, we will do mock testimonies, grill you, and pin you into a corner. That way, when Anders tries to do it for real, you'll be ready."

"Okay," Jenna muttered, still terrified. "When will my deposition happen?"

Jim responded, "We don't have a firm date or timeline, but I would expect not for a while. Probably about six months from now. Our trial date has been set for January 30, 2012."

"Wow," said Jenna, sounding depressed. "So this lawsuit is going to be hanging over my head for over a year? How do people deal with that?"

Nancy spoke, "That's a good question. There's no denying that it's extremely stressful and constantly present. Some people go see a therapist, which you may want to consider."

"I don't need a therapist," snapped Jenna.

Nancy tried to smooth things over, "I'm sorry, Jenna. I didn't mean to insinuate that you do. I just know it helps some people to have someone besides us and their spouse to talk to."

"No, I'm sorry," Jenna said. "It's just that it's bad enough that this is happening. The thought of seeing a shrink is just too much right now. I'm not ready to be sued and crazy all at the same time."

"Don't give it a second thought. Jim and I have pretty thick skin, so no worries. And no one thinks you're crazy."

"So this really could take over a year?" asked Jenna, attempting to get back on target.

Nancy responded, "The only way things may conclude sooner is if we settle with Ms. Hollings. At this point, I think it's premature to pursue that option. We have no idea if what they wrote in this complaint is true. For all we know, Michelle Hollings may have had hepatitis C before she ever came to St. Augustine for her surgery. The discovery process will help sort that out. As things start to take shape, we may come to the conclusion that settling is in your best interest."

"You mean," asked Jenna, "if it looks like we're going to lose?"

"Basically, yes," replied Nancy. "Some cases are stronger than others. I'm not saying that we feel that way about your case right now, but things can and do change. Just so we are clear, the decision to settle is ultimately yours. We can give you our input and advice, but neither we nor your malpractice carrier can force you to settle."

Jenna asked, "After the discovery process and all the depositions are taken, then what?"

Jim replied simply, "Then we go to court next January. Our trial has been scheduled to last three weeks."

Jenna sighed. "It's the gift that keeps on giving."

Neither of her attorneys replied. There was really nothing either of them could say. The air in the room was thick with emotion. Jim finally asked Jenna if she had any more questions.

There were so many things she did not understand. Jenna felt like a traveller in a foreign country where every aspect of life was different – the language, the logic, the customs. She was an uninvited visitor in a world she did not recognize.

"First of all, if this patient is suing St. Augustine and me together, do we have to coordinate our legal defenses? I don't see how that would work."

Jim set his pen down and rested his hands on the conference table. "Most likely, if the case ends up going to trial, the jury will be asked to determine the percentage of liability for each party, Hillary Martin included. For example, they may find that Hillary Martin is ninety percent responsible, the hospital is eight percent responsible, and you are two percent responsible. Then whatever amount the jury chooses to award, if it goes that way, will be applied to each of the three parties according to their degree of responsibility. You and St. Augustine will both be on trial together, but not necessarily on the same side. Each party is going to be looking out for their own best interests."

Jenna's eyes bore into Jim's as she said, "Which means that, more likely than not, the hospital is going to sacrifice me."

"They can and probably will try to do that, at least to some degree," Jim admitted. "The facts are that Hillary Martin was *their* employee, not yours. They hired a drug addict. We strongly suspect their background check on Ms. Martin was inadequate, at best. Otherwise they would have uncovered truths about her that certainly would have precluded her from being hired. If Hillary Martin had never been employed by St. Augustine and had never been permitted to be in the operating rooms, this whole catastrophe would never have occurred."

"I have another question," said Jenna, wild-eyed. "I know this sounds irrational, but it really scares me. What about the media? Do you think I'll end up in the press?"

"Anything's possible," answered Jim. "As you probably know, a case filed against one of your partners ended up on the front page of the Sunday paper. Anders just so happens to be the attorney on that case, too. She loves the press and uses it to trash and intimidate the doctors she sues. I don't see any imminent stories coming out, but it's something you have to prepare for. You will need to prepare your family, as well."

Mental images flashed in Jenna's head of Mia going to school and having some other kid say, "Hey, my mom saw your mom on TV. Did your mom really give some lady a bad disease?"

Not to mention her colleagues. Jenna could easily picture them turning on her. Goosebumps raised the hair on her arms as she imagined their critical stares and condemning comments about her inadequacies and failings.

Then there would be the everyday people – her neighbors, her hairdresser, other parents. Would they go out of their way to avoid her? Would they also judge her?

Jim had no way of knowing the destructive thoughts that were running rampant in Jenna's head, but the expression on her face spoke volumes. Her skin was as white as the snow covering the city.

Trying to nudge Jenna back on track, Jim asked, "Do you have any more questions about the complaint or what to expect as things move forward?"

"No," answered Jenna dryly. "I think you guys covered it pretty well."

"Well then," Jim continued, "we have copies of your anesthesia paperwork for Ms. Hollings. If you feel up to it, we would like to go through it with you. However, if you've had enough for one day, we understand. We can reschedule for later this week."

Jenna was tired and emotionally drained. However, the last thing she wanted was to have to come back tomorrow or the next day.

"No, I'm okay. Let's keep going. I just need five minutes to use the restroom and call home."

"Absolutely," Jim replied. They all stood, and Jenna left the room.

TWENTY-EIGHT

In the restroom, Jenna splashed cool water on her face. Although it did not ease her pain, it did help to revive her. She called Tom and told him she would probably be several more hours. He asked how things were going, but Jenna did not want to discuss it, certainly not in the women's restroom at her attorneys' office. Jenna hung up with her husband and made her way through the labyrinth of cubicles back to the conference room.

She took her seat, and Jim handed her a stack of papers.

"We would like to go through all your documentation, piece by piece, so that Nancy and I are sure we understand everything. Let's start with your pre-anesthetic assessment sheet."

Jenna rifled through the stack of papers laid out in front of her and found the copy.

Jim asked, "As you look at your preop assessment, is there anything remarkable about Ms. Hollings as a patient?"

Jenna traced her finger over every word and shook her head. "The patient is completely straightforward. Ms. Hollings was young, thin, and healthy."

Instantly, Jenna was consumed with self-reproach. *Michelle Hollings was healthy*, she thought, *up until the point I injected hepatitis C into her bloodstream.*

Next, Jim asked Jenna to refer to the anesthesia record. Jenna found her copy and motioned for Jim to continue.

"Can you walk us through this record? It would be particularly helpful if you could read and explain your notations and abbreviations, the drugs you gave and why, and Ms. Hollings' vital signs during the procedure."

For several minutes, Jenna silently scrutinized the anesthesia record. She felt a small amount of relief in being the one who understood everything, rather than the one who understood nothing. At least for now, Jenna was the expert. She slid her chair closer to the table and tucked her hair behind her ears.

"To start with, I documented that she had a peripheral IV in her left upper extremity, and it ran well. She was NPO, meaning no food or water, nothing by mouth, since midnight. The patient was brought to OR 2 and placed in the supine position, meaning that she was laying on her back on the operating room table. She had a smooth IV induction, which indicates that I gave her the intravenous medications to knock her out, and there were no complications. Her eyes were taped shut, to protect them from inadvertently being scratched."

Jenna shifted her attention from her document to her lawyers. Reassured that they were following her, she continued.

"She was easy to mask ventilate, and her intubation was uncomplicated and atraumatic. I noted that her arms were extended from her sides for surgery. Her extremities were padded, to avoid nerve injury. The last notation I make about the start of the case is that a warming blanket was placed over her lower body.

"Further down, in the notation section, I document that at the end of the case, the patient met all the criteria for extubation. Once the breathing tube was removed, the patient was taken to the PACU – the recovery room – in stable condition with supplemental oxygen delivered through a nasal cannula."

Jenna's attorneys furiously scribbled notes on their copies as she spoke. Jenna waited for them to catch up. She was starting to calm down. Going through her anesthesia record felt safe and familiar.

Jim stopped writing and glanced up at Jenna. "Now I'd like you to look at the drugs you gave, the corresponding vital signs, and explain Ms. Hollings' operating-room course."

Jenna moved her finger along the anesthesia record. "It looks like Michelle Hollings got 2 milligrams of Versed in preop, before she got to the OR, to help her relax. That's pretty standard. Apparently, she must have not have felt much of an effect, because I gave her 2 more milligrams of Versed in the operating room, before putting her off to sleep.

"Her first blood pressure upon entering the room was 140/80, and her heart rate was 105. That would indicate that she was probably nervous, which is very common. Then it looks like I induced anesthesia, meaning I knocked her out. I gave her 100 milligrams of Lidocaine, 250 micrograms of Fentanyl, and 200 milligrams of Propofol – Michael Jackson's milk."

Jim and Nancy, caught off guard by Jenna's humor, started laughing. Nancy looked at her client and realized this was the real Jenna Reiner – spunky, off-color, and down to earth.

Jenna smiled at their appreciation for her joke and continued.

"The last induction drug I gave was 50 milligrams of Rocuronium, a paralytic. Once the patient was intubated, I secured the breathing tube in place with tape. Then I turned on the Sevoflurane, which was the anesthesia gas I used to keep her asleep during the procedure. After induction, her blood pressure dropped to 90/60, and her heart rate was in the 90s. That's a very typical response. Most of the anesthesia medications and the gases used for induction dilate blood vessels and depress the heart to a certain degree. As a result, most patients will show a drop their blood pressure and heart rate.

"Then, it looks like, right at the time of surgical incision, Ms. Hollings' blood pressure rose to around 160/90, and her heart rate increased to over 100. I gave her 10 milligrams of Morphine and increased the concentration of the gas."

Jim interrupted, "Why did you switch narcotics?"

"Morphine lasts longer. I'm sure I figured it would help her wake up more comfortably. Anyway, it looks like her blood pressure remained elevated, even after the first dose of Morphine should have kicked in. I administered another 5 milligrams and further increased the concentration of Sevoflurane. After that, her blood pressure came down to around 100/50, and her heart rate dropped into the 90s. Her vital signs stayed in that range for the rest of the case.

"During the surgery, Ms. Hollings also received some anti-nausea medications and an antibiotic."

"Do you see any evidence that she didn't respond to the Fentanyl you gave at the beginning of the case?

What I'm getting at is whether it looks like she got Fentanyl or saline?" asked Nancy.

Jenna studied the chart closely. Looking at Nancy, Jenna replied honestly, "I would say, based on this record, Ms. Hollings responded appropriately to the Fentanyl. She dropped her blood pressure following intubation, which is a very stimulating and painful event if a patient is inadequately anesthetized. There is nothing in my documentation that leads me to believe that it wasn't Fentanyl.

"It's not uncommon to see patients require additional narcotics once the surgical incision has been made. After intubation, there's a period of about ten minutes where the patient is being positioned and prepped. Since none of that is painful, you often see their blood pressure and heart rate decrease as the vasodilating effects of the gases and medications are unopposed. At the time of incision, the noxious stimulus causes the patient to release adrenaline, and their blood pressure and heart rate increase. Not every patient needs additional narcotics at the time of surgical incision, but it's not uncommon, either."

"What about the Morphine?" Jim asked. "You indicated that 10 milligrams was a pretty hefty dose, and she got a total of 15 before her vital signs settled down. What do you make of that?"

Jenna replied quickly, "It tells me that Ms. Hollings, like many other young people, probably likes to party. When people routinely drink, do drugs, smoke pot, things like that, it's not uncommon to see their anesthetic requirements increase. According to the record, I gave her 10 milligrams of Morphine, and she showed virtually no response. It took another 5 milligrams before her vital signs indicated the drug was having any effect.   For whatever reason, she had an apparent tolerance."

Jim asked, "Jenna, I know from the records that you drew up the Fentanyl in advance, but what about the Morphine? When would you have accessed that drug?"

"I would have obtained it during the case, when it became apparent that additional narcotic was required. I would have checked it out from the Accudose machine and injected it immediately."

Jim placed his elbows on the table and moved closer to Jenna.   "Just so I'm clear, there would be absolutely no way that anyone could have tampered with the Morphine that you administered to Ms. Hollings? And, furthermore, she required high doses of that drug before you saw the desired effect?"

Jenna could see where Jim was going with this. Grinning, she replied, "That's one hundred percent correct."

Jim then said, "Let's move on to the Accudose record that we obtained. The Accudose is the machine from which you check out narcotics, correct?"

"Correct," replied Jenna.

"So," Jim continued, "it looks like you checked out 250 micrograms of Fentanyl and 2 milligrams of Versed at 7:38, but Ms. Hollings' case didn't start until 8:27. Can you explain why you checked out the narcotics in advance and what you did with them from 7:38 until 8:27?"

Jenna wanted to lie. She wished she could tell her lawyers that she kept the drugs in her pocket the whole time. Nancy's advice rang through her head – the way doctors hang themselves is by being dishonest. Besides, Jenna was not a liar, and she would not start now.

Peering down at the record, Jenna locked her sight on the documented times. With downcast eyes, she said,

"Most likely, I checked them out and drew them up around 7:38. My practice was to always be prepared. I would have all the routine drugs drawn up and ready to go before each case started. That way, if any issues arose, any unanticipated emergencies or whatnot, I wasn't caught off guard. Then I probably stuffed them in a drawer of my anesthesia machine and went to interview the patient."

"You never left your drugs out on top of the anesthesia cart in plain sight?" asked Jim.

This time, Jenna raised her head and faced Jim directly. "Never. I always hid them in a drawer under supplies."

"Had that always been your practice with respect to your drugs?" asked Nancy. "To draw them up in advance and hide them in the anesthesia cart while you tended to things outside the OR?"

"Yes," said Jenna. "That's what I was taught to do in residency and what I continued to do in private practice."

Jim and Nancy could see Jenna starting to fade. They had been going strong the entire afternoon.

Nancy looked sympathetically at Jenna and said, "Kiddo, I think we're done. Do you have any questions?"

Jenna knit her brow. "How do you both feel about the strength of our case, right now, based on what we've talked about?"

Jim cleared the table in front of him. "Jenna, I've been a malpractice attorney defending doctors for over twenty years. I've tried a lot of cases, and I've settled a lot of cases. I'm pretty good at sniffing out the ones that stand a chance with a jury. I think your actions are defendable. There are a lot of holes in this story that we can use to our advantage."

"Such as?" asked Jenna skeptically.

"To begin with, there is no proof that Hillary Martin stole your syringe of Fentanyl. There is no proof that Michelle Hollings became infected from a contaminated Fentanyl syringe. Even if Ms. Hollings did acquire hepatitis C from Hillary Martin, it still doesn't explain *how* it happened. Hillary Martin could have used saline from the surgical table to refill syringes that she stole from other doctors. That saline, not your Fentanyl syringe, could have been the source of contamination.

"There's also the issue of standard of care. We've done some preliminary investigation and the consensus, so far, is that there really was no clearly defined, nationally accepted standard of care when it came to securing narcotics in the OR. Your practice was absolutely not out of line with what many, if not most, other physicians were doing.

"As far as the negligence per se claim, we will poke holes at what it means to have drugs secured. Our contention is that the operating room itself was a secure environment. Hillary Martin changed that, of course, but prior to her crimes, operating rooms were considered protected areas. Therefore, storing your drugs in your cart within the operating room should constitute securing your drugs. The key here is the law that Anders refers to in the complaint is extremely vague. It states that drugs should be secured, but doesn't go on to clearly define what 'secure' means."

"That's the most encouraging news I've heard all day," said Jenna, with a hint of optimism.

Exhausted, Jenna swiveled her chair around and stole a glance out the window. Only then did she realize the sun had set. At least six hours had passed since Jenna first arrived. Her stomach grumbled, and her eyes burned.

Jenna retrieved her purse and stood to leave. She was almost out the door when she heard Nancy say, "We'll be in touch."

Unfortunately, Jenna knew they would.

TWENTY-NINE

Jenna drove home with the music blasting at full volume, hoping to drown out her thoughts. Although she wanted to cry and release her emotions, she could not. She was completely spent.

Reviewing the events of the day, Jenna could not comprehend how such horrific allegations could be attached to her name. Heartless words replayed in Jenna's head. In spite of the music booming from the speakers, all Jenna could hear was Jim's voice as he read the complaint:

"If it weren't for the carelessness of Dr. Reiner, Michelle Hollings would not have contracted hepatitis C."

"Had Dr. Reiner shown diligence in her duties to protect her patient by detecting the syringe of Fentanyl had been tampered with, Ms. Hollings would not have been infected with the hepatitis C virus."

"It was the ultimate act of Dr. Reiner injecting a syringe contaminated with hepatitis C into Ms. Hollings' bloodstream that resulted in her infection."

Driving down the highway, Jenna started to doubt herself. Maybe it was her fault. What if she had ruined Michelle Hollings' life? What if Michelle Hollings ended up dying from end-stage liver disease? What if every day of the rest of her patient's life was spent in pain, fear, and uncertainty? It would all be a result of what was in that syringe – the very syringe Jenna had held in her own hands.

Rolling down the window, Jenna allowed an arctic gust of December air to enter the car. It was painfully refreshing.

In an instant, Jenna's emotions shifted to ire and repugnance. She was outraged at Allison Anders' characterization of her as a careless and incompetent doctor. How could someone write such vile statements about somebody else? What would possess someone to be so ruthless and cruel?

Jenna could not shake the words, "Michelle Hollings prays . . ." from her mind.

"Give me a break!" Jenna shouted into the dark emptiness of her car.

Before Jenna knew it, she had arrived home. She pulled into the garage and rolled up the window. Her cheeks were icy, and her hair was a tangled mess.

Jenna had not yet reached the door of her house when Mia flung it open and ran toward her yelling, "Mommy, Mommy! You're home!" Mia flung herself into the arms of her mother. "Where have you been, anyway?"

She released herself from Mia's embrace and kissed the top of her head. "Mia, I'm so sorry. Can you give me a minute to change clothes and settle down? Then I'll explain things to you."

"I guess," said Mia, not sure what to make of the bizarre expression on her mother's face.

Jenna walked inside. The scent of garlic permeated the air, and Jenna knew instinctively that Tom had spaghetti cooking on the stove. She strolled into the kitchen, grateful he had been considerate enough to have dinner waiting. Tom heard her come in and looked up as he stirred the sauce. For a moment he barely recognized his wife. Dropping the spoon on the counter, Tom came over to Jenna and wrapped his arms around her. His act of kindness was all it took for Jenna to crumble.

With their daughter staring at them with concern, Tom held Jenna as she buried her head into his chest and wept. Soon, Mia came up and wiggled her way into the mix.

"Mommy, please don't cry," Mia begged. "Everything will be okay. Daddy and I promise. Don't we, Daddy?"

Tom looked at their precious child. At only eleven, Mia possessed wisdom and compassion well beyond her years.

"Yes, Mia," said Tom, as he looked at his wife and back at Mia. "We promise. Let's take care of Mom tonight, okay?"

Mia tenderly took her mother's hand and said, "Come on, Mom. Let's get you changed and out of those icky scrubs."

Jenna blindly followed her daughter into the bedroom. For Mia's sake, Jenna let her pick out a pair of sweatpants and a T-shirt. In a reversal of roles, Mia helped Jenna pull her cotton scrub top over her head and tossed it into the hamper. Jenna pulled the T-shirt on and changed into the sweatpants. She was deeply touched when Mia emerged from the closet, carrying her slippers. Jenna sat on the edge of the bed, allowing her daughter to slip the footwear on her feet. Indulging her daughter was the best thing that had happened to Jenna all day.

Mother and daughter walked back into the kitchen, hand-in-hand, to find dinner waiting for them on the table. Tom handed Jenna a generous glass of Merlot, which she gratefully accepted. The three of them sat down at the table, and Mia immediately asked, "Mommy, what's wrong?"

Jenna took an oversized gulp of her wine. The warmth of the spirits slid down her throat and hit her stomach.

"Mia," Jenna began, "remember how there was that awful lady at my hospital who stole drugs?"

"Yes." Mia's expression grew more intense. She maintained laser-beam focus on her mother.

"And remember how I explained to you that she had a really bad disease, called hepatitis C?"

Mia nodded.

"Well, it turns out that woman may have stolen one of my syringes that was meant for one of my patients. Then, so I wouldn't catch her stealing, she put a dirty syringe in its place. The dirty syringe had her disease in it, but it looked exactly like the real medicine. I didn't know it, but I gave the dirty medicine to my patient, and my patient got the disease."

Jenna took another large drink of wine. She could feel dampness trickling from her eyes. "Does that make sense so far?"

"Yeah, Mom. It makes sense. So are you crying because you feel bad for the patient?"

"Partly. And partly because I feel bad for *me*. My patient got hurt, and now she wants somebody to be punished for what happened to her."

"Well then, they should punish the lady who stole the drugs. She's the one who did the bad thing," replied Mia, with her very astute eleven-year-old logic.

"They did punish her," Jenna explained. "They sent her to jail for fifty years. But that's not all the patient and her lawyers want. When people get hurt, especially at the hospital, they want someone to make up for it by paying them money. They file a lawsuit against hospitals or doctors or whomever they think they can blame for what happened to them. My patient filed a lawsuit against me."

A rancid lump surfaced in Jenna's throat as she heard the word "lawsuit" slip past her lips.

Mia's face turned blotchy, and her arms flung violently as she spoke. "How can they do that? You didn't do anything wrong! It was that stupid lady. Why don't they get money from her?"

Explaining the lawsuit to her daughter allowed Jenna to see things more clearly. She realized this was a big money grab and nothing else. Her newfound clarity did not take the sting out of the accusations leveled against her, but it did offer her new focus.

"Well," said Jenna, "that lady who stole my drugs is a loser. She doesn't have any money. If she did, maybe they would have left me alone and gone after her. As it turns out, I have something called malpractice insurance. I pay an insurance company a bunch of money every year. Then, if I get sued, they pay the patient for me. My patient wants to get that money. In order to do so, my patient has to prove that I was at least partly responsible for her getting the disease."

"You're a good doctor," said Mia, defensively. "It wasn't your fault! How much money does she want you to give her?"

Jenna replied sorrowfully, "As much as she can get. My insurance company will pay up to a million dollars."

"Wow!" exclaimed Mia. "That's a lot. It's totally unfair. She doesn't deserve a million dollars from you or your insurance company."

"I don't think so, either. But now, I have to meet with lawyers, and we have to figure out a way to show that I'm not the one to blame. If we can do that, she'll get nothing. We just found out about the lawsuit today, and I had to meet with my attorneys all afternoon. I'm so sorry I missed out on time with you."

"It's okay," Mia said sympathetically. "Will you have to go to court, like on TV?"

Jenna studied her plate of cold spaghetti and inhaled the last bit of her wine. Tom automatically refilled her glass. Sadly, she confessed the ugly details of her future to her daughter.

"Maybe. Probably. But that won't happen for a long time. In the meantime, the patient and her lawyers are going to try to make me look like a bad doctor and a bad person. They are going to say a lot of mean things about me. And sometimes, it might hurt my feelings and make me cry."

Mia stood and hugged her mother. "Mommy, I'm so sorry for you. Daddy and I will take care of you. Don't let those people make you sad. It's like when people say bad things to me at school. You tell me to ignore them. So now, you have to do the same."

"I know, baby," said Jenna, choking on tears. She was surprised and touched by her daughter's insight and guidance. "But, just like with you, sometimes the words still hurt, no matter how hard you try to pretend they don't."

Tom sat in silence, watching the exchange between the two loves of his life.

Softly, he said, "Jenna, eat. I'm going to get Mia to bed, and then we can talk."

Mia resisted. "I want to stay with Mommy." Her eyes welled up.

Jenna looked at her daughter compassionately and said, "Mia, it's getting late. Why not let Daddy put you to bed, and I'll come up and snuggle with you later?"

"Okay," Mia said reluctantly, refusing to release her hold on her mother. Jenna kissed her daughter's curly locks and took in the scent of her skin. Tom gently peeled their daughter away from Jenna. Both of his girls had tears running down their checks.

THIRTY

It took Tom over half an hour before he was finally able to get Mia to sleep. Returning downstairs, he found his wife sitting at the table with her bowl of spaghetti barely touched and pushed off to the side. Jenna's head was buried in her hands, and her body was wracked with sobs.

Tom pulled up a kitchen chair and scooted it close to his wife. Lifting Jenna's chin, Tom forced her to look at him. Her eyes were swollen. He poured them both another glass of wine.

"Do you feel like talking?" asked Tom cautiously.

Jenna sighed, pushed her chair back, and rested her feet in Tom's lap.

She said miserably, "Well, I guess it's official. No more wondering when it's going to happen. I have formally been sued."

"Yeah," replied Tom, with a serious tone. "So, what did you guys talk about for six hours?"

"Pretty much everything. It took three hours just to get through the twenty-six-page complaint. Jim read it aloud, line by line, and clarified all the legal terminology."

"Sounds excruciating," said Tom.

"Yeah, but it was necessary. I don't think I would have understood half of it if Jim hadn't decoded it for me.

You should see the things they wrote about me. It was awful."

"How so?"

On her third glass of wine, Jenna was slurring her words, and her voice was high-pitched and edgy.

"They came right out and said that if it hadn't been for my negligence, Michelle Hollings wouldn't be a victim with a deadly virus."

"Jenna, you can't buy into that bullshit. *You* are not responsible. You are being sued because they think you're a rich doctor who has deep pockets, plain and simple, nothing more. I assume they are suing St. Augustine, too?"

"Yep! Get this, we're co-defendants! How great is that? The big, powerful corporation all lawyered up sitting side-by-side with the dispensable, little doctor – both trying to escape blame. I'm sure that will go well. Nancy already told me they'd probably serve me up as a scapegoat to save their own greedy hides. At least she's honest."

Jenna took another swallow of wine. She clumsily sloshed her glass around as she spoke. Tom was relieved she had drained most of it, or else it would have spilled by now.

"What exactly are you being sued for?" Tom asked, as gently as possible.

A shiver coursed through Jenna. If seeing the lawsuit in print had not made it real, articulating it to her husband most certainly did.

"There are two claims against me. I guess I should feel lucky. St. Augustine got nailed with eight. The first one is medical malpractice. You know, basically I'm a rotten doctor, sub-par, I suck. The second one is negligence per se. That means I'm also a terrible person who doesn't obey the law."

"Jenna, did they say how much they want? What kind of demands are they making?"

"Apparently, the sky's the limit."

"They didn't specify an amount?" Tom asked, trying to keep Jenna on track.

"Nope. I guess that's up for the jury to decide."

"So what did you spend the remainder of the time discussing?"

Tom could tell his wife's level of coherency was fading fast, but he was not about to take her glass of wine away from her. If Tom were in Jenna's shoes, he'd most certainly be drinking himself into oblivion right now, too. Yet, he also wanted to get as many details as possible from Jenna before her drunken haze clouded her memory.

Jenna relaxed a little, grateful to be off the topic of the complaint itself. "Jim and Nancy wanted me to go over my pre-op assessment and anesthesia record for Michelle Hollings. I basically had to do for them what they did for me – translate my world into something they could understand. It was uneventful."

"Did they ask you what you did with your drugs?" asked Tom.

"Yes."

"And," Tom pried, "what did you tell them?"

Jenna hung her head. In hindsight, she felt so foolish for thinking her drugs were safe.

"I told them the truth."

Tom was rubbing Jenna's feet. Between that and the wine, she started to feel relaxed and groggy.

Tom asked her, "Jenna, do you *feel* guilty?"

Jenna thought for a minute. Fresh tears came to her eyes.

"I don't know. What kills me is I actually held that syringe in my hand. The very syringe Hillary Martin had used to get high. I pushed a deadly virus into my patient."

"Jenna?"

"Yes?"

"Never admit that to anyone else. Not even your lawyers, okay?"

"I'm not stupid," Jenna responded defensively.

Jenna drained the last of her wine and stumbled across the kitchen to the cupboard. Tom watched her swallow a couple of sleeping pills.

"Are you going to be okay to work tomorrow?" Tom asked, worried about her impending hangover and her current emotional state.

"No, and maybe not the next day, either. I'm not going in."

Tom looked at his wife. Not having the heart to judge her, he did not say a word.

THIRTY-ONE

June 22, 2011

It was a warm, sunny Wednesday afternoon. Over six months had passed since Jenna first learned she was being sued, yet the intensity and pain of the situation never seemed to ease. Today was no exception. In two days, Allison Anders would do her best to destroy Jenna. She had precious little time to learn how to keep that from happening.

Jenna arrived early for her pre-deposition meeting with Jim and Nancy. With an hour to kill, she decided to stroll the streets of the downtown shopping district. She hoped that some fresh air would help calm her nerves.

The outdoor mall was active with professionals on their lunch breaks, women shopping, tourists taking pictures, and panhandlers begging for change. It felt good to be lost among them, simply another unknown face in the crowd. Jenna wandered around for blocks, savoring the afternoon sun as it beat down upon her tan skin. Sensing her reprieve was close to an end, Jenna checked her phone for the time. Her hour of freedom was nearly over. She had ten minutes to make it back to the steel skyscraper where her unpleasant fate awaited.

Jenna entered the lobby to find Jim and Nancy waiting for her. After exchanging hellos, they led her back to the all-too-familiar conference room.

Consumed by anxiety and dread, Jenna reminded herself to focus. This meeting was survival training. It was imperative that she absorbed every bit of advice her lawyers offered.

Jim spoke with fatherly concern, "Jenna, we know this is your first deposition. We don't want anything to surprise you, so we are going to prepare you for the worst."

Nancy interjected, "The thing you need to know about Anders is that her objective is to ruin you. She will search for your weaknesses and shamelessly exploit them. She will use intimidation, degradation, deceptive kindness – anything that she thinks will successfully lure you into her den."

"She sounds lovely," replied Jenna mockingly. "What specifically will she do to trap me?"

Jenna sat up straight, pen in hand, ready to take notes on every detail. Nancy was encouraged to see Jenna so attentive. So far, Jenna did not seem to be cowering. It was a positive sign.

Nancy elaborated, "One of Anders' favorite tactics is to ask the same basic question repeatedly, until she finally gets the answer she wants. She'll tweak the question by changing a couple of words, but it will be essentially unchanged. Listen carefully to what she's asking you, and stay consistent in your responses. It's critical that you don't contradict yourself.

"Anders also likes to ask long-winded questions. Don't let the length of her questions confuse you. Often, Jim and I have a hard time remembering the first part of her question by the time she gets to the end, and we're used to it. If you can't follow, ask her to repeat the question. If it's still too long and confusing, ask her to break it down. Whatever you do, don't answer anything that is not completely clear.

"Also, the best answers are the shortest answers. Whenever possible, keep it to 'yes,' 'no,' 'I don't know,' or 'I don't recall.' Once you state your answer, don't elaborate. Anders may ask you a question, and you may answer with a simple 'yes' or 'no.' Then, she will sit there and just look at you. The silence will make you feel uncomfortable. In normal conversation, you'd be inclined to fill in the void. *Don't.* Just stare back at her, no matter how awkward it makes you feel. Make her fish for information, but never hand her anything! Understood?"

"Yes," said Jenna, grateful for the coaching. She quickly shook the cramp out of her right hand as she jotted down every word. Without this advice, she knew Allison Anders would devour her within minutes.

Jim spoke up, "Unfortunately, however bad Allison Anders may be, she's not as bad as her partner, Lyle Silverstein. He is truly an evil man. And, Jenna, you have to be prepared to face both of them, because it's highly likely he may be there, too. You're in a high-profile case with a lot of money on the line. Lyle loves money. He may show up for all or part of your deposition. I'm not going to downplay it for you. Lyle is downright mean. I've seen him scream at defendants, get right up in their faces, and tower over them. He's a large man, and he uses his size and aggressive personality to his advantage. He can be very threatening."

Jenna's throat became tight and dry. Her eyes darted back and forth between Jim and Nancy.

"C-can they really do that? Get in my face? Yell at me? Mock me?"

Jenna was losing control. It was heart-wrenching to observe. Jim tried to restore confidence in his client. "That's why we will be there, right at your side. If either of them steps out of bounds, we will immediately object. There are limits as to how abusive they can be toward you, and we will not let them exceed those limits.

"However, you have to be prepared. Just because we're there to reel them in, doesn't mean they won't push the envelope. You need to know with absolute certainty that they will attack you. It may not happen right off the bat, but it will happen. Expect it at every turn. Never let your guard down. Never relax."

Jenna knew the deposition was going to be rough, but this surpassed her most pessimistic expectations. Ravaged by self-doubt, Jenna knew that somehow, in two short days, she was going to have to change dramatically in order to survive.

Nancy smiled gently at Jenna as she spoke. "You do have something within you that may give you an edge over both Anders and Silverstein."

"I do?" asked Jenna, completely taken aback. "What?"

"Exactly what you see as your biggest weakness. Simply stated, Jenna, you're *nice*. They don't know what to do with nice.

"Jim and I have tried many cases and gone through countless depositions against both Anders and Silverstein. Their modus operandi is to rattle the defendant, to provoke them into anger, and then to show that to the jury. Usually their job is made easier by the mere fact that most physicians are defensive when their skills or judgment are questioned.

"You're not the typical doctor. Your identity, as far as we can tell, is not built upon your status as a physician. You're a mother and a wife. That's what defines you and gives you strength. Being a doctor is what you do, not who you are. They aren't going to know what to do with that, or what to do with you."

Jenna's face reddened at Nancy's assessment.

"Okay, so maybe I'm nice. How does that protect me from being destroyed on Friday?"

Jim locked eyes with Jenna. "The way you survive is that you consider this a game. It's a very cruel, heartless, and vindictive game, but a game nonetheless. Know that if you start to succumb to their tactics, you lose. Every minute you keep it together, you win. We'll help you through the rest. Jenna, we have faith in you. You can do this."

Jenna pulled in a deep breath and exhaled. Standing to stretch her legs, she turned her back on her lawyers. Her mind drifted back to the four years spent in college, studying nonstop, maintaining a perfect GPA, and graduating with honors. Following college, there were the four arduous years of medical school where she was perpetually deprived of sleep, exercise, and daylight. From there, she moved onward to four years of residency where attending physicians belittled her on a daily basis, leaving her feeling completely defeated.

In fact, the only good things that happened to Jenna during those years were her marriage to Tom and Mia's birth. It was her family that had literally saved her from giving up or being destroyed. After residency, it took years of constant and patient reassurance from Tom before Jenna reached the point where she did not believe that she was worthless.

Jenna recognized this was a pivotal event in her life. She could allow herself to be beaten down again, or this time she could fight back. For the sake of her reputation, her family and, most importantly, herself, Jenna decided to not only defend herself, but to win.

With new resolve, Jenna turned back around and faced her attorneys. With a devilish grin, Jenna said with conviction, "Okay, let's get ready."

THIRTY-TWO

Jenna looked like a different person. Her eyes glimmered as she held her head high. There was a radiant glow in her cheeks. Taking her seat again, Jenna sat with perfect posture as she rested her hands comfortably on the table. Jim and Nancy had not yet witnessed this side of their client. There had been hints of it, but nothing quite like this.

Energized by Jenna's demeanor, Jim beamed, "Okay, then. Let's do it!"

He pulled his laptop in front of him and called up his calendar. "The deposition is set to start at nine o'clock. Nancy and I will meet you in the building's café, which is located on the ground floor, at 8:30. That way, if you have any last minute questions, we can answer them without being rushed.

"Your deposition will be videotaped. At the other end of the table from where you will be seated, there will be the videographer with a large camera focused on you. I know it sounds intimidating, but try to ignore it. You don't have to look right into it, which helps. Most people forget that it's there after a short while.

"Nancy and I will be seated on your left, with Nancy closest to you. Immediately on your right will be Allison Anders. She's the person you're talking to, so keep your attention focused on her. You can look at Nancy or myself if you have a question, but try not to do it excessively. We don't want to give the impression that we're coaching you – it diminishes your credibility.

"On Ms. Anders' side of the table, there may be Lyle Silverstein or any other member of their firm. You also need to be aware that Michelle Hollings might show up. We don't think she will, since Anders hasn't had a patient present at any of the other depositions, but anything is possible. If she's there, it's for the purpose of intimidating you and getting under your skin. Don't let it. Don't look at her. Keep your focus on Anders. There will also be a stenographer in the corner of the room, recording every word.

"Everything sound okay so far?"

"I wouldn't go so far as to say everything sounds okay. Everything sounds completely horrid, but at least I know what to expect."

Jim chuckled at Jenna's honesty and continued, "The deposition will start with you raising your right hand and swearing, under oath, to tell the truth. The camera will start rolling at that time.

"Everyone present at the deposition will state their name and their reason for being there. After that, Anders will explain the rules of conduct. She will tell you that if you don't understand one of her questions, you have the right to ask for clarification. Like we've said countless times before, we encourage you to do this. Remember, she is the master of confusing questions. If you are the least bit confused, *ask*!

"She will tell you that you have the right to request a break any time you need it. The only constraint on that right is if she has a question pending. If that's the case, you can't ask for a break until you've answered.

"Anytime you start to feel overwhelmed or want to talk to us, ask for a break. I'll keep my eye on you, too. If I feel like you are starting to look worn down or need some guidance, I'll make the request. Even if everything seems to be going along fine, I'll still make sure we take a breather every hour or so, just to help you stay fresh."

Jenna considered what it was going to be like to face Allison Anders. From the very moment Jenna saw Allison at the courthouse, she had disliked her. Since then, she had grown to despise her. To Jenna, this lawsuit had become very personal. It was a battle between her and Allison Anders.

She looked up, deathly serious. "So, let me make sure I understand this. They can ask me anything. They can make me look like an idiot, call me an idiot, or worse. They can get in my face and yell at me, and my job is to not flinch. I'm supposed to go through hours of verbal abuse and intimidation, all the while acting polite, and never reacting to their taunts."

Jim raised his eyebrow and pointed at Jenna. "If you can pull that off, I personally guarantee you the satisfaction of winning this battle."

Jenna asked, "So when we take breaks, how long do we get and where do we go?"

Jim answered, "We either huddle in their lobby or they leave us alone in their conference room. We can take as long as we want, but typically we try to keep it to less than fifteen minutes."

Jenna cried out, "You mean to tell me we are supposed to talk in secret, on *their* turf? Are you kidding me? I wouldn't put it past them to have the place bugged. Do we have to stay in their office?"

There was no way Jenna was going to relinquish that much control to the enemy.

Jim steepled his fingers in front of his face as he contemplated Jenna's request. "Well, there's no rule that says we can't leave. We never have before, but if it makes you more comfortable, we can go down into the lobby or even outside."

Jenna's face grew red with anger. The room was silent as her lawyers watched her. Jenna glared at them and smacked her palms on the table. "There's no way I'm talking about *my* secrets on *their* territory."

Jim and Nancy were left speechless.

Attempting to steer the meeting back to more productive matters, Jim handed Jenna a pile of documents.

"All the documents that you see here are what we have provided to Anders. During your deposition, she's going to ask you about each of these. It's all stuff you've seen before. I don't anticipate any major landmines here. Just make sure you look through these before Friday so they are fresh in your mind, okay?"

"Will do," Jenna replied, still rattled after her outburst.

Jim continued, "One of the most important topics that will inevitably come up is how you stored your narcotics. Our defense is going to depend on proving that your drugs were stored in a secure environment. As we've mentioned before, the DEA rules for narcotic storage are vague. The guidelines use the terms 'locked' and 'secured,' but they don't adequately define what qualifies as such. Whenever you hear Anders say 'unlocked and unsecured,' your immediate response should be that your drugs were secured. Do not deviate from this answer, no matter how many times and how many ways she asks you."

"Got it, my drugs were secured. The operating room was considered to be a secure environment and, by storing my drugs within that environment, they were secured." Jenna repeated the statement, making sure she said it correctly.

Jim and Nancy smiled at her like proud parents. Nancy simply said, "Perfect."

"Are there any more traps to watch out for?" Jenna asked.

"Just one," Nancy said. "Anders might bring up the possibility of punitive damages."

Jenna put her pen down and asked, "What are punitive damages?"

"That's where, under extraordinary circumstances, they not only sue you within the limits of your malpractice policy, but they also sue you personally."

Jenna's heart started to race. "You mean they could take my personal possessions?"

Nancy tried to console her. "Before you get too worked up, let me explain. In order to prove their case for punitive damages, they would have to show that you acted with willful and wanton disregard for the safety of Michelle Hollings. Hillary Martin's actions meet the criteria for punitive damages, but yours definitely do not."

"So, it's just an empty threat designed to scare me?"

Nancy responded, "Yes, so don't let it upset you if she brings it up."

"I'll do my best."

Jenna was beginning come to terms with the rules of this game. This was not a gathering of civilized, educated professionals in a room trying to get to the truth. Quite the contrary, this was a firing squad, where the bullets were in the form of words. Success, it seemed, would be measured not by victory, but by lack of defeat.

Sensing their meeting was over, Jenna stood to leave. Jim pushed his glasses up on his nose and gestured for her to sit back down.

"We have one last issue to discuss."

Jenna took her seat. The subdued expression on her lawyers' faces startled her. The room was quiet. Neither Jim nor Nancy could look directly at Jenna. Jim rubbed his forehead as he struggled to find the best way to tell her the news. After concluding that there was no best way, he finally spoke.

"We wanted to let you know that St. Augustine settled with Michelle Hollings."

"They settled?" shrieked Jenna. "When? Why?"

"We found out yesterday. Apparently, the settlement occurred last week. The exact amount and terms are undisclosed and confidential."

"I'm sure it was a huge amount," said Jenna indignantly.

"I'm sure you're right," said Jim. "I can only speculate, but I think it's safe to assume that Ms. Hollings is set for life, both financially and with respect to medical care."

"So, they got their stack of money, and they still want me? Why? Why would it be worth it to them to pursue me?"

Jim, ashamed of this particular side of his profession, said regretfully, "They want all they can get, every last penny."

"Why do you think St. Augustine settled?" Jenna asked, rubbing her temples.

Jim's body stiffened. He carefully considered his options. After several moments of introspection and uncomfortable silence, he decided to tell Jenna the truth. She deserved nothing less.

He lowered his voice, "What I'm about to tell you never leaves this room. Are we clear?"

Jenna suspected Jim was about to divulge a very dangerous secret. She was right.

"Yes, absolutely. I won't tell anyone." She inched her chair closer to the table and leaned forward.

"When Hillary Martin was deposed in front of the federal prosecutor after her plea agreement, she admitted she shared syringes of Fentanyl with others in her social circle. These people could have had hepatitis, HIV – you name it. The investigation has only focused on identifying those patients that have hepatitis C with a viral DNA sequence matching that of Hillary Martin's. However, many other patients turned up to be hep C positive, just not with Martin's exact viral sequence. So far, St. Augustine has only taken responsibility for a select few. Lucky for the hospital, the court has sealed her deposition, but they know what Hillary Martin said in her testimony. They also know the repercussions if this information ever leaked out."

"They need to bury this as quickly as possible," Jenna concluded. The game had become much more dangerous. Jenna's blood turned cold, and her hair stood on end.

Nancy replied, "It's in their best interest to do so."

"So what's in *my* best interest?" Jenna asked, outraged.

"For now," said Jim, "I think we should continue to fight. We have a defendable case. If things change, we'll discuss it. For us to settle now would be premature."

THIRTY-THREE

June 24, 2011

The alarm clock sounded at 4 a.m. on the day of Jenna's deposition. Jenna threw on her jogging clothes, and she and her dog quietly left her house. Outside was dark and quiet. The rest of the world was sleeping. Jenna took comfort in the sound of her feet hitting the pavement. She looked down at Ginger, running faithfully at her side.

"Well, girl," Jenna said as much to Ginger as to herself, "today's the big day. Think I'll do okay?" Ginger looked up at her owner affectionately and wagged her tail in response to Jenna's words. Jenna convinced herself that the tail wagging was a sign. Even her dog thought she would survive the battle.

Jenna continued her run and soon sweat soaked her hair and shirt. Fueled by adrenaline and nervous energy, her pace was considerably faster than usual.

By the time Jenna got home, the sun was beginning to rise. She paused to enjoy the glory of the pinks, blues, and purples of the morning sky as the enormous, orange sun peeked over the horizon. She bent down and kissed the top of Ginger's head. "Everything's going to be okay, girl. I promise. Everything's going to be okay." Like earlier that morning, the words were for her own sake.

Jenna showered and dressed in the plain, black skirt and cashmere cardigan that she had bought for the occasion. Mia watched her mother do her hair and makeup. When Jenna was ready to leave, both Tom and Mia gave her big, tight hugs.

Mia said, "You look really pretty, Mommy. I bet you're prettier than that mean lawyer woman."

Jenna giggled at the sweetness of her daughter's compliment. "I don't know about prettier, but I bet I'm nicer!"

Tom looked at his wife. He could sense Jenna's inner tension, but he was proud at how well composed she appeared. "You'll do great. Jim and Nancy will take care of you. Stay strong, and don't let that bitch win!"

Jenna moved forward to kiss Tom goodbye and whispered, "Thanks."

At exactly 8:20, Jenna parked her car on a side street near Allison Anders' office building. She had taken a beta-blocker on the drive over, in hopes of dulling her nerves. On her walk toward the building, she could feel the effects of the medication. Her hands weren't shaking, her pulse was slow, and she felt calm without feeling sedated. Without her adrenaline surging, Jenna was much more able to focus.

She sat down in one of the lobby chairs and tried to give the appearance of someone she knew she wasn't. She did her best to sit up straight and appear confident and in control. Minutes later, Nancy walked up wearing a beige pantsuit.

Jenna stood to greet her and was immediately embraced in a hug. Nancy pulled back and looked Jenna over. "You look very nice. Your outfit is perfect. How are you doing on the inside?"

"Scared to death," replied Jenna, without hesitation.

"Did you take the beta blocker you were talking about?"

Jenna proudly extended her steady hand. "Can't you tell? I think it's helping. It's kind of slowed me down enough to feel somewhat normal."

"Good," said Nancy. "Whatever works."

At that moment, both women spotted Jim entering the lobby. He approached and put a hand on Jenna's shoulder.

"You ready for this?" Jim asked.

"No. So let's go." Jenna forced herself to smile in spite of her sense of dread.

Jim and Nancy led the way. They were clearly familiar with the building. Jenna followed them into the elevator, and Jim hit the button for the sixth floor. Equal to the offices of Moore and Everett, Allison Anders and her partners had apparently done well enough to occupy an entire floor. The threesome solemnly stepped out of the elevator and found themselves immediately at the reception desk. Jenna did not dare look around. She was completely focused on her lawyers and nothing else.

Jim, Nancy, and Jenna took a seat on a leather couch in the lobby. The conference room was directly in front of them, encased in glass walls. The first thing Jenna noticed was the bulky camera positioned at one end of a long, rectangular conference table. A stocky man past his prime was adjusting the camera's settings. He wore a distastefully bright aloha shirt, which was unbuttoned down to his sternum, revealing his gray, curly, and unruly chest hairs. The man looked like a caricature, dressed more for a night at a casino than for a deposition.

There were other people in the conference room, but Jenna would not allow herself to look at them. Then, Jim whispered something that broke Jenna's attention away from the cameraman. "Looks like Ms. Hollings showed up after all."

Jenna caught her breath. She could easily guess which of the people in the conference room was her patient. Michelle Hollings was the one with the perky, oversized breasts. The plaintiff had been well prepped for the occasion, wearing a conservative, straight black skirt that went past her knees, a silk blouse, and black pumps. Her long blonde hair had been pulled back into a tight bun. Jenna wondered if Hollings kept the clit ring in.

Someone from inside the glass conference room motioned to Jim and Nancy, and they stood. Nancy leaned in close to Jenna and whispered, "It's time."

Like a prisoner being marched to the execution chamber, Jenna followed her lawyers, emotionless and compliant. They entered the room, and Jenna instantly recognized Allison Anders. Jenna frowned at her, consumed with pure hatred.

Jim waved his hand to the head of the table, and Jenna took her seat. As she did, Allison approached. Instinctively, Jenna stood. Before Jenna knew it, she found herself gripping the hand of the devil. Allison's hands were frigid, her grip severe.

"Dr. Reiner, I'm Allison Anders, Ms. Hollings' counsel."

Jenna nodded and took her hand back as quickly as possible. She did not say a word. As quickly as Jenna found herself locked in a handshake with Allison Anders, Michelle Hollings was standing in front of her, extending a hand. Jenna stiffly reciprocated. Ms. Hollings introduced herself, and Jenna only nodded. She had nothing to say to

Michelle Hollings. Most certainly, she was not about to apologize to her for what happened or offer any sympathy. Jenna remembered the warnings – remorse implies guilt. Staring blankly ahead, Jenna sat back down. All she could think about was how desperately she wanted to scrub the skin off her hands.

Within moments, everyone had taken their seats. Jenna was sworn in, and the ground rules were explained. Less than five minutes into the deposition, Allison bared her fangs.

Allison wagged her finger in Jenna's face, inches from her nose. "Are you aware that, during your deposition, if you testify to something that is inconsistent with any of your own medical records or inconsistent even with a different portion of your deposition, that could be pointed out to a jury, if this went to trial?"

Jenna refused to pull back. Instead, she stared Allison dead in the eyes and firmly replied, "Yes, I'm aware of that."

Allison's next question deeply offended Jenna. "Is there anything today, whether you're under the influence of a drug or alcohol or not feeling well, that would affect your ability to give open and honest answers?"

Jenna never diverted her gaze from Allison. She would not give Allison the satisfaction of being shamed into looking away. Jenna said coolly, "No."

"If today, during the deposition, you are not being direct and are being evasive, are you aware that could be pointed out to a jury?"

Maintaining her stare and intensity, Jenna simply said, "Yes."

The next hour was filled with basic questions, establishing basic facts. Allison's tone was one of complete disapproval of Jenna. Even the simplest questions were asked with mockery. Jenna, determined to do her best, had not yet fumbled. She kept most of her answers to "yes" or "no."

Over time, Allison's tenacity started to wear on Jenna. She could feel her attention lapsing. Jenna kept hoping that Jim would call for a break, as he had promised, but he never did. In the meantime, Allison kept firing questions at her.

Finally, Jenna decided to take matters into her own hands. At the end of the answer to the next question, Jenna said, "No, and I need to take a break."

Allison slammed the screen of her laptop closed, clearly annoyed that Jenna had slipped in her request for a break as part of her answer to a question. Sighing in disgust, Allison said, "Okay. Let's take a break. We'll meet back here in fifteen minutes."

Jenna led the way this time, with her two lawyers on her heels. She marched directly to the elevators without saying a word. Covertly, Jenna glanced at the conference room while waiting for the elevator to arrive. Allison's eyes narrowed and her mouth was pinched tight. Apparently, Allison was not accustomed to defendants leaving *her* floor and escaping *her* control during a break. Jenna smiled slightly, feeling as though she had just scored one point, albeit a small one. Once on the ground floor, Jenna marched outside into the warm summer air. It was only then that she spoke.

Biting her thumbnail, she asked, "Have I screwed up yet?"

She was certain she had made nothing but mistakes. Allison was so relentless and nasty. Every one of Jenna's answers caused Allison to respond with a look of dismay and disgust. Since Jenna was instructed to avoid looking at her attorneys, she had no feedback other than Allison's patronizing reactions.

Jenna's gaze alternated between her attorneys. She was anxious for their feedback, regardless of how bad it might be. Then Jim and Nancy did something that stunned Jenna. They both smiled.

Nancy was the first to speak, "Jenna, you are doing great. Honestly. I know it doesn't feel like it, but you are."

Jim actually chuckled, "I think you're the first person I've seen who has succeeded in flustering Allison Anders."

Jenna regarded him with disbelief, "What do you mean?"

Jim replied, more serious this time, "I mean, you're not responding the way she's accustomed to. She hasn't gotten you to raise your voice or lose your temper. You've been polite, forthcoming, and unshakable."

"It doesn't feel like I'm doing well. She talks to me like I'm an imbecile. She acts like I'm lower than scum."

Nancy cut in, "That's her way, and it usually works well for her. She may be getting to you on the inside, but it's not showing on the outside. That's all that matters. Just keep it up. Keep your focus. We still have many hours ahead of us, so don't let your guard down."

Jim checked his watch, "Well ladies, time's up."

THIRTY-FOUR

Jenna and her lawyers returned to the conference room and took their assigned seats on the enemy's turf. The cameraman tersely announced, "We are back on the record. Time is now 10:45 a.m."

The red light on the camera flickered. Jenna did her best to ignore it.

Allison leaned back in her chair and asked Jenna, "Are you aware of the claims that have been made against you by Ms. Hollings?"

"Yes."

Allison's tone was venomous. "Tell me, Doctor, what are those claims, as you understand them?"

Jenna felt the weight of Michelle Hollings' eyes upon her, but refused to look in her direction. Instead, she kept her focus directly on Allison and replied calmly, "As I understand things, Ms. Hollings claims that she contracted hepatitis C during her surgical procedure at St. Augustine. She thinks that I am, at least partially, to blame."

"Do you dispute the fact that Michelle Hollings contracted hepatitis C during her surgical procedure at St. Augustine?"

Jenna spotted the red flag in the question. Her lawyers' advice was paying off.

She answered defiantly, "I don't have any solid evidence to support or refute the claim. At this point, I can't say with certainty either way."

Allison fired back, "Does it upset you that one of your patients contracted hepatitis C?"

Jenna responded carefully, "My job, as a doctor, is to take excellent care of my patients. I care deeply about what I do and who I care for. If anything unfortunate happens to one of my patients, for whatever reason, it deeply upsets me."

"And, in fact, something did happen to one of your patients on January 20, 2010. Michelle Hollings walked into St. Augustine Hospital for a simple, outpatient surgical procedure and walked out with a deadly virus. This happened under your care. Based on what you just said, you are upset about that, correct?"

Jenna was unwilling to be provoked. She succinctly replied, "It's upsetting to me that Ms. Hollings has hepatitis C."

Allison abruptly shifted gears. "Doctor, didn't you sign a sworn affidavit stating that it was your *usual* procedure to draw your drugs up in advance, place them in a drawer of your anesthesia cart, and hide them under various anesthesia supplies? Is that what you did with the drugs intended for Michelle Hollings?"

In spite of the beta-blocker, Jenna could feel her pulse quicken. She paused for a moment to think about her answer. Jenna knew this question was inevitable, and she had rehearsed her answer many times. Still, she wanted to make sure she did not inadvertently say anything wrong. Jenna took a cleansing breath and a sip of water before she answered.

"I can't recall specifically what I did that day. It was over a year ago."

"But your affidavit states what you did with drugs. So were you lying then, or are you lying now?" Allison's lips pursed as she blinked at Jenna.

Nancy jumped in, "Objection. You are mischaracterizing her testimony, and your tone and accusations are inappropriate. Jenna, you may go ahead and answer the question."

The objection gave Jenna the brief amount of time she needed to regain her composure.

Jenna responded steadily, "Neither. I don't lie. My affidavit attests to my *usual* practice. Just because I may do something the same way ninety-nine out of one hundred times, doesn't mean that there is never an occasion where I may deviate from my common practice. Because I can't specifically recall the events of that day, I can't say with one hundred percent certainty that I did things any particular way."

"Why would you hide your drugs?" Allison asked indignantly.

Jenna sucked in a deep breath, buying a precious few seconds, and then evenly stated, "Because in my training I was taught that if narcotics came up missing, the procedure was to call the police, and they would come and question you. Of course, if you did nothing wrong, you'd be cleared, but you still had to go through the ordeal and disgrace of being questioned. I never wanted that to happen to me."

"Then you must agree that the operating room is not a secure environment. If it were, how could your drugs go missing? You must have been worried that someone might steal your narcotics?" Allison suppressed a grin, certain this would be her kill shot.

Jenna shook her head earnestly, "No, it wasn't that at all. Mostly, I was concerned that if I left them out, either housekeeping or an anesthesia tech might innocently discard them, thinking they were waste."

"Tell me . . ." said Allison as she drummed her fingers on the surface of the table. "Tell me specifically about the training you received concerning the handling of controlled substances in medical school and residency."

Jenna took a second to assemble her thoughts. "There really wasn't any formal instruction during either time period of my training. We had pharmacology courses in medical school, but that was it. During residency, there weren't any formal lectures or in-services instructing us how to handle narcotics. We learned on the job by following the example of our attendings and senior residents. We were expected to have everything prepared before the patient entered the OR, including all of our drugs. It was common practice to leave medications in the OR, either in a drawer or on top of the cart. The OR was considered to be a secure environment."

Allison then asked with condemnation, "*Who*, who specifically led you to believe that the operating room was a secure environment where you could leave controlled substances unlocked and unattended?"

Jenna kept her cool. "The attending physicians, who were my supervisors and mentors, watched over me like hawks. If it had been inappropriate for me to store my drugs in my anesthesia cart, I would have been reprimanded. I did it that way, and my fellow residents did it that way. It was acceptable practice. The attendings knew what we were doing, and they never advised us otherwise."

Allison leaned in closer to Jenna. "Doctor, you didn't answer my question. I asked you who! Give me a name! Who told you the OR was an environment where you can leave narcotics unlocked and unsecured?"

"I never left my drugs unlocked and unsecured. My drugs were in a secure environment."

Allison countered, her frustration escalating, "And again, I know that is your mantra, but that's not what I am asking. Tell me a name of an attending, a mentor, anyone who would say that your practice regarding the storage of narcotics was acceptable."

"I can give you the names of the attendings that I can remember, if that's what you want."

"Please do," replied Allison snidely.

Jenna searched her memory. "Well, there was Dr. Brad Thomas, Dr. Bob Watkins, Dr. Jim Bloom, Dr. Bonnie Monroe. That's all I can remember off the top of my head. It was over ten years ago that I trained."

Allison then asked, "Are you telling me that any of these doctors that you just named, doctors that were involved in your training during residency, would be happy to testify, under oath, that the operating room is a secure environment where it is acceptable to leave narcotics unattended?"

Jenna responded with a hint of agitation. She was starting to slip. "I can't tell you what somebody would or would not say under oath, but I can tell you that, if they told the truth, they would agree with my testimony. As to whether or not they would be happy to come and testify in front of you or a court, I don't think anybody would be happy about having to do that."

Before Allison could fire her next question, Jenna quickly added, "I'd like to take a break now."

Allison commanded, "No, we are not taking a break! I still have questions!"

Nancy jumped to Jenna's defense, "Allison, there are no questions pending. If my client needs a break, she is entitled to a break."

"Your client," Allison scoffed, "has wasted a great deal of time reciting her mantra and evading my questions. I still have questions. We can break in a few minutes."

Jenna's bladder was painfully distended. Not only did Jenna need an emotional break, but she also seriously needed to relieve herself. Annoyed that Allison Anders was changing the rules midstream, and certain that it was completely inappropriate, Jenna spoke up with determination.

"You said in the beginning that I could take a break whenever I needed one. I answered your last question. I'm requesting a break. I have to use the restroom . . . badly. I need a break, and I'm taking one. Now!"

Jenna stood and was already at the door by the time Allison was able to respond. Jim and Nancy were right behind her. Left behind at the table, Allison pouted. Throwing her hands up in the air, she said, "Fine, let's take a break. Why not make it a lunch break while we're at it? We'll meet back here in thirty minutes."

A smirk crept across Jenna's her face as she punched the button for the elevator.

THIRTY-FIVE

Jenna, Jim, and Nancy rode the elevator in silence down to the ground floor and headed to the building's café. Jenna quickly used the restroom and then joined Jim and Nancy at the deli counter. Her attorneys each grabbed themselves a sandwich. Jenna felt mildly nauseated, and the prepackaged food was enormously unappealing. Nancy knew Jenna needed something in her stomach to sustain her for the afternoon. In a motherly tone, she said, "At least grab a salad or some chips. You need to eat." Obediently, Jenna chose a Caesar salad and went to find a table where they could be alone.

While she waited for Jim and Nancy to pay the cashier, Jenna inconspicuously swallowed another beta-blocker. The pill Jenna had taken earlier that morning had helped her keep her cool, but she could feel its effects beginning to wear off. Jim and Nancy each sat on opposite sides of Jenna.

Jenna looked at her lawyers and unloaded. "That woman," Jenna said with unbridled fury, "is a cunt! And trust me, I don't use that term indiscriminately!"

Jenna was careful not to say the word too loudly. It was not her style to use such extreme vulgarity, but in this situation, she felt it was justified.

Neither of her lawyers reacted to Jenna's swearword with disapproval or judgment. Nancy simply nodded, as she replied matter-of-factly, "Yes, she is."

Jenna continued to rant, her face contorted with rage. "How can she act like that? First of all, who is she to tell me that I can't go to the bathroom? I obeyed her every rule, exactly how she laid them out, and she has the nerve to forbid me from peeing? Is she really that petty and immature?" Jenna was livid.

Jim spoke up, "That was clearly out of line on her part, and she knew it. But you handled it beautifully. You remained calm, you threw her rules right back in her face, and you refused to be held hostage. In fact, I think her little spat back there shows that you are getting to her.

"Overall, Jenna, your deposition is going exceptionally well. There haven't been any major blunders. You've been polite, kept your answers brief, and haven't shown any hint of being intimidated. Just keep it up."

"Seriously?" Jenna craved their reassurance.

"Trust us," replied Nancy, "you're doing great."

The three of them sat quietly at the table. While Jim and Nancy devoured their sandwiches, Jenna pushed her wilted lettuce back and forth with a plastic fork. At Nancy's insistence, she took a couple of nibbles, but that was all. She felt like they had just taken their seats when Jim checked the time.

"We've got about eight minutes before we need to go back up there. Jenna, would you like to go outside and get some fresh air?"

Jenna felt frozen, like her muscles would not budge.

Jim touched her shoulder. "Jenna?"

Her body shuddered as she broke out of her spell. "Huh? Yeah, sounds great," she said, anxious to escape of the confines of the building.

The three of them stood outside while the midday sun cast short shadows on the ground. Jenna was quiet and lost in thought. So much so that she did not notice Michelle Hollings walk past them and head to the parking lot, with car keys in her hand.

Jim pointed it out. "Looks like Ms. Hollings won't be joining us for the afternoon session."

"Maybe she's got some shopping to do with her newly acquired wealth," said Jenna contemptuously.

THIRTY-SIX

Their thirty-minute reprieve came to an end, and the threesome took the elevators back up to the sixth floor. Jenna marched past the receptionist and entered the conference room. Allison walked in behind them looking extremely uptight and ready for an ambush. Jenna scrutinized her adversary. Allison held her head high, her mouth was in a grimace, and her eyes were menacing.

The revolting cameraman once again acknowledged that they were back on record. He then flopped into his leather chair and leaned back as if he were watching his favorite sports team.

Allison had not yet scooted in her chair when she resumed her interrogation of Jenna. "Dr. Reiner, are you familiar with the DEA rules and regulations concerning the dispensing, handling, storage, security, and administration of controlled substances?"

Jenna inhaled and responded, "I'm aware that there are DEA guidelines."

Allison did not blink as she scowled at Jenna. Her words were loud and unnaturally slow, like she was communicating with a foreigner. "Let me repeat my question, because you failed to answer it. This time, I'd like a direct answer. Dr. Reiner, are you familiar with the DEA rules and regulations concerning the dispensing, handling, storage, security, and administration of controlled substances that would apply to you as an anesthesiologist in the operating room?"

Jenna reminded herself to stay calm and maintain a slow, even tone.

Refusing to shy away from Allison's penetrating gaze, Jenna rested her arms on the table and leaned slightly closer to her nemesis. "I know that the guidelines are overwhelmingly vast, comprising thousands of pages of documentation. Furthermore, most of the guidelines apply to hospitals, doctors' offices, and pharmacies where medications are stored – not to individual practitioners."

Allison clutched her pen tightly between her thumb and index finger as she attacked Jenna with the same question, for the third time. "So your answer is 'no'? You don't have any familiarity with the DEA guidelines as they pertain to you as an anesthesiologist?"

Jenna remained still, her back straight, and her eyes wide and attentive.

"It is impractical to expect that I would be intimately familiar with the DEA guidelines. I feel it is reasonable and legitimate to rely upon the hospital administration, through their policies and procedures, to guide me in such a way that I am in compliance."

Allison let out a theatrical sigh and asked Jenna with reproach, "Dr. Reiner, do you understand that your evasive answers and failure to answer questions directly can be pointed out to a jury at trial?"

Nancy interrupted, "Objection, form and argumentative."

Toying with Allison Anders was a dangerous endeavor. However, the glimmer in Jenna's eyes exposed the fact that she was beginning to enjoy frustrating the attorney. Jenna turned her head in Allison's direction.

With the front of her face out of view of the camera, Jenna batted her eyelashes before answering.

When Jenna responded to the accusation, her face was full of innocence and sincerity. "Truly, I'm not trying to be evasive. I'm just trying to be honest and make sure that I explain myself."

Allison snorted in exasperation. "Dr. Reiner, do you have any specific knowledge regarding any specific rule or regulation from the DEA, other than what you infer from hospital policy?"

Jenna felt slight defeat, but she was not about to let it show. Without any hint of humiliation or regret, she said, "No."

Allison hastily changed the direction of the conversation. "Doctor, how do you keep up to date with your profession?"

Jenna was inwardly grateful for a lighter topic. "I go to medical conferences, I read textbooks, and I look up things on the Internet."

"When was the last medical conference that you attended?"

Jenna sensed this was leading up to something, but she was not yet sure what. Treading carefully, she answered, "This past January."

"Which specific websites do you get your information from?"

"No website in particular."

Jenna was starting to grasp Allison's tactics. Allison reveled in starting with simple, seemingly innocuous questions. Questions that Jenna had no reason to fear and no reason to hesitate before answering. Then Allison would try to keep her responding quickly, in hopes of preventing her from thinking things through. All the while, the questions became increasingly perilous. To her credit, Jenna was fighting back. She refused to let Allison set the pace, and it was effective.

"So you don't know any of the websites you reference for your medical knowledge? Wikipedia, perhaps?" Allison ridiculed Jenna. At the other end of the room, the cameraman snickered.

"No, I do not get my medical knowledge from Wikipedia," Jenna snapped. Although she wanted nothing more than to dive across the table and gouge Allison's eyes out, she never let it show.

"I usually Google a topic and then browse through the search results, so it varies."

"Do you read newspapers?"

Jenna was perplexed as to what that had to do with anything. "I peruse the news websites, if that's what you mean."

"Are you aware of any stories where nurses, doctors, or other health-care workers have drug-addiction issues and have diverted drugs at hospitals?"

Jenna promptly understood the objective behind Allison's media question. Taking a second to collect her thoughts, she proceeded with vigilance.

"I think everybody in the health-care field has heard stories about people stealing drugs. It's pretty much urban legend. That being said, I have never heard stories about people stealing drugs and doing what Hillary Martin allegedly did. Before this story broke, I would never have conceived that someone would have stolen drugs, replaced them with contaminated syringes, and ultimately infected patients."

"Do you feel like you have a duty to prevent the diversion of narcotics?"

Not a question that Jenna had anticipated, she was unsure how to respond. She sensed the word "duty" was a snare. Although her palms were becoming damp, she did not dare wipe them dry. Swallowing hard, Jenna answered, "No, I don't feel that I have a duty to prevent diversion of narcotics."

Allison responded with a scornful tone. "You don't feel as if you have any duty, any responsibility whatsoever, to make sure someone doesn't steal your drugs?"

The room was soundless and the air heavy as all eyes bore down on Jenna.

She responded with composure and grace. "My *duty* is to provide anesthesia care for my patients. I have a duty to be prepared for and handle intraoperative and perioperative events, whether the events are anticipated or emergent. My duty, my focus, and my responsibilities revolve around patient care. Just as it is not my duty, or my designated role, to mop the floors, it is also not my duty to be focused on the prevention of drug diversion."

"Doctor, are you aware that St. Augustine Hospital reported they had ten separate incidents of narcotic theft in the twelve months prior to January 2010?"

"No," replied Jenna, expressionless.

Allison called up a document on her laptop. Reading from the screen, she asked, "Are you aware that one of these thefts involved the diversion of fifteen syringes of Fentanyl by a floor nurse? Another theft involved twenty tablets of Oxycontin that were taken from the top of a medication cart. In yet another case, a staff member from St. Augustine was found in a break room of the hospital with several vials of Fentanyl in front of her and several more confiscated from her locker. Were you aware of any of these diversions?"

"No."

"Do you think you should just remain in the dark when it comes to diversions at your hospital? Does that absolve you from the responsibility to assist in preventing future diversions? You see no evil, so you expect no evil. Is that how you operate?"

Nancy interjected, "Object to form."

Jenna shifted in her chair. The skin on the back of her legs peeled away from the leather as Jenna crossed them.

"I don't see myself as remaining in the dark, so I can't answer your question if it's based upon that premise."

Allison's tone was becoming steadily more insulting. She furrowed her brow and said, "You told me a few minutes ago that, in your wildest dreams, you could never think that someone would divert Fentanyl and substitute it with a syringe containing saline. Isn't that true?"

Nancy objected, "Objection, misstates her testimony."

Jenna jumped on Nancy's lead. "That is *not* what I said. I stated that before Hillary Martin and this ordeal came to light, I would never have imagined, based on my previous knowledge and experience, that someone would do something so sinister. I would never have thought that a member of the OR staff would have been so evil as to steal a syringe intended for a patient and replace it with a contaminated syringe, knowing that the contaminated syringe would then be used on a patient. There is a big difference between substituting a syringe for one containing sterile saline and one contaminated with hepatitis C."

"Doctor, are you aware there is an anesthesia journal published by the American Society of Anesthesiologists?"

The way she said "Doctor" made Jenna's skin crawl. It sounded like an accusation, like Jenna was an imposter.

"To which journal, specifically, are you referring? There are several."

Allison's voice became tense. "It's called 'Anesthesiology.'"

Recognizing the testiness in her rival, Jenna responded unpretentiously, "Yes, I'm aware of it."

Jenna straightened her posture and folded her hands in her lap. Every muscle in her neck and shoulders was tight. She longed to crack her neck and relieve some of the tension, but she resisted the urge.

"Do you receive the journal?"

"No," replied Jenna.

"*You don't?* I would think as a member of the American Society of Anesthesiologists, you would receive that publication just like every other member."

For a fraction of an instant, Jenna shifted her gaze downward. "I'm not a member of the ASA."

"You're a practicing anesthesiologist, and you're not a member of your professional society?"

Heat rose up Jenna's neck, as she explained, "No, I'm not. My husband is cheap, and the dues are expensive. It never seemed necessary."

Out of the corner of her eye, Jenna saw Nancy grin at her answer.

"Are you aware," Allison continued, undeterred, "that in 2008, there was an article titled 'Addiction and Substance Abuse in Anesthesiology' published by the ASA? In that article, they state that the power of the disease of addiction and the need for the drug is so overwhelmingly strong, that otherwise reasonable and intelligent people will resort to seemingly incredulous behavior in order to obtain their drug of choice. Would you agree with that statement?"

Jenna stalled before answering, reminding herself of the ground rules of this game.

"I wouldn't agree or disagree. I would need to read the article in its entirety and take time to think about it."

Allison appeared unfazed. "The article also says that addicts may substitute a syringe containing their drug of choice for one containing saline or a mixture of Lidocaine and Esmolol during a relief break. Have you ever heard that before?"

"No," said Jenna. "And I'd like to take a break."

THIRTY-SEVEN

The threesome strode outside on to the front steps of the building. Jenna drew in a deep breath of the summer air. She felt like she were being released from jail and tasting freedom for the first time in years. Jim sensed her discontent. Standing in front of his client, he placed his arms on her shoulders and grinned.

Jenna, perplexed by Jim's expression, stood still.

Jim exclaimed, "Jenna, you are doing great! I hope you don't take this the wrong way, but it's actually been fun to watch. I have never seen anyone get under Allison Anders' skin before. *Never.* You heeded our advice, and it shows. My guess is we're headed for the home stretch, so keep up your focus just a little while longer. I'm being completely honest when I tell you that you are doing better than any of your colleagues have done against Allison."

Jenna shifted her focus to Nancy. With her arms folded across her chest, she asked, "What do you think? And *don't* lie to me."

Nancy chuckled, "I wouldn't lie to you, it's not my style. Not even to protect your feelings. Everything Jim said is true, especially the part about it being fun to watch."

Jenna wrinkled her forehead. Unconvinced, she confessed, "I can feel myself getting snippy with her. And even though I know it's unwise, I have to admit that I can't help messing with her when I get the chance. I'm trying to keep it as subtle as possible, but every little dig helps to keep me going."

Nancy replied with kindness, "Jenna, I think your version of a dig differs radically from what people like Allison Anders might think. Yes, I can see you pausing before each question, but not excessively, and it's keeping you focused. It's also pissing her off, which is great. What you are doing is not out of line. The little jabs you have gotten in on her have been pulled off with innocence and poise. In fact, most times it has taken Allison several moments to realize she's been hit. Keep doing what you've been doing all day. We're almost there."

Jenna nodded. Knowing the break was over, she pulled in one last breath of fresh air and followed Jim and Nancy back into the building. Jenna prayed this would be the last time the three of them made the death march back to the enemy's chambers.

In the conference room, Allison was already seated and impatiently tapping her pen on the table.

Jim and Nancy entered the conference room through the front door and quickly took their seats. Nancy explained Jenna's absence, "Dr. Reiner is using the restroom and will be here shortly."

Moments later, Jenna entered through the back door. No one seemed to notice her presence. Jim and Nancy were huddled over Jim's laptop, and Allison was sorting through a stack of documents.

Standing behind the cameraman, Jenna poured herself a glass of water. The sound of fluid striking the glass filled the room. The cameraman looked at Allison as he repugnantly said, "Well, I hope that's not her behind me, urinating on the floor." He snorted at his own joke. Allison worked to suppress a grin.

Jenna returned to her seat and slammed her glass down on the table, creating a thud that caught Allison's attention. Water sloshed over onto the tabletop. Allison peered down at the mess, wrinkling her nose at the small puddle. Jenna refused to wipe it up.

The entire room had heard the remark, but nobody acknowledged it. Jenna glared at the brash man seated behind the camera, refusing to take her eyes off of him. For a few minutes, he returned Jenna's stare, but then he grew uncomfortable and looked away.

Pretending to adjust his equipment, the man announced, "Time is now 3:10 p.m., and we are back on record." The red light clicked on, signaling that combat was to recommence.

Allison stopped tapping her pen and held it to her mouth.

"In January 2010, at St. Augustine hospital, was there a mechanism to lock up your drugs?"

"No."

"Do you think that you had any reason to foresee that there would be a healthcare worker diverting drugs in the OR?"

Jenna had tired of Allison's questions. While Jenna considered her response, she briefly allowed her mind to wander. Jenna envisioned Allison as a blonde-haired dragon, constantly encircling Jenna, and snorting flames at her. All Jenna could do was continue to jump out of the fire's path. She was growing weak, however, and the flames were getting dangerously close.

Allison jostled Jenna back to the task at hand. "Doctor, please answer the question."

Jenna refocused. "I don't think I can answer that. I don't know what other people's motivations are. I do know, based on my experience, that I trusted my OR staff. Prior to this unprecedented event, I had no reason not to trust them. I fully expected that St. Augustine would hire quality people, and I had no reason to question that belief. I can't foresee whether or not someone would commit a crime any more than I could foresee what you're going to eat for dinner."

"So what you're telling me is that you had no worry, no concern, that any of the nurses or other people that you worked with would ever divert drugs? You could never have imagined such a thing?"

Nancy interrupted, "Objection, form, misstates."

Jenna replied with conviction, "I don't agree with your statement. I never said that."

Allison blasted back, "So then, would you agree that it would be foreseeable that health-care workers, including scrub techs, may divert controlled substances?"

Nancy again said, "Objection, form, misstates."

"I don't agree with that, either."

It was a battle of wills. Jenna fully recognized that Allison desperately wanted to put condemning words in her mouth, and Jenna was determined to keep it from happening.

Allison slapped her palm on the table. Surprised by the action, Jenna caught her breath.

"So you don't agree with that, either? Which is it, Doctor? How foreseeable is it that a nurse or scrub tech would divert controlled substances in a hospital setting?"

The room was focused on Jenna. She did not blink once as she replied, "In January, 2010, I don't think the actions of Hillary Martin were at all foreseeable."

Allison stood and rested her hands on the edge of the table, towering over Jenna. With malice, she asked, "Are you aware that if a judge and jury determine your failure to lock and secure controlled substances was willful and wanton conduct, they could award for punitive damages?"

Jenna silently thanked her lawyers for preparing her for this topic. Although she had been forewarned, she decided to feign ignorance.

With bright, wide eyes, Jenna replied, "I'm not a legal expert. In fact, I understand law about as well as you understand medicine. I don't know a whole lot about punitive damages."

Allison harrumphed. Jenna had not intended to become confrontational, but the words slipped out. Secretly, she did not regret it. Especially when she looked over and saw the cameraman roll his eyes at her comment. After enduring hours of verbal assaults, sarcasm, and scrutiny, this one little comment vindicated Jenna.

Acting as if nothing had happened, Jenna waited patiently for the next question.

Allison remained standing. "Just to enlighten you, punitive damages are not covered by your insurance policy."

Jenna deeply wanted to enlighten Allison Anders that humans aren't supposed to be cannibals. Instead, she refrained from responding and stared blankly at her nemesis.

Allison sat down and pulled a document from a stack of papers in front of her.

"Looking at your anesthesia record for Ms. Hollings, which you have in the papers in front of you, would you agree that her vital signs and response to the initial dose of Fentanyl are consistent with her receiving saline and not Fentanyl?"

Jenna made a display of rifling through the stack, painstakingly searching through each page. Meanwhile, Allison gritted her teeth.

After several minutes, Jenna had the record in front of her. She raised her head and replied with conviction, "Absolutely not."

"Why not?"

"Because her vital signs show a completely normal response to the induction of anesthesia. Both her heart rate and blood pressure drop."

"Would you agree that the fact that she required additional narcotic, in the form of Morphine, is evidence that the initial dose of Fentanyl was, in fact, saline?"

Jenna spoke slowly, enunciating every syllable, "Ab-so-lute-ly not."

"And again, I ask you, why not?"

"Because if you look at what she received in total, it demonstrates that, for whatever reason, Ms. Hollings had a tolerance to the effects of narcotics. If she didn't have tolerance, 10 milligrams of Morphine should have been more than sufficient to carry her through the entire procedure, with or without the initial dose of Fentanyl. The fact that she required a total dose of 15 milligrams of Morphine, which is substantial, proves nothing more than Ms. Hollings requires more narcotic than the average person."

"Yes, but it's also consistent with the fact that Michelle Hollings did not receive 250 micrograms of Fentanyl, but instead received saline. Wouldn't you agree that this could also possibly explain her need for additional narcotics?"

"No," replied Jenna, refusing to fold.

Allison's back stiffened and she pounded her fist on the conference table. Her face was beefy red.

"Tell me, Dr. Reiner!   Tell me why it's not consistent with this anesthesia record, her vital signs, and the drugs you dispensed and administered. Why is that not consistent with the possibility that she received saline versus Fentanyl?"

Nancy cried out, "Objection, asked and answered."

"No!   You're not answering my questions!" Allison shouted back at Jenna. "You're saying why it's not consistent with . . . or why it's fine . . . or why it's patient dependent.   My question is, do you have any evidence to the contrary, looking at this anesthesia record, that Michelle Hollings received saline rather than Fentanyl?"

Jenna decided to push things. "Can you please repeat the question?"

It was all Jenna could do to refrain from laughing as she said the words.

Allison's nostrils flared. "You heard the question, Doctor."

Jenna replied smoothly, "I need you to repeat it, please."

Shaking her copy of the anesthesia record at Jenna, Allison shouted, "Do you have any evidence to prove that Michelle Hollings did not receive saline instead of Fentanyl?"

"I don't see anything in this record that would support your speculation."

Allison strained to maintain her composure. She took a moment to look up something on her laptop. Jenna figured it was Allison's way of taking a very necessary time out.

After several minutes, Allison asked Jenna, "Do you think Hillary Martin is at fault for infecting Michelle Hollings with hepatitis C?"

Although Jenna hated Hillary Martin for her crimes and for the lives she had ruined, including her own, Jenna also detected another trap in this question.

She answered carefully, "I honestly don't know. I'm not sure if any of us will ever really know what happened in that operating room. So, without knowing the truth, I can't really answer one way or the other."

"Do you blame St. Augustine Hospital at all for the fact that Ms. Hollings contracted hepatitis C?"

Again, Jenna repressed her true feelings. "I don't have enough information right now to make a decision on that. If I had all the information, I'd be able to sit down, digest it, and decide where I stood."

Allison shot daggers at Jenna. "Dr. Reiner, if you had reasonably locked the controlled substances that you dispensed for Michelle Hollings, or waited to dispense them from the Accudose until Ms. Hollings was present in the operating room, she would not have contracted hepatitis C, correct?"

Jenna sat with perfect posture and returned Allison's stare. In a clear voice that resonated throughout the room, Jenna boldly stated, "Incorrect. I disagree."

The afternoon was dragging on. Jenna glanced out the window and noticed the sun starting to descend over the western mountains. She was anxious for this to end.

As if a higher power heard her request, Allison blurted, "No further questions."

The cameraman grunted, "This concludes the videotaped deposition of Dr. Jenna Reiner. The time is 4:47 p.m. on this 24th day of June, 2011."

Jenna grabbed her purse and left without saying a word. Jim and Nancy lingered to discuss some issues with Allison Anders. Jenna was not about to wait for them. She knew she would meet them outside. Marching proudly to the elevators, Jenna stepped in alone. Once the doors closed, Jenna lifted her middle finger to the savagery she was escaping.

THIRTY-EIGHT

Jenna bolted from the building. After being held prisoner in an artificially lit conference room for hours, the late afternoon sun blinded her. She put on her sunglasses and waited for her lawyers. The buzz of the Friday afternoon traffic on the nearby highway made her long to be on the road, heading home. Reaching into her purse, she pulled out her phone.

There was a text message from Tom. "What do you want to do for dinner?"

Jenna quickly texted back, "DRINK!" and silenced the phone.

Sitting on the hard, dirty concrete steps, Jenna stretched her legs out in front of her, tilted her head back toward the blue sky, and closed her eyes. She was completely worn-out. Lost in thought, Jenna jumped when she felt Jim gently tap her shoulder. She turned her head toward her attorneys.

"Let us walk you to your car," said Jim. "We can talk along the way."

It was evident to Jenna that Jim wanted to get beyond both earshot and eyeshot of Allison Anders. Hastily, Jenna stood, and the three of them walked along the sidewalk. It felt like an eternity had passed since she parked along the street that morning.

Once they were away from the building, Jenna stopped and asked everything she wanted and needed to know with one word, "So?"

Jim and Nancy were beaming. Jenna never imagined either of them being giddy, but they were. They both started their praises at the same instant, talking over each other in short spurts.

"You were great."

"You surpassed our expectations."

"You should become an expert witness. You held yourself together so well."

Then came the most important compliment, "You won!"

Jenna looked at them in disbelief. "Really? I'm sure I must have messed up somewhere."

Jim, the more solemn and reserved of her two attorneys, said with absolute conviction, "If you messed up somewhere, I'd tell you. Of course, when we get a copy of the transcript, we'll go through it and maybe catch a flaw or two. But being witness to things today, I think you did great! If we go to trial, and I hope we do, I think you are going to make a phenomenal witness. What about you, Jenna? How do *you* feel right now?"

"I'm relieved it's over. I feel a hell of a lot better than I expected I would. I'll tell you one thing. If anyone tries to tell me this isn't personal ever again, I think my head will explode. Allison Anders made it very personal today. Maybe she talks to every defendant like that, but I will never forget the things she said and the way she said them. I truly hate her. You'd have a hard time convincing me that the feeling wasn't mutual. There's no way she could have acted that way toward me if she felt otherwise."

Jim rubbed his chin and agreed, "Maybe you're right."

Jenna interrupted, "And another thing . . . I will *not* settle this case. I'd rather go to court, defend myself, and lose, than to concede defeat without a fight. I will never bow down to Allison Anders. Ever."

Suddenly, something occurred to Jenna. "Lyle Silverstein never showed up. Does that mean anything?"

Jim shrugged his shoulders. "You're the first woman physician to be deposed. Maybe they thought another professional female would get to you more than a male. I consider it a lucky break."

"Yeah, me too," Jenna agreed, unable to imagine anyone worse than Allison Anders.

Nancy said, "We'll be in touch with you early next week. The next few months will be filled with more depositions, document gathering, et cetera. We'll keep you informed every step of the way. For now, you've had a long day, and you did great. Go home. Hug your husband and your little girl. Relax. Have a cocktail. You've earned it."

"Do I have to do those things in that order?" Jenna joked as she got into her car.

Jim and Nancy stood on the sidewalk and watched Jenna drive away. Although her attorneys were genuinely thrilled for the day's outcome, they knew Jenna's newfound momentum would only carry her so far.

Jenna's attorneys watched her car disappear around a corner. Nancy looked at Jim with a regretful frown. "When should we break the news?"

Jim absentmindedly looked down at the concrete. Finally, he said, "She's been through a lot. Let's allow her to savor today's victory. She and her family leave for Hawaii next week. Let's give her a little peace. We'll tell her about the additional charges against her when she gets back. Nothing is going to change between now and then."

****

On the way home, Jenna called Tom. He had been emotionally prepared for tears and devastation. Instead, Tom was pleasantly stunned to hear elation, confidence, and spunk in his wife's voice. While Jenna yammered about what details she could remember, a glimmer of hope began to surface in Tom.

Maybe, things would be okay. Maybe, this would not destroy Jenna after all. Just maybe, his wife finally had the backbone to stand up for herself.

THIRTY-NINE

Allison peered out of the conference room windows, down to the steps in front of the building. Dr. Jenna Reiner sat alone, with her legs stretched out in front of her. From Allison's perch six floors above the ground, she scrutinized the doctor. Allison found her exasperating and completely unpredictable. Jenna, with her big, blue eyes full of innocence, her unpretentious demeanor, her calm, unhurried responses. Allison had neither expected nor prepared for this encounter. Replaying the day's events in her mind, Allison concluded that Jenna was either incredibly cunning or unbelievably stupid. Either way, Allison painfully admitted that she had lost this encounter.

Catching her own reflection in the window, Allison appeared worn down. Her lipstick had worn away hours ago, exposing her pale lips. Allison's silk blouse, once perfectly pressed, was wrinkled. Smudged mascara had pooled at the bottom of her eyes.

Through the window, Allison spied Jim and Nancy as they approached their client. The three of them were walking away from the building when she heard the sound of Lyle Silverstein behind her, clearing his throat. Inconspicuously, Allison wiped the mascara from below her eyes and spun around, flashing a confident smile at her partner.

Lyle had been secluded in his office for the duration of the deposition. He watched the events unfold from a live video stream supplied by multiple hidden cameras embedded at strategic locations within the conference room. His entire day was spent dissecting the facial expressions, body language, and mannerisms of everyone in the room, particularly those of Dr. Reiner. On more than one occasion, Lyle fought the impulse to barge in and attack her. The doctor's soft-spoken nature and composure incensed him.

Adding to Lyle's frustration was his profound disappointment in Allison's performance. Her mission was to brutalize Jenna Reiner. Lyle did not care if that meant bringing the doctor to tears or provoking her into anger. By whatever means necessary, by the end of the day Jenna Reiner should have been destroyed.

Allison did not say a word as she focused on Lyle, watching him shut both doors to the conference room. Lyle pressed a control button on a panel in the back of the room, causing the windows that faced the lobby to become opaque. Allison braced herself.

Grimacing, Lyle strode across the conference room, towering over Allison, as they stood face-to-face. She reminded herself to breathe.

"What the fuck was that?" Lyle hissed.

Acutely cognizant of her failings, Allison did not answer. Instead, she stood tall and did her best to hold Lyle's sharp stare.

"You let that little bitch of a doctor run the show. She set the pace, not you. Jenna Reiner played you like a fiddle. You were supposed to rattle her – not the other way around."

His words boomed throughout the confines of the conference room. Allison was certain that the receptionist and anyone in the lobby could overhear his lashing. However unpleasant, she knew she deserved his reproach.

"Lyle," Allison said, "I was as surprised as anyone by Dr. Reiner. Unfortunately, I underestimated her. Let me assure you, that won't happen twice."

"See that it doesn't. You didn't get one helpful admission from her. Dr. Reiner handed your ass to you. It was embarrassing to watch."

Lyle's words stung. He was Allison's mentor and senior partner, and his validation and approval meant everything to her. He was one of the few people that she actually admired.

Attempting to redeem herself, Allison spoke. "Today wasn't a complete loss, Lyle."

Silverstein took a seat at the table. Allison sat across from him, opening her laptop.

Lyle gripped the edges of the dark cherry table tightly, leaving oily impressions from his fingers on the surface. Chuckling, he said, "Help me understand, Allison, how today was not a complete loss."

Allison leaned back and grinned, appearing infinitely more confident than minutes before. "First of all, now we know Jenna Reiner. She was very well prepared for today, but I also think that it was all she could do to keep it together. Toward the end, I sensed her starting to falter. She may have had the strength to go up against us once, but I don't think she could do it again. I think we should file a motion to have her redeposed."

Lyle's face relaxed. Intrigued, he asked, "On what grounds?"

"On the grounds that her answers were exceedingly evasive. I will have the motion prepared by Monday and file it with the court immediately."

Lyle nodded, "All right. Let me review it before you send it out. We can't afford to screw this up, Allison. She needs to disappear. This case cannot go to trial."

"You have my assurance. Jenna Reiner will not be a problem."

FORTY

July 16, 2011

Jenna, Tom, and Mia were at the end of a trip of a lifetime. The beach house they rented in Poipu was more amazing and beautiful than any place they had ever stayed before. For two blissful weeks, the three of them never stopped moving. The Reiner family hiked, swam, surfed, played games, read books, and made sandcastles. More importantly, they laughed, teased, cuddled, and talked. The one thing the Reiners did not do was bring up the lawsuit. Jenna, Tom, and Mia had made a pact before they left. If only for two weeks, the lawsuit did not exist. They had each kept their word.

Their last night arrived sooner than any of them would have liked. Although she would not admit it to Tom or Mia, Jenna was nervous about going home and found herself on edge. While Tom and Mia reminisced about the high points of their trip over dinner, Jenna said very little. Before they left for the flight home, Jenna snuck out into the backyard alone. She descended the lava rock steps that led from their perch above the ocean down to the water. In her bare feet, she precariously hopped from one jagged patch of black rock to another, making her way out to a solitary mound of stone that jutted up from the sea. Twenty feet from shore, Jenna sat on the rock and listened to the rhythmic crashing of the waves. The tears trickling down her cheeks dripped into the ocean, blending in with the saltiness of the sea.

Tom saw his wife, sitting alone, her legs curled up into her body. She was surrounded by the froth and mist of the ocean's tides. He called her name from the yard, but she couldn't hear him over the roar of the waves. Following Jenna's earlier maneuver, Tom made his way out to the solitary rock. Instantly, he noticed Jenna was crying.

He sat down next to her, and put his arm around her. Splashes of water hit their feet and bottoms, threatening to soak their shorts. Neither of them cared. Jenna rested her head on Tom's shoulder and whispered, "I'm scared. I don't want to go back."

She looked so innocent and frightened, like a young child. It pained Tom to see his wife in so much turmoil.

Tom held Jenna tight, hoping to make her feel some level of comfort and protection. She melted into him. At last, Tom knew it was time to leave. He whispered into Jenna's hair, "I don't want to go back either, but we have to. Whatever happens, I'll be there for you."

He held his hand out to Jenna, but she remained planted on the rock. Her eyes were bloodshot and wet, her face puffy and blotchy. "Can you give me just a minute alone? I promise, I'll be right up."

Tom nodded and made his way back to the beach house.

Jenna stood alone, looking out at the horizon and the sinking sun. The ocean had always captivated her. She tried to take everything in – the blues and greens of the water, the reflection of the sun glistening off the rippling waves, the smell of the mist. Tom whistled at her. The piercing screech got her attention. Before she headed back to the demons at home, she held two fingers to her lips, kissed them, and extended her arm toward the Pacific Ocean.

She whispered to the waves, "Good bye, for now. Please take care of us."

Jenna turned and made her way back to the house. With each step forward, she was distancing herself from what she loved and moving closer into the jaws of evil.

At the airport, Tom dropped Jenna and Mia off with the luggage, while he returned their rental car. Preoccupied by what faced her when she arrived home, Jenna did her best to check their six bulky bags.

Tom returned to the main terminal to find his wife in a raging argument with a local airport employee about the weight of their luggage. Jenna had three suitcases splayed open. She was sitting on the floor in front of an airport scale shifting their belongings from one suitcase to the next. Clothes, bathing suits, towels, underwear, and shoes were strewn across the floor, in direct view of other mainlanders returning home. The humidity, combined with Jenna's frustration, caused her to perspire, and her damp shirt stuck to her skin.

Jenna was in the middle of frantically moving shoes from one suitcase to another when Tom discretely bent down and asked, "What in the hell is going on?"

"What's going on?" shrieked Jenna, a little too loud. Her hair was a frizzy mess, and her face was flushed. "What's going on is that the luggage Nazi over there is making me move our underwear around in front of the entire island, so that we aren't a single ounce over the limit." Jenna pointed to the offending airport employee. The local woman shook her head in disgust.

It was unlike Jenna to become so agitated. Tom recognized Jenna's angst about returning home, but it didn't justify her behavior, especially in front of their daughter. To Mia's credit, she sat dutifully by her mother's side and helped her sort out their luggage. Tom was not sure for whom he felt more sympathy. His wife, who was causing quite a scene and making a complete fool of herself, or their daughter, who was getting her fair share of pity stares from the strangers in the airport.

Tom pulled Jenna up from the floor and told her firmly, "Go take Mia and stand in the check-in line. I'll take it from here."

Jenna scowled at the airport worker as she left.

While Tom successfully evened out their luggage, while Jenna and Mia stood in the ticket line. After surviving a grueling check-in process, the Reiners reached airport security to find it completely backed up. Sweltering tourists were crammed into the maze. The line was not moving, and Jenna was uncomfortably hot. She wiped the sweat from her forehead as she asked snidely, "Can they move any slower?"

Tom looked at Jenna with reproach and whispered, "Please, Jenna, calm down."

Mia, unaccustomed to Jenna's lack of patience, moved closer to her father. For the remainder of the process, no one spoke.

The Reiners barely got through security in time and nearly missed their flight. Jenna trudged through the narrow aisle of the crowded aircraft, clumsily bumping annoyed passengers in her path. To Tom's relief, once seated, she shut her eyes. An hour into the flight, Jenna had just drifted off to sleep when Mia woke her to ask for a snack. Jenna snapped, "Goddamit, Mia! Go to sleep. You just had dinner. You don't need any snacks!"

Tears of shame and shock filled Mia's eyes. People in nearby rows witnessed the exchange in dismay. Tom frantically reached into their carry-on bag and found some crackers. Jenna tried unsuccessfully to go back to sleep.

The next morning, on the drive home from the airport, Jenna was mortified at her behavior. She apologized no fewer than twenty times to both Mia and Tom. Jenna had never barked at Mia like that before, for any reason. The rest of her antics she could live down, but she had a hard time recognizing herself as *that* woman on the plane, yelling at her child over an innocent request for a snack.

The Reiners stumbled into their house in a complete fog. The red-eye back from Hawaii was always a dreadful experience, but this trip was exceptionally painful. To add to Jenna's misery, her head pounded and her eyes burned.

Mia immediately fell sound asleep on the couch, and Tom carried in their luggage. Jenna trudged into the office and checked her email. She had intentionally not allowed herself to look at it during their entire vacation, but the vacation was officially over.

FORTY-ONE

Ironically, at the same moment Jenna's plane was touching down, Jim Taylor was sending her an email about the lawsuit. The time had come for him to inform Jenna that Allison Anders had filed a motion to amend the initial complaint, which included the addition of two more charges. The "Second Amended Complaint for Damages, Certificate of Review, and Jury Demand" was attached, for Jenna's reading pleasure. More recently, Allison had also filed a motion to compel additional testimony from Jenna. According to Jim, Allison stipulated that Jenna had been excessively evasive in her answers during her first deposition. She argued that a second deposition was not only warranted, but necessary.

Jenna's gut cramped. Reading the document, she was appalled. Speculations were stated as if they were facts. Allison accused Jenna of having prior knowledge of the complaints and suspicions about Hillary Martin that were shared amongst the medical and hospital staff. The complaint went on to state that Jenna was aware of prior and similar diversion activities, both at St. Augustine and at other facilities. In spite of this alleged knowledge, the complaint asserted that Jenna routinely left her drugs unattended, unlocked, unmonitored, and unsecured for extended periods of time.

Her mouth agape, Jenna could not believe the lies. She had never known anything about Hillary Martin until the news story broke, four months after Hillary stole Jenna's drugs. Moreover, she never had any specific knowledge about staff members stealing drugs at St. Augustine. In fact, Jenna clearly told Allison as much in her deposition.

The stakes had increased substantially. Whereas there had previously only been two claims against Jenna, now there were four.

There was a claim added for "Medical Monitoring." Allison maintained that Jenna should establish a fund that would be made available to Ms. Hollings for future treatment of her hepatitis C infection.

Jenna wondered how they could demand such a thing. St. Augustine already promised free and unlimited lifetime medical care for all infected patients.

Allison also added a claim for "Reckless and Intentional Infliction of Emotional Distress." The claim stated that Jenna's conduct was extreme, outrageous, irresponsible, and intentional.

Jenna grabbed the phone and dialed Jim's cell phone. He answered on the first ring.

"So this is my welcome back?" asked Jenna with an odd mixture of sarcasm and fear.

Jim fully expected the call. He decided to forego the pleasantries about her trip and got right to the issue at hand. "I take it you read the email."

"Yeah, I read it alright. So, Allison Anders loses on round one at the deposition, and that means she gets another chance to have a go at me? If I had lost, like she wanted, I'm pretty sure I wouldn't be granted the luxury of requesting do-overs!"

Jim tried to keep calm, hoping to bring Jenna's emotions down to his level. "For one thing, understand that this is just a motion to compel you to be redeposed. We have written a very persuasive counterargument. The judge has yet to rule on it. I sat through your entire deposition and listened intently. You were not being evasive, by anyone's standards. I would be very shocked if the judge ruled in their favor."

"Then what about this amended complaint? Now they double the number of claims against me? And how can they state as if it were fact that I knew about Hillary Martin's diversion practices? I didn't know anything! St. Augustine made sure of that. Then what about the second claim? Is that the same as punitive damages?"

Between sleep deprivation, her guilt over her actions the night before, and Jim's email, Jenna was rapidly escalating into a fit. In anger, she slammed the glass French doors to the office shut, causing the panes to rattle.

Tom walked past the office door with the last 50-pound suitcase in his grasp. Behind the closed doors, he heard his wife shrieking as she spoke on the phone. Tom figured it was either the airline calling about Jenna's misconduct last night or her attorneys. For Jenna's sake, he secretly hoped the airline had caught up with her. He motioned for Jenna to turn the phone on speaker as he silently entered the office.

Jim's voice filled the room. "I know you are upset. I'm so sorry you have to come home to this. As far as making claims about what you did or didn't know, right now they can basically say anything they want. When it comes time for trial, that's our chance to prove those claims are untrue."

"What about the reckless and intentional claim? Does that mean what I think it does?"

"Yes, I'm afraid it does. It doesn't mean that the judge will accept it, but it definitely lays the groundwork for a punitive damages claim against you. As we discussed, if a jury is allowed to rule on that and finds against you, those damages are not covered by your malpractice policy."

Jenna looked at Tom and shook her head sadly.

Jim continued, "Jenna, you have to understand that a lot of this is just posturing. Most cases settle out of court. Every other hepatitis case that has been filed so far has settled. Allison Anders and Lyle Silverstein do *not* want to go to court. Every hour, every minute they spend preparing for trial is money that they won't see in the end. This is the phase where things can get really ugly. They will use words, accusations, and threats to intimidate you and wear you down. They hope that you'll do what most doctors do."

"Which is?" asked Jenna.

Gravely, Jim responded. "Reach a breaking point. The point where the stress on you, your family, and your existence is so excessive and relentless that you just want it to go away. They want to get you to the point where you are chronically worried, you can't function, and you can't focus. Whether you allow them to get you there or not is up to you, but we are here for you whenever you need us."

"What about punitive damages? The thing is, Jim, we don't have much. We own a house that's under water. We have very little in savings. Our retirement accounts have been decimated over the past several years by the stock market. What can they take if we have nothing?"

"I suppose they can go after what little you have and then garnish your wages."

Jenna's words were as cold as ice. "I'd quit my profession and live as a vagabond before I'd work a single second of the day to give money to that slime ball attorney and her lowlife client!"

Jenna had clearly made the leap from simply hating Allison Anders to hating Michelle Hollings, too.

FORTY-TWO

October 2011

Jenna came straight from the hospital to meet her attorneys. She was still wearing her blue scrubs and brown, soiled OR clogs. Over the past several months, since her deposition, they had exchanged countless emails and phone calls. The time had come for them to once again meet face-to-face.

Nancy ran out to grab some documents. Alone with Jenna, Jim looked at her compassionately and asked, "How have you been doing?"

Jenna paused for a second. "Do you really want the truth?" Her annoyance and frustration were evident.

Jim sat back, stunned at Jenna's tone. "Of course," he said. Suspecting an imminent meltdown from Jenna, Jim stood and closed the door.

Jenna shuddered, "Every day, I think about this. Even when I try not to, there's no escaping it. I'm bombarded by emails or phone calls from you guys requesting this or updating me on that. I look at every patient and wonder which one is going to sue me next. I second-guess every decision I make at work. I used to be relaxed, easygoing, even funny. Now, I'm filled with hostility. I hate Allison Anders. I hate Michelle Hollings.

I hate all of the legal mumbo jumbo. I hate my job. I hate every other doctor around me who loves what they do. I'm completely exhausted. So, you asked for honesty . . . there it is."

Jim slid his chair closer to the table and removed his reading glasses. He was a bit taken aback by Jenna's frankness, but not completely. Jenna had proven to Jim and Nancy numerous times that she saw no need for false pretenses. He thought back to the afternoon of her deposition. Jenna had been so energized, so ready for battle. Jim and Nancy both knew that Allison would eventually wear her down, but he was hoping, somehow, he could prevent that from happening.

Jim tried his best to console Jenna. "What you're feeling is completely normal. This is a relentless process. There's always something that comes up. You think it can't get any worse, and then it does. I understand where you're coming from. If things are becoming unbearable for you, we can always initiate settlement negotiations. Nothing is worth living in hell."

Although Jim had not intended for his words to come out threatening or condescending, that was how Jenna interpreted them. Jenna thought back to the deposition and the brutality of spending seven hours being interrogated. She recalled the indignity of the cameraman's insinuation that she was standing behind him, urinating on the floor. The lies Allison had written about her in the most recent complaint created another fresh, seeping wound.

Jenna was determined to be strong. There was no way she would give up.

Staring intently at Jim, she said, "No! I absolutely will not settle. We go all the way. It may be hard. I may have my bad days, but there is no way I'm giving up!"

"Okay," Jim replied. Inwardly, he wondered how much more Jenna could endure before she broke. Right now, he thought Jenna was teetering precariously close to the edge.

A light rap on the door interrupted their conversation. Nancy entered, smiling and cheerful. Her smile quickly vanished when she saw the serious expressions on Jim's face.

"Did I miss something?" Nancy asked with hesitation and a hint of dread.

Jenna shook her head, and Jim shifted his eyes. Nancy knew to let this one go and quietly took her seat. Besides, she was certain that Jim would fill her in later.

Unsure of what to say, no one spoke. Finally, Jim broke the silence. "Jenna, we wanted to go through the case with you today, piece by piece, to let you know where things stand and how they are shaping up. Why don't we start with some good news?"

Jenna smiled weakly. "I didn't think there was such a thing as good news where this lawsuit is concerned."

Jim overlooked her pessimism. Jenna was testy today, which was not like her. "In this case, I think you will find it very good news. The judge ruled on Anders' motion to redepose you."

The words slowly registered. Jenna stiffened her posture and raised an eyebrow. "Go on."

Jim passed Jenna a copy of the court ruling. "The judge ruled in our favor. In her motion, Anders sent him cherry-picked excerpts from your deposition. The statements were manipulated and taken out of context in an effort to make you appear evasive. In our counterargument, we sent in the entire transcript and videotape of your deposition. This judge is a fair and thorough man. I'm certain that he either watched or read your entire deposition before he made his ruling."

Nancy added, "And if he really did read your entire deposition, it helps us in another way."

"What's that?" asked Jenna.

"Even in print," Nancy explained, "Anders does not come off favorably. Hopefully, this opens the judge's eyes to her antics. That should benefit us on future rulings."

Jenna's eyes lit up. Letting out an enormous sigh, she said softly, "Thank you. Thank both of you for whatever you did to get me out of that. You're right, this is good news."

She felt like a pressure-valve had been released.

Nancy said, "As you know, your court date is January 30, 2012. The trial is scheduled to last for three weeks. At this point, you will need to notify your office that you will need the entire time off. Your presence in court will be required every day during the trial."

"Isn't three weeks an awfully long time? I thought it was rare for even a big murder case to last that long. How could this possibly drag on for three weeks?"

"Your trial is going to be complicated. The world of medicine is foreign to most people. There are a lot of issues to be covered and explained in terms that a juror can understand.

"This afternoon, we want to go over our strategy and theirs. We have their expert witness disclosure list, and we have also assembled ours. It's your choice, Jenna. Which side do you want to go over first?"

Jenna swallowed against her dry throat. "Let's start with the devil's version of things. Then at least we end on a more positive note."

FORTY-THREE

Jim methodically organized the documents in front of him. "To lay the groundwork, we know that Anders' strategy is to show that it was below the standard of care to leave narcotics unattended and unsecured. She's also going to try to prove this violated DEA rules. If successful, she will then argue that if you hadn't violated the guidelines, Hillary Martin would have never had the opportunity to contaminate the syringe. Furthermore, Ms. Hollings would not have contracted hepatitis. It will all point back to you."

His last words ripped through Jenna like a blade. Struggling to keep afloat, Jenna asked, "I thought that the standard of care was defined by what other reasonable physicians in the same specialty were doing or would have done under similar circumstances. How can they claim I violated the standard of care? Maybe not every anesthesiologist would like to admit that they left their drugs unattended, but I know for a fact that most did."

"We agree with you. However, the problem for us is two-fold. First of all, just because many, if not most, doctors do something a certain way, it doesn't make it right. Standard of care isn't defined by majority rule. It's defined by what experts say was the right thing to do.

"Which leads us to the next issue – their expert witnesses. They have two anesthesiologists who have given depositions. These doctors are fully prepared to enter the courtroom and testify that what you did with your narcotics did not meet the standard of care. I don't want to get ahead of myself, but just to reassure you, we have our own experts that will testify to the contrary."

The thought of being publicly attacked by strangers left Jenna feeling vulnerable. She rubbed her eyes, trying to make sense of it all. "What kind of doctor would come into court with the intention of destroying a fellow physician? Particularly over something like this, where I was the victim of a criminal act? I was *not* the criminal."

Jim responded, "Unfortunately, the plaintiff's attorneys aren't the only ones that can say anything they want. So too, can the expert witnesses who are well compensated for their testimony."

"Who are these people? These so-called 'experts?'" Jenna was practically shouting, shaking her head in disbelief. Jim was thankful that Nancy had closed the door when she came into the room. Glancing up at the window to the hallway, he noticed one of his colleagues looking their way. Fortunately, he thought, Jenna's back was to the window. Jim subtly motioned to Nancy with his pen, and she stood and lowered the blinds.

Meanwhile, Jim referenced his notes. "Their first witness is Dr. James Jenkins. He's an older gentleman and, unfortunately, very likable. Dr. Jenkins has given expert testimony many times in the past, and he is very polished and well spoken.

"The good thing for us is that Dr. Jenkins hasn't done a case in the OR for over seven years. That will allow us to cast doubt on his credibility."

Jenna's pupils were large, like saucers. Her head felt like it were being squeezed in a vice – tighter and tighter with each passing word.

"Their second expert witness is much less likable. His name is Dr. Joseph Monroe. He's from the East Coast and has the accent, abrasiveness, and arrogance to back it up.

"This is his first testimony as an expert witness, and it showed in his deposition. You would dislike him instantly, and hopefully the jurors will, too.

"Over the course of his career, Dr. Monroe has served extensively on committees that have dealt with patient safety, including the handling of narcotics within the operating room. Even with his impressive credentials, he makes some pretty outlandish claims. That's where Nancy and I think we can question his credibility."

Jenna sunk in her chair, her head dropped. "Like what?"

"Dr. Monroe is exceedingly rigid in his opinions. For example, he maintains that narcotics should either be locked or under the direct control of the anesthesiologist at *all* times, including during surgery. We questioned him as to whether he ever left drugs on the top of the anesthesia cart during a case while he turned his back to attend to the patient or do a procedure. He adamantly denies that he has ever done so, even in the face of an unstable patient. Clearly, that is a ridiculous and impractical assertion."

Jenna's hope was rapidly fading. Somberly, she asked, "What do these guys get paid to slaughter me?"

Jim leafed through the documents filed by Allison Anders, found the page, and handed it to Jenna. Her mouth dropped when she read the amounts. The two anesthesia experts each earned $500 per hour to review records and another $500 per hour for deposition testimony.   If the case went to trial, they would each receive $6,000 per day, plus all expenses.

Jenna slammed the document down on the table. "Pretty nice chunk of change to destroy my career, my reputation, and my life!"

Nancy shifted gears, "Besides the anesthesiologists, Anders will call other experts that help establish a case for damages.

"They will have Ms. Hollings' clinical psychologist testify that Hollings suffers from post-traumatic stress disorder, anxiety disorder, and panic attacks.   The psychologist will state that these conditions are a direct result of her infection with hepatitis C.

"Anders also has an economist that will testify that the probable losses to Ms. Hollings, based upon her contraction of hepatitis C and the lifelong repercussions related to loss of earning potential, emotional damages, and health care costs range from $1,200,000 to $2,000,000."

"You can't be serious!" Jenna roared.

Nancy empathized with Jenna's indignation.   "I know, go figure.   The woman works at a strip club and, up until the time when she settled with St. Augustine, she didn't even own a car."

"Wait a minute," Jenna cried out in disbelief.   "I didn't know any of this.   What else do you know about her?"

Nancy wore an ornery smirk of satisfaction. "Quite a bit, actually.   We took her deposition last week. Michelle Hollings is not at all the clean-cut, poster child that Anders would like us to believe.

"Ms. Hollings dropped out of high school when she was seventeen.   Her mother threw her out of the house for using drugs.   On the streets, Hollings prostituted for a while, until she found a girlfriend that hooked her up with a job at a local strip club. Hollings moved in with that friend and has been dancing ever since. She claims that she hasn't used any illegal drugs in more than four years, with the exception of an occasional joint."

Jenna squinted at her lawyers, her voice curt, "So that prissy little blonde that came to my deposition, all prim and proper, wearing a prudish skirt and pearls, is really a stripper and a whore?"

Nancy knew this information was invaluable. "That's what I'm telling you."

Finally, Jenna felt her suffocating pessimism begin to fade. "So this is really good news, right? I mean, how could a jury possibly side with someone like her?"

Nancy told Jenna the other side. "Her occupation and her past will certainly make her less likable. However, she's still an attractive, previously healthy woman that came in for breast augmentation and left with hepatitis. She claims that during her twelve months of treatment for hepatitis C, she slept most of the time and was unable to work. Socially, she became withdrawn and rarely went out with her friends. Her boyfriend left her after finding out about the infection. It wasn't until we pulled it out of her through repeated questioning that she admitted he was also married and has two kids. Maybe that had something to do with his ending their relationship, as well.

"We also got Ms. Hollings to admit, albeit reluctantly and after many heated objections from Anders, that since completing treatment she has no detectable hepatitis C virus in her bloodstream. Essentially, she's cured. Although, Hollings did make certain we were aware that the doctors told her there is a chance that the virus could reactivate at any time.

"Just so you know, Jenna, we have two experts in the field that will testify on your behalf that reactivation is virtually impossible.

"We also found out, since her settlement with St. Augustine, Michelle Hollings moved into a brand new townhouse and quit her job. She's also made some interesting purchases, including a loaded Hummer SUV, a new Mustang convertible, and a good deal of jewelry. Not bad for someone with no education and no employment."

Jenna was encouraged by Ms. Hollings' less than stellar lifestyle. At least it made Michelle Hollings look less like the poor, frail victim and more like what Jenna now saw her as – a greedy good-for-nothing looking for the winning lottery ticket.

"She also had plenty to say about you," Nancy added. Jim and Nancy eyed Jenna keenly, gauging her response.

Jenna raised her right eyebrow. "What did she say?"

Nancy continued, "At the end of Michelle Hollings' deposition, Anders asked if you had ever apologized to her in any way for her contracting hepatitis C. Michelle Hollings said that you had not. Anders then asked her whether she felt that you had shown any sorrow or regret at your deposition. Ms. Hollings said she never got that impression from you. In fact, she said that your attitude during the deposition was so upsetting to her that she had to leave."

Nancy was playing Jenna. She knew that fueling Jenna's rage was the key to keeping her in the game.

Jenna said harshly, "I was told, *explicitly*, by Randy Stevens, Rob Wilson, and the two of you, not to contact her! I'm sure Allison Anders knew I had been given those instructions. What did she expect at my deposition? Did she think I was going to give Michelle Hollings a big hug and tell her how sorry I was? Anders knew I wasn't allowed to apologize, even if I wanted to. And to use the rules of engagement against me? Unbelievable!"

Burying her head in her hands, Jenna pleaded with her attorneys, "Please, please tell me we've got a way to fight back."

Jim was quick to reassure her, "Jenna, for the past couple hours, you've been hearing *their* side. Now, you get to hear *ours*."

Jenna propped her elbows on the table, giving her attorneys her full attention. "Okay, show me what we've got."

The edges of Jim's lips turned up slightly. "Our first expert witness is Dr. Phillip Ramano. He is the Chair of Anesthesia at Good Samaritan Hospital, right across town. Dr. Ramano's our ace-in-the-hole. Basically, everything that Anders' experts say against you, Dr. Ramano is prepared to testify otherwise. Even though Dr. Ramano has never given expert testimony before, he's competent, well spoken, sincere, and a man of principle. These traits are immediately apparent, and they will mean a great deal in the eyes of the jurors."

Jenna could not believe what she was hearing. She had never crossed paths with the doctor before, but Phillip Ramano was a Godsend. After being bombarded with experts intent on demonstrating her incompetence, finally there was someone who thought differently. For hours, Jenna had listened to the bad things. At last, she began to feel hopeful.

Smiling, she asked with bewilderment, "Who is this guy? And why would he go out on such a limb for me?"

Jim spoke softly, "Dr. Ramano is a good guy, and he came to his conclusions on his own. He has told us flat out that he doesn't think you did anything wrong."

Jenna was dumbstruck. "I don't know if it's appropriate or if you are allowed to relay communication between the two of us but, if you can, can you please tell him thank you?"

She blinked rapidly to hold back tears.

Jim nodded, "We'll make sure he knows."

He paused for a moment to stretch his back and then continued, "Our second expert is Dr. Richard Muzzani. He's a practicing anesthesiologist and Professor of Anesthesia in Seattle. Dr. Muzzani has testified as an expert witness numerous times, and he's very professional and convincing.

"Dr. Muzzani will testify that in 2010, there was considerable debate about the acceptable means of storage and security of controlled substances within the OR. Furthermore, he will state that even today, there is no established or nationally agreed upon standard of care.

"According to Dr. Muzzani, your practices were the norm rather than the exception. In fact, he will go so far as to say the that gold standard for an anesthesiologist is to be prepared to take care of his or her patient, including having all medications drawn up before the patient enters the room.

"He also intends to state unequivocally that there was no way you could have foreseen Hillary Martin would engage in criminal activity which would result in Ms. Hollings being infected with the hepatitis C virus."

Jim paused for a second while Jenna poured herself a glass of water. Her mouth felt like cotton.

Nancy interposed, "With respect to the remainder of Dr. Ramano's and Dr. Muzzani's testimony, their opinions are very congruent. That's good because it will demonstrate to the jury that two respected and practicing anesthesiologists, one local and one not, agree with each other that you did nothing wrong.

"Each of them will testify that placing the medications in a drawer of the anesthesia cart and leaving them unattended was consistent with the standard of care, because the OR was considered to be a secure environment.

"Both doctors have reviewed the anesthesia record for Ms. Hollings, and they agree that the record is consistent with Michelle Hollings having received Fentanyl and not saline.

"Our experts have each read your deposition. They will testify, contrary to what Anders and her experts might claim, anesthesiologists do not have a duty to prevent diversion of controlled substances within the operating room. Furthermore, they will attest that anesthesiologists are not expected to understand the myriad of DEA rules and regulations regarding controlled substances."

Jenna was about to speak when Nancy held her hand up and grinned, "Wait! There's more."

"More?" Jenna asked, astonished.

Nancy beamed, "Our experts will testify that anesthesiologists were not, in 2010, required to keep controlled substances locked in the OR at all times, and that anesthesiologists were not responsible for monitoring their drug cart at all times during a procedure.

"Furthermore, both doctors will state that it is impossible to know, with reasonable medical probability, how Hillary Martin transmitted her hepatitis C virus to Ms. Hollings. It could have been a contaminated syringe just as easily as it could have been contaminated saline used as an irrigant during surgery.

"Finally, Drs. Muzzani and Ramano will testify that diversion of controlled substances within the OR is not rampant, and that your alleged ignorance of the prevalence of diversion in operating rooms is not outside the standard of care.

"Both of these gentlemen feel very strongly that Hillary Martin, not you, is to blame for Ms. Hollings' development of hepatitis C."

Jenna simply shook her head. At first, she could not believe two doctors would come to her defense. The specifics of how far they were willing to go left her dazed.

"Oh my God," Jenna smiled. "These guys are saying that everything that Anders claims is complete nonsense. I never would have expected such strong testimony."

Jim said, "Jenna, there are people out there, us included, who believe in you. You just have to remind yourself to listen to them and not to the opposition."

Nancy looked over at Jenna, whose face was full of confusion. "Feeling a little better about things now?"

"I . . . I don't even know what to say. Up until now, everything seemed so bleak. Now it suddenly feels like things could possibly go in my favor. I'm having a hard time absorbing it all."

Nancy said warmly, "Jenna, why don't we take a short break? Stretch our legs a little bit?"

Jim stepped out to use the restroom. Jenna headed out to do the same. At the door, Nancy reached out for Jenna's arm and asked, "You okay?"

Before Jenna knew it, she had melted into Nancy's arms. Pools of emotion poured from Jenna's soul. After a couple of minutes, Jenna backed away.

Between hiccups, Jenna replied, "Honestly, I don't even know where that came from. I'm sorry. You must think I'm an emotional train wreck."

Nancy put her hands on Jenna's shoulders. "Not at all. I think you're human. We may not be used to seeing that in our professions, but we can still recognize it when we come across it. You're just a normal woman in a really bad situation. Now go take a quick break, and then let's get back to work."

On her way out, Jenna whispered, "Thank you."

FORTY-FOUR

In the ladies' room, Jenna splashed cool water on her face and blew her nose. Five minutes later, she returned to the conference room. Out of respect, Jim overlooked Jenna's bloodshot eyes and red nose.

Once Jenna took her seat, he resumed outlining their lineup of expert witnesses.

"Getting back to our defense, Dr. Arlene Myer is a nationally recognized hepatologist. She will testify that hepatitis C could have been transmitted to Ms. Hollings by either contaminated saline or contaminated medication.

"Dr. Meyer will also state that Michelle Hollings' hepatitis infection is cured. According to the doctor's extensive experience, the fact that Ms. Hollings has had no detectable virus since completion of her treatment indicates that, without repeat exposure, there is essentially zero chance of recurrence. Furthermore, she will state that Ms. Hollings has no current symptoms related to her prior infection or its treatment."

Jokingly, Jenna said, "Maybe I should have asked to hear our side first. Knowing all this, their case is starting to sound like a crock. What else do you have?"

The irritation in Jenna's eyes began to clear. Gradually, she appeared calmer and more confident.

Nancy was openly grinning. "It keeps getting better. We have a psychologist that has reviewed Michelle Hollings' records. According to Dr. Joyce Boden, Ms. Hollings' diagnoses of PTSD, panic disorder, and anxiety disorder are not supported by her symptoms, and the criteria for diagnosis of any of these disorders has not been met."

"Big shocker there," interjected Jenna with spite.

Nancy continued, "Dr. Boden will also testify that any psychiatric symptoms that Ms. Hollings currently suffers from are unrelated to her infection with hepatitis C.

"Our last expert witness is a human resources vice president by the name of John Rhodes. He has more than thirty years of experience in hiring practices for large corporations. Mr. Rhodes plans to testify that St. Augustine Hospital was grossly negligent in its pre-employment investigation and retention of Hillary Martin.

"More specifically, he will testify that St. Augustine did not require Ms. Martin to account for gaps in her employment. These gaps should have been red flags, and should have prompted further inquiry. He will attest to the fact that St. Augustine failed to contact the hospitals where Hillary Martin was employed in the past, and they failed to do a criminal background check.

"Mr. Rhodes has harsh criticisms of St. Augustine's response to Hillary Martin's employment health screening. Martin stated on an employment screening form that she was negative for a variety of infectious diseases, including hepatitis C. As we all know, her pre-employment blood work showed otherwise. Nothing was done to determine whether Hillary Martin knowingly lied on her health screening. She was never questioned with respect to when and how she could have possibly become infected with the hepatitis C virus. Mr.

Rhodes' testimony will show that a reasonable investigation should have either revealed her infection was a result of intravenous drug use, and/or she falsified her pre-employment screening form. Either way, her job offer should have been withdrawn."

"Wow," said Jenna, shaking her head. "It's so much to comprehend. Listening to their side, all I can picture is the jurors taking out the guilty stamp and branding me on the forehead. Then I listen to our side and think, how could we lose?"

Jim replied honestly, "If you see it that way, then you are very perceptive. The trial will be a series of tit for tats. It will ultimately boil down to who the jurors find most believable, who they like the best, how they perceive you, and how they perceive Michelle Hollings. Unfortunately, it is these intangibles, rather than the facts, which most often determines who wins and who loses. That being said, I think we have a very credible list of expert witnesses, and we feel very positive about this case."

"So," asked Jenna "what exactly is our strategy?"

He looked directly at her, his hands clasped behind his head. "We attack."

Jim's face grew more animated and energized. The twinkle in his eyes told Jenna that this was the part of his job he relished. Jenna glanced at Nancy, whose enthusiasm mirrored that of her colleague's.

Even though Jim's expression was filled with excitement, his words were menacing, "Jenna, this is the point where we go for the jugular."

To Jenna, nothing sounded more enticing.

Jim smirked, "We start by suggesting that there is a distinct possibility that it wasn't even your syringe of

Fentanyl that served as the source of Michelle Hollings' infection."

Tilting her head in Jim's direction, Jenna asked, "I know you alluded to that with respect to Dr. Meyer's testimony, but what exactly do you mean?"

"Hillary Martin testified that she stole Fentanyl syringes, filled the used ones with saline, and replaced the stolen syringes with contaminated syringes. In the entirety of her testimony, Martin *never* singled out any particular anesthesiologist. Never once did Hillary Martin come out and say, 'I stole from so and so.' This got us to thinking. What if Martin never touched your syringes? What if the contamination came from saline?"

Nancy could not contain herself. "It's more than just an outlandish excuse, Jenna. This is a *plausible* explanation for Ms. Hollings' infection. It is completely possible that it had nothing to do with you or your drugs. We were thinking about it. Where would Martin have had the easiest access to saline?"

Jenna challenged herself to think like Hillary Martin as she contemplated Nancy's question. "Well, there are vials of saline in the anesthesia cart, but that would mean Martin would have to spend that much more time snooping around where she did not belong. From her perspective, that probably was not the best source. There are one liter and half-liter bags of saline everywhere, but they are prepackaged in a protective wrapper. It wouldn't be very practical to steal a liter bag, draw up five milliliters of saline, and then throw the whole bag away without being caught."

Her attorneys patiently waited for Jenna to come to the realization they had already reached.

Jenna considered other sources of saline. All of a sudden, it hit her. Without warning, Jenna leapt from her chair, snapped her fingers, and pointed at her lawyers.

"The back table! There's always a bowl of saline on the back table with all the sterile surgical equipment. If I were Hillary Martin, that's where I'd refill. It's just sitting there, ready to be used. It would be the quickest and easiest way to refill a syringe without being caught. If that were the case, the saline on the back table would become contaminated. That saline is used to irrigate open wounds and comes in direct contact with a patient's blood."

Jenna sat back down, pondering this explanation. Doubt soon overshadowed her initial elation. "The problem is, how would we ever prove that?"

Nancy answered, "The beauty is, we don't have to. The only person in the world who knows what Hillary Martin really did is Hillary Martin. Look at her credibility. She's a drug addict, a convicted felon, a proven liar, and a thief. No lawyer in their right mind, not even Allison Anders, would ever call her to the stand as part of their defense. There's no way Hillary Martin will be present at trial to contradict our theory. Anything that Hillary Martin has ever said up to this point is suspect, at best. All we have to do is show this explanation is possible."

"I like it," said Jenna, sneering. "If the jury becomes uncertain as to whether or not my syringes were ever diverted, a huge part of Anders' ammunition against me disappears. Then we have our anesthesia experts come in and testify that, even if Martin did steal my drugs, I wasn't doing anything wrong."

"Exactly," said Jim proudly. "It's a million little holes that will make their case disintegrate in the end."

"What about St. Augustine?" Jenna asked, concerned. "You said Mr. Rhodes would testify that their hiring practices were inadequate, at best. Exactly how far are we going to go with attacking the hospital?"

The prospect of revealing St. Augustine's mistakes made Jenna's stomach burn. She was certain there would be damaging repercussions for her career. On the other hand, Jenna acknowledged that they had to do everything they could to win this case.

Although Jim correctly suspected Jenna did not feel an overwhelming sense of loyalty to the hospital, he realized that confronting St. Augustine would be difficult for her.

Choosing his words carefully, Jim said, "There is no doubt that St. Augustine failed to follow adequate screening procedures when they hired Hillary Martin. I would venture to say that McDonalds does a more thorough background check on its potential employees than St. Augustine conducted for Hillary Martin. And there's a big difference between flipping burgers and being granted access to an operating room."

Jim stalled for a moment, struggling to read Jenna's emotions. A strong strike on the hospital was critical to their defense. It was imperative to convince Jenna of the same.

"Jenna," he argued, "if St. Augustine had done the proper background check and had asked the right questions, Hillary Martin would never have been hired. If that were the case, Martin would never have had the opportunity to infect patients. In essence, St. Augustine placed you in a position to be victimized by a criminal. St. Augustine put you *here*. Don't forget the patients who may have been infected by Hillary Martin's drug buddies. St. Augustine is actively trying to cover up their existence and deny them care. The folks at St. Augustine aren't the good guys."

Since the beginning, Jenna had grown increasingly hostile toward the hospital administration. St. Augustine had made an epic hiring mistake. To Jenna, it was apparent that the administration was willing to do whatever was required to make this mess go away. Jenna considered Jim's words and understood that he was right. St. Augustine had started the cycle that was threatening to ruin Jenna's life. If the situation were reversed and St. Augustine's existence depended on exposing Jenna's flaws, the hospital would heartlessly and swiftly annihilate her. In the interest of self-preservation, she had no choice but do to the same.

Jenna shivered as she said, "Even though I know you're right, I'm scared to death to go up against them. St. Augustine wants this to all go away, and we'll be flaunting their mistakes and culpability for all to see. What do you think they'll do to me?"

Nancy spoke up, "Legally, the hospital can't do anything. If St. Augustine revoked your privileges, they'd have to do the same for every other anesthesiologist affected by this ordeal, and that's unlikely."

"I'm sure they could make life difficult for me," Jenna said, hanging her head.

"They would proceed very carefully before they did anything like that. The last thing they want is more bad press, and mistreating a doctor because her case went to court would bring plenty of undesired attention. That being said, you have to be prepared for the worst and willing to accept that possibility before we move forward."

Jenna rubbed her eyes, contemplating the consequences. She raised her head and brazenly concluded, "We have no choice but to go after St.

Augustine.   I'll deal with the fallout if and when it happens."

FORTY-FIVE

Jenna felt like a gambler sitting at the blackjack table, having lost everything but her last twenty dollars. Taking a big breath, she decided to bet her remaining chips and play to the bitter end. There were so many other players who had precious little to lose and so much to win. Worse, these players were intimately familiar with the rules of the game. They knew how to read the cards, stack the odds in their favor, and game the system. Jenna, on the other hand, was competing for the very first time, and the stakes could not be higher. In the end, it remained to be seen who would fold. The plaintiff's expert witnesses? Michelle Hollings? Allison Anders? Or would it be Jenna?

Thoughts of Michelle Hollings filled Jenna's consciousness. If part of their defense relied upon attacking St. Augustine, destroying Michelle Hollings seemed like the next logical step.

Looking at her lawyers, Jenna asked, "What about Hollings?"

Nancy reached for her laptop, clicked on the mouse pad, turned her computer around, and pushed it across the table toward Jenna. Jenna positioned the screen in front of her and gasped as she found herself looking at Michelle

Hollings' Facebook page. She was dumbstruck as she scrolled through the pictures.

Michelle Hollings was beautiful, seductive, and sexy. One picture captured Michelle Hollings on a tropical beach lying in the sand, wearing a skimpy bikini that barely covered her enormous breasts. Her brown skin shimmered in the sun, as she held a Dos Equis up to the camera. In another picture, Michelle posed in cutoff shorts and a push-up bra on the hood of her shiny, red convertible.

Jenna's eyes were blazing. "So *this* is the face of chronic fatigue, PTSD, anxiety, and panic attacks? We can show this to the jury, right?"

Somberly, Jim explained, "We can, and we will. The tricky part is that you never know what jurors find offensive and what they don't. We have to be very careful how we go about it."

Incredulously, Jenna asked, "So, we downplay this?"

"Not at all. We fully intend to introduce it, but very cautiously. We can't hold up a picture of Michelle Hollings with a beer in her hand and tell the jury she's a bad person. Instead, we ask Hollings if she has any activities she enjoys. Regardless of her answer, we introduce the photo and gently point out to the jury that Michelle Hollings seems pretty happy drinking on the beach.

"We ask Hollings if there's any other way she could have contracted hepatitis C. If she denies any such possibility exists, and she probably will, we pull out the photos showing her body piercings.

"We'll get these images into play, but we will do it in a way that keeps us from looking as though we are attacking the victim. We don't want to turn the jury against us. It's a tenuous exercise, but trust us, it's one we are very good at."

Jenna grew cold with anger. "Just promise me that you will work this stuff in. If they get to trash me for days on end, we should at least get revenge whenever we can."

Jim's eyes bore into Jenna's. "I give you my word."

Nancy reached back for her computer. "Just so you know, all of these photos are new, since Hollings' settlement with St. Augustine. Frankly, the girl is an idiot for posting them. I'm shocked that Anders hasn't caught wind of this and forced her to pull them off the Internet. The oversight is too bad for Anders, but lucky for us. You might also want to know that we are setting up surveillance on Ms. Hollings."

Never having considered such a thing, Jenna was intrigued. "Surveillance? You mean private eye, stakeout kind of stuff?"

"Exactly," replied Nancy. "We know Michelle Hollings is not the incapacitated introvert she claims to have become. That much is evident from her Facebook page. If we can catch Hollings in action, we'll have more powerful evidence to present to the jury. Randy Stevens has authorized us to have her monitored for two entire weekends. The private investigator will follow her everywhere, taking pictures and video of any indiscretions."

A chilling thought gripped Jenna. *What if Allison Anders was watching her?* Did she know where Jenna lived? What about Mia and Tom? Could Allison have some stranger stalking her family? The concept of someone tracking her daughter left Jenna feeling paranoid.

"Could they be following me?" Jenna whispered.

Nancy was quick to comfort her. "It's unlikely. Your character is not on trial here. The same is not true with respect to Michelle Hollings."

Jenna did not completely believe Nancy. If Allison Anders did not have a tail on her, maybe St. Augustine did. This whole thing had evolved into something much larger than Jenna had ever anticipated.

FORTY-SIX

November 2011

Saturday night, Mia was spending the night with a friend, allowing Tom and Jenna to enjoy a rare evening alone. Jenna cuddled up on the couch, sipping herbal tea, and watching a television documentary. Her eyes were trained on the program, but her mind was elsewhere.

Tom snuggled up next to Jenna, muted the TV, and began kissing her neck. Involuntarily, Jenna's back stiffened. She felt dirty and worthless. The burden of being intimate was more than she could bear. For her husband's sake, she forced herself to reciprocate. Within minutes, they were undressed, lying on the shaggy carpet with the television flickering in the background. Tom was aroused. Jenna felt like a corpse. Tom fondled Jenna's breasts, gently kissing her nipples. Reflexively, her nipples hardened, and Jenna moaned on cue. He kissed his way down her stomach. She tried to relax, but could not. More than anything, she just wanted to finish the act and get it over with. She rolled Tom over on to his back and mounted him. Tom, pent up with desire, rocked his hips against Jenna's. Their bodies collided, hard and forceful, until he exploded inside his wife.

In the darkened room, tears slid down Jenna's cheeks as she rolled off of her husband. In the shadows of the night, Tom heard Jenna sniffle. He turned off the television, switched on the fireplace, and lit a couple of candles. Jenna sat motionless, her knees drawn toward her chest. Tom sat beside her and wrapped a blanket around them.

Jenna was unable to face her husband. Instead, she picked at a loose piece of yarn in the weave of the blanket. Tom reached over and held his wife's face in his hands.

With gentleness and concern, he asked, "What's wrong?"

"I'm sorry. Maybe I'm just tired." She sounded sad, exhausted, and powerless.

"I'm not talking about tonight. I'm talking about *you*. Every day. All the time. You're distant, distracted. You're here, but not really. You have to talk to me. Please, Jenna. Don't shut me out."

Jenna's wall of bravado crumbled, and the floodgates of defeat and humiliation opened wide. Meeting Tom's gaze, she felt like a failure.

"I'm so stressed. The lawsuit follows me every second of the day. I worry that somebody is watching us, like our people spy on Michelle Hollings. Every morning, the first thing I do is check to see if there's a news story about me. At work, I feel like tainted goods. I don't trust myself anymore, and I certainly don't trust my patients. I wanted to be strong. I wanted to fight. Part of me still does. But part of me feels like I'm breaking."

For a minute, Tom did not know what to say. He knew the lawsuit was taking a toll on Jenna, but she seemed determined to see it through. Up until now, he never questioned her commitment. Knowing how strong-willed Jenna could be, he assumed that surviving this ordeal was no exception. Yet now, he could see, bit by tiny bit, the lawsuit was crushing her.

"Do you want to settle?" Tom asked hesitantly.

Tom could hear Jenna's hair whip back and forth as she shook her head. "No! Absolutely not! I'm not giving in to those bastards!"

Tom knew his wife better than anyone. Regardless of the words spewing from Jenna's mouth, she had reached her limit.

"Do you want to talk about it?" Tom asked.

"I guess," Jenna replied, shrugging her shoulders. She reached for a Kleenex and blew her nose. Her lower lip trembled as she bit the inside of her check.

"Let's look at our options," said Tom, doing his best to sound objective and methodical. "Our first option is to continue to trial. That's in January, which means two more months that are only going to get more intense as the court date grows nearer.

"The second option is to settle and end this. Put it behind us and get on with our lives. Is that a fair assessment?"

Jenna kept her gaze downward, her voice was frail. "Yeah. The real sad thing is, either way, I lose. If I settle, I have a black mark on my record, not to mention the personal pain of giving up and handing Michelle Hollings and her wicked attorney a fist full of cash.

"If I go to court, the jury will most likely find that I share at least some of the blame in Hollings' infection. I don't think my percentage of liability will be anywhere near St. Augustine's or Hillary Martin's, but it's still a judgment against me. A black mark is a black mark, regardless of whether it happens now or in January. And it's pretty much guaranteed either way.

"If this thing goes to trial, it's going to be a media circus. It made national news when the Hillary Martin story first broke. Of course I'm worried about what that will do to me. More than that, it makes me sick to think about what it might do to you and, even more so, to Mia. What if some kid comes up to her at school and says something cruel? What if other moms decide their daughters can't play with Mia and she becomes an outcast? What if her picture somehow ends up in the news and some psychopath tries to hurt her?

"So far, I've escaped any media attention, but I feel it coming. It's my biggest fear."

Tom put his arms around his wife, wishing he could take this burden away from her. He would support Jenna in whatever decision she made. Secretly, however, Tom longed for the nightmare to end.

Jenna laid her head on Tom's shoulder as they sat nuzzled up on the couch, her warm breath against his cheek.

"What do you want to do?" he asked.

Jenna broke down, "What do I really want to do? I want to go back to being normal, whatever that is. I want to take a trip, get away, go to Hawaii. I want all this to be over. I can't do it anymore. The vultures are going to get their money one way or the other. I can't take two more months of this."

Tom's words were gentle, as the light from the fire cast shadows across his face. "Then settle. You could meet with Jim and Nancy first thing Monday morning and sign the papers. My guess is Michelle Hollings would have a check in her hot little hands by the end of the week.

"Then, maybe *we* should splurge. We've earned it. Let's go to Maui for two weeks around Thanksgiving.

We'll take Mia out of school, relax, forget, reconnect, and get your orgasm back."

For so long, Jenna had resisted the temptation of quitting. To her surprise, now that she and Tom were discussing it, she felt instant relief.

Laughing seductively, Jenna reached over and kissed her husband. She felt like she could breathe again. The oppressive cloud of misery had lifted. Playfully nibbling at Tom's ear, Jenna's voice was husky as she whispered, "Make love to me."

Tom pushed Jenna to the ground. Tenderly, he did all the things to her that she loved. Things felt right again.

FORTY-SEVEN

Sunday, Jenna spent the entire day, followed by a sleepless night, contemplating what she was about to do. By Monday morning, Jenna was convinced that settling the case was the right thing to do, both for her and for her family.

At 4 a.m., Jenna crawled out of bed and sent off two emails, one to Jim and the other to Nancy. She politely, but firmly, demanded a face-to-face meeting later that day. She also texted each of their cell phones and left voice messages at their work numbers. By 9 a.m., both attorneys replied that they were free all afternoon.

Jenna fought to make it through the day. At 2 p.m., she signed out her last patient to the recovery room nurse and headed straight to her attorneys' offices.

After exchanging the obligatory pleasantries, Jenna and her attorneys took their seats in the conference room. For the first time, Jenna noticed that neither Jim nor Nancy arrived with a handful of legal documents or a laptop computer. The only items each of them carried were a blank legal pad and a pen. It was a refreshing change.

Jim and Nancy sat with their hands folded and resting on the table. Jenna's posture was straight. She appeared dignified and confident. Slowly and clearly, she said four simple words, "I want to settle."

Once the words passed Jenna's lips, they became more than a mere thought or a contemplated course of action. They became *real*. She felt the words mocking her, causing her to feel exposed and weak. Jenna strived to remain stoic, but her eyes betrayed her as they filled with salty drops of shame.

Nancy placed a tissue box in front of her. Jenna did not thank her. It was too humiliating.

Jim spoke, "We had a feeling this is what you wanted to discuss. And you certainly have every right to demand that we settle. Can I ask you why? Why now?"

To Jenna's relief, there was no hint of condemnation or reproach in Jim's voice.

Jenna's breath caught in her throat. "I-I c-c-can't sleep. I hardly eat. I'm failing as both a mother and a wife. I've thought it through and, either way, settle or go to trial, I lose. Even though we have a compelling case with great expert witnesses, the same argument could be made for the other side."

She eyed her attorneys with scrutiny. Leaning forward, she raised her finger at them. "Tell me this. Do you really expect, in your heart of hearts, that I could go to trial and be found completely innocent?"

Jim answered honestly, "Like we've always told you, juries are unpredictable. Do I think it's possible? Yes. Do I think it's likely? If I had to give you percentage odds, I'd say maybe a ten to fifteen percent chance of that happening."

"So that's about a ninety percent chance that it won't! And, if that's the case, is it worth it? So far, the media has left me alone, but that's a ticking time bomb waiting to go off. The amount of stress will only get worse between now and January. I want out, and I want out *now*!"

Jenna's fragile composure completely disintegrated. She put her hands over her face and cried, her shoulders heaving as she struggled for air. This was not how Jenna had planned their meeting. She anticipated it would be liberating to end the process. Now, in front of her lawyers, seated in their conference room high above the city, all the feelings Jenna had suppressed since the suit began were coming out with a vengeance.

Jim and Nancy looked at Jenna. She was a wreck. No matter how badly they personally wanted to see this case to trial, no matter how many hours, days, and weeks of work they had invested in Jenna's defense, they had the decency and respect for Jenna to accept her decision.

Nancy pushed her chair back and walked toward the door. "I'll go print off the form."

Jenna took deep, slow breaths, trying to control her sobs. After several minutes, she started to calm down.

She asked Jim, "So what's the process from here on out?"

Nancy reentered the conference room with a one-page document in hand, which she handed to Jenna.

Jim began to explain the process. "First, you sign this consent for settlement. Then we call Randy Stevens and inform him of your decision. Randy will make a settlement offer to Anders. After that, Randy and Allison Anders will throw counter-settlement amounts back and forth, until they finally reach common ground.

"One thing you need to understand is Randy Stevens can settle for whatever amount he feels necessary in order to get the job done. That could be ten thousand dollars or one million dollars. Higher settlement amounts tend to attract more scrutiny from licensing boards, which will follow you for the remainder of your career. Once you sign this consent, things are out of your hands. But, to reassure you, Randy Stevens feels very strongly that none of you did anything wrong, and I don't see him giving away one penny more than he needs to."

"What do you see it settling for?" Jenna asked.

"Several of your partners have already settled cases with Anders. Of course, settlement amounts are confidential, and I can't divulge that information. I can tell you, though, that a settlement somewhere in the middle of twenty-five to seventy-five thousand dollars would seem like a reasonable expectation."

Jenna always appreciated Jim's uncanny ability to tell her what she wanted to know, yet still play by the rules.

"How long will it take? We are leaving for Hawaii on Thanksgiving Day, and it would be great if this were all behind us before we left."

Jim checked the calendar on his phone. "That gives us about three weeks. I think things should be settled by then."

Nancy handed the consent form to Jenna. Pen in hand, Jenna signed over her pride. She dropped the pen on the table and studied her signature. The shaky scribble was unrecognizable.

With tears streaming down her cheeks, Jenna apologized to her attorneys. "I'm sorry I gave up. I know I let both of you down. I've let myself down. This is harder than I ever anticipated, and I've had enough. I'm so sorry for all the work you've done, all for nothing. Mostly, I want to thank you for your guidance, support, and friendship."

Both Jim and Nancy bore melancholy smiles as they told Jenna, "You're welcome."

Jim said, "Until this case is settled, we are going to continue to forge ahead as if we were still on course for trial.   Although I don't see it happening, settlement negotiations have been known to fall through. Until the deal is officially done, we go along, business as usual. We'll keep you updated."

The meeting was over, and Jenna stood to leave. Jim and Nancy walked her to the elevator. Jim shook Jenna's hand and then pulled her in and hugged her. He whispered, "Things are going to get better."

Unable to talk, Jenna desperately needed to leave. She gave Nancy a quick hug, as she fought back grief.

The elevator doors opened, and Jenna silently stepped inside. Punching the button for the ground floor, Jenna waited impatiently for the doors to close. Once they did, even though Jenna was the only passenger, she moved into the back corner, buried her head in the wall, and cried.

At the fifth floor, the elevator stopped. Jenna barely had enough time to wipe her tears away and look at the ground before an elderly, African American woman with kind eyes and freckled cheeks stepped inside.

She glanced at Jenna. "Oh Honey, you gonna freeze out there without a coat."

The stranger turned to face Jenna directly and saw pure devastation. "Oh Lord. Are you okay?"

At that moment, the elevator reached the ground floor, and Jenna bolted out. Wracked with sobs, she called back to the compassionate stranger, "I need to go home."

The woman exited the elevator behind Jenna, shouting after her, "Sugar, you get home. God bless you."

Jenna ran to her car, jumped in, and locked the doors. In the chilly, desolate parking lot, she sat in the driver's seat and wept. Twenty minutes later, she was finally composed enough to drive home.

FORTY-EIGHT

Thanksgiving, 2011

Tom, Jenna, and Mia were elated to spend Thanksgiving Day flying over the Pacific Ocean. By the time their plane landed on Maui, the sun had set. The sky was thick and black. Famished and anxious to get settled, the Reiners loaded their luggage into the rental car and headed to their oceanfront condo. For the next two weeks, this would be their home.

Thanksgiving dinner was perfect. Jenna and her family feasted on hamburgers at the Barefoot Beach Bar on Ka'anapali Beach. Situated only a few feet from the Reiners' table, a jubilant, Hawaiian singer serenaded them with island tunes while Jenna and Mia buried their bare feet in the warm sand. In spite of the lack of a turkey dinner and family members gathered around with football games playing in the background, the Reiners were infinitely thankful.

Although Jenna's lawsuit had not officially settled, Randy Stevens and Allison Anders were engaged in intense negotiations. Jim and Nancy assured her that a settlement would be finalized by the time their vacation was over, and she was safe to consider the lawsuit behind her. Jenna took them at their word and relaxed.

According to the Reiners' Thanksgiving tradition, Tom, Mia, and Jenna each made a toast. Mia went first, with her tropical pineapple-orange-guava drink held high in the air. Her eyes sparkled with excitement.

"I'm thankful for my mommy and my daddy. I'm thankful to be here in the place we love most in the world. Oh yeah, and I'm thankful that I get to miss two weeks of school." Mia giggled as she clinked her glass with Tom's and Jenna's Mai Tais.

Next, it was Jenna's turn. She was in a reflective mood and knew that special moments like these needed to be cherished. This vacation was the beginning of a fresh start.

Raising her glass adorned with a paper umbrella, Jenna proclaimed, "I'm thankful for my husband, who has stood by me through such trying times. I'm thankful that I have the most beautiful, special, sweet, and sensitive daughter in the world. I'm thankful that the nightmare is over. And, I'm really thankful to be sitting by the beach in the place where my heart will always live."

"Hear! Hear!" said Tom, as they tapped their glasses together again.

"Daddy's turn!" exclaimed Mia with delight.

Tom cleared his throat and stood, making a big production of his toast. Holding his glass in the air, he said, "I'm happy to be able to spend time with the two most beautiful girls in the world. Let's make this vacation all about us and do whatever we want. No matter the cost. We all deserve it."

"I'll drink to that," Jenna said, lifting her glass to Tom's.

The next morning, Jenna woke early to the soothing sound of waves gently rolling on to the shoreline. Quietly, she crept out to the lanai and looked out at the deserted beach. She was so grateful for the trip. Hawaii was part of her soul. It gave her peace and tranquility. A salty ocean breeze swept over her body. The sun was just coming up, casting a dim light along the coastline.

Mesmerized by the beauty of the ocean, Jenna did not hear Tom as he snuck up behind her and wrapped his arms around her waist. Happily surprised, Jenna quickly turned around and kissed her husband. Her mouth relaxed as Tom's tongue pirouetted around her own. The sensuality caused butterflies in Jenna's stomach.

"What about our daughter?" she asked, breathless.

Tom tiptoed away, returning moments later with a boyish grin. "Fast asleep and sawing logs."

Jenna turned back to the ocean, with Tom standing behind her. Tom pressed his erection into Jenna's back, and she giggled like a young girl.

"Aloha to you, too," Jenna whispered with hot breath.

Jenna felt more playful, carefree, and young than she had in months. Tom covertly lifted her robe, pulled down her panties, and made love to her right there on the lanai. Life for the Reiners was already improving.

FORTY-NINE

Katharine Harper arrived promptly at 3 p.m. for her meeting with Keith Jones. Keith's secretary had paged Katharine earlier that day to schedule the appointment. Since that time, Katharine had a sense of impending doom.

The CEO was seated behind his oversized, vintage desk when his assistant, Candace, escorted Katharine into his opulent office. She entered, and Keith stood and approached her, shaking her hand.

"Katharine, thanks for coming on such short notice. Can I have Candace get you something to drink?"

His assistant smiled politely, awaiting an answer. Katharine, wary of the situation, said flatly, "I'm fine. Thank you."

Nodding, Candace left the room, closing the door securely behind her.

Katharine sat in one of the burgundy leather chairs angled in front of Keith's desk. Keith circled behind his bureau and took his seat. For several moments, Katharine found herself locked in a disconcerting gaze with Keith Jones. His eyes were intense, his focus sharp. The CEO remained motionless.

Katharine shifted in her chair and crossed her legs. Not one to be intimidated, she confidently initiated conversation. "What can I do for you, Keith?"

Keith spun his chair around, contemplating his response. Once his revolution was complete, he asked Katharine, "How well do you know Dr. Reiner?"

Caught off guard, Katharine blurted, "Jenna?" Immediately, she regretted referring to her friend by her first name.

Keith rested his elbows on his desk and clasped his hands in front of his mouth, holding his thumbs to his lips. "Your sense of familiarity indicates that the two of you are more than just acquaintances. Would that assumption be correct?"

Katharine stiffened. "I'm on friendly terms with many of the staff physicians, Dr. Reiner included."

Keith leaned toward Katharine. From her seat, she could see the pores in his skin and the slight stubble on his chin.

"Katharine, as you are well aware, this hepatitis debacle has cost St. Augustine dearly."

"I'm fully aware," Katharine responded, her expression blank. Inwardly, Katharine's pulse quickened, fearing where her long-time friend fit into Keith Jones' agenda.

Keith lowered his eyebrows. "As you know, every doctor involved in litigation to this point has surrendered without incident. The lawsuits have been settled discreetly, and the physicians have been allowed to continue unhindered in their careers."

Eager to get to the point, Katharine demanded, "And?"

Keith's grin was so sinister, it caused Katharine to catch her breath. She did her best to conceal her discomfort.

"There seems to be a little problem with Dr. Reiner." Keith searched Katharine's face for any hint of knowledge as to Jenna's position.

"What kind of problem?" Katharine uncrossed her legs and clutched the armrests of her chair.

Keith stood and paced behind his desk. After several passes, he stopped and glared at Katharine Harper.

"Jenna Reiner's in the midst of settlement negotiations, which is a smart move on her part. The problem is, the attorney from her malpractice carrier, a Mr. Randy Stevens, and the plaintiff's attorney don't see eye-to-eye on a reasonable settlement amount. I get the impression that Randy Stevens has taken a special interest in Dr. Reiner. In other cases, Mr. Stevens has readily compromised. With Jenna Reiner, however, he seems to have a personal mission to save her honor."

Katharine intuitively surmised where the conversation was headed, but chose to play the fool. "What does this have to do with me?"

Keith walked around his desk and sat next to Katharine. He reached out and grabbed the armrest of her chair. Katharine glanced down. Keith's skin nearly touched her arm, and she felt the heat of his flesh radiate from his hands. Ironically, the contrast in their skin color, dark black against pasty white, exemplified the stark contrast in their motivations and sense of honor.

The CEO spoke in a low, soft tone. Katharine was forced to move closer to him in order to make out his words.

"I know you and Jenna Reiner are personal friends. I saw you two last summer, in the courtyard. Jenna Reiner was crying. The two of you hugged. You know her. What will break her?"

Shaking her head in disbelief, Katharine said, "You're mistaken. We are nothing more than colleagues. I'm afraid I can't answer your question."

Keith walked over to a concealed liquor cabinet and poured himself a glass of scotch. With his back to Katharine, he asked, "Can I get you some?"

Katharine's mouth went dry. "No. Thank you," she replied coldly.

Taking a drink, Keith turned around and directed his power and ruthlessness at Katharine. "You know, Katharine, I have great admiration for you. You are an incredibly gifted physician. Additionally, you have overcome the burden of being a woman in a male-dominated profession and have very successfully climbed your way to the top."

He let his words sink in.

"Your re-appointment as Medical Staff President occurs in less than six months. I've reviewed your file. It's impeccable. It would be such a travesty after all those years of scratching your way to the top, to end up all for none. So, let me ask you again, what will break Dr. Reiner?"

Katharine's gut turned, her mouth salivated, and she was certain she might vomit at any moment. Closing her eyes, Katharine thought about Jenna. Jenna, the one who had always been there to encourage her. Jenna, the one who had never once failed her. Then Katharine thought about her own family. She was the martyr – the only one of her six siblings who had escaped the confines of poverty to rise to the top. Katharine thought of her mother, sacrificing herself as she tirelessly worked two jobs and single-handedly raised her children. Now that her mother had passed, that responsibility fell onto Katharine's shoulders. She could not let her mother down.

Slowly, Katharine opened her eyes and bore into the gaze of Keith Jones.

In barely more than a whisper, Katharine replied, "The press. She's terrified of the press."

A smile swept across Keith's face. Not waiting to be excused, Katharine stormed out of his office, slamming the door behind her.

Silently, Katharine prayed for forgiveness.

FIFTY

The Reiners were enjoying their second week of paradise. Jenna started to relax and become her old self again. Sprawled out under a beach umbrella, soaking up the tropical sun, Jenna heard the muffled sounds of her phone ringing from inside a beach bag. Digging through the bottles of sunblock and beach toys, she found the phone by the third ring. Caller ID displayed "Mountain Anesthesia Consultants." Jenna wondered what would compel her office to intrude on her vacation.

Curtly, she answered, "Hello?"

"Jenna? This is Rob Wilson. I know you're on vacation, and I'm sorry to bother you."

Rob's voice sounded off. Maybe it was the connection, but Jenna sensed danger.

Jenna stood, walking away from the crashing waves and the laughter of the beach crowd. "What's up?"

"I hate to be the one to tell you this."

Suddenly oblivious to her surroundings, Jenna could no longer hear the ocean or feel the warm, moist air upon her skin. Her entire world filtered down to what Rob was about to disclose.

"Tell me what?"

Rob felt sorry for Jenna. Knowing how hard this lawsuit had been on her, it was anguishing to be the bearer of bad news. He hesitated for a second and then forced himself to speak.

"We got a call this morning from a reporter, Kyle Lewis, from the Tribune. He's demanding a statement from you. Jenna, you need to call your attorneys. Immediately."

Jenna's world spun as she stood alone in the sand with her phone to her ear. A child ran by and scattered sand in her direction, bringing her back into reality.

"Jenna, I'm so sorry."

"Me too," Jenna said as she hung up the phone.

Tom and Mia approached her, and their smiles instantly faded. Jenna's entire body was trembling. Mia was frightened. Instinctively, Mia threw her arms around Jenna and asked, "Mommy, what's wrong?"

Looking at her family, Jenna said callously, "Well, it looks like I made the news!"

Jenna watched Tom's face as he registered the words. "I need to call Jim and Nancy."

Jenna walked away from the crowded beach and dialed her lawyer. Nancy answered on the second ring.

"Nancy, what the hell is going on?"

"I'm honestly not sure. Kyle Lewis from the Tribune has called both Jim and me repeatedly this morning. We are not responding. You should not respond either, understood?"

"You know I'm smarter than that. Why would the press bite on this now? You said this would all be over!"

Nancy reminded herself to keep her calm, for Jenna's sake. "What is going on is that we are miles apart on dollar amounts for settlement. Anders is demanding eight hundred thousand dollars. That's higher than any other demand she's made so far. Randy Stevens started his negotiations at fifty thousand. He's playing hardball, and he's not willing to budge.

"Obviously, Anders has members of the press in her back pocket. She can't get Randy to budge, but she knows if she puts pressure on you through public humiliation, you can pressure him to settle."

"Why didn't you tell me the negotiations weren't going well? You made it sound like this was a done deal." Jenna tried to keep her voice down, but she was furious.

Nancy responded with remorse, "At first, we truly believed that both sides would reach a compromise. We didn't foresee any problems, and we wanted you to be able to go away and not have to worry about this. Now both sides have clearly drawn a line in the sand, and Allison Anders just increased the stakes."

Jenna sighed heavily into the phone, "When is this story supposed to print?"

"The reporter wanted us to comment by Wednesday, so I'm assuming it will print on Thursday or Friday."

Seized by bitterness, there was nothing more for Jenna to say. Even the distance of the Pacific Ocean could not hinder Allison Anders from taking yet another part of Jenna's life away from her.

The only thing Jenna could be thankful for was that Mia would be three thousand miles away from home when the story broke.

FIFTY-ONE

Jenna, Tom, and Mia arrived home early Saturday morning. Nauseated and exhausted from the red-eye flight, Jenna and Mia stumbled up to Mia's bedroom, and Jenna tucked her in for a nap. Once Mia fell asleep, Jenna rushed down to the computer and checked for the story in the Tribune. Nancy thought it would have been published a couple days prior, but so far nothing had materialized. Unable to deal with her mounting anxiety, Jenna called Nancy.

"What do you think is going on? Do you think they're waiting for Sunday?" Jenna asked, panicked.

Nancy replied, "I have no way to know for sure. It's highly probable that the Tribune's editor rejected the story. It's clearly not newsworthy. There have been no recent developments, and the trial is two months away. We've seen stuff like this before. Reporters contact us for comment, and the story never transpires. This is beginning to have that sort of feel.

"Besides, there are bigger stories to put in the Sunday paper. I know this is the last thing you want to hear, but all we can do is sit back and wait until tomorrow."

For the remainder of the day, Jenna moved like a zombie. Attempting to suppress the thoughts of seeing her name in the Sunday paper, Jenna tried to keep herself occupied. She put away the luggage, did the laundry, walked the dog, and watched a movie with Mia. Still, Jenna remained plagued by her fear of the unknown.

Sunday morning, Jenna woke before sunrise and proceeded into her home office to check the Tribune's website. Her hands trembled as she manipulated the mouse, fearing that around the next virtual corner, her name would appear. To Jenna's relief and astonishment, however, there was nothing. She hoped Nancy was right, and the story would never be printed. Relieved, she slipped back into bed with Tom, but never fell back to sleep.

Monday morning at five o'clock, Jenna's alarm clock blared, shaking her from a fitful sleep. She reached over, shut it off, and reluctantly got out of bed. Jenna shuffled through the dark into the office. She felt less anxious after Sunday passed without incident, but was compelled to check nonetheless.

Jenna clicked the mouse, and the Tribune's home page displayed on the computer screen. She could hear her pulse bounding through her temples as she read the top headline, "Anesthesiologist Disregards Practice Guidelines in Hepatitis C Outbreak."

"No, no, no!" Jenna nearly jumped out of her skin. She could barely manipulate the mouse, but she forced herself to read the text.

The article began by recapping Hillary Martin's crimes. The next four paragraphs provided a heart-wrenching account of Michelle Hollings and how her life had been destroyed.

Then came the assault on Jenna.

"Prominent doctors argue they don't have a duty to lock up narcotics, despite the 2010 operating room theft and fraud by Hillary Martin. Martin's diversion of Fentanyl resulted in the infection of over thirty patients with hepatitis C.

"Dr. Phillip Ramano, a local anesthesiologist, will testify that doctors don't have a duty to lock up drugs like Fentanyl. He will serve as an expert witness in the January trial of Dr. Jenna Reiner.

"Dr. Reiner also maintains that she did not have that responsibility. According to court documents, Dr. Reiner considers drug diversions part of 'urban legend.' Dr. Reiner is expected to testify that her practice was reasonable and met the applicable standard of care. In her deposition, Dr. Reiner contends that anesthesiologists do not have a duty to prevent diversion of controlled substances within the OR."

Jenna could hardly focus on the words through her tears.

"The defense strategy and expert testimony by Dr. Ramano contradicts federal guidelines and practices of other anesthesiologists.

"Reiner's attorneys present an alternative theory for how patients were infected with hepatitis C. A defense expert will testify the infections could have come from contaminated saline that Hillary Martin used to refill stolen syringes. The defense will argue that if the infection came from the saline, and not from the Fentanyl syringe used by Dr. Reiner, that would be an intervening cause that would remove blame from the doctor."

The article concluded with a message aimed directly at Jenna.

"There is still the potential for the case to be settled before trial, but Michelle Hollings is ready to see these issues aired again in public.

"'More people need to know what's going on in their hospitals. It's stupid for the anesthesiologists to say they have no fault whatsoever, when they were the ones in control of all of it,' said Hollings, whose hepatitis C counts have been tamped down by treatments, but will always have a chance of recurring."

Jenna could not believe the extent of mischaracterization and slander. The article served as the ultimate checkmate. For Jenna, the threat had been acknowledged, and the message had been received.

FIFTY-TWO

Jenna stumbled past Tom on her way to the bathroom. Standing in front of the mirror, she tried to put in her contact lenses. Lifting the lens to her eye, her hand shook so wildly that she was forced to give up. Tom walked in behind his wife, unaware of what he was about to encounter.

"Good morning," Tom said, smiling sleepily. He rubbed the growth on his chin and snuggled up behind Jenna, kissing her neck. Jenna remained still, paralyzed. Once Tom caught Jenna's reflection in the mirror, his heart sank. "What happened?"

Jenna attempted to answer, but could not. Her emotional state went beyond tears, grief, and agony. She was only able to mutter, "Article. Tribune. *So bad.*"

Tom darted off to the office and returned ten minutes later, looking nearly as ghastly as Jenna. However, whereas Jenna was broken and devastated, Tom was consumed with fury.

Forgetting about their sleeping daughter, Tom started ranting. "That article is complete bullshit! It's so totally biased, I'm shocked they can get away with publishing it. I'll bet Anders wrote it herself and then passed it over to the reporter. Everything in it was taken out of context and manipulated to make you look like the devil. How can they print such crap?"

Jenna was oblivious to her husband. Her mind raced in a million directions. *She had cases scheduled to start in ninety minutes. There was no way she could go to work. She could not let Mia see her like this. She wanted to die.*

"I have to call Katharine Harper."

Sitting alone on the stairs in the dim morning light, Jenna dialed Katharine's cell phone. It was 6:15, and Katharine would certainly be awake.

"Hello," Katharine Harper answered, sounding sluggish.

Jenna tried to speak, but only sobs emerged from her mouth.

Unable to identify the voice from the unintelligible grunts on the other line, Katharine held the phone away from her ear and read Jenna's name from caller ID. Jenna sounded so distraught, Katharine feared something catastrophic had happened to Tom or Mia.

"Jenna? What's wrong?"

Jenna inhaled and spilled the horrid details. "Katharine, the Tribune ran an article on me today. It's bad. Really bad."

Katharine's throat tightened.

"What am I going to do?" Jenna wailed. "What if a patient sees the article and recognizes my name? What if my partners shun me? What if the surgeons don't want to work with me?"

Ravaged by guilt, Katharine attempted to console her friend.

"Listen here, you're one of the best damn anesthesiologists around. I don't give a rat's behind about some article in the paper."

"But Katharine, now everyone will know."

"Know what? That a drug addict preyed upon you? That you are one of many other doctors in the same boat? That some reporter is corrupt?"

Jenna was breathing in ragged gasps. "They'll think I'm worthless, stupid, and incompetent. They'll think I destroyed my patient's life."

Pools of saliva flooded Jenna's mouth. She could not swallow quickly enough to keep it down.

"I've got to go."

"Wait . . ." Katharine called out as Jenna hung up. Sitting alone in her kitchen, listening to the dial tone, Katharine said, "My God. What did I do?"

****

Jenna made it to the bathroom just in time to lift the toilet seat and wretch. She spit the taste of bile into the toilet and wiped her mouth with a tissue. Her legs wobbled as she stood to flush the toilet. Staggering into her closet, she did her best to dress herself.

"Are you going to be okay?" asked Tom. He sat on the edge of the bathtub, watching Jenna battle to pull a shirt over her head.

She responded honestly, "No, I'm not."

Jenna glanced at her reflection in the mirror. Her eyes were bloodshot and hollow, like her soul had been scooped out of her body, leaving her with nothing.

Before Jenna left for work, she sent emails to her attorneys. The correspondence was blunt. "We need to meet TODAY. I will head over when done with cases. DO **NOT** PROCEED WITH ANY FURTHER SETTLEMENT NEGOTIATIONS UNTIL WE TALK!"

"Please take care of Mia," she said to Tom as she left the house. Refusing to let her daughter see her in such a state, Jenna forfeited their daily ritual of kissing goodbye.

Miraculously, Jenna arrived at the hospital without crashing her vehicle. She had no memory of the drive. In the parking garage, she circled through several levels until she reached the top. It was deserted. Jenna shut off the engine and stared vacantly out the window at the early morning sky. Clutching her stomach, her eyes overflowed and her shoulders heaved as misery seeped from Jenna's pores.

Minutes later, another car pulled up and parked near Jenna. Wiping her face, she collected her things and walked to the elevator.

Inside the hospital, Jenna crossed the window-encased bridge on her way to the operating rooms with her head hung low. Passing a set of chairs and a table along the wall, Jenna spotted a pile of copies of the Tribune. Her heart stopped. The headline appeared in the boldest font of any other text on the cover, "Doc Defies Rules Regarding Narcotics."

To Jenna, this was clearly as malicious as it could get.

Grabbing a copy of the paper, she ran into the women's locker room. Fortunately, it was empty. Jenna picked up the phone, bracing one hand in the other in order to steady her fingers, and dialed Tom. He answered immediately. Jenna's voice was barely more than a whisper, broken by gulps for air.

"It's on the front page!"

"What?"

"It's on the fucking front page of the Tribune. Top story. Bold print."

"Oh God, Jenna! I'm so sorry. Are you going to make it through the day?"

Jenna heard the locker room door creak open.

"I have to. Someone's coming. I've gotta go."

Jenna swiftly hid the newspaper in her bag and stepped into a bathroom stall. Sitting on the toilet, she buried her head in her hands hoping to muffle the sound of her sobs. Eventually, her tears ran dry, and Jenna left to prepare for her first case.

To Jenna's relief, she arrived at her operating room to find it unoccupied. She entered and moved glumly to the head of the bed. Jenna stared at the anesthesia machine as if it were a foreign object. A few minutes later, Jody, the circulating nurse, walked in, her arms loaded with supplies. Jenna glanced up and feebly attempted a friendly smile.

"Hey, Dr. R. What's shaking?" Jody asked.

Jenna was unable to speak. Tears stung her eyes as she tossed the newspaper toward the nurse.

Jody grasped the paper and read the first portion of the article. Shaking her head in disgust, she dropped the paper on the operating room table and walked over to Jenna.

Putting her arm around Jenna's shoulder, Jody asked, "Do you think you should be here?"

Jenna answered bitterly, "No, I don't. But we are short-staffed today, and there's nobody to cover for me."

Rubbing Jenna's arm, Jody said, "Well, somehow we'll get you through this. I'll have your back, all day. If you want to talk, we can talk. If you want me to keep the conversation away from you, I'll do that, too."

"Thank you," said Jenna, grateful for the kindness. "I don't want anybody to talk to me. If you could keep the conversation on the other side of the drape, that would be great."

"You got it."

Before Jenna could face her first patient, she had one more call to make. She phoned her office manager, Julia.

Upon hearing Jenna's voice, Julia said, "Dr. Reiner, I'm so sorry. Is there anything I can do?"

Jenna gulped, amazed at how fast the news of her tragedy had spread.

"Thanks. Look, I know it's our busy time of year, but I need the rest of the week off. I shouldn't even be here today. Can you make that happen?"

"Consider it done."

FIFTY-THREE

Jenna walked into the preoperative area to meet her first patient. Her colleagues immediately noticed her presence and conversations ceased. In the silence, Jenna felt the enormity of their collective judgment. Marching directly into her first patient's room, Jenna pulled the door closed behind her. For a moment, it dawned on her how disheveled she must look. Her eyelids were swollen, her nose red, and her hair untamed. The patient, consumed by her own anxiety, did not appear to notice.

Mid-morning, between cases, Katharine Harper walked into Jenna's operating room. Jenna fiddled with her equipment, attempting to look busy. Katharine knew better. Jenna was hiding out.

"I just read the article," Katharine said sadly.

Jenna unleashed. "Now do you see why I am so upset? It's a bunch of lies, but the people who read the paper don't know that. The article makes me look like some callous, ignorant, reckless bitch! I've read the comments posted online. People I have never met are calling me lazy, heartless, and negligent. They think I'm a criminal, for Christ's sake!"

It crushed Katharine to witness the pain she had brought upon her friend, but Jenna's anger gave Katharine hope.

Grabbing Jenna by the arm, Katharine commanded, "You have to fight this! You cannot settle! You'd never be able to live with yourself. Do you hear what I'm saying?"

Jenna nodded. "I came to the same conclusion the moment I read the article."

Katharine was thankful that Keith Jones' plan had backfired. Instead of breaking Jenna, the media coverage had given her new strength and determination.

Jenna pulled the crumpled newspaper out of her bag and waved it at her friend. "This article was fully intended to pressure me. Well, screw them, because their ruthless tactic failed. I did want to settle. I wanted this to go away. My biggest fear was this story making the press. Now it has. There's nothing more they can do to hurt me. There's no way I'm backing down now."

Katharine started to respond, but stopped when Jody wheeled the next patient into the operating room. Jenna methodically administered anesthesia, and Katharine slipped out of the room. Once the patient was unconscious and the surgical drapes were up, Jenna hid behind them and wept. Out of respect, no one in the operating room acknowledged Jenna's sniffles or tried to engage her in conversation.

By early afternoon, Jenna managed to finish her cases. On her drive to meet with Jim and Nancy, her pager went off.

She moaned, "Please, leave me alone." Unclipping the pager from her waist, Jenna read the message. It was Julia's number from her office. Reluctantly, Jenna called her back. As soon as Jenna identified herself, Julia said, "Hello, Dr. Reiner. Dr. Wilson wants to talk to you. He's sitting right here."

Before Jenna could assemble her thoughts, Rob Wilson was on the phone. "Hi, Jenna. I just wanted to see how you were doing?"

"Not Good." Jenna could barely speak. Once again, she lost her composure. Her emotional instability was exhausting.

Rob continued, "I'm so sorry about the article. I just wanted to call and check on you. I also wanted to make sure you know the corporation and the anesthesia department stand behind you. We all recognize that the article is full of fabrications and distortions, and no one thinks differently of you. Okay?"

"Okay." Regardless of what she said to Rob, Jenna remained unconvinced.

"Where are you now?" Rob asked. "Are you still at the hospital?"

Jenna stared blindly out the windshield. "I'm headed to my attorneys' office."

"Could you call me when you're done?"

Normally, Jenna would obediently accommodate her superior's request, but this one made no sense to her. There was a point where Jenna had nothing else to give, and she had reached it.

"Rob, I really appreciate your call and your kind words. If your reason for calling was to offer me your sympathy, I am extremely grateful. If there's another reason, I'd rather deal with it right now."

Rob, stunned by Jenna's uncharacteristic boldness, paused for a moment.

"Listen Jenna, I'm sorry to ask this of you, but we really need you to work tomorrow. We are overbooked, and we are going to have to give cases away if we can't get them covered. I really hate to ask this of you, but could you do two short orthopedics' cases tomorrow morning? That's all we need."

Jenna grunted, "Fine," and hung up. She knew this was a command, disguised as a request. All she wanted was to hide from the world, but so far, the world would not allow it.

FIFTY-FOUR

Jenna sat across from her lawyers. Her voice sounded like shattering crystals and reflected her state of mind.

"*Why?* Why would this come out now? The very day I go back to work after vacation?"

Jim and Nancy appeared nearly as shaken and surprised as their client. The article in the Tribune was one of the most vicious attacks on a physician either of them had witnessed during their careers.

Nancy spoke, "It's an obvious pressure tactic. I'm not sure how this story made it past the editors of the Tribune, but it did. It's a blatant one-sided attack against you.

"And the fact that they waited to publish it until you got back into town seems an unlikely coincidence. Anders must have obtained your vacation itinerary. I'm sure she wanted to make sure you were around so the article would have maximum impact."

Jenna snapped back, "Well, can I sue the Tribune? They took words from my deposition and printed them out of context. Isn't that slander?"

Nancy shook her head. "I spent the entire morning analyzing this article. Every single word they printed can be supported either by your deposition or other public records. Newspapers know the game. They are very cognizant of exactly how far they can push the boundaries. Unfortunately, there's nothing in the article that would support a lawsuit."

"So yet again, I'm the one who gets screwed," Jenna fired back.

Jim said sadly, "I can appreciate that you feel that way."

Jenna had more clarity than she had all day. For the moment, she had no urge to cry. Her hands remained shaky, but she made no attempt to hide her tremor from her attorneys. After a day like this, she felt entitled to look, act, and say anything she wanted.

Confidently, Jenna declared, "There will be no settlement. I want to revoke my consent to settle, effective immediately. We're going all the way."

Jim fixated on Jenna. "Are you absolutely sure?"

Jenna stared back. "Absolutely. Anders' little game was unsuccessful. I'm sure she intended to disgrace me, which she did. She also aimed to terrorize me and weaken me to the point that I'd do anything she or Michelle Hollings wanted. That's where she misjudged me. I've spent my entire life backing down and being belittled by people like her. Not this time! If I don't do this for me, then I'll do it for my daughter. How can I expect Mia to respect me and to look to me as her role model, if I back down to this? All I want to know is, where do we go from here?"

Jim said, "I know today's been rough for you. This isn't a decision you have to make right now. I have to be honest. A month ago, you came in here and completely broke down. Now you're saying you're ready to go to trial again? I want to make sure you think things through. It's going to get ugly, and we have to know that you have the strength to persevere."

Miffed by Jim's words, Jenna felt her lawyers did not completely trust her. She knew it was time to act like an adult. Whether she truly felt strong and self-confident was irrelevant. She needed to portray that image to Jim and Nancy.

Jenna said defiantly, "I will not let you down. I give you my word. I also will not settle. So, again, I'm asking, where do we go from here?"

Her determination eased Jim's doubts slightly, but he was still troubled by her emotional state.

Jim said, "First of all, we recommend that you obtain personal counsel."

"Personal counsel? What's that?"

"It's an attorney you hire to protect *you*. It's someone whose sole interest is in your well being."

"What do you mean, someone who is looking out for my best interests? Isn't that what *you* guys do?"

Jim replied, "We do look out for your best interests, as far as the case is concerned. But your malpractice carrier employs us. Ultimately, we answer to Randy Stevens. There may be things that come up where our hands are tied on what advice we can give you because of our obligation to Randy. That's when it's in your best interest to have your own private attorney. When we hit bumps along the road where we think you should consult your personal counsel, we'll advise you of such. This is all to protect you."

Jenna focused on maintaining her composure.

"Is this something that's covered by my malpractice policy?"

"Unfortunately, no. But the people we would recommend are reasonably priced. At the most, it should cost a couple thousand dollars."

"Okay. That's fine. I'll do whatever it takes. How soon do I need to do this?"

Jim replied without hesitation, "Immediately. We'll give you a short list of names. The one I'd recommend most highly is Walter Morey. We've referred people to him before. He's been very accessible, helpful, and reasonable."

"Well, let's go with him. I trust your recommendation."

Nancy stood and said, "I'll go get his contact info."

As Nancy walked out, Jim said, "I'll contact him and let him know to expect your call tomorrow. If he's unavailable, I'll get in touch with you tonight and give you another name."

Nancy returned with Walter Morey's contact information written neatly on a sheet of yellow legal paper.

Jenna said, "I'll get in touch with him tomorrow. What else do we need to do? Shouldn't I sign something that officially revokes my consent for settlement?"

Jim answered, "For right now, Jenna, go home. Get some sleep. Talk this over with your husband, and call Walter. We will not proceed with any further settlement negotiations for now. I want you to be sure about your decision. It's going to take a toll on you and your family. Think about that. Let's meet later this week after you've had a few days to digest everything. Are you free on Thursday or Friday?"

"I took the rest of the week off . . . with the exception of tomorrow morning." The burden of being forced to work the next day only increased Jenna's overall resentment.

"Then call us after you get in touch with Walter. For what it's worth, Nancy and I are so sorry this happened. It's not fair."

"No," said Jenna, "it's not."

FIFTY-FIVE

The early winter sky had grown dark by the time Jenna made it home. She opened the door and overheard Mia and Tom chatting in the kitchen. Both her husband and daughter stopped talking when she entered the room.

Jenna looked raw, destroyed, and empty. Mia ran over to her mother. Tom approached them and cocooned his wife and child. Jenna held on to each of them tightly, as if they were her life preservers in a stormy sea. For close to a minute, no one made a sound. Finally, Mia, her eyes wet with sorrow, said, "Mommy, I'm so sorry."

Choking on her own tears, Jenna whispered, "Me too, baby."

Tom sent Mia upstairs on a mission that would grant him a few uninterrupted minutes with Jenna. As soon as Mia was out of earshot, Jenna grabbed a bottle of beer from the refrigerator, took a large swig, and filled Tom in on her day. By the time the Reiners sat down for dinner, Jenna was well into her second beer. Oddly, she felt no calming effects from the alcohol – her hands continued to shake violently, her nerves were rattled, and her heart hammered in her chest.

During dinner, Jenna barely ate anything. She sat motionless at the table while Tom tried to keep a normal conversation going with Mia.

Eventually, she said, "I'm going to go lay down for a while."

Grabbing another beer along the way, she lay down on the couch, alone in the unlit family room. She was consumed by thoughts of the article, her attorneys, and talk of personal counsel.

The ringing of the telephone caught her attention. Jenna heard Tom answer it from within the kitchen. She was instantly overcome with anxiety. What if it was a reporter? Jenna and Tom had not discussed screening calls, and she was not sure it would occur to him.

"She's busy right now. Could she call you back?" Tom's words were followed by a long pause as he listened to the person on the other end.

Whatever the unknown caller said to Tom, it must have been convincing because Jenna heard him say, "Uhm, okay. Just a minute."

Tom covered the receiver with his hand. Jenna looked up at him, shaking her head no.

"It's Katharine. She *really* wants to talk to you. She says she knows what you're going through. Even if you don't want to talk to her, she at the very least wants to hear your voice to make sure you're okay. She sounds really concerned. Maybe you should take her call."

The last thing Jenna wanted was to speak with anybody, but it did not sound as if Katharine would take "no" for an answer. Jenna grabbed her beer and sat at one of the barstools in the kitchen. Tom took Mia into the other room, giving Jenna some privacy.

"Hi, Katharine."

The alcohol was finally kicking in. To her own ears, Jenna's speech sounded slurred, but she did not care. After what the Tribune had printed for the world to see, having the Medical Staff President catch her drunk seemed like a non-issue to Jenna.

"Jenna, are you okay? I've been thinking about you all day."

"At this point, I'm just numb. This has been, undeniably, one of the worst days of my life."

Katharine could hear the crack of a bottle being opened on Jenna's end. Without judgment, she asked, "What are you doing to cope with all this?"

"So far, I've been trying real hard to get drunk. The problem is, I keep drinking, and I don't feel anything. I was hoping I'd pass out by now, but it's not working."

Katharine gathered by Jenna's garbled speech that the alcohol was working better than her friend thought.

"Okay, you've got to listen to me. I've been sued before. First piece of advice, stop drinking. It will only cloud your judgment and may even compromise your performance at work. Second thing, if you don't have a primary care doctor, get one now. I have a female internist I've been seeing for years. If you want, I'll call her tomorrow and get you in right away. You need to get a basic physical exam, have your labs checked, and get some meds to help you sleep. The next couple of months are going to put a huge strain on your health. You need someone qualified to help you through it." She paused for a moment to allow Jenna to absorb her advice.

Cautiously, Katharine asked, "Have you thought about seeing someone?"

"You mean like a therapist?" asked Jenna.

Katharine sensed Jenna's reluctance.

"Yes, Jenna, a therapist. Seeing one doesn't mean you're crazy. The amount of stress you're under is something very few people face in their life. I'm not a psychiatrist, but to me you sound clinically depressed. I have this guy that I have seen off and on for years. He's used to working with doctors, and he isn't some lay-on-my-couch, psychobabble freak. His approach is very clinical."

"I'll think about it," Jenna said, hoping to lay the subject to rest.

Katharine, tenacious as always, refused to let Jenna off the hook. "Let me ask you a few things. Have you been sleeping well?"

"No."

"How about your appetite? Have you lost weight?"

"Just a few pounds."

"How about sex? Not to intrude."

Katharine had hit a nerve. Jenna could handle the effects of stress on herself, but she detested the impact it had on her family.

"I have absolutely no interest. None. I know it bothers Tom."

Jenna took another long drink. Answering Katharine's questions made it apparent that she needed help.

"Okay," Jenna relented, "I get your point. I'll call the guy tomorrow, right after I try not to kill my two patients."

"You're working tomorrow?" asked Katharine, astonished.

Sourly, Jenna replied, "Not by choice. Rob Wilson called to tell me how sorry he was and, by the way, there are still cases to do. Too bad my life is going up in flames, but the corporation needs to make money."

Jenna noticed her hands were still trembling, and she started to cry into the phone.

"Katharine, I can't stop shaking. Ever since this morning, my hands have been unsteady. It's like I can't turn it off. Has that ever happened to you?"

"Yeah," Katharine replied honestly. "It's not going away on its own. Your adrenaline is sky high. Go see my shrink. Get some anti-anxiety medication. You're going to need it."

Exhausted, Jenna slurred into the phone, "Katharine, I'm gonna go now."

Then she hung up the phone, lay down on the couch, and passed out.

FIFTY-SIX

The next morning, Jenna managed to crawl out of bed, in spite of her grief and pounding headache. She stumbled into the bathroom, brushed her teeth, combed her hair, and threw on a pair of scrubs. There would be no makeup today, no shower. Her only goal was to finish her two short cases uneventfully and then begin preparing for war.

Jenna was back home before 10 a.m., and the first thing she did was to call Walter Morey. His secretary answered. Jenna identified herself and was immediately patched through.

"Hello, Dr. Reiner. This is Walter Morey, but I insist that you call me Walt."

Jenna had not planned what she was going to say to the attorney. In fact, Jenna expected several hours, if not days, of phone tag before they actually spoke. The fact that Walter Morey took her first call threw Jenna off guard.

"I'll call you Walt, but only if you call me Jenna. Jim Taylor and Nancy Guilding referred me to you. I'm being sued and . . ."

Jenna choked. Hearing the words come out of her mouth confirmed that her life was in shambles.

Walter was supportive and soothing. "Yes, Jim called me last night and filled me in. Sounds like the Tribune had a heyday with you. I'm really sorry about that."

Jenna tried to pull herself together, but she could not conceal the sound of her whimpers. She decided to ignore it and hoped that Walt would, too.

"Thanks. So I guess I need personal counsel. Can you help me?"

"Jim's an old friend and a wonderful attorney. He and I go way back. When he called me last night, he told me all about your case. He said you're a fine lady and, coming from Jim, that's good enough for me. How soon can we meet in person?"

Once again, Jenna was surprised. She had not anticipated that things would move so expeditiously. It caused her to worry that matters were more serious than she realized.

"I guess I could meet you anytime this week."

"How's one o'clock today?"

"Uh, fine," replied Jenna, still crying. Not trusting her memory, she jotted the time down on a piece of scratch paper.

"Just a couple of details before we meet. First of all, are you married?"

"Yes."

"Well then, since my role is largely to protect you and, by extension, your family, from any personal financial insult related to this lawsuit, I would strongly recommend that your husband accompany you today. Although you are my client, attorney-client privilege extends to your spouse, so we are free to discuss matters in his presence.

"Also, I will require a five thousand dollar retainer. Usually, my retainer fees are higher, but I don't anticipate that you will require extensive services from my end. Any portion that remains unused when this is all done and settled will be refunded to you."

Five thousand dollars was a lot of money and yet another thing to worry about. Jenna was unsure if she and Tom had that kind of cash. Unfortunately, she had no choice but to come up with the money by any means possible.

"Okay," she said, "my husband, Tom, and I will see you at one. Is there anything else?"

"Jenna, I can tell you're very upset. I know your lawyers have told you whom you can and cannot discuss this case with, which doesn't leave you many options. Have you considered seeing a psychiatrist?"

"Not really."

Katharine's lecture from the night before echoed in her head. Walter was the second person in less than twenty-four hours who thought Jenna needed professional help. Maybe they were right.

"I think it would be a good idea. In fact, as your attorney, I strongly advise that you do so as soon as possible. As I'm sure you are well aware, this is an enormous stress. I can tell from our brief conversation how distraught you are. I have some names of people who have helped other physicians in the midst of a lawsuit. Anything you say to a psychiatrist is protected conversation, which is another reason why they are a good resource."

"Actually, I have a name from a trusted colleague. I guess you're right. Maybe I do need some outside help. I'll make the call, and Tom and I will see you at one o'clock."

FIFTY SEVEN

At ten minutes to one, Jenna and Tom arrived to meet with Walter Morey. A secretary escorted them into his office, which was impressively large with a beautiful, brick fireplace and rich oak furniture. Walter's cluttered desk sat in one corner, and an oversized mahogany conference table lined with leather chairs filled the remainder of the room.

Jenna and Tom entered, and an older man of impressive height and build stood and walked over to greet them. Walt had the swagger and mannerisms of a cowboy. After shaking each of their hands, he asked the Reiners to take a seat at the table.

Once everyone was seated, Walt spoke. "Look, my time is your money, so let's not waste it. Like I told you on the phone, Jim has brought me up to speed on your case. It sounds like right now, you've told Jim and Nancy to revoke your consent for settlement. Is that correct?"

Jenna nodded and said assertively, "Yes, that's right."

Walt stared at Jenna with a perplexed expression. It made her uncomfortable.

"What I'd like to know is *why* you don't want to settle? What are your reasons?"

Tom and Walt both focused on Jenna. She felt like she had a spotlight on her, and she did not appreciate it.

"Well, I guess there are a lot of reasons. First, I don't think I did anything wrong, so why shouldn't I get the chance to defend myself? Second, why should I just roll over and die, while Allison Anders and her client get rewarded with a huge check just because they are aggressive and ruthless? Third, we have a young daughter. Mia's eleven. I want to show her that, even if I lose, at least I stood up for what I believed was right. I would expect nothing less from her in life. Lastly, my worst fear already came true yesterday. They smeared me in the press, for all to see. I know they could do that again, and probably will, but it will never hurt the same way twice. I have nothing to lose."

Walt paused for a moment. Jenna sensed he was the kind of man who chose his words very carefully.

"Your reasons are very typical, very emotional, and dangerously short-sighted."

Jenna was stunned and insulted by Walt's candor. She wondered if Tom had given the same answer, would Walt have called it "emotional," too? Even Tom stiffened at Walt's assessment.

Walt quickly added, "I know that isn't what you were expecting to hear, and I hope you don't take offense. I'm not paid to tell you what you *want* to hear, I'm paid to tell you what you *need* to hear. What you need to understand is that this lawsuit is *not* about justice. It's not about right versus wrong, good versus evil. It's about one thing and one thing only. *Money.* The sooner you come to terms with that and accept it, the better off you'll be.

"You say you want to go to trial and clear your name? Based on what I know of your case, I'd say your chances of being completely exonerated are about forty percent. That means there is a sixty percent chance that you go to trial and lose. In the meantime, you drag yourself and your family through the mud. Or, you do the smart thing and settle. Get rid of this.

"Besides, the emotional state you're in is no way to start trial preparations. You look weak and wounded, and I don't blame you. But that's not going to win over a jury. If you went to trial looking like you do right now, you would single-handedly destroy your case."

Abruptly, Walt turned his attention to Tom, "How do you feel about things?"

Tom looked at his wife and then back at Walt.

"I'm not sure. I've watched this destroy Jenna for nearly two years. It's turned her against her career. She's lost her self-confidence. I know how upset she is and how badly she wants to give it back to these sons-of-bitches. Honestly, I'm afraid it might ruin her in the process."

Walt nodded in agreement.

Looking back at Jenna, Walt said, "The decision is yours to make. I am only here to offer you legal advice. If you choose to proceed to trial, I will respect your decision and offer you counsel, as needed. My recommendation, based on what this has already done to you personally, is to settle. I know you're meeting with Jim and Nancy at the end of the week to formulate a plan. I suggest you think this over for a few days. I am more than happy to chat with you again before you meet with them."

Jenna felt the need to defend herself. Walt had pieced together an impression of her that was inaccurate.

"I'm taking your advice, by the way. I have an appointment with a psychiatrist tomorrow morning." Jenna hoped to prove to Walt that she was taking control.

Walt said, "Great. Who is it?"

"His name is Evan Kendall."

"I know him well. In fact, he's one of the names I would have offered to you. He's a good guy. I think seeing him is a very good idea."

Jenna and Tom stood to leave, but not before handing Walter Morey a check for five thousand dollars.

FIFTY-EIGHT

Jenna arrived at Dr. Kendall's office fifteen minutes early. Sitting in the parking lot, she watched her hands shake as she rested them on the leather steering wheel. For Jenna, this was truly rock bottom. It was one thing to be emotional and stressed, but it was quite another to admit that your emotions were out of control.

Worker bees poured into the office complex. Remaining in her car, Jenna watched the clock. With exactly seven minutes to spare, she exited the warmth of her Land Rover and felt the frigid winter wind whip across her body. To escape the bitter chill, she bolted toward the building.

Jenna took the elevator up to the fourth floor and walked into Dr. Kendall's office. The waiting room was dimly lit, with a couch along one wall. Classical music played softly over the speakers. On a coffee table sat a collection of magazines – *National Geographic*, *The New Yorker*, and *Newsweek*. There was another door, which apparently led to Dr. Kendall's office. On it was a sign that read, "Please be seated until the doctor arrives."

She nervously took a seat on the couch and pulled out her phone, pretending to check email.

At exactly nine o'clock, the doctor's door opened. A middle-aged man in a suit walked out, avoiding eye contact with Jenna. On his heels, Dr. Kendall emerged. A slender man, Dr. Kendall was clean-shaven with gray hair that was freshly trimmed. His pants and dress shirt were meticulously pressed. He extended a hand toward Jenna.

"Jenna Reiner? I'm Dr. Kendall. Please come in."

The office had soft lighting and was furnished with two oversized leather chairs and a leather couch.

"Please, make yourself comfortable."

Jenna started to panic. Even the insignificant decision of where to plant her body strained her coping abilities. She settled on sitting in the center of the couch. Dr. Kendall seated himself in a leather chair across from her.

"I know from what you said on the phone that you're going through a tough lawsuit, and things have reached a peak. I read the Tribune article after you called me. I can imagine that you're devastated. Why don't we start with you telling me how you're doing?"

Wetness dripped from Jenna's eyes. Dr. Kendall kindly slid a Kleenex box toward her.

"I'm doing awful. My hands won't stop shaking. My mind is racing. I can't concentrate. I cry all the time. I can't sleep, and I hardly eat. I'm angry, disgraced, and beaten down. I can barely function. Sometimes I don't even know how I get from the morning to the night. I live in constant fear of which patient is going to sue me next. Besides all that, things are great."

Dr. Kendall listened intently. Much to Jenna's relief, he did not sit there scribbling her words onto some note pad. Nor had Dr. Kendall asked Jenna to tell him about her mother or her dreams or any other kind of Freudian nonsense.

"How do you feel toward the patient that's suing you?"

It had been so long since Jenna considered Michelle Hollings as a patient and not as a plaintiff, it took her a moment to compose a response.

"At first, when I learned of the suit, I felt incredibly guilty. People around me kept telling me that I hadn't done anything wrong, but I still could not shake the image of me plunging a deadly virus into my patient's bloodstream. From the beginning, though, I knew I'd grow to hate her, and I do. She's a lowlife scavenger. It's surreal to think that she once trusted me enough to place her life in my hands. Now, she turns around and does everything she can to destroy me."

"Every emotion you're having is completely normal," said Dr. Kendall.

"Oh, so losing your mind is just part of the process?" asked Jenna, her voice filled with sarcasm and pain.

"You're not losing your mind. What you're describing is a normal response to an escalating situation over which you have little control. I've treated many physicians over the years that have been in the middle of a lawsuit. All the feelings you're describing – guilt, anxiety, dread, sadness, frustration, insomnia – these are all very typical.

"That being said, we need to get you on some medication that will help stabilize your mood, so you can focus. I also think we need to continue to meet. For now, I'd like that to be at least twice a week. You're going through an intense ordeal, and things aren't going to get any easier. Once I see how you respond to the medications, we can back off on the frequency of the visits. Does that sound like a reasonable plan?"

Jenna blew her nose and nodded. "What medications were you thinking of?"

"I think a benzodiazepine would be a good choice. Hopefully, it will help with your tremor, and it will also help you sleep."

"What about taking it at work? Won't I get in trouble?" Jenna asked with concern.

She knew benzodiazepines were a controlled substance, and the last thing she needed was to be caught with a mind-altering drug in her system.

"If I prescribe it, then it's fine. In fact, you don't even need to divulge it. If there is ever an issue, I will defend you as your physician. I'd also like to start you on an antidepressant. The combination should help you feel much better."

For the first time in days, Jenna felt hopeful. The notion of not feeling miserable was invigorating.

"How soon should I expect to feel any changes?"

"With the benzodiazepine, right away. With the antidepressant, you may feel some changes immediately, but it typically takes four to five days before patients start to notice any effects, and then about two weeks to reach maximal effects."

Jenna changed topics. "Can I ask for your advice on something?"

"Sure."

"We were in the process of settlement negotiations when the Tribune story broke. The story made me so furious, I met with my lawyers on Monday and told them I will not settle. On their advice, I had to meet with personal counsel yesterday. That attorney's advice was to settle. He said, in my emotional state, I'd ruin the case.

"I know that settling would make this go away, but in my heart of hearts, I can't do it. Every time I think of handing over a huge check to the patient and her scumbag attorney after what they did to trash me, I feel like part of my soul is dying."

"Well," said Dr. Kendall, "let me preface things by reminding you that I'm not a lawyer. That being said, I've treated many physicians facing a medical malpractice suit.

"My personal opinion is that from the onset of this story, going back to when Hillary Martin first made the news, I never thought the doctors were to blame. Hillary Martin? Absolutely. St. Augustine, as her employer? Probably. But the anesthesiologists? That seemed like a stretch. If you trust your attorneys and they have a strong defense, I would think you'd stand a reasonable chance of vindicating yourself.

"As for your personal counsel, I'm sure he's a solid attorney, but to make a judgment about your emotional fortitude one day after your being thrashed in the paper seems premature and presumptive. As your psychiatrist, I think you'll be fine by the time the trial comes around.

"With respect to settling or going to trial, I've seen many doctors face the exact same dilemma. Of the doctors who chose to settle, I would say at least ninety percent of them, when they look back on things six months or even years later, wish they hadn't. Of those that continue to trial, it's as stressful and awful as everyone says, but most are glad they did it."

Jenna thought about her doctor's advice and smiled slightly. She was starting to calm down.

"Usually, I get the lecture that this isn't about me. But it is about me. My pride is at stake. My sense of right and wrong is on the line. I can't stomach the thought of rolling over and letting them rip my beating heart from my chest. To me, that's what settling feels like."

Dr. Kendall replied, "It sounds like your decision is made. Trust yourself. When all is said and done, and the sun sets on this chapter of your life, the lawyers and all their advice will be long gone. They'll be on to the next lawsuit and the next set of victims. You'll be alone standing in front of the proverbial mirror. The only person you'll ever have to answer to is yourself."

Jenna felt the burdens of her reality lighten tremendously. Her perspective shifted to a brighter, more positive outlook. Jenna's attorneys were correct on one account – this was *her* decision to make. For most of her life, she had cowered. Jenna viewed this battle as an embodiment of every defeat she had ever endured. This time, she was determined to prevail.

FIFTY-NINE

On Friday morning, Jenna phoned Walter Morey. She felt more empowered than she ever had before.

"Walt, this is Jenna Reiner. I just wanted to inform you that I am meeting with Jim and Nancy this afternoon. I've given my decision careful consideration, and I will not settle." Her tone was unwavering.

In stark contrast to his judgmental stance only days prior, Walt told Jenna, "You certainly sound less emotional than you did earlier this week. Keep up this demeanor, and you'll be fine. I'll be there when you need me."

"I'm sure you will, Walt," Jenna said with a hint of mockery, as she hung up the phone. So far, she was unimpressed with Walter Morey. He had not yet offered Jenna anything of substance, and she could only imagine what his services had cost her so far in legal fees.

After calling Walt, Jenna drove to her attorneys' office. Once they were seated in the conference room, Jenna eyed each of them, attempting to determine their sentiments. Their faces revealed nothing except anticipation. With the aid of her chemically-induced sense of calm, Jenna assertively proclaimed, "I refuse to settle. I demand that we take this to trial. I'm certain about my decision, and I will not waiver. With that out of the way, I want to be brought up to speed on everything as it pertains to my case."

This was the side of Jenna that both attorneys knew existed, but they rarely saw. They only hoped it would last.

Giving Jenna the respect she deserved, Jim began to explain where things stood. "Our first issue is that our judge will be turning over after the first of the year. So far, Judge Krantz has been a stroke of luck. He's been fair and has ruled in our favor several times.

"The new judge, Judge Wilson, is more of an unknown. Judge Wilson has a reputation of being objective and honest, but he's also a relatively new judge on the bench. That means he may be less likely to make risky rulings, even if they are the right thing to do. If that happens, it increases the likelihood that Allison Anders and Lyle Silverstein would have free reign in the courtroom. All we can do is hope for the best."

"Great," said Jenna, with blatant pessimism.

Hesitantly, Nancy said, "I got a call from Anders yesterday."

"Oh yeah?" Jenna said, with the sourness of hatred rising in her throat.

"She offered to settle for five hundred thousand dollars. It was what we call a 'drop-dead' settlement demand. Basically, we had until 5 p.m. to respond, or the offer would be revoked. We called Randy Stevens, and he said to tell them to take a hike. I knew you'd say the same, so I didn't bother you with it."

"You're right about that. Do you think this means anything?"

Nancy replied, "It could mean a number of things. Just as much as going to trial is a gamble for us, it's also a gamble for them. Anders may not be quite as certain about the case as she would like us to think. Plus, we are approaching the most costly phase of trial preparation. The upcoming expenses will eat away at their profits if they win or cost them dearly if they don't. It could also mean that Michelle Hollings doesn't want to wait for her money. Maybe she isn't willing to risk a loss. It's hard to say, but any way you slice it, it shows some form of desperation."

Jenna reveled in the thought of Allison getting nervous.

"So what happened when you didn't respond? Do you think they realize settlement-negotiation days are over?"

"The fact that we didn't validate their offer with a response or even an acknowledgement sent a very clear message. Which brings me to this morning. Anders called and wanted to know if you had retained personal counsel. If so, she wanted to know who you're using."

In spite of her medications, Jenna started fuming. Her face looked like thunder.

"Anders has no right to that information. What did you tell her?"

"I told her that whether you had or had not retained personal counsel fell under attorney-client privilege. She reminded me that this case may be subject to punitive damages, and that any defense lawyer with a functioning neuron would be a fool not to advise their client to seek personal counsel at this point. She's demanding to know who you're using."

"No way!" shouted Jenna, pounding her fist on the table. "What purpose could she possibly have for wanting to know that, other than to somehow hurt me? At the very least, she could tie Walt up in hours of conversation that ends up costing me a bundle. Does he know about this?"

"Yes, I spoke with him just before you arrived. He sees no problem with them chatting. However, it's your decision. He's retained by you, so you call the shots."

Jenna tried to calm down. "How could he possibly see no reason not to question Anders' motives? She's a snake."

"He sees things from a different perspective. He has a professional relationship with Anders and Silverstein. Not friendly, but not adversarial. Their relationship is based upon mutual respect. He thinks he may be able to fish around and see if he can get Anders to slip up. Maybe, she'll tell him something that might help us. Jim and I tend to agree. We don't see any harm in it, and there truly is the potential for gain."

Jenna was not sure what to think. Knitting her brows, she asked Nancy, "And what if Walt is the one who slips up and gives her something useful?"

"I know Walt, and I can guarantee that won't happen. If it makes you feel better, you can send him an email and cc Jim and me. In it, you explicitly state that he is not allowed to divulge anything about you or your case. If he violates your directive, he could lose his license to practice law."

"You guys really believe this is the right thing to do?"

"We do," Nancy said firmly. Jim nodded as well.

Against Jenna's gut instinct, she trusted her attorneys' advice.

"Okay, then. I'll fire off an email to Walt this afternoon. Let me know what happens."

SIXTY

Less than two hours had passed since Jenna emailed Walt, granting him permission to speak with Allison. Walt was sitting behind his desk working on another case when his secretary buzzed him and disclosed that Allison was on the phone.

"Allison! It's been a long time. How have you been?" he asked politely, doing his best to appear surprised by her phone call.

"I've been great, Walt. Just trying to keep my head above water with all of the hepatitis C cases. Which brings me to why I'm calling you, other than to hear your sexy voice," Allison chuckled seductively into the phone.

Walt detected an echo as Allison spoke and instinctively knew he was on speaker. Most certainly, Lyle Silverstein was at Allison's side. Walt decided to disregard it.

Allison continued, "I understand that you are personal counsel for Dr. Jenna Reiner. Tell me, Walt, what is she like? I mean, I spent seven hours with her during her deposition, but surely she must have a side to her that's more flattering than what I witnessed."

"She's very nice, especially to people who aren't suing her or trashing her in the press."

Allison countered with feigned innocence, "I can't control what the Tribune chooses to publish."

"I'm sure you can't," replied Walt with a subtle, yet sarcastic, bite. "Anyway, Allison, what can I do for you?"

"I was just wondering if Dr. Reiner is aware that we have filed a motion for punitive damages to be included in her trial?" Allison asked with venom dripping from her voice.

"When did that motion get filed?"

Allison snapped back, "This morning, at 8:30, to be exact."

Walt shot back, "Allison, you and I both know that this is not a punitive damages case. Whatever Jenna Reiner's actions were, they were not willful and wanton. You'll never get a judge to rule in your favor."

"We'll see," Allison said, barely loud enough to be heard. "Did you know we sent over a settlement offer to her attorneys yesterday? We're thinking they must not have received it, because they never responded. Frankly, it was more than a little rude. It seems like, with all the uncertainty and negative publicity that Dr. Reiner faces if this goes to trial, she'd be chomping at the bit to settle. Does she realize how serious things are? Does she know we fully intend to go after her personal assets?"

"What makes you so sure you'd win?"

"We've got solid expert witnesses. Dr. Reiner has admitted she left her drugs alone in a room with a drug-addicted thief. And then there's our young patient, whose entire life has been tarnished by Dr. Reiner's carelessness."

Allison paused for a moment, and then asked candidly, "So, what we'd like to know is why it seems

like she's dug in her heels? Why is she refusing to settle?
Hasn't she been through enough? If I were her, I'd greatly
fear what could happen next."

Refusing to violate his client's demands, Walt
simply said, "Goodbye, Allison. I hope you have a good
day, and good luck with your case."

Before Allison could respond, he hung up the
phone.

Walter Morey had the uneasy premonition that, as
was the case with Jenna, this had become personal for
Allison, too. For Jenna's sake, he feared Allison's next
move.

SIXTY-ONE

Allison hung up the phone and stared directly at her senior partner. Lyle Silverstein's face was red and tight. He stood, sending his chair sailing behind him. Baring his unnaturally white teeth, Lyle shouted, "Does Jenna Reiner really think she can beat this? She has no idea what she's up against."

Over the years, Allison had become accustomed to Lyle's tirades. She sat calmly at the table, respectfully waiting for Lyle to finish. When he had raged long enough to release his pent up frustration, he looked at Allison and asked, "Okay, so what's your take on things?"

She thought carefully about her conversation with Walt before answering.

"I think, as things stand now, Dr. Reiner has decided there will be no settlement. Looking back, it was a mistake to attack her in the media. Prior to that story, settlement negotiations weren't going well, but at least they were underway. Then the story prints, and all negotiations come to a screeching halt. Based on what Keith Jones told us, I fully expected the story would break her, but, once again, she's surprised me. We can call in more favors and give her more negative publicity, but I think it's only going to add fuel to her fire."

Lyle was frustrated. Because of Jenna Reiner's stubborn resolve, this case was going into the red quickly.

Glaring at Allison, he said, "Every other doctor, without exception, has settled and done so quickly and quietly. Not only is pursuing this case costing us a small fortune, which we may never make back, but I've also got Keith Jones breathing down my neck. He's fuming over this. He says St. Augustine can't afford the negative publicity that would come with a trial, and he's right. If we don't get this case to end, and soon, he's threatening to stop paying us."

From the beginning, Allison and Lyle were the only members of their practice to have any involvement with the hepatitis cases. That was by design. Keith Jones agreed to pay one hundred thousand dollars directly to Anders and Silverstein for each case that settled. It was a hefty price, but it was miniscule in comparison to what Keith Jones stood to lose if this ordeal bankrupted his hospital. So far, Anders and Lyle were each half a million dollars richer than they were before Hillary Martin started stealing drugs and infecting patients.

Closing her eyes, Allison replayed the phone conversation with Walt in her mind. He had given nothing away. However, as Allison reflected on the call, she thought she heard him catch his breath at the mention of the punitive damages filing. Allison guessed that Jenna would sacrifice herself and her career, but not her family.

Allison opened her eyes and smirked. Snapping her fingers, she said, "Punitive damages. That's where the money is, so to speak. The question is, how do we get a judge to rule in our favor? My guess is that Judge Krantz will leave that ruling to Judge Wilson. That bodes well for us, because I don't think Krantz would buy the argument that this is a punitive damages case."

"That leaves us with Judge Wilson," said Lyle, rubbing the stubble on his chin. "I don't like him. He's young, and he's trying to prove himself. Ruling in favor of punitive damages is going to draw attention, and he's not going to like that. Somehow, we have to get Wilson recused."

Allison contemplated the situation. She had some vague memory, something about Judge Wilson that had circulated through the rumor mill, but Allison could not pull it into her consciousness. In a flash, it struck her. She turned to face Lyle with a wicked grin.

"Do you remember hearing about a judge's wife who had surgery at St. Augustine during the period when Hillary Martin worked there?"

Lyle tried to shake the cobwebs from his memory. "Holy shit! How could I have forgotten about that? Wasn't it Judge Wilson's wife?"

A malicious look swept across Lyle's face, like a tiger about to pounce on its prey.

Allison gloated. "I strongly believe it was. I heard he was really torn up about it, as was his wife. I remember thinking, I pity the anesthesiologist that infected a judge's wife."

"Then why would he have accepted the case? Surely he would know it's a conflict of interest," Lyle replied.

"Unless . . ." said Allison.

"Unless what?"

"Unless he wants revenge, and he planned on using this case to get it. Regardless of his motives, this is definitely grounds for recusal. I have a contact at St. Augustine. I'll have them check the medical records to confirm our suspicions." Allison quickly picked up the phone.

Fifteen minutes later, the two attorneys had their answer. Mrs. Wilson had undergone a cosmetic procedure during the critical period. She was tested for hepatitis C, and the results were negative.

****

Later that evening, Allison Anders sat crouched in the driver's seat of her BMW. She had been waiting for over an hour in the dingy parking garage attached to the courthouse. It was well past 7 p.m., and only a few cars remained. Allison, however, cared about only one.

From her rearview mirror, she spied Judge Wilson. He had nearly reached his car when his phone vibrated. He pulled it out of his pocket to check the screen. The text message was from an anonymous number.

"How's your wife? Still hep C negative?"

The judge scanned the parking lot, fearing someone was watching him. He never noticed Allison Anders sitting in the front seat of her sedan, hidden behind heavily tinted windows, and gauging his reaction.

SIXTY-TWO

January 16, 2012

Late in the afternoon, Jenna and Mia were snuggled up in front of the fireplace on a cold and snowy Monday. Jenna was about to make some hot cocoa when she received a call from her attorneys.

"Hey guys, how's everything going?" Jenna asked, never knowing what to expect.

Jim took the lead. "We just wanted to touch base with you. There were some, well, interesting developments today."

Jenna sat up straight. She had developed a profound distaste for the word "interesting."

"What happened?" she asked anxiously, leaving Mia for the privacy of her office.

"Judge Wilson recused himself from our case. He didn't provide an explanation."

"So what does that mean?"

"It means he's removed himself from your case. It will be up to Chief Judge Hastings to appoint someone else."

Jenna's mind started projecting forward. Her trial date was only two weeks away. She instantly feared this could delay things, which was more than she could handle.

Jenna had mentally prepared herself to be sitting in a courtroom for three weeks starting at the end of January. She could last that long, but no longer.

"Will this delay the trial date?" Jenna asked, fearfully.

Jim answered, "It may. It depends on how quickly a new judge can be assigned and how quickly that person can get up to speed."

Nancy's voice came over the phone. "There are a couple of other issues we need to talk about. We have some bad news. We have decided not to use Dr. Ramano as one of our experts."

Flabbergasted, Jenna asked, "Why not? He's local, respected, and accomplished."

Nancy tried to explain, "When the story broke in the Tribune, Dr. Ramano got a pretty heavy beat down from the higher ups at his hospital. The administrators had a heart-to-heart with him. They threatened his job.

"When he came in to do his deposition last week, he was a mess. In spite of all the pressure he faced, he still believed in your practice strongly enough to proceed as your expert witness.

"In good conscience, we could not put him or his career in jeopardy. We are also concerned that the damage done to him by the Tribune's article would lessen his credibility. There was no choice – we had to let him go."

For a moment, Jenna forgot about herself and what this ordeal had done to her. To see what it had done to someone who was merely on the sidelines left her saddened and repulsed. She felt guilty for bringing Dr. Ramano into this, even if she was not directly responsible.

"What does this do to our case?"

Jim replied, "I don't see it as a huge blow. We still have Dr. Muzzani, who makes a great expert witness."

Jenna was not completely convinced. It seemed like things were falling apart.

"Anything else?" asked Jenna, silently praying for the bad news to end.

Jim cleared his throat. Jenna could hear the clicking of his keyboard in the background. Once the clicking ceased, he said, "We got a letter from Allison Anders today. It's a posturing letter and nothing more, but you should know about it."

"Go on," Jenna grumbled into the phone.

"I'll email you a copy as soon as we hang up, but it basically advises us that you could face punitive damages in excess of your one million dollar policy limit. Anders felt obliged to remind us of the dire ramifications to you personally if the jury finds in favor of exemplary damages. This letter is intended to scare you. Don't let it. As we've discussed before, this is not a punitive damages case. No judge would see it that way."

SIXTY-THREE

Lyle Silverstein and Allison Anders huddled at a back table in a dark, obscure tavern in lower downtown. Each of them sipped on a glass of scotch. There were a few other patrons scattered throughout the bar, but since it was mid-afternoon on a Tuesday, the tavern was not yet crowded. In the somber atmosphere, Lyle and Allison blended into the scene. Neither of them spoke a word to the other. They were each lost in their own thoughts.

The front door to the bar opened and a large man sauntered in. Only his silhouette was visible as the daylight illuminated him from behind. The door closed, and the man's presence darkened, melding into the surroundings. He exchanged glances with no one. Purposefully, he strode over to Lyle and Allison. Lyle covertly motioned to the bartender to bring their guest a scotch.

"Grant Hastings!" said Lyle with warmth and familiarity, as he shook the man's hand.

Lyle was a man of considerable stature, but Grant Hastings clearly outsized him. In the grasp of his acquaintance, Lyle's bulky hand seemed feminine and small.

Allison sat back and quietly watched the exchange.

"Grant," Lyle announced, "I'd like to introduce you to one of our shining stars, Allison Anders. Allison, Judge Hastings."

Appearing infinitely confident, Allison was poised, polished, and intensely focused. Firmly, she exchanged a handshake with the Chief Justice for the Thirteenth District Court. Although the judge dwarfed her in both physical presence and professional rank, Allison never demonstrated any hint of weakness or intimidation. By the time the introductions were completed, Judge Hastings sat down and took a drink of the scotch that had been placed in front of him.

"Good stuff," he said.

"Nothing but the best," replied Lyle with a sinister grin.

The judge's expression turned stern and serious. "Okay, Lyle. Let's cut to the chase. I know you must need something on a large scale for you to lure me out of my chambers during the middle of the day."

Lyle also preferred to avoid wasting time on idle chitchat. The three of them sat clustered around the table. Lyle quickly glanced around. Nobody was paying them any attention.

"We have a sticky situation, and I need your help. The hep C cases. As you know, we are representing the bulk of the patients. St. Augustine is making it well worth our while to make the cases against the anesthesiologists go away quietly. The hospital can't afford any more press. But we have a case coming up with an anesthesiologist who seems to have a wild hair up her ass."

Grant Hastings knew the cases well. They had all been filed in his court. He was acutely aware of how close the case in question was to going to trial.

"This troublesome doctor," asked the judge, "what's her name?"

Allison snatched the opportunity to become part of the conversation.

"Her name is Jenna Reiner. So far, Your Honor, our efforts to convince her that settling would be in her best interest have only seemed to further motivate her to pursue a trial. She's truly an enigma. On the outside, she seems unworldly, weak, and vulnerable. We thought she'd be one of the easiest to bring down, but we were wrong. Dr. Reiner is irritatingly unshakable."

"Judge Wilson was supposed to preside over her case . . . until he recused himself," Judge Hastings recalled. "It's interesting he forgot about his wife's surgery and potential exposure to the virus, until now."

"Yes, it is interesting," said Allison.

Judge Hastings took a moment to sip his scotch. He did not respond to Allison as he glanced from her to Lyle. The two men had once been friends – close friends, in fact. Until the day Lyle came home early from work to find Grant Hastings in Lyle's bed, with Lyle's wife.

Back then, in his youth, Lyle's career meant much more to him than his trophy wife or his dispensable friend. He could have easily divorced his wife and left her penniless. Likewise, he could have confessed the affair to Mrs. Hastings, ruining Grant Hastings' marriage and reputation. Instead, Lyle viewed the affair as an opportunity – an opportunity for future blackmail.

Over the course of his career, many other "opportunities" had fallen into Lyle's lap. He patiently stored each and every one of them, like pennies in a piggy bank. When necessary, Lyle would use his stash of secrets to achieve his goals.

Today, Lyle intended to use the affair against his old friend. Grant Hastings realized as much when Lyle had called him for the meeting. The judge also appreciated how dangerous Lyle Silverstein could be if he were crossed. For years, Grant Hastings feared this day – the day he would have to make a deal with the devil himself in order to bury his past.

Grant asked bluntly, "What is it that you want?"

Lyle never took his gaze off Grant. "A one hundred percent guarantee that this case never makes it to trial."

Grant Hastings was an extremely intelligent man and a talented judge. Throughout his career, he had seen defendants come and go in medical malpractice cases, and he knew their breaking points. So far, Dr. Reiner had withstood the typical tests. Even the beating she had taken in the press had not caused her to back down.

Judge Hastings recognized Jenna Reiner as a woman of principle, as those are the only ones that make it this far. However, he also knew that even the most determined defendants are unanimously intimidated by one thing – the threat of personal financial exposure.

Grant took another sip of his scotch. Looking Lyle directly in the eyes, he said tersely, "You want punitive damages, I presume."

Lyle nodded. "Dr. Reiner has a husband and a young daughter. I think she's willing to risk a lot, but not her family's future. Certainly not her precious daughter's college fund."

Grant looked down into his near-empty scotch glass. "You've got a problem, Lyle. This is *not* a punitive damages case. It's a tough sale."

Lyle Silverstein smirked as he went in for the kill. "Maybe it's a tough thing for a younger, more inexperienced judge to allow into trial. Our argument in our motion is very compelling.   I think a more experienced, senior judge might see things differently."

"You want *me* to preside over this case?" Saliva caught in the back of the judges' throat, provoking him to cough.

Lyle did not respond. To him, the answer was obvious.

Grant Hastings sat back in his chair. For the judge, there was no option. He regarded his ex-friend with a mixture of respect, disgust, and fear.

Glaring at Lyle, Judge Hastings said, "Then, we're even."

Lyle held up his glass and gestured a toast. "Even."

SIXTY-FOUR

At 10 a.m. on Wednesday morning, Jim and Nancy called Jenna. Nancy barely allowed Jenna time to say hello before she started speaking.

"Jenna, the strangest thing just happened. A new judge has been assigned to your case. You're getting the big Kahuna! Judge Grant Hastings."

"Nancy," Jenna said impatiently, "his name means nothing to me. You're going to have to fill me in. Is this good or bad? What does this all mean?"

"Judge Hastings is the Chief Judge for the Thirteenth District Court. He rarely presides over cases, but apparently he's decided to take on your case. He's a good judge, Jenna. We actually could not have done any better." Nancy sounded euphoric.

"What does this mean for our schedule? We're less than two weeks away from the scheduled trial date," Jenna said, biting her lower lip.

"We've also learned that Judge Hastings intends to keep our trial on schedule."

Jenna exhaled loudly. The words brought more relief to her than her lawyers would ever know. The end was in sight, for better or for worse.

Nancy continued, "As the Chief Judge, he's aware of all the cases in his court, yours included. He won't be starting from scratch in an attempt to familiarize himself with your case. Also, he's stated that he will rule on all motions for your case by next Monday. He's not messing around. We'll be working all weekend to get things ready, but at least this judge seems like he's on it."

Jenna perked up. Nancy's enthusiasm was contagious. Maybe things were finally falling into order. Maybe things would actually go her way.

SIXTY-FIVE

Judge Hastings sat alone in his elegant chambers. The sunlight from the early morning sky crept in through the windows, casting a yellow glow across the room. In front of Judge Hastings lay a stack of motions for the case of Michelle Hollings v. Dr. Jenna Reiner. Of the numerous arguments in front of him, only one mattered. Grant Hastings genuinely detested what he was about to do.

He picked up a picture of his wife from his desktop. After thirty years of marriage, Julie still took his breath away. She was kind, loving, selfless, supportive, intelligent, and sexy. To Grant Hastings, his wife was absolutely perfect. Julie was the love of his life.

The judge thought back to the affair he had with Lyle Silverstein's wife, so many years ago. He and Lyle had both been young stars, quickly bounding the stairway to enormous success and wealth. Grant met Alicia Silverstein at a black-tie affair. He found her exotic and intoxicating. Subconsciously, Grant also knew that part of Alicia's allure was about taking something that belonged to Lyle.   Grant and Lyle had been friends, but very competitive.   The act of ravaging Lyle's wife was the ultimate power trip.   One thing led to another, and Grant Hastings found himself in a full-blown affair with Alicia Silverstein.

The day that Lyle caught Grant and Alicia in his bed had been a wake-up call for the judge.   He feared losing everything, which to him meant only one thing – his wife.   The guilt of what he had done never stopped haunting him.   Grant Hastings never again violated his wedding vows.   In fact, the judge spent every waking moment of his life since that fateful day making it up to Julie, secretly paying for a sin that he prayed his wife would never discover.

Grant's mind wandered to the other woman in this dilemma, Dr. Jenna Reiner.   Over the weekend, the judge watched Jenna Reiner's entire seven-hour deposition, curious about this woman who refused to give up.   His impression was that Jenna Reiner was an ordinary, honorable person caught up in a terrible situation.   He felt genuine empathy for her as he read the article from the Tribune.   Grant was disgusted by the one-sided slant, and he knew it came directly from the mouths of Silverstein and Anders.   Nobody deserved that kind of public humiliation, most certainly not this woman.

Grant placed his hand on the motion for exemplary damages, as he considered the merits of the case.   From his experience, he estimated Jenna Reiner had about a fifty-fifty chance of being cleared of any medical malpractice.

Judge Hastings tried to justify what he was about to do.   Maybe, he reasoned, he would be saving Jenna Reiner from herself.   By forcing her hand into settling the case, perhaps Grant could spare Dr. Reiner the demoralization of a very public and high-profile trial.

Over the years, Judge Hastings observed countless physicians sit in his court, for weeks on end, as plaintiff's attorneys scorned and chastised them in front of strangers. He saw firsthand the damaging effects as physicians' integrity and honor were destroyed. Day by day, he'd watch dark bags grow underneath the defendants' eyes. He would see their shaking hands and their sinking souls.

Grant studied the picture of his wife. Sometimes, he thought, others must be sacrificed for the benefit of another.

Picking up the motion for punitive damages, Grant started reading. By any standard, the motion was biased and inflammatory. It was a ruthless attack on Dr. Jenna Reiner. Yet, at the same time, the argument was very persuasive.

Although Lyle Silverstein was a cold-hearted bastard, he was incredibly gifted when it came to the practice of law. Lyle and his sidekick, Allison Anders, had drudged up prior rulings which strongly supported their motion for the inclusion of exemplary damages. By virtue of Lyle's genius and tenacity, things had become easier for Judge Hastings. Regardless of being blackmailed, the argument in the motion was so compelling, Judge Hastings was inclined to grant it. Even so, he felt no less shame for what he was about to do to an innocent doctor.

SIXTY-SIX

January 23, 2012

Less than a week had passed since Judge Hastings officially took over Jenna's case. All motions had been filed, including Allison's motion to add exemplary damages against Jenna. Jenna's nerves were frayed as she and her attorneys awaited the judge's ruling.

Desperately wanting to escape reality, Jenna decided to take the day off. She planned to spend the time indulging herself. She had definitely earned it. At 9 a.m., she dropped Mia off at school and headed to the spa for a massage. The rubdown helped Jenna feel relaxed, pampered, and special.

Later that morning, Jenna returned home to shower. Stepping under the showerhead, Jenna delighted in the hot, steamy water beating down over her body. Closing her eyes, she let the water run over her head. She felt completely at ease, her mind filled with nothing. There were no thoughts of Michelle Hollings, hepatitis, man-eating attorneys, or court dates.

Jenna was savoring her brief interlude with inner peace when she heard the phone ring. She counted the rings — one, two, three, four, and finally, five. When she stepped out of the shower, she thought she heard her cell phone ringing in the kitchen. There was no denying it. Someone was intent on reaching her.

Jenna wrapped a towel around her head and ran naked into the kitchen to check her phone. She had not received only one phone call. Jim and Nancy had called her several times. There was an ominous text message from her attorneys, "Call us immediately."

Reluctantly, Jenna placed the call. She dialed Nancy's direct line and was immediately placed on speaker. Jim was already present. Something serious was happening.

"Jenna," said Jim flatly, "we need to see you. How soon can you come in?"

"What's going on?" asked Jenna, her wet body dripping on the kitchen tile.

"We'd prefer to discuss things in person. How soon can you get here?" Jim's demeanor rattled Jenna.

Jenna looked up at the clock and quickly calculated the time it would take her to dress and drive downtown. "I'll be there in an hour."

"Good," said Jim. "And we'd like your husband to come with you."

Jenna thought about asking why, but correctly assumed Jim would not tell her.

"We'll be there in an hour," Jenna said numbly.

Hanging up, Jenna felt dead inside. She suspected she was being summoned to her own execution.

Jenna called Tom and told him about the phone call.

"What do you think this means?" he asked. "They've never wanted me involved before."

"I have no idea, but it doesn't feel good. I'll pick you up in thirty minutes. I gotta go get dressed."

Jenna did not wait for Tom to confirm if he *could* come. There really was no choice, for either of them.

SIXTY-SEVEN

Jenna and Tom entered the offices of Moore and Everett. For Jenna, the surroundings were intimidating, but familiar. In contrast, for Tom, everything was foreign. As soon as they entered, the receptionist buzzed Jim to announce their arrival. In less than a minute, both Jim and Nancy approached. Both attorneys appeared gravely serious. Jenna introduced Tom, and Jim and Nancy escorted them back into the meeting room.

Jenna rounded the corner and was stunned to see Walter Morey seated at the conference table. Puzzled, Jenna looked from one attorney to the other and then the other. "Walter? What are you doing here?"

Jim interrupted. "Jenna, why don't you and Tom take a seat? We asked Walter to join us. At this point, you need advice from your personal counsel, in addition to us. Also, Randy Stevens is on the line."

"Hi Jenna, thanks for getting to Jim's and Nancy's office so quickly," Randy's voice boomed from a speaker placed in the center of the table.

Jenna sat down, terrified. Her mouth became dry, and she felt slightly woozy.

Tom took the seat next to her.

"What's going on?" she demanded.

Under the table, Tom put his hand on Jenna's thigh – a reminder that he was there for her. It did little to help.

Jim took the lead. "We were informed this morning that Judge Hastings has made a ruling on the claim for exemplary damages."

Jenna felt the room spin. Everyone was watching her for a reaction. A wave of nausea flooded over her. She could not breathe – the air was too thick to draw into her lungs. Tom instinctively reached across the table for the pitcher of water and poured them each a glass. Jenna had to grasp it with both hands in order to take a sip.

Tom knew his wife was overwhelmed. The silence in the room was becoming uncomfortable to everyone. Tom cleared his throat and asked, "What was the ruling?"

Jim could not look Jenna in the eyes. Watching her reaction was too painful – like watching an animal being euthanized. Instead, Jim looked at Tom and said with sorrow and regret, "Judge Hastings ruled in favor of the plaintiff. Exemplary damage charges will be included in the charges against Jenna."

Jenna erupted into sobs. She had fought so hard, remained so strong and determined, and endured so much. Jenna was completely devastated. Looking up at Jim and Nancy, she whispered, "I need a moment alone. Can I go somewhere?"

Without a moment of hesitation, Nancy stood and put an arm around Jenna, helping her to stand. She led Jenna into her office, miraculously avoiding contact with anyone along the way. Nancy went to shut the door behind her and give Jenna some privacy. Before she could leave, Jenna whimpered, "Please stay."

Nancy closed the door and came over to her. Jenna buried herself in Nancy's shoulder and wept. Eventually,

Nancy sat Jenna down and took a seat next to her. She had tears in her eyes, too.

"Jenna, I am so sorry. I have never met anyone quite like you. I've seen the personal struggles that you've overcome over the course of this lawsuit. I've watched you grow as a person, and I deeply admire you. Rarely do I have clients that I connect with, that impact me. You have. Jenna, I'm proud of you, and I rarely say those words to my clients or my friends. You should be proud of yourself."

Overwhelmed by Nancy's works, Jenna calmed down just enough to regain the ability to speak.

"Thank you. I'm proud that someone like you would say that to someone like me," Jenna responded with pure humility.

The two women, who had become friends, hugged each other tightly. Nancy whispered to Jenna, "I'm going to give you a few more minutes alone. When you're ready, come back in, and we'll get back to business."

Jenna and Nancy had been gone for over fifteen minutes, leaving Jim, Walt, Tom, and Randy alone. The men tried to fill the void with innocuous discussions of sports and weather, but they were all grateful when Nancy finally returned.

Tom looked at Nancy with concern in his eyes. "Is Jenna okay?"

Nancy smiled kindly at Tom, "She's just taking a couple of extra minutes, but she's doing better."

Five minutes later, Jenna reentered the room. Trying to appear strong, she said, "My apologies. It won't happen again."

Her attorneys all muttered some variation of "Don't worry about it."

Jim figured the best thing to do was to proceed. "Just so you both are clear on what exemplary damages entails, let me explain. In order for Jenna to be found guilty of these charges, the opposing counsel will have to prove that Jenna's actions demonstrated willful and wanton disregard. In law school, the analogy often provided is taking a machine gun and running down the street, shooting everyone in sight.

"As we've said all along, we don't believe Jenna's actions even come close to this standard. We were as shocked by the judge's ruling as you both are. However, now that the ruling has been made, it holds serious repercussions. If the jury ruled against you, it could decimate your assets. That's why we wanted Tom and Walt here. Jenna, your decision on how to proceed affects not only you, but also your family. They could take everything you have."

Jenna looked at Jim in disbelief. "How could the judge rule in favor of including these charges? You said – you, Nancy, Walt, your colleagues – that nobody thinks this is a punitive damages case. Can't we appeal the ruling?"

Jim conceded, "I've already looked into that. Basically, we'd have to appeal it to the State Supreme Court. The general consensus is that it would be nearly impossible to get them to overturn a ruling made by a chief judge. In the unlikely event that they did rule in our favor, we would still have to try the case under Judge Hastings. Under those circumstances, I would have serious concerns as to whether he'd act favorably toward our side."

Exploring every angle, Jenna searched for anything that would keep her afloat. "You said that the charges would be decided upon by the jury. If it's such a preposterous allegation, wouldn't a jury be likely to see things in my favor?"

Walt spoke up, "I would strongly advise you *not* to take your chances with a jury. Like we've told you all along, juries are fickle. Even when things seem logical and clear-cut, a jury could see them in a completely different light."

Clearly frustrated, Jenna looked back at Jim and Nancy. "Are there any other ways to fight this?"

Jim spoke up, "There is one last option. I feel compelled to tell you about it, but I wouldn't advise it. In trial, the prosecution's side will go first. They are going to butcher you, which we know and expect. Once they rest, we can make a motion for the judge to dismiss the exemplary damages charge. The problem is, at that point in the trial you look your worst. We haven't yet had our chance to erase the damage they've done. Based on that, it's unlikely that the judge would dismiss the charge.

"After our side rests, we can again file a motion for the dismissal of the charge. At that point, it would be our hope that you would look better in the eyes of the judge and the jury. However, most judges are unlikely to reverse a ruling they've already made. More likely than not, at that point the judge would throw it to the jury and let them decide. Which brings us back to Walt's points."

Jenna directed her voice to the speaker, "Randy, what do you think?"

"I've always felt very strongly that the doctors being prosecuted because of Hillary Martin's crimes did nothing wrong. You're all victims of a criminal act. I still think this is a defendable case, a winnable case. In my experience of over thirty years of defending doctors, I have never seen punitive damages awarded. That's true even in cases where I thought the charge might apply. The odds are on your side. That being said, your case could be the one that stuns us all. I want to try this case. I want to see you win. But, if it were myself and my family on the chopping block, I'd settle. It's not what I want, but I think it's the safest move."

Jenna stood. "Nancy, can Tom and I have a couple minutes in your office to discuss things?"

"Absolutely." Nancy stood and led Tom and Jenna down the hall.

Once they were alone, Jenna clutched her husband, burying her head in his chest. After several minutes, Tom pushed Jenna back just enough so that they could see each other's faces. Tom looked tired and shell-shocked. Jenna looked defeated and wounded beyond repair.

"For nearly two years," Jenna shrieked, "this has dominated my life. They've belittled me, embarrassed me, harassed me, called me names, and said I did things that are completely untrue. I was prepared to fight. I wanted to fight. It was the only thing I controlled – my decision not to give up. Now they've taken that away, too. I think the only thing that could ever hurt me more than this is if something ever happened to you or Mia."

Tom's heart broke for his wife. Jenna's pain and grief were palpable. Staring down at her, he asked, "Jenna, it's still your choice. What do you want to do?"

Jenna's legs started to give out from beneath her. She gripped Tom tightly, shutting her eyes, and falling into a chair. In her mind, Jenna pictured herself lying face down on the ground, with Allison Anders standing over her. Allison had a bow and arrow, and her weapon was aimed directly at Jenna's heart. The only thing preventing Allison from releasing the arrow was a clean shot. Allison flashed a diabolical smirk. Overpowered, Jenna rolled onto her back and stared into the piercing, green eyes of her adversary. Jenna simply muttered two small words, "I'm yours." With malice and precision, Allison released the arrow. It penetrated Jenna's chest, slicing her heart.

When Jenna opened her eyes, tears of failure were streaming down her cheeks.

"There is no choice. Game over."

SIXTY-EIGHT

January 30, 2012

It was mid-morning on a blustery Monday. The sky was gray and gloomy, mirroring Jenna's mood. An angry wind shook the windows, threatening to intrude. Fresh snow on the ground swirled violently and gathered in heavy drifts.

Mia was at school, and Jenna sat alone in her empty house trying to figure out how to put her life back together. She made a cup of tea and sat on the fireplace hearth. The blazing fire warmed her back, but brought little comfort. This should have been Jenna's first day in court. It was a day that was stolen from her. A lump of rancid bitterness rose in her throat.

Above the loud wind gusts whipping through the trees, Jenna heard the incessant ringing of her cell phone. She had no intention of answering it, but caller ID showed Nancy's number. Jenna fantasized that perhaps Nancy was calling her to tell her that the judge had reconsidered, and her appearance in court was required immediately. Waiting until the fourth ring, Jenna picked up the line.

Although Jenna was alone, she inexplicably felt the need for privacy. Walking into the office, she shut the French doors and sat down in the leather chair. Jenna cradled the phone against her left shoulder while she held the oversized mug of tea with both hands, warming her palms.

"Hey, Jenna. I just wanted to see how you were doing?" Nancy's voice sounded flat and forced, as if the wind had just been knocked out of her.

"Awful," Jenna replied bleakly.

Nancy was speechless. She felt like someone had died – there really was nothing she could say. Mere words could not begin to heal the hole in Jenna's heart.

"If it makes you feel any better, Jim and I feel the same. The judge's decision was unconscionable. Every lawyer in our firm is talking about it. We're all shocked."

"Then, why? Why would he make such an outrageous ruling? Why would he do this to me?"

"I don't know." Nancy had no other reply.

Jenna slammed her cup down on the desktop. Her resentment had reached a crescendo.

"Don't give me that! What the hell is 'I don't know' supposed to mean? You and Jim must have some idea! You owe me the truth. I've got nothing else."

Nancy stood up and closed the door to her office. She sat down on the edge of her desk and stared at the copy of the Tribune with Jenna's story on the front page. From the day the story was printed, Nancy had kept it on display, tacked to her corkboard. It was her constant reminder of the doctor she was working to save.

She lowered her voice. "Let me start by saying that all this is speculation. Even Jim and I will probably never know for certain what motivated Judge Hastings to make the ruling. That being said, our impression is that, for whatever reason, he did not want to see this case reach trial. Maybe he was concerned about publicity, maybe somebody got to him. For whatever reason, he knew how to make sure the trial would never come to pass, and he acted."

Jenna swiveled her chair around toward the bookshelves and glanced up at the rows of anesthesia and medical textbooks – books she had spent countless hours studying, memorizing facts and concepts. She wondered how much of her life she had given away to those books. How many precious moments had she missed?

Spinning back around, Jenna studied her medical school diploma, displayed prominently on the wall. It was elegantly framed in oak with solid-gold inlays. She remembered the day she took it to the framing studio. Jenna had strutted into the store with her precious diploma rolled in a protective cardboard tube. She unrolled it in front of the framer and imagined the other shoppers glancing at the degree in awe. For the first time in her life, she felt like she had made it. She was . . . a doctor.

Since then, her life had been sucked away. Her career was a parasite – always taking, but never giving anything back. Now it had taken her honor.

Jenna knew what she needed to do. She spoke discreetly, "Nancy, I need to ask you a favor, off the record. If you can't do it, I understand, and we can forget I ever mentioned it."

Nancy muttered, "Tell me what you need."

Jenna continued gazing at her diploma, with animosity and sorrow swelling within her. "I want to confront Judge Hastings. Privately. How could I do that?"

Nancy felt her heart skip a beat. "Are you sure about this Jenna? You're contemplating something that could turn out to be very dangerous."

"Will you help me, or not?"

The boldness in Jenna's voice made Nancy wish they were in court, as scheduled. In this state of mind, Jenna would have been invincible.

"I'll help. Just give me a minute to find my file."

"What file?" Jenna asked, accusatorily. From Nancy's end, Jenna heard the sound of drawers opening and closing, and papers shuffling.

"We have a file on every judge. It contains their professional bio, past rulings, and personal information. The kind of stuff that gives us insight on how best to deal with each of them."

"I never knew about that."

Nancy replied sternly, "And you still don't. Okay, I found it. Graduated from Harvard, married to wife, Julie, for thirty years, three kids, blah, blah, blah. Here we go – home address. You got a pen ready?"

Jenna hurriedly retrieved one from the cluttered desk drawer, along with an old, tattered envelope to write on.

"Ready."

"Fifteen Holden Road in Greenbrier Village."

Jenna scribbled down the address. "Got it. Thanks, Nancy."

Nancy shook her head, unsure of what she had just unleashed. "Be careful, Jenna."

SIXTY-NINE

Jenna hung up the phone and began executing her plan. First, she called Tom.

"Hey, babe. What's up?" Tom asked.

Jenna struggled to sound normal and keep the pitch in her voice even. "Nancy just called and asked me to dinner. Normally I wouldn't go, but maybe it will help me get some closure. She also wanted me to drop by her office this afternoon to tie up some loose ends. Is there any way you can get Mia after school?"

"Sure. When do you think you'll be home?"

Jenna hated lying to him, but she knew he'd disapprove of what she was about to attempt. "I don't know. Maybe not until late. Is that okay?"

Tom hoped the meeting would bring Jenna some relief. "It's fine. Tell Nancy hello from me, and I'll see you when you get home."

Before Jenna left the house, she conducted a quick Internet search on the judge. It did not take long before Jenna knew exactly what he looked like. Armed with an address and a photo, Jenna dressed quickly in jeans and a sweater and left her house.

Driving across town, Jenna played things out in her mind. She planned on waiting as long as necessary for the judge to come home, and then she would confront him.

Her GPS directed her into a very elite neighborhood. Mansions were perched along the hillside, offering panoramic views only bestowed upon the wealthy. The grounds were meticulously maintained, not a single tree branch was out of place. Even in the dead of winter, blades of green grass poked through the snow. Unfortunately for Jenna, the community was gated – something she hadn't anticipated. She pulled off into a small parking area and watched as a security guard questioned each driver before granting access.

"Shit," she muttered, as her strategy unraveled. There was no way she would make it past the guard. Gazing out her windshield, Jenna watched as Mercedes, BMWs, and the occasional Bentley passed through the security screen. Jenna was about to give up when she noticed a large man with a full head of white hair leaving the subdivision. He was driving a silver Lexus sedan. Her glimpse at the driver was brief, but Jenna was sure it was the judge. She put her car into drive and pulled out on to the road. Careful to keep at least two cars between them, she followed Judge Hastings.

Her head was buzzing as she pursued the judge through the congested mid-day traffic. At one point, several cars merged into the lane in front of her, and she was sure she had lost sight of him. After several anxious minutes of craning her neck to see past the other vehicles, she glimpsed the rear of his car. Changing lanes, Jenna accelerated, passing several of the cars and pulled in behind Judge Hastings. Before she got too close, she slipped on her dark sunglasses and a wool, winter cap – not the best masquerade, but better than nothing.

Fifteen minutes later, he pulled into the parking lot of a country club and parked in the outermost row. Jenna strategically parked between the judge's car and the building's entrance. He would be forced to walk past her on his way in. Glancing in her rearview mirror, Jenna spotted Judge Hastings gather a tennis bag from his trunk and make his way toward her. When he was ten feet away, she removed her sunglasses and stepped out of her car.

The air was frigid, and a biting wind chilled Jenna's cheeks. She put her hands in her coat pockets and rushed toward the judge. Jenna stopped directly in his path. They were the only two in the icy parking lot. Jenna stood in front on him, and the judge smiled politely. In a flash, his smile faded as he recognized Jenna from her deposition tape. Standing only a few feet apart, neither of them moved.

"Judge Hastings?"

"Dr. Reiner," he said suspiciously. "What are you doing here? Are you following me?"

Jenna had come for a purpose, and she refused to be sidetracked.

"I just have to know. *Why?*"

Grant Hastings had never been tracked down and confronted by a defendant before. His instinct was to be indignant and harsh. However, as Jenna stood in front of him, her cheeks red from the cold and drops forming at the base of her nose, he was riveted. The woman in front of him was so much softer than what he saw from Jenna during her deposition. Her deep, blue eyes revealed a sense of great loss and immeasurable pain. The way she stood, unpretentious with her shoulders slightly hunched, made her look battered and crushed. Mostly, Jenna looked empty.

She continued, "Do you know what you took from me?"

Judge Hastings bowed his head, partly in shame and partly because looking at Jenna was too agonizing. He had ruined this woman.

"Look at me!" Jenna insisted. She struggled to maintain her composure as anger welled up inside her.

The judge raised his head and beheld the victim in front of him.

Jenna erupted. "I have lost everything – my dignity, my integrity, my reputation. You took away the only chance I had to redeem myself. You took that from me!"

Black streams ran from Jenna's eyes and down her face. She refused to wipe them away. Judge Hastings deserved to see every aspect of her anguish.

Jenna pulled a picture of Mia from her coat pocket and thrust it at the judge. At first, he made no effort to accept it. Jenna shook the photo in front of him.

"Take this!" she insisted.

The judge reached for the picture. He studied the young girl in the photo. Instantly, he recognized her eyes. They were the same as her mother's, except the girl's eyes were happy and full of life, whereas Jenna's were hollow and dead.

"She's beautiful," Grant Hastings said softly, rubbing his thumb along the edge.

"Yes, she is. Not only that, she's smart and kind and funny. Now, thanks to you, she's also jaded. We taught her to follow the rules and stand up for what she believes. Then, she watched me cower and say nothing, as I was slayed by Allison Anders. Right now, I should be in your courtroom making my daughter proud. Not here, in some parking lot, begging you for answers!"

Grant Hastings handed Mia's picture back to Jenna. With his arm extended, he said, "I'm sorry."

She kept her hands buried in her pockets. "Keep it. Maybe one day, you'll look at it – look at her – and realize what you've done."

Jenna turned and walked back to her car. Watching her drive away, in the quietness of a frosty January day, the judge felt the sting of tears.

SEVENTY

June 2012

Jenna and Mia, donned in summer dresses and sandals, met Tom downtown for lunch. Sitting at an outdoor table, sipping ice tea, Jenna could not have been happier. Tom reached across the table and held her hand. He admired his wife. She looked so beautiful with a light summer tan accentuating her striking eyes. What Tom noticed most, however, was how peaceful Jenna had become since leaving medicine. Her face no longer appeared strained, her voice was softer, her frown gone. Reflecting on the contrast from then to now, Tom wondered how Jenna lasted as long as she did.

"Have I told you lately how pretty you are?" he asked.

"Yes," Jenna giggled, "but you can always tell me again."

"You look so content and relaxed. It suits you well."

Jenna leaned across the table and kissed Tom passionately. Mia rolled her eyes, but her grin gave her true feelings away.

Life had changed dramatically in the past six months. Since the day Jenna had crumbled to Allison

Anders, she never returned to medicine. The perks of her salary were gone, but so was the antipathy and pessimism. Her marriage to Tom had never been better, and her relationship with Mia had never been closer.

"You want to hear something kind of crazy?" Jenna asked.

"I love crazy," Tom teased. "Lay it on me."

"In a way, I'm almost grateful to Allison Anders."

Mia shrieked, "Mom! How can you say that? She ruined our lives for a long time. She's an awful, wretched woman."

Jenna reached over and brushed Mia's hair out of her face, caressing her daughter's cheek as she pulled her hand away. "That's all true. The thing is, look how much better our lives are now. If this whole thing hadn't happened, I'd still be stuck in a career I despised, and I'd still be miserable. As painful as the lawsuit was, I would have never quit medicine for any other reason."

"We're glad you did. Now we get you all to ourselves, right, Dad?" Like her mother, Mia had blossomed over the past six months. She was starting to become a spectacular, young woman, with her own thoughts and attitudes.

Tom winked at his daughter. "Right."

The threesome finished their lunch, happily chatting over hamburgers and fries.

After a wonderful meal, they stood to leave. Before heading back to work, Tom teased, "So what kind of trouble are my ladies going to get into this afternoon?"

Mia planted her hands on her hips. "Uh, duh! We're packing for our trip."

Tom laughed, knowing full well how Jenna and Mia would spend the rest of their day. In the morning, they were returning to Hawaii – this time for an entire month and with an agenda. They would be house shopping.

"Mom?" Mia smirked.

"Yes?"

"This time, no fighting with the luggage Nazi, okay?"

Jenna chuckled. Her outlandish behavior had evolved into a family joke. She and Mia locked pinkies.

"I promise."

SEVENTY-ONE

At 5 p.m., Jenna and Mia were in the bedroom packing when Tom came home from work. Jenna had the news on the television, but the sound was muted. Tom came in and kissed her on the cheek. When she looked up at him, the video on the screen caught her attention. She dropped a shirt she was folding and lunged across the bed for the remote. Anxiously, she turned up the volume. She and Tom were locked on the TV.

A reporter stood on the steps outside an office building. Jenna immediately recognized the location. A year ago, she had found herself numb and alone, sitting on those very steps after her deposition.

The newswoman held a microphone to her mouth and narrowed her eyes as she spoke into the camera. "We are standing outside the offices of Silverstein, Howell, and Anders. Prominent malpractice attorneys Lyle Silverstein and Allison Anders were arrested today on a variety of charges, including extortion and perversion of justice."

The video streamed to a clip of Allison, her hands cuffed behind her back, being placed into a patrol car. Her face was turned away from the camera, her head bowed.

The reporter continued, "Also arrested was CEO of St. Augustine Hospital, Keith Jones. The three are accused of devising an intricate plot to bury evidence.

Channel 8 News has learned that former St. Augustine scrub technician, Hillary Martin, may have exposed more patients to infectious diseases than originally thought.

"In a court-sealed, videotaped deposition released today under the orders of Judge Grant Hastings, Martin admits to sharing stolen Fentanyl syringes with others within her social circle. Those people may also have been carriers of hepatitis C, along with other forms of hepatitis and HIV.

"During Hillary Martin's deposition, she admits to exchanging syringes of Fentanyl intended for patients with contaminated syringes – ones filled with saline and labeled identically to the stolen drugs. Anesthesiologists at St. Augustine unknowingly administered the tainted medications to their patients during surgical procedures, exposing them to deadly viruses.

"Until this recent development, it was believed that Hillary Martin was the only one whose blood contaminated the syringes that were later used on patients. Testing done by St. Augustine two years ago focused only on identifying patients who met two criteria – those who had surgery during the time period when Hillary Martin was employed and also had a strain of hepatitis C that was genetically linked to that of Ms. Martin's. In light of these latest developments, Hillary Martin's crimes my have introduced other strains of hepatitis C into the contaminated intravenous medications. It also introduces the possibility that patients were infected with diseases besides hepatitis C, including hepatitis B and HIV.

"St. Augustine had previously promised to provide free, lifelong medical care to all infected patients. In light of this new information, the number of infected patients could escalate dramatically, possibly financially crippling St. Augustine Hospital. Keith Jones, Lyle Silverstein, and

Allison Anders are accused of attempting to suppress this information in hopes of minimizing St. Augustine's financial exposure to victims.

"Attempts to contact representatives from St. Augustine Hospital and Silverstein, Howell, and Anders have gone unanswered. We will continue to bring you updates on this story as it evolves."

Mia walked in to the bedroom, carrying an armload of beach gear. She heard the last bit of the news story. Her eyes darted between her parents. "What's going on?"

Jenna led Mia over to the bed, and they sat on the down comforter. Cupping Mia's cheeks in her palms, Jenna said, "Mia, I think fate just stepped in and taught Allison Anders a lesson."

Mia had seen the images of the lawyer being led away in handcuffs. She knew all too well the identity of the gorgeous blonde who tried to destroy her mother. "Is she going to jail?"

Jenna's voice was smooth and tranquil. "I think she may be. And a couple of other bad guys, too."

Grinning, Mia said, "It's Karma. Like that boy in first grade who used to kick me on the playground. Then one day, we saw him at the mall in a wheelchair with his leg in a cast. Remember that, Mom? Just like back then, Karma was looking out for us."

Jenna pulled her daughter close, melding their torsos together. She kissed the top of Mia's head and whispered into her ear, "Good people usually win, Mia. Sometimes we just have to be patient."

The sound of the doorbell interrupted Jenna's moment with her daughter. In her bare feet, shorts, and a tank top, Jenna ran to get the door. When she opened it, she gasped. Judge Hastings stood on her doorstep, with Mia's photo in his hand.

"Did you see the news?" he asked, solemnly.

"I did," replied Jenna.

The judge shifted his weight. It was odd to see such a powerful man look uncomfortable and awkward. He handed the photo of Mia back to Jenna. As he did, Mia came running up behind her mother.

"Hey, Mom, have you seen my blue bikini?" When Mia saw the stranger at the door, she immediately apologized. "Sorry, I didn't know you were talking to someone."

"I'm just leaving." The judge headed back to his car. When he reached the bottom of their porch, he turned back around and smiled at Mia. "You should be proud of your mother."

The stranger caught Mia off guard, but she sensed something significant was transpiring. She looked into his eyes. With the wisdom and confidence of a woman, not a child, Mia said, "I am."

The mysterious man nodded and walked away. Jenna and Mia stood in the doorway, holding hands, and watched him drive off. The judge rounded the corner and disappeared from view. Once he was out of sight, Mia grabbed her photo from her mother's hand. Although it was her most recent school picture, it looked tattered and frayed. The edges were worn and uneven. Mia regarded her mother with bewilderment.

"Who was that?" she asked.

Jenna squeezed Mia's hand. "That, my sweetness, was the judge that gave me back my life."

Jenna squinted into the blinding afternoon sun. A single, salty bead escaped from her eye and traced an erratic path down her cheek. The tear slithered its way to Jenna's mouth, where it settled on her lips. She licked it away. For the first time in years, the saltiness was sweet, rather than bitter. It was a blessed tear of joy.

ABOUT KATE O'REILLEY

Kate O'Reilley is a practicing physician and the author of two novels, *It's Nothing Personal* and *In Good Hands*. She lives in Colorado with her husband and daughter. Visit her website at www.kateoreilley.com

IN GOOD HANDS

COMING SUMMER 2013

MARCUS

Sounds. I hear strange sounds – machines beeping, metal clanking, bodies rustling, and wheels rolling. Warped voices come from every direction. I can't understand what they are saying. From my belly and my side, there is sharp, stabbing pain like I've never felt before. I can't figure out where I am.

Panic sets in. My heart races and pounds within my chest. I should be breathless, but something isn't right. My chest slowly inflates and deflates like a balloon being overblown and then emptied, over and over again. The air is being forced into my lungs from somewhere else. I don't like the way this feels.

Come on Marcus, focus! Where the hell am I?

Slowly, my mind starts to clear. I force myself to tune out the pain and concentrate. One thing I know for sure is that I am lying on my back on something that is cold, hard, and scratchy. My arms are out to my side, like I'm Jesus on the cross. I try to lift my hands and move my legs, but nothing happens. I strain to open my eyes, but there is only darkness. I struggle to scream, but my mouth is frozen. I realize there is some kind of tube down my throat – very far down my throat. It seems like I should be gagging on it, but that doesn't happen either. Nothing about my body is working right.

What kind of sick, twisted shit is going on here?

Suddenly, my heart rate slows. It shouldn't have, because I am freaking out. My heart should be beating a million times a minute. I can no longer hear the blood swooshing in my skull. Instead, I hear the voices of strangers.

"How far up the abdomen do you want me to scrub, doctor?" asks a woman with a raspy voice. She sounds like she is standing right beside me.

"To the nipples," replies a deep, male voice that seems further away.

I feel the splash of something cold and wet on my belly and chest. My mind wants my arms to reach up and wipe away the liquid, but I am quickly reminded that my arms are dead weight, completely useless. I want to get up and run, but my muscles are disconnected from my thoughts. My body has become a trap, and I am at the mercy of strangers.

A scratchy pad touches my belly button. It moves outward in circles all across my stomach. Whoever is doing this to me is being rough, pressing hard, and scraping my skin. The stuff stings, and it's making me freeze. I should be shivering, but I can't. Finally, the scrubbing stops.

Music is playing in the background, but I don't recognize the song. It's nothing I would listen to.

Think. Where am I? Think.

My chest blows up with air again and then empties.

In bits and pieces, things come back to me. I remember being at Freddie's party and getting really messed up. In the back room, I snorted a little blow and took a couple hits of acid. When I walked out to the kitchen to grab a beer, Lacey showed up with that guy. She looked right at me, gave me a nasty little smile, and then started making out with him. Little whore! She's only with him to piss me off.

Again, my chest expands against my will.

After that, everything happened so fast. When I think about it, it's more like seeing a bunch of random pictures scattered in front of me, like I wasn't really there. I do remember that I pulled out my knife and walked up to Lacey. Her boy toy said something like, "Oh Shit!" and backed away from the two of us. Other people screamed and ran. But not Lacey, she just stood there, mocking me.

"Look at you, with your big, bad blade. What are you going to do with that, Marcus? Hack me up for the world to see?"

Something happens inside my head, and I snap. I don't remember slicing her, but I can picture Lacey standing in front of me. Her skin is completely white, and her eyes are wide and round. Her hand is over her cheek, which is slashed open in a clean, long line. Blood pours down her face. The next thing I know, I am pulling the knife out of her belly, and there is warm, sticky blood trickling from the silver and red blade onto my hands. Next, I remember a man shouting.

"Police! Freeze! Drop the knife!"

Male voices boom from behind me. I don't turn around to face them. Instead, I just stand there, frozen, staring at Lacey. She's crouched down on the floor, crying and screaming, as she clutches the hole in her belly. Blood is everywhere, dripping from her face and gut. It soaks into the cheap carpet, surrounding her red.

Her crying is too much, and I can't take the sound of her. I've got to make it stop. My right hand still grips my knife as I raise it over her chest.

"Shut up!"

She continues to cry.

"Drop the knife!"

The cops have circled around me, two of them, one of either side. I take my eyes off of Lacey for just a second to look at them. Their guns are pointed at me. At first, nobody moves. Then I see Lacey trying to squirm away, and I lunge at her with the knife.

Pop! The explosive sound of gunshots fills the air. My ears are ringing, and I fall to the ground. Blood starts to gush out of my stomach, but I don't feel any pain. The world begins to spin. I drop the knife as I fall to the floor. Then, there is only blackness.

My chest blows up again.

I try to remember what happened next, but there is nothing, until now.

There are people on both sides of me, placing some kind of cover or sheet over my legs, chest, and arms. I know my stomach is uncovered because I can still feel the icy air hitting my skin.

"Okay to start?" asks the deep, male voice.

Okay to start what?

"Absolutely," says a woman's voice. It sounds like she's right by my head. I can hear her body moving around.

Just below my breastplate, fingers press on me. They are covered in some kind of rubber, like a glove. In the next instant, fire rips down my abdomen – a straight line of flames that goes from just below my ribs to just above my pubs. There is nothing I can do to make it stop.

I nearly pass out from the excruciating pain, but I'm brought back when I hear a high-pitched sound. It buzzes on and then off, in short bursts. *Zzzzzzzp. Zzzzzzzp.* Each time, a blast of electricity sears the skin on my belly. There is a foul odor, like something burning. It's the scent of my own flesh.

The pain is more intense than the highest high. There is no escaping it. Still, my heart rate remains steady and slow, even though my mind is exploding.

I know I am cut open. Cold air saturates my insides. There is something being shoved into my belly cavity, something cold, metallic, and large. The sound of gears cranking fills my ears. With each turn, the metal thing gets bigger and bigger, stretching me open.

Next, I feel tugging. It's not like anything I've ever felt before, and it makes me want to vomit. On my skin, there is something warm and slippery.

Oh my God. It's my guts!

Time stands still. I can't tell if it's been minutes, hours, or even days. The pain never lets up. I am freezing. Every once in a while, I try again to move or scream, but my muscles are dead. Eventually, I give up and stop trying. There's no point. I'm starting to lose my mind. All I can think about is the pain and what will come next. This is hell.

At some point, my guts are no longer laying on my skin. There is a lot of pressure in my belly. They must be putting my parts back inside me. There is the sound of gears cranking again, and the thing that was ripping me open seems to be getting smaller. Finally, I no longer feel it in my stomach.

"All right Mandy. We're closing." I hear the same male voice from before shout out towards my head.

I realize that the spiky thing piercing my skin is a needle. They are sewing me back up. Every time the needle spears a little higher, I can feel a wiry thread being pulled behind it. I make it through one stick, only to know that it's going to be followed by another.

I am surprised to feel moist, warm air on my left ear, and then I hear her. It's the woman who said,

"Absolutely," so long ago. Her voice is cold, almost dead, and barely more than a whisper.

"This is what you get for slashing up that girl."

The voice sounds familiar, but I can't figure out where I've heard it before. The needle driving up my belly continues. Then blackness takes over. I slip away into nothingness.

****

"Wake up, Marcus. Open your eyes! I can't take that thing out of your mouth until you open your eyes."

Everything is foggy, but I can hear voices.

"Marcus, wake up!"

It's her! The voice. She did this to me. I'll kill her!

Someone grinds their knuckles into my chest. It's pissing me off. I want to punch them, but my arms are too floppy and uncoordinated. I'm gagging on something. I open my eyes, just a crack, and I am instantly blinded by the brightness of the room. My stomach is killing me.

"Marcus!" I hear the woman's voice. It's soft and soothing, so different than before. "You've just had surgery. You need to open your eyes. Time to wake up."